Broken Toys
By Brian Schreiber

This book is a work of fiction. Names, characters, places, and incidents either are products of the author's imagination or are used fictitiously. Any resemblance to actual events or locales or persons, living or dead, is entirely coincidental.

Copyright © 2019 by Brian Schreiber

All rights reserved, including the right to reproduce this book or portions thereof in any form whatsoever. For more information send correspondence to bschreiber215@gmail.com.

ISBN 9781694277619

Opening Credits

There I lay, on Michael Moltanato's couch for yet another consecutive Wednesday. I had found Michael by doing a mental health search on the internet, and he fortunately had an office located a mile from work. I had been going to therapy for about seven months at that point and was beginning to really experience breakthroughs. I never comprehended the science behind recovering repressed memories but there I was, remembering another one.

I was about the age of five and playing in the middle of a sprawling, overgrown field in Oklahoma. There was a broken swing set, a rusted out roundabout and a slide missing one of the rungs on the ladder. This playground had seen better days. I'm unsure if the next part was real but I recalled, vividly, a locust invasion while playing in that "park." The sky turned black and I ran as fast as I could back to the apartment complex. At the time, it seemed less dangerous. The next image in my mind was of my mother shamefully walking naked through the apartment. This was something I later saw my father do during the times I lived with him, and a behavior I assume he forced upon my otherwise modest mother. The final image was an incident of rage where my father hunted us through the apartment complex with a sawed-off shotgun. We hid in a nest of bushes fearing for our lives, my mother's hand wrapped over my mouth. It would not be the last time I saw that gun.

I'm not Brady

Growing up, my brother Brady was an all-star baseball catcher in New Jersey. He was in state tournaments and a standout in his youth. My father groomed Brady early and, being a huge sports fan himself, showed tons of interest. This drew Brady close to our father. After my parents split, but before we lived in the apartment on Westfield Avenue, we lived with my grandmother for a short time. Early one Saturday morning, I was playing on the swings in the back yard. Brady was throwing a tennis ball against the stucco wall. When the repetitive thump of the rubber ceased, I looked over and saw Brady running along the side of the house towards the street. A few minutes later I went searching for him, but he was nowhere to be found. I ran into the house screaming. Completely and understandably panicked, my mom started walking the streets looking for her missing son. I watched her disappear as she turned the corner at the end of the block. Meanwhile, my grandmother called the police. I had no concept of time but would say it took my mother fifteen minutes to resurface. She had circled several of the surrounding blocks hoping Brady would be close. He wasn't. Soon after mom returned home, there were three cop cars pulling up, blocking the street. My mother, now in full voice, was in a desperate conversation with an intimidating-looking police officer. He was talking to her with his hand in the stop position like a traffic cop. She was frantic, and he was admirably handling her. "How could an eleven-year-old boy just disappear in broad daylight?" she cried. The police took down all Brady's information and interviewed me. —*Did you see what direction your brother headed?* —*No.* The police convoy rode off.

After a frantic couple of hours, my father called to tell my mom he had picked up Brady. Unbeknownst to anyone, Brady had called dad. He wanted to go live with him, so they had arranged a time he would be picked up. The plan was never vetted with mom, and since they were still officially married, although separated, there was no custody agreement in place. My mother was screaming at the phone. She cried incessantly for days, but the end result was Brady lived with my father for a few months only to come home when we were moved into the apartment. I never learned what happened during that time, but I also never heard him speak of our father again. I always wondered but never dared to ask. From experience, living with dad for any stretch of time can crush your spirit.

A few months later, I was around six and going to my father's house for bi-weekly day visits. Never overnight. My parents never divorced so there was no court-ordered visitation. Somehow my mother agreed to let him see me every other Saturday, and we would meet him in the parking lot of McDonald's on Route 130 in Pennsauken. In retrospect, the best part was the Big Mac and fries. Sometimes mom and I would sit there for an hour before coming to terms that he had better things to do that day. In some twisted way, I was extra happy when he actually showed up.

He was no longer in contact with my brother, but it was really my brother he wanted. Brady was the athlete. Despite my dad's continued *efforts*, I wasn't. My father would take me out back to play catch. He would put me through drills where I fielded ground balls and pop-ups. As more balls either got past me or dropped to the ground, his frustration grew. He then started throwing pop-ups high in the air and before the balls descended, he threw one at me. It was to improve my concentration on the pop-ups, he said. After several of these incidents I went home with bruises I couldn't hide, and the visitation ended. No more Big Macs. No more fries.

1977

I was born in West Jersey Hospital in Camden, New Jersey in 1970. By the time I was seven, we had already lived in a trailer park in South Jersey, moved to Oklahoma for an indeterminate period of time, and then, after my mother and father separated, lived in an apartment on Westfield Avenue in Camden. It was culturally diverse, and, as white kids, my brother and I were in the minority. My two best friends, Robert and William, were both black, and apparently, we were thick as thieves. I truly don't remember them, but they both reached out when Facebook came along and provided me the Cliffs Notes. The apartment was a small row home, and we lived next door to my Aunt Betsy and my cousin Nicole.

That year, I learned to spin tops behind the pizza place a block from the house. We used to scrape money together and go the *five-and-dime* store and buy them. It was so much fun but a source of heartbreak for me. See, spinning tops was a game where you had a wooden top you would wrap in thick string and with a flick of your wrist the string would unravel, and the top would jump to life on the pavement. Traditionally, the idea of spinning tops was to spin them into a chalk circle and see whose would remain in the circle and spin the longest. However, that was not the objective in this neighborhood. The goal of the game was to attack the other spinning tops. The idea was to aim your top at your opponents with the purpose of cracking it. All the tops had a divot on the topside of them and if you hit it just right the top would split down the middle. It was a skill I never mastered. I even began to sharpen the metal tip to make mine more lethal. I just wasn't very good and often would find myself walking home carrying the two cracked halves in my hands, dejected. To Brady's credit, he always tried to avenge my losses. Looking back, it was one of very few bonding moments I shared with my brother.

Late in the afternoon of August 16, 1977, I walked out of the house and found my mother and aunt sitting on the steps. I remember thinking how dissimilar they looked given they were siblings. My mother, standing at five-foot-ten, took much of her looks from my grandfather. She was a busty and a big-boned woman just scraping past her thirtieth birthday, but she wouldn't be considered overweight until a decade later. Over the years, her hair color vacillated between brunette and dirty blond. Her sister Betsy was the spitting image of my grandmother, short and stocky with curly auburn hair. They looked nothing alike.

The row houses on Westfield Avenue were elevated a few feet off the street and there was a staircase leading down. The two sisters were sitting on opposite sides of the railing that drove down the middle. They were both leaning into it as if they were hanging on for dear life. As I got closer, I realized they were sobbing. Elvis Presley had died that day. He was a musical and cultural icon even though he had been deteriorating in front of the world's eyes for the last few years. He died from heart failure, but when the toxicology report came back a few weeks later, there were high doses of Dilaudid, Percodan, Demerol, Quaaludes and codeine in his system. My mother was devastated. Years later, I would watch a documentary on his rise to fame and tragic death and understand, in some small way, what my mother and aunt felt that day.

One morning I was lying in bed yelling at my brother for something he did. My mom stormed in screaming. Minutes later I had a bar of soap being wedged into my mouth. Apparently, whatever I said to my brother was misheard, and now I was paying for it. It was the first time I heard the word *cunt*.

I had a tendency to laugh whenever my mom would strike me. She wasn't an abusive parent, but she did believe in a good ass smacking when it was warranted, and I got my fair share. The problem was my laughter. It wasn't on purpose. I couldn't help it. The harder I laughed the more force she would put into hitting me. There was one time she needed to be pulled off. She was incensed by my laughter and lost complete control. A few years later she would tell the story as thinking she might have killed me that day. Obviously, she was being a bit dramatic; still, being on the wrong end of that beating, I saw her rage.

Barbie Doll

In 1978, we lived in Washington Township, New Jersey with a woman named Heidi and her two children, Aaron and Nancy. That was the year I became a shoplifter; I was eight years old. It was winter when we moved in. There wasn't snow on the ground, but I remember it being very cold. Aaron seemed to be a couple years older than my brother. My mother always made Brady take me with him which probably was one of the reasons he later pushed me away. One day, Brady, Aaron and I were out in the back yard. Brady heard traffic coming from the woods behind the house. Aaron told Brady there was a highway beyond the woods and so we went to investigate. I remember the trip down, thinking how steep the hill was and wondering if we would even be able to climb back up the incline. The ground was full of dense brush and if it had been summertime, we surely would have had a hard time making the trip. On the way down, I could see through the trees the occasional car passing by. We finally reached the edge of the tree-line and were confronted with a chain-link fence. Past the fence was a patch of grass before the paved highway. There were two roads going in opposite directions separated by one hundred feet of grass. The closest was going to the right, east. We hopped the fence and sat in the grass for a while. Brady noticed there was water beyond the trees across the roads, so it was time to play Frogger. We managed to cross the highway without much fanfare and continued through the wooded barrier protecting what turned out to be a lake. After we skipped rocks for a while, the adventure was over. I would later find out the road we crossed was the Atlantic

City Expressway. Today, with the increased traffic, that frog would surely be dead.

Nancy was about my age, and I think I must have been smitten, but I can't say for sure what I was feeling. Whatever it was, I was seemingly willing to do anything to see her smile. You'll find this a common theme for me. Within walking distance from the house was a retail store called Two Guys. I guess you can compare it to K-Mart but given they went bankrupt in 2018, that reference may not stand the test of time. Look it up on Wikipedia. One of the ways we used to kill time was to walk over to Two Guys and amuse ourselves running around in the store. We were in the toy department one day, and Nancy was ogling this Barbie doll. She put it down and walked to the end of the aisle and disappeared. I can't say what came over me, but I picked up the Barbie doll and slid it under my jacket. I was terrified the rest of the time in the store. We eventually walked out, and it wasn't until the next day that I put the doll on her bed. In future visits, I stole Barbie accessory boxes. They included clothes and tiny bathroom shit like brushes and handheld mirrors. The craziest part was I never stole anything for myself. All for Nancy. I never got caught; well, not yet.

While we were living with Heidi, who as it turns out, was really only a friend, my mother met Sophia. She had been seeing Sophia secretly. Well, meaning Brady and I had not met her. My father managed to find us, and after forcing his way into the house, he dragged mom out to the street and whaled away until the police arrived. We would flee to Indiana a few days later.

Indiana Bound

I was not sure who this Sophia Martin was but here we were, Brady and I, riding in the back of a pickup truck. She was my mom's new friend and the person who would help raise me for the next decade. We were fleeing the scene of my recent Barbie doll abductions and as it turned out, much, much more. Looking back, I realize my mother's type in women was pudgy and shorter than her. Sophia always seemed to have a smile on her face and even her own catch phrase. She would always say, "I 'magine." Cutting off the *i* in the word *imagine* gave it a more hick tone and always made me smile. I often tried it on for size, but the phrase was all her own.

There was a cap over the truck bed, and it was full of the few scraps we owned in this world. No seat belts, hell, no seats! We were literally sitting there at the end of the truck looking through the filthy back window as we watched the miles pile up behind us. I cannot recall if we stayed overnight anywhere or drove straight through. All I can tell you is we wound up spending my fourth-grade school year somewhere in Indiana. I became best buddies with a boy my age, but half my size, named Moose. Not sure if that was his birth name or a nickname, but Moose and I were inseparable.

Some of these timeline details were filled in years later with the help of my mother. Funny, she rarely supplied the *whats* and *whys*, mostly the *whens*, almost in a protective manner. We arrived in Indiana in the early summer of 1979. Moose and I spent the season building a fort in the nearby woods and searched for crayfish in the stream. We were innocent and had no cares in the world. Except for the bully that picked on Moose, and now that I was around, me. I may have been taller than Moose but was skinny as a rail. We must have resembled the adolescent version of Laurel and Hardy.

One day, I was riding my bike around the neighborhood when the bully came barreling up behind me, screaming. About a week earlier, Mr. Bully had thrown a rock that split open my forehead. We couldn't afford to go to the hospital, so mom cleaned the wound and put a butterfly band-aid over it. I can still feel the indentation in my skull where the rock hit. So, there I was, hauling ass on my bike trying to escape. I managed to get to the trailer where Sophia's brother, Bill, lived. It was closer than trying to get home. I dropped the bike and ran into the trailer panting and out of breath. "Uncle" Bill was home and yelled at me for slamming the screen door.

"Boy, what's wrong with you?"

"Nothing."

After a handful of seconds and lots of cursing later from Uncle Bill, I told him the boy that hurt me the previous week was outside. He said, "Boy, if you don't go out there and beat the shit out of that kid right now, I am going to beat you where you stand."

Bill opened the screen door, and I found myself being launched over the threshold. He slapped the back of my head as I left. I don't remember the fight but heard Bill tell the story a few times over the years, always painting me the victor. I also don't remember any more bullying incidents after that day.

I smoked cigarettes for many of my late teen and adult years on and off. Sometimes packs a day and sometimes only on occasion. My smoking habit began during that summer. Moose was my pusher. He was stealing cigarettes from his father and smoking them in the woods. I started taking puffs, and after the coughing fits subsided, I convinced myself I liked it. Now I was stealing cigarette butts from the ash tray in our trailer and the occasional full cigarette when I was feeling bold. My mom and Sophia smoked Winstons, so they became my preferred choice.

One day, Moose and I were on the swings in the park seeing who could get the highest when these older girls showed up. I'm not sure how this happened but the next thing I knew we are swinging with the girls scissored across us, face to face. The challenge of who could go the highest was still in play. Once a victor was declared, Moose lit a cigarette. He offered to share, and one girl took a drag.

The taller girl said, "So what are you boys doing now? We could go back to my house and listen to music? My mom won't be home from work until like six-fifteen."

I looked at Moose, and before I could even give him the facial equivalent of a thumbs-down he was already saying, "Let's go!"

There wasn't much conversation among the four of us. When we reached the trailer, it seemed almost at random we paired up by height and started making out while The Knack were singing the newly released, *My Sharona*, in the background. Yes, I know, we were both around nine years old. What's worse is these girls were practically teenagers. It was pretty innocent, and it never happened again, but it turned out to be my first kiss. I don't count it.

Summer turned to winter. Times were tough, and although I didn't really understand the economics of life, I did know we were poor. As the calendar flipped to December, people were starting to put up Christmas decorations around the trailer park. I came home from school one afternoon in mid-December, and my mother sat me down. She told me there would be no Christmas for us that year. I remember not believing it. *I had been losing faith that Santa even existed so this would turn out to be the final nail in his coffin.* As Christmas approached, there was no tree or presents under it. I went to bed Christmas Eve and woke up at some ungodly time as kids tend to do. Full of excitement, I raced from my room and saw my mother wasn't tricking me. That day wasn't Christmas; it was just Tuesday. I knelt on the couch looking out the bay window that spanned the front of the trailer, in a trance, and not really believing this was my life. I felt my mom's hand squeeze my shoulder three times, and after choking back tears all she could say was, "I'm sorry, Brian." I never took Christmas or anything for granted again and don't regret the day Santa died.

Right after Christmas, we drove back to New Jersey in that same beat-up pickup; again, stuffed in the back, like luggage. I pulled out a cigarette butt and matches from my bag and started to light it up. My brother yelled at me to throw it out and then said the words that stopped me smoking for years. "Mom knows."

Mickle Boulevard

I didn't realize that when I came home from Indiana I would be going to live with my father. I had always thought we fled to the Hoosier State to escape him. My brother had had a falling out with him a couple years prior, so he stayed with mom. I have no memory as to how or why the exchange happened and didn't think of the intricacies of the parental swap until years after my mother passed away. I wish I had thought to ask more questions when she was alive.

So here I was in 1981 and living with my father in a senior citizen high-rise on Mickle Boulevard in Camden, New Jersey. I remember falling asleep on the couch as my father and his co-workers screamed at the television. The Eagles lost to the Raiders in Super Bowl XV. The final score was 27-10, and although the Eagles were favored by three points, they did not play like it. After Ron Jaworski threw an interception on his first pass, the Raiders scored two first quarter touchdowns and never looked back. This marked the first time a wildcard team had won the Super Bowl. My father was a huge, disappointed, Philadelphia Eagles fan but wouldn't live long enough to see them exorcise the ghost of Super Bowl XV.

My mother had always painted my father as an evil person. She described his Jekyll to Hyde transformation as a direct result of his alcoholism. I was ten, and I must say I didn't see it. He was great to me during this period of my life. It was summertime, and even though he worked as the superintendent for this senior citizen building, he was painting houses on the side. Whenever I was off from school, I went with him to assist and was paid for my efforts. It was fun to wake up early and jump in the van. Nothing fancy but I never forgot how huge that white panel van seemed to me at that age. I felt like I needed a running start to hurdle into it. In the morning, he would make two cups of instant Maxwell House coffee and let me put the cream and sugar in mine. I like mine extra light and sweet. I wouldn't realize for years just how awful instant coffee tastes. I'm sure there are many of you that can relate to their father's driving with a can of beer between his legs but not all of them did it at seven a.m. Dad would double fist coffee and beer in the morning. But, to me, it didn't seem wrong. He didn't appear drunk. At least not during the day.

    Months before that big Eagles loss, I started playing basketball at school and fell in love with the game. My father and I would watch the Philadelphia 76ers on TV. They were a couple years away from getting Moses Malone in a trade and subsequently winning the NBA Championship, but the team was competitive, and it was a bonding experience. I wouldn't be with him when they finally won, but my love for the game was not lost on my father.

On Christmas morning, I woke up and went out to the living room. We didn't have a tree and I guess I was getting used to that idea. It did not bother me, and my belief in Santa's existence was already in the rear-view mirror; innocence lost. I opened my presents. We sat for a while longer, drinking coffee. My father kept staring holes through me. Finally, I figured out there was something he wasn't telling me. He had a smile that kind of slanted to one side and it looked like only half of his face was happy. He called me Boog. Not sure why but he said, "Boog, we need to go to the shop." The shop was where all the tools, equipment and landscaping gear were stored. I looked at him with the strained eyes of someone knowing he was up to shenanigans. His eyes got big and he raised his eyebrows a couple times, pursed his lips and nodded his head in the direction of the front door. I jumped up and ran out. The shop was down the hall from the first-floor apartment where we lived. I ran and thrust myself against the shop's double doors. It didn't budge. The door was locked. I waited for dad to slow play this reveal as he sauntered down the hall twirling keys around his finger. Thinking back, I could see pride in his eyes as he came to unlock my surprise. The doors swung open and the room was no longer a disheveled collection of scattered tools and lawn equipment. In fact, the room looked less like a workshop and more like a gymnasium. Dad told me his two maintenance men, Carl and Jose, worked nights the entire week prior getting it ready. Now, all you could see was a 94' long basketball court complete with full-sized basketball rims on each side, spray painted lines and both home and away benches on the far side. I was speechless. There was a basketball sitting alone in the center of the court; waiting for me. I ran and grabbed it. I dribbled and shot that basketball the entire day. At that time, my father could do no wrong. Throughout the rest of the Christmas break from school, I played horse with Carl and Jose. Carl was a tall black guy who was super strong and always smiling. He would put me on his shoulders and let me dunk the basketball. It is one of my favorite memories of childhood.

As a child, you never see race, and prejudice is learned not innate. The fact we were two of the very few white people in the building was completely lost on me. I recall on a Saturday afternoon my dad took me for a walk around the neighborhood. From what I've been told, the area wasn't safe during those years, but my father never seemed to show fear or even have a reason for it. He took me into a local shop in a completely black neighborhood, and we got ice cream. He ordered for both of us, and although my favorite flavor is vanilla, I heard him order me a double scoop of *Caucasian*. I didn't sense any tension, and, in fact, the nice older black man serving us laughed when he said it. I think about how that comment would go over today and wonder how different the reaction would be. Regardless of color or race, everyone who came across my father seemed to love and respect him. He was very raw in his approach but seemed to exude the confidence to pull it off without making people angry. He treated the seniors with the respect they deserved, but if you weren't collecting social security you were fair game. In public, I never saw him overtly racist to people of color or misogynistic towards women, but he flirted dangerously close to the borders. However, in the privacy of his own home, you would swear he was both a racist and a misogynist. Whenever he spoke about people, he used graphic, potentially hateful, descriptors. It's not worth going through the list of derogatory slurs; he used them all, and you get the idea. It was difficult for me to wrap my head around my father's seemingly contradictory behavior.

We spent Thanksgiving that year with relatives of Art Still. Art was a NFL football defensive end for the Kansas City

Chiefs. That year, the Detroit Lions hosted the game, and, unfortunately, the Chiefs fell to the Lions 27-10. It was my first time eating with a black family and also my first time eating black-eyed peas, collard greens and pickled pigs' feet. I could have done without the pigs' feet. I became close with not just the Still family but many folks in the community. Being eleven made it easy for me to work my way into many situations. I learned to play chess and billiards during that year, and there were always seniors ready to challenge me. I was not the only one attached to these people; my father became very protective of them and made sure they were well taken care of. He sent me, at least once daily, to the corner store for Mrs. Such-and-Such for milk, bread or cigarettes. Back then, all you needed was a written note to buy cigarettes. It was a more trusting time. I would deliver the groceries, and the seniors would try to give me money. My father instructed me never to take it.

One night, I was woken up by the fire alarm. It wasn't the first time and always seemed to happen in the middle of the night. One of the building alarms was located in our living room, and I cannot describe the decibel level of the shrieks emitted by this device. I walked out to look for my father, but he was nowhere to be found. The front door was open, so I went through it and headed right. There was much commotion as I turned the corner. The lobby was laid out with a security office to the left, a single door meant for deliveries as well as the handicapped entrance and, finally, a revolving door for general admission. The doors were magnetically locked, and tenants needed a key fob to enter. There was an armed guard posted in the security office twenty-four hours a day. The red and blue jackpot lights outside the front windows caught my attention first. Still wiping the sleep from my eyes, I saw my father surrounded by police officers; there must have been three or four of them. I was still groggy, so the lights hurt my eyes, and I was a little disoriented. Then I saw the blood. The bodies of two men lay on the tiled floor, about a dozen feet apart. Sheets covered their bodies, but the blood refused to be concealed. On one corpse, the sheet was soaked around the midsection. I couldn't see much of the other body as it was farther away and covered with a slightly darker cloth. I stood there until one of the officers ushered me back to my apartment. My father was never arrested. He would later tell me the two men broke into the building, setting off the alarm. There had been no security guard on duty for whatever reason. He confronted them, and, at some point, the shotgun went off, and the two men were gone. At the time, I did not realize I had seen the gun before. I had nightmares about this tragedy for years. Sometimes, I still do.

First Real Home

In '81, I turned eleven. I went back to living with mom and we relocated to the town I would affectionately consider my hometown. Mom and Sophia got back together, and we moved into the first floor of a two-story house. Until I was an adult, I wouldn't realize it was considered a duplex, and there were actually people living in the same house, above us. We occupied the first floor, and it was the biggest place I had lived to date. I was happy. The back yard was immense and mine to explore. When we pulled up for the first time, I ran out to the backyard. I stood there imagining what I would do over the next couple years. I gazed at the majesty of the trees I would climb and games I would eventually play with the neighbors' kids. I imagined waking up on Saturdays, watching the Smurfs and Scooby-Doo and running to the backyard to carve endless chasms into the dirt and make a mini-metropolis for my matchbox cars.

"Brian," my mother yelled. "We're not done, monkey!"

I refocused and helped finish moving our belongings in, and over the next couple hours our house was taking shape and becoming home. *—To me, wherever mom was was home.* It was a little past noon when my mother asked me to run to Wawa and pick up lunch. The order was very specific. Bologna, cheese (both sliced extra thin), Stroehmann's white bread, Hellmann's mayonnaise, whole milk, and a two-liter of Coke. I got ready to go, and my mom gave me money; well, actually it wasn't money. She handed me a book of food stamps. My heart sank. I knew we were poor; we had always been poor. But this was a new beginning, wasn't it? I hid the shame from my mother because I knew she did the best she could for us. I walked over to the store and gathered the groceries. I nearly had everything together when a group of kids my age swept through the front doors, laughing. I imagined a scenario where those children took turns lobbing verbal grenades at me. They were the villains in my own personal spaghetti western, *The Welfare Kid*. To avoid pulling my daydreams into reality, I milled around the store for as long as I could. My mother would start worrying soon. I mustered the courage to finally go the cash register and check out my purchase. The process seemed endless, and once all my items were rung up, I handed the cashier the book of stamps, head down. She gently ripped out the required amount and gave me the rest. I was as horrified as an eleven-year-old boy could be and imagined the worst. I would forever be the poor kid in school, and everyone would laugh when I was around. In actuality, none of that happened. I went home, and we ate lunch. I never told my mother. Looking back, this would be the first time I put on a façade to paint a picture of an alternate reality. That time, I did it to spare my mother's feelings. As I evolved as a person, I would learn to create this false front to protect myself.

Our financial situation did not change, but I learned to view it differently as I got older. It is probably the reason I began working at age thirteen.

First Crush

I was sitting in my room on a warm, rainy summer day in 1981. I wasn't sequestered of my own accord; I was being punished for some egregious act. My mom liked to stretch out my scoldings and make me appreciate my misdeeds by grounding me for whole days instead of mere hours. There weren't many portable devices in the 80's for boys my age other than television and my brother's Boombox. Those were off limits and I wouldn't own a Sony Walkman for another two years. I sat there beside my window staring into the rain. I probably would have been in my room anyway, considering the foul weather, but I was being treated like a prisoner for some mundane transgression and the thought of that incensed me. Sitting there, brooding, I was now fixated on a carving I discovered on my windowsill. MELANIE. Who was Melanie? I imagined her sitting at that very window on a similarly gloomy day making her mark. I imagined we knew each other, and we would become boyfriend and girlfriend. I imagined loving her.

My neighborhood consisted of one street with only four houses containing kids. The houses were all in a row. It was Chris and Garritt Moore on the corner. They were the rich kids, at least from my perspective. Chris was a chunky kid with blond hair and a speech impediment. He would stutter when he talked and blink really fast when he got nervous. Garritt was entirely forgettable, and I didn't like either one of them much, but I did like their Atari 2600 gaming console. For the time period, it was revolutionary and something my family could never afford. Pitfall and Missile Command were my favorite games. I used to go to their house after school as long as my homework was finished. My mother was a stickler about that. I would rush over and watch Star Blazers on their color television and then talk them into letting me play Atari.

I lived to the right of the Moores in an ugly green, two-story house. We lived on the bottom floor and Jim and his wife Betty lived above us. He was a long-distance truck driver and would be gone for what felt like months at a time. I remember every time he was around, he felt the obligation to pull out a wad of folded cash. To this day, I cannot understand his motivation, but I did imagine snatching it and running.

To the right of my house was Thomas Gallagher, and there was a short time when I considered him my best friend. He was about two and a half years older than I, but that just drew me closer. He was a gangly, awkward guy with a disheveled blond mop but the coolest as far as I was concerned. He got me into Ozzy Osbourne, Judas Priest, and heavy metal in general. He built on the musical foundations my brother had laid but unlike my brother, Thomas wanted me around. He and I also shared a passion for collecting comic books. We would go to the Berlin auction (basically, a flea market) every month. There was a makeshift store in the center aisle that was completely dedicated to comics. The smell of ink and paper was unmistakable. I would often close my eyes and take deep breaths. I was in heaven and also penniless. I eventually became frustrated at not being able to afford them, so I began stealing the ones I wanted. I can't recall if Thomas did as well, and that is certainly not to protect his good name. You'll recall my history of stealing

Barbie accessories for Nancy, so I certainly had thievery in my DNA. I got really good at it. I was stealing about twenty a month on average. As Hans Gruber would say, "I am an exceptional thief." Or so I thought until I was arrested stealing fourteen dollars' worth of comic books from a local convenience store. I had been stealing from there for months, and the owner ended up bringing in an undercover detective to work the cash register. I was young and stupid. Like clockwork, I would go the day the new comics were delivered and literally pillage the display. The police came, cuffed me, threw me into a police car and then locked me to a bench. Mom eventually came to collect me and beat the shit out of me as we drove home. That day, as she beat me, I didn't laugh. Years later, she confessed that the police called and told her to wait a few hours before coming into the station. Sitting there chained to a bench gave me the perspective I needed. To this day, I still cannot walk out of any store without the feeling someone is going to stop me and accuse me of shoplifting. Lesson learned.

Finally, to the right of Thomas were Julie and Nelson. They were brother and sister and couldn't look more different. Julie was my age and reminded me of Little Orphan Annie with her curly red hair. Scrawny Nelson was a few years younger and always looked like he just crawled out of the mud. Hygiene was not yet his priority. He was also a little pain in the ass. Their yard reminded me of the junkyard from the sitcom *Sanford and Son*. It was full of car parts and miscellaneous junk strewn everywhere.

This collection of misfits constructed the memories I would forever compare as the perfect display model for childhood.

We would all play together, no fighting. We played cops and robbers, freeze tag, and my personal favorite, jailbreak. Actually, I think jailbreak was the consensus favorite. One day we were all outside, and I saw Julie had a friend with her. I'm not sure she noticed but I couldn't stop staring. There was something about her big doe eyes that captivated me, and when she flashed the smile that always looked like she had a secret she wanted to tell you but couldn't, my stomach felt funny. It turns out she wasn't just Julie's best friend but also Thomas's cousin. Her name... Melanie Palermo. *Could it be? Yes!* She had lived with her family in the house I now lived in. Slept in the same room where I now slept. My daydreams could come true!

We all played outside every day and into the night during that summer. I think back to the warm suffocating nights where the fireflies blinked in random patterns. I felt so alive in those moments as my feelings of competition and infatuation clashed. I was disappointed when Melanie wasn't there. I remember being in my room running my finger across her name etched on my windowsill. I loved it best when we played jailbreak, and I could chase her. I felt the true joy of young, innocent love. I'm not sure if you could describe it to that extreme, but I would tell myself I did love her. There were many nights when Melanie slept at Julie's, and I would sneak out my window and go climb the roof and talk to them. I only recently found out they both liked me, but I only had eyes for one. Melanie was very shy, and I teased her a lot. She tells me I was mean, but I think it was a nervous reaction. Yes, we still talk to this day. We reconnected on Facebook some years ago. She is married with grown children at this point, but we reminisce, and I validated some of these memories through our talks. She was truly my first crush. Her family eventually moved, so we spent many hours talking on the phone. They only moved about twenty minutes away, but it might as well have been around the globe. I missed her and thought about her endlessly. Every time "Jessie's Girl" came on the radio or MTV I would think of her. I remember experiencing what I felt as physical pain, thinking of how I had lost her before we ever even had a chance. It's crazy the perspective you have in your adolescence, and how quickly everything can change.

Kissing Cousins

My brother, Brady, and I shared a full-size bed. He stood about six-three. I was quickly catching up, so the accommodations were getting cozy. It was unbearable to sleep in the summertime. Air conditioning was unheard of, and the welfare office wasn't giving out box fans. Our room was located on an obstructed side of the house, so a cross-breeze was out of the question. This day was an exceptionally warm one, even for June.

Around mid-morning, my brother was sitting on the bed listening to the radio. WMMR was and is a local Rock and Roll station in Philadelphia that, at the time, played what would now be considered oldies. Brady was really into classic rock bands, and, wanting to be like my brother, I was too. His favorite band at was relatively local to us; George Thorogood and the Delaware destroyers. *Bad to the Bone*, their breakout album and title track, wouldn't come out for a couple more months. On this day, there were probably songs by Led Zeppelin, Pink Floyd, and Eddie Money coming through my brother's boombox. Looking at him in admiration, I found his tall, slim frame and floppy side-parted hair to be my current definition of cool. I would replicate his image for a few years. Unfortunately, Brady seemed to have zero interest in my existence.

I heard voices coming from the living room and soon our cousin, Nicole, was opening the bedroom door. You couldn't miss her bob-cut, curly, flaming-red hair. She wasn't much to look at and had always been overweight. Nicole laboriously squatted on the floor, Indian style, between where my brother sat on the bed and the table housing the radio. Her head bobbed up-and-down, scanning through my brother's collection of audio cassettes. There were six rows of them, neatly and alphabetically aligned. She would, seemingly at random, pull one from the stack as if she was a magician tugging at a tablecloth. Nicole was around Brady's age so my non-existence in the conversation may have been expected, warranted even. I was desperate to be included and even crafted the responses I might have, otherwise, added. They continued their A to B conversation about which album was better, Led Zeppelin IV or The Wall by Pink Floyd. —*This was an A and B conversation and we're not going to bother telling you to C your way out of it*— I felt like a fly on the wall. About an hour later, my brother was off to meet his best friend.

Once Brady left, Nicole jumped into his spot next to me on the bed. I was singing along with the music trying to keep up with her and it was all normal enough. Abruptly, she asked me if I had been with a girl yet. "No." I'm not sure I knew what she was asking. She offered to be my first kiss, and I declined. She then jumped off the bed and locked the door. She promised I would like it. I was wearing a pair of Brady's hand me down jean shorts. Back in the 80's, they were super popular. It took a very long time to get the fringes just right. See, back then you couldn't buy cut-off shorts with fringes, so you needed to take an old pair of dungarees and cut them at the thigh. You then took something thin and sharp, like a razor blade, and slowly worked to remove about an inch of the horizontal threads, leaving the vertical ones; the fringe. Much shorter than you would think was in style. I nicked my finger once. It didn't hurt as much as I thought. Looking down I saw my shorts around my ankles, and she was kneeling before me. Thankfully, the memory fades from there. What happened in that room got buried inside me that day. At the time, I was twelve years old.

Summer of '84

After my eighth-grade year, my mother broke the news that I would, once again, be shipped off to live with my father. Over the previous months, I had noticed mom and Sophia arguing more often than not. Sophia was spending more time away and would usually come home smelling like stale Miller High Life. Unfortunately, this was a scenario my mother had grown accustomed to over the years. I think she began viewing alcoholism as a required skill mastered by her partners since both her father and her husband had advanced degrees on the subject. Mom and Sophia's domestic partnership had come to a conclusion. Sophia left the house, and my mother had no choice but to follow suit. She felt her only option was to stay with my grandmother since she had no job and couldn't afford to live on her own, let alone support a fourteen-year-old teenager. My brother had graduated high school in 1984 and had since joined the Air Force.

Sunday, May 27, 1984. It was Memorial Day weekend. My father pulled up to the front of the house and honked the horn. He didn't bother to get out of the car. I hugged my mother goodbye and when I pulled away, she clutched both sides of my face. Her fingers stroked the back of my hairline, and her bloodshot eyes affixed to mine.

"You be a good boy you hear me, Bri? This is only until I get back on my feet, I promise. You believe me, right? I love you."

I guess I did. She hugged me again, and her warm tears struck my neck like the first few drops from a rainstorm on a sweltering summer day. The pungent odor of cigarettes on her breathe only exacerbated the queasiness in my stomach.

"Don't forget to call me! You have Grandma's number. It's in your bag," she called as I walked down the porch stairs.

I didn't look back as I listlessly walked to the car. "Hey, Boog," my father said. As we drove away, I did everything I could to hold back the tears. Thinking of the friends I was leaving behind felt like a gut punch, and I couldn't get Melanie out of my head. Because of the shame I felt over my mom not being able to keep us together, most of my friends were not aware I had left until I was already gone. A true Irish exit.

We drove to the edge of my hometown where my father made an unscheduled left hand turn across the Black Horse Pike into the parking lot of the Alpine Lounge. I couldn't believe it. I had been with him for barely fifteen minutes, and we were already stopping at a bar. He told me he wanted to buy me lunch. —*No more Big Macs. No more fries.* As I walked behind him into the bar, I saw him differently than I had four years prior. Since I had had a growth spurt over the last year, I was now five-foot-ten and taller than he was by a few inches. He had held a job painting bridges when he was in his twenties, so his leathery skin was stained dark brown. It's a wonder he didn't die from skin cancer. Dad gestured for me to sit on the stool next to him. I know what you're thinking, I was underage and not legally permitted to sit at the bar. I can't tell you how, but my father seemed to possess this Jedi mind trick ability, and I was not the droids they were looking for. He ordered a pint for himself, a Coke for me and asked the bartender for a menu. I ordered a cheeseburger, fries, and a Halloween costume to disguise my shame. Across the bar, I saw two teachers from my middle school, and though they may not have known exactly who I was, I knew them. I was mortified. They stared at me and whispered to each other, which made me even more uncomfortable. I'm not certain if they recognized me or were just appalled at this man for bringing his kid to a bar. By the time I was finished eating, my father had downed at least five beers. I asked if he was ready to go, and he told me to relax and ordered us both another round. It was only about two o'clock in the afternoon. We finally left after what felt like days and began our journey to what was to be my new "home."

We drove down Route 42 and got off the Route 130 exit heading toward Cherry Hill, New Jersey. He took a short cut through Cooper River Park. We drove down Route 70 in Cherry Hill and pulled into the parking lot of a high-rise apartment building. This place reminded me of the senior citizens building where I had last lived with my father on Mickle Boulevard in 1980. We entered the building and proceeded to the elevator. The elevator stopped at the seventh floor where we took a left turn down a long hallway. Our apartment was on the right, number 723. Was this my new home? Never. It would be a place I slept, watched TV and did homework, but that place and this man would never give me the feeling of home.

I had only been in this place a few days when a sea swell of homesickness overcame me. I needed a lifeline. Finally, I was able to reach Melanie on the phone. The call provided temporary relief, an emotional *fix*. My father put me to work, and it was a welcome distraction from my homesickness.

He was the superintendent of the building and was in charge of a crew of guys that did various jobs. He may have been the boss but was never afraid to roll his sleeves up and jump in to help. I think that is why his crew had such staunch respect for him, and among other traits, I feel I inherited his work ethic. One of my first tasks was helping him paint a recent vacancy on the fourth floor. We started at six in the morning, and I think I was sleep walking for the first couple hours. My father had introduced me to coffee about the time I was able to walk. Ever since, caffeine and I have been cell mates. Dad taught me to do basic handyman tasks over that summer. One day, he needed to swap out an electrical outlet in one of the apartments. I watched over his shoulder as he dismantled the receptacle. He turned to tell me the first test was to make sure there was current going through the line. He spread the black and white wires apart and looked back again so I would see him lick one of his fingers. With one hand, he placed one finger on the white wire and dragged the moistened finger across the black wire in a quick flicking motion. He didn't flinch. His dark, emotionless eyes didn't even blink. He stepped away from the outlet and told me to perform the same test and tell him if the problem was the receptacle or the wire leading to it. I knelt down and tried to replicate his exact steps, but the result was much different. When I placed my moistened finger on the wire, I felt the electricity course through my body, and I let out what I can only describe as a screech you might hear from a seven-year-old girl. He laughed and asked where the problem was. I told him the receptacle must be bad, and he smiled. Even though he tricked me into electrocuting myself, it was more shock than pain. I never felt like he did it to hurt me. We shared a laugh and I learned to be careful when working with electricity. In retrospect, he should have taught me where the breaker box was located. Even though he gave me questionable advice, it was a bonding moment.

Over the next several weeks I began taking jobs on my own and even had a schedule with a list of tasks to perform each day. I was getting paid, not much, but when I went to the convenience store, I no longer needed to use food stamps and look over my shoulder in shame. I began to build confidence in my growing abilities to be a maintenance man just like my father. I felt he was proud of me, and I tried to take full advantage of it. I worked as hard as I could and tried to be around him as much as possible during the day. The days were always good because he would be relatively sober. He would start to drink in the early morning, and by the time six or seven came calling, the downhill spiral would commence. That's when the evil would speak through him, so I tended to embrace the daylight.

My boyhood crush was about to be superseded and would lack the innocence of its predecessor; it was bound to happen. At least weekly, I had to clean the in-ground pool located at the rear of the complex. One sunny Saturday morning, the pool area was vacant except for two teenage girls sunbathing on the far side. I couldn't help but notice. I tested the chemical levels and would need to add chlorine after I finished vacuuming. I tried to focus on the vacuum dragging across the gritty cement floor. I stole a few glances in their direction and tried to eavesdrop.

"I love your hair color. It's almost, like, black silk and your eyes look super green today."

"I nearly cut if off last week. I *fucking* hate it."

"Oh, my God, what are you talking about, I'd totally kill you if you did that."

"You would be doing me a favor."

"You seem super annoyed today. You okay?"

The brunette said, "I fucking hate my step-father. He's such a creeper and I totally saw him looking at my boobs the other night."

"*Shut up*! No way. What were you wearing?"

"*Uhhhh, way*. And he didn't even really hide it! I was about to go to bed, so like a t-shirt and shorts, probably. My mom totally needs to fuck him more or something."

The blond girl's laugh trailed off and after a few moments of awkward silence, "Your suit is *super* cute. Where'd you get it?"

"Thanks, it's okay. I got it from Deb Shop. It was like 50% off."

"Totally?"

"Yeah, totally."

I didn't yet possess the gift of gab with girls. Even if I did, there was no good part where I could have jumped in. What would I have said? "Hey, Dark-Haired-Girl, I think you have nice boobs, too. Your step-father has good taste." I was actually terrified to say anything. The taller of the two was a straight-haired blonde with full breasts and long legs; she was lying down, but I would say she was practically my height. Her sun-kissed skin was too perfect this early in the summer and suggested a tanning salon membership. She seemed as bubbly and sweet as a root beer float. The other girl had dark hair and a vinegary disposition. There was a constant crinkle in her nose as if someone had farted. I was drawn to the blond, but, listen, they were both hot by whatever my current standards were. I would later find out the blond's name was Jessica and the brunette's, Alex. I finished cleaning the pool in what would certainly have rivaled a Guinness record. I packed the equipment away in the pool house and pulled out the five-gallon bucket containing chlorine tablets. After dropping a few into the pool's filtration system, I went back to the apartment. Later that night, with my hands still faintly smelling of chlorine, I masturbated over the images of the girls lying by the pool. I manufactured a scenario in my mind vastly different from the reality of the day.

Early one Saturday morning, my father threw me the keys to his '78 Oldsmobile Cutlass Supreme.

"Nice catch. Let's go."

"Go where."

"I hope you don't think I'm going to be carting you around everywhere."

This was totally out of the blue and I had an excited but nervous feeling come over me.

"Dad, I don't even get my permit until I'm sixteen."

"So, it's only a year away. Move your ass."

We went down to the parking lot, and I climbed into the driver's seat while he rode shotgun. All my senses heightened by this experience, I noticed how heavy the door was as I pulled it closed. The leather on the steering wheel was worn through, and there was the unmistakable stagnant smell of cigarettes. I must have turned stark white as I turned the key, and the ignition fired leaving only a grumbling hum. Dad told me to drive around the parking lot and try not to hit anyone's car. I backed out in a series of starts and jerks as I apprehensively tapped the brakes. He was oddly considerate and made me feel comfortable. I was soon driving around the parking lot at an unremarkable ten miles an hour. I practiced pulling into parking spots and eventually between cars. The session lasted about twenty minutes, and I was elated. This would be another of my father's shining moments.

I was getting on the elevator to go down to the pool one weekend morning; it was about eleven a.m. The elevator door opened, and my eyes widened as I saw the blond was in the elevator alone. I got on in silence and didn't even acknowledge her presence.

"Hi! Don't you work for the building? I think I saw you cleaning the pool a couple weeks ago." Her welcoming smile should have put me at ease.

"Yes, I live on the seventh floor."

She looked at me curiously, "I assumed that since you got on from that floor in your bathing suit." She giggled.

I grinned bashfully and asked, "Where do you live?"

"The tenth floor. I'm Jessica."

"Hi, I'm Brian." This wasn't so scary after all.

I paced ahead of her, threw my towel on a chair in the shade, and immediately dove headfirst into the deep end. I swam a couple laps and got out to retrieve my towel. I sat on the front of the lounge chair and dried off. A few minutes passed, and we made eye contact.
She gestured to me, "Why are you sitting all the way over there? Come keep me company." I took the seat next to her.

"Do you go to West?"

"West?" I said as if she was speaking Portuguese.

"Cherry Hill West."

"Oh, I don't know."

"I go to West. I'll be a senior. You?"

"Freshman"

"*No way*"

"Yeah. Why."

"Oh, no reason. That's cool. I just assumed you were older." I could not tell you what she thought of me, but I felt like my words must have been coming out in gibberish. Moments later, her brunette friend showed up.

"What's up, slut?"

"Ew, like, whatever. Alex, this is Brian. He works here. Remember, he was the guy that cleaned the pool that one day."

"Hey." She said making me feel as if I'd sat at the wrong lunch table in middle school.

Alex lubed up with sunscreen and lay face down on the towel she draped across the chair. We lay there for a while with intermittent conversation. They exchanged inaudible whispers. I caught Alex looking at me a few times, but my attention was on Jessica. It was an extremely hot and humid day in early July, and as the sun reached its pinnacle I spent much of the day in the pool. They got in to cool off but obviously tanning was the day's objective. Waterlogged, I lay down next to Jessica on my stomach facing away from them.

After some time passed, Jessica said, "Brian. Hey Brian, you awake?"

I played dead.

"I think he's asleep," Jessica said in an almost silent whisper. The rest of the conversation was held at the same volume.

"He's *cute*."

"Yeah, but *super* young. He's only going to be in ninth."

"Shut up."

Jessica said, "*I know*. Too young for me."

"I still think he's cute. I'd do him."

"Ew, skank."

"Whatever, don't act like you are so pure."

"Oh my God, you're like so evil."

"Whatever, bitch," Alex said, dismissively.

I was crushed. Jessica wasn't interested. I lay there until they both left. I waited a few more minutes and went back to the apartment totally dejected.

The conversation with Jessica led me to wonder if I would be going to school with these girls. I asked my father what was going on with my school situation for the fall. I would be entering my first year in high school, after all, and started to realize the terror in that revelation. He told me he wanted me to go to Cherry Hill East and continued to explain that East would give me a much better education than West. Since our apartment building was zoned for West, he asked a friend to use their address to register for school, another one of his magic tricks that would never be possible today. This only fueled the dread I felt in attending a new school where I was a total stranger. School would begin in a little over seven weeks.

A couple more weeks passed. It was early on a Sunday morning, and my father and I headed to my grandmother's house. She made breakfast and did our laundry while we visited my grandfather. He was probably the kindest man I've met in my lifetime, and I wondered where my father had inherited his rage. We sat and watched a Phillies game. I was so happy to be around this great man. My pop-pop took me into the basement with him so he could roll a cigarette. He pulled out a can of tobacco and rolling papers, and I watched the slight tremble of his hands as he carefully twisted the tobacco into this thin piece of paper. He was only allowed to smoke in the basement or outside. When the game was over, and my grandmother had finished washing our clothes we left. She had a habit of ironing our underwear and folding our socks up. Seriously, she would take a pair of socks, roll them together and bind them with a rubber band. It was glorious for anyone suffering from a minor obsessive-compulsive disorder. I tried to emulate the habit as I grew older. It never stuck.

On the way home, we stopped at a place called Rexy's. The *one-beer* promise turned into eight. My father must have been a regular there since everyone said hello when we came in. You could never tell with him because complete strangers took to him quickly. He didn't bother introducing me until the woman sitting next to him inquired, "Your kid?"

"Yupper."

"He's cute. Takes after his father, I see."

He turned, winked at me and then turned back to her. Then, without breaking their stare, my dad said the bartender, "Please buy this beautiful woman a drink for me will ya, Stan?" He moved over a stool to sit next to her. They were now breathing each other's air.

Still trained on this woman, thumbing back in my direction, "And, Stan, get my son whatever he wants."

I got a coke and a handful of quarters. "I'll just put the quarters on the tab," Stan said with a smile.

There was a *Three Stooges* pinball machine and a *Ms. Pac-man* arcade style cabinet sitting side-by-side. I bounced back and forth between them until my pockets were empty. Every once in a while, I looked and saw my father bouncing back and forth between a lively conversation with guys across the bar and whispering into this woman's ear. About an hour and a half later, dad was on his feet and pointing towards the door. He curled his tongue and whistled, "*Shweeeer-shweeet*, Let's go, Boog."

My father weakly saluted the guys across the bar, shook Stan's hand and kissed the woman on the cheek. She tucked a napkin in his shirt pocket and whispered for him to call her.

I realized dad was drunk but kept my mouth shut because I didn't want to tug at the veil covering the evil just beneath the surface. We drove along and made a right onto the road running parallel to Cooper River Park. Here we were again. We got about three quarters of the way down the road when he slammed directly into the back of a parked car. I was thrust forward and hit my head on the dashboard. Unfazed by the accident, he backed up and continued driving. It didn't occur to him to ask if I was hurt. I was about to become unhinged. We reached the apartment and I boiled over with anger.

"I can't fucking believe you."

"Watch your mouth!"

I let out an angry bark of laughter and snapped, "we were just in a fucking car accident! Do you get that?"

"Don't be a goddamn, *sissy*. Fucking drama queen! And I told you to watch your mouth. Don't make me say it again!"

"*Drama queen? Are you kidding me? I just slammed my head against the dashboard, and you're worrying about me cursing?* Wow, that's *rich*, Dad. This is getting out of control. *We could have been killed.*"

"I think you're over reacting. And *who the fuck do you think you are talking to?*"

"A pathetic drunk, that's who. How can you even say I'm overreacting?"

The lines on his forehead deepened and the ones on his cheeks formed parentheses that bracketed his scowl. He stood there measuring me silently. Then he walked slowly towards me, his voice gravelly and focused.

"Don't you ever talk to me that way again. You hear me? Comprende, chief? You may have grown a few inches, but I will still whoop your ass. You *fucking* respect me! I'm your father."

I said, "It's hard to respect you. Respect's earned. This, what happened tonight? That doesn't deserve respect. You're an alcoholic. Don't you see that? Did you see that car? Did you see the damage you did? You didn't even care. Whether you're hitting cars or threatening to hit me, it's not right. And certainly not to be respected."

"Don't you fuckin' lecture me, boy. I am in no mood for you. You're making too big a deal out of this. You're fine. I'm fine. Everything's fine. *So shut the fuck up and get out of my face.*" His eyes were on fire and I knew there was no reasoning with him.

"Whatever, Dad. I'm going to bed."

A few years later, I would act the quarrel out in my drama class with my best friend. My drama teacher approached after class and said she was submitting an entry to the committee for the annual Teen Arts Festival. After auditioning we found out we had been picked to represent our county. Here is the letter we were sent.

Dear Student,
Congratulations! You have been selected to represent Gloucester County at the 1988 NJ State Teen Arts Festival on June 1, 1988. The festival will be held at the Mason Gross School of Arts, Douglass Campus of Rutgers, The State University., in New Brunswick.

The information regarding your performance at the Gloucester County Teen Arts Festival is being forwarded to the State Festival Office. They will contact you with specific details about June 1st.

Thank you for participating, and the best of luck at the State Festival!

The morning of the festival I was a nervous wreck. I wasn't sure I would be able to pull this off. It was emotionally exhausting. I had performed on stage for school drama and musical productions. Stage fright wasn't my issue. It was the anxiety of baring my soul. Even though no one knew this piece was a depiction of actual events, I couldn't help but *feel* they did. I was embarrassed to have this life. I do an excellent job painting pictures of how I want the world to see me. I don't mean I am fake, I'm far from it. I just tend to obscure the parts I don't want the world to see. Only the people close to me get to see the fractures. And sometimes only I get to see them.

We stood in the wings of the stage, and our time was finally here. We walked out already in character and played out the story of the events after the accident. I lived the experience all over again, but this time it ended with a rousing ovation from a crowd of about two hundred. I stood on stage taking my bow fully engulfed in tears. My father's drinking never stalled.

The air settled over the next few days and life went back to normal. At least as normal as it could be for my father and me. One Saturday, I was working in the lobby painting the trim in the vestibule when Jessica walked through the front doors.

"*Hiiiii Brian*, how are you?"

"Oh, hey. I'm great. Where are you headed?"

"Home, I just went for a run." She was wearing the right attire and glistening like a golden goddess. I found it hard to concentrate.

"Do you party?" she said abruptly.

Unsure of what she meant and still distracted by the length of her legs, I nervously told her, "Of course. Yeah, yes. Why?"

"We should totally hang out," she said. I found it hard to maintain eye contact. I looked to the floor and then back at her.

"Yeah, yeah, absolutely. *Yes*."

"Can you get in the empty apartments?"

"Of course. I can get into every apartment." I overshared. I really shouldn't have told her I had the master key to every door in the building on my keyring.

Jessica turned and walked over to the security desk. When she returned, she grabbed my hand and wrote with the pen she had borrowed. I looked down and read my palm. No name, just a phone number and a heart with an arrow through it, written in blue ink.

She smiled, pursed her lips, and was on her way. As she turned, I focused on the Rorschach sweat blot that formed on the lower back of her light blue tank top. I continued staring at the closed elevator doors in some quasi-trance. I only remembered why I was standing in the lobby when I looked down and saw the paint brush still in my hand. I kept staring at the other hand in disbelief. *How she gripped my hand when she wrote it.* I finished painting, took everything back to the maintenance office, and went to the apartment. I was lying in bed listening to Billy Squier telling me that everybody wanted me, thinking about this girl and when it would be right to call her. I had no experience with courting girls. I didn't want to look desperate and was a bit intimidated, so I didn't call her. I saw Jess in the elevator a few days later, and she asked why I didn't reach out. I made up an excuse and told her my father was working me to the bone, and I would call her that night. I did, and after a bumpy start, we talked for hours, and she told me she thought I seemed much older. This was a nice revelation since I overheard her tell Alex I was too young, and now here we sat talking endlessly on the phone.

"What are you doing Friday? Wanna hang out?"

"I gotta check my calendar." I said sarcastically.

"Jerk."

"Totally kidding, I'd love to hang out."

Friday came, and I was a little too excited. And nervous. She was way out of my league. As she had suggested, we were planning to hang out in one of the vacant apartments. Against my better judgment, I let my hormones lead the way and agreed it was a great idea. I told my father I was going to a movie. I nervously fumbled for the key to apartment 511 and went inside. I waited there for about twenty minutes and finally heard a light knock. I opened the door to find Jessica. I was shocked to see Alex standing next to her, but that would not ruin my excitement. They came in, and I noticed Alex was carrying a backpack. From the backpack she pulled out a large bottle of vodka and a few smaller containers of orange juice as well as a sleeve of plastic cups. Since the building never shut the power off in any of the units, we put the juice in the refrigerator. Jessica was standing there in a tight top, and I couldn't help but stare.

"Let's get this *fucking* party started," Alex yelled as she poured three shots of vodka.

"*Shhh*. We're not supposed to be in here," Jessica whispered. I thanked her with my eyes.

"Oh, my God, whatever, bitch. Fine. Drink up. Cheers, losers."

We all downed our shots, and I tried to stop my face from showing how awful that tasted. Jessica made screwdrivers and handed me one. This was more my speed. Other than sipping my father's beer every now and again, this was really my first drinking experience and, at first, I was a little apprehensive, given my father's addiction. After the shot, I drank very slowly, taking calculated sips. About an hour later, Jessica pulled out a small baggie.

"Joint, joint joint, jooint, jooooint, JOINT!" Alex was super happy.

She went to the window, opened it, and Jessica lit up. *Now*, I was terrified! I had taken my first real drink, and now drugs had come on the scene. At this point, I had no idea how to act, but I didn't want to appear like a child, so I played it as cool as I could. Alex then got up and took a hit and she and Jessica were passing the joint back and forth. She asked if I wanted some, and I said, "Of course!" I went over and took a hit, and quickly exhaled. I coughed a bit. I felt nothing, so I took deeper drags; the coughing worsened, but I still felt no different. Now that was probably a good outcome, but I was thinking I should feel differently. The night progressed, and the girls were most definitely high. They giggled back and forth incessantly. It put me off a bit, but I was bewitched by Jessica. She could have been wearing a clown costume with full makeup and the big red nose, and it wouldn't have mattered. As the night progressed, we made eye contact that let me know she was either interested in me or completely fucked up. I would have taken either at that point. I was pretty in control since I was practically pretending to drink, and the pot had no effect on me. The adrenaline also didn't hurt. The three of us were sitting in a circle in the middle of this empty apartment when Jessica leaned over out of nowhere and kissed me. I think it was meant for my lips but somehow wandered and landed on the corner of my mouth. I wasn't expecting it as I was in mid-sentence talking to Alex. I looked at her and leaned forward to meet her waiting lips. We kissed for a few moments, totally forgetting Alex was still in the room.

After that kiss, the mounting tension became too heavy to carry. The light-hearted hangout-session had come to an end. Alex seemed put off by the turn of events, and within fifteen minutes she left without a goodbye.

I drew in a deep breath and blew the air out slowly making a face I might make trying to walk unnoticed through a lion's den. "I'm sorry."

"Why are you sorry? Alex is just disappointed. She really likes you. We both do. We talked about this the other day and agreed if one of us hooked up with you the other would back off. I made my move, and I think that upset her. It's my fault, not yours."

"Well, I can't say I'm upset by *that*. I really only like you. Alex is a little... mean. Maybe mean is the wrong word. I don't know how to describe it."

"She just has like a super shitty home life. Her parents split up when she was really young, and her stepfather is a real douche. Her mom totally always takes his side, too. And he's kind of creepy. She sleeps over like all the time. She was supposed to stay over tonight. Guess not now."

"That sucks."

"Yeah."

We talked a bit longer, and the alcohol was beginning to take effect. I was no longer nervous. We began to make out,

Broken Toys

and she slid her hand down and touched me over my jeans. I was at full attention, and she seemed pleased. I pulled her t-shirt over her head and fumbled with her bra. She saved me the embarrassment and took it off herself. I could hardly believe my eyes. I had only seen tits like these in my father's Playboy magazines. I was like an uncoordinated newborn fumbling around. She unbuttoned my pants and began stroking me as we kissed. Foreplay, at that point, was over. I slid my shorts off, and she did the same. I lasted as long as I possibly could; maybe a couple minutes. I finished inside of her. She didn't seem to be put off by this, and, no, there was no protection to speak of during our encounter. *I know... I KNOW*, but as you will learn moving forward, I often rolled the dice. Anyway, I lay there on top of her fully naked, on the floor, in the middle of a totally vacant apartment. It was perfect. Maybe it was the alcohol or the weed. It was probably the sex, but whatever it was, it felt right. I would always remember the three songs that played leading up to and during our encounter. They remain, to this day, reminders of that night. They were, in order, *Drive* by the Cars, *The Warrior* by Patty Smyth, and *Sunglasses at Night* by Corey Hart. When we finally fled the apartment, I was totally in love. This was different from how I felt about Melanie. We still talked occasionally on the telephone, and she would always be my first young love, but the stakes just got higher. I no longer felt like the innocent boy who had left Melanie behind.

After that point, I saw Jessica nearly every day. We had sex a couple of times, and I referred to her as my girlfriend to my father. We were lying in my bed listening to music one morning when dad came calling.

"Boog, you here?"

"Boog?" Jessica whispered. I shook her question off.

My dad came in the room, "Whoa, who's *this*?"

"Dad, this is Jessica. I told you about her. She the girl that lives up on the tenth floor."

"Yes. *Yes,* you did."

Jessica jumped off the bed to greet my father. "Hello, it's nice to meet you."

"It sure is," he said. I could feel her skin crawling as he efficiently scanned her body.

I was struck by how Jessica towered over him. "What did you need, Dad?"

"Oh, nothing. It can wait. Have fun." He stole one last glance in her direction before closing the bedroom door behind him.

I think she was being kind when she told me he was nice. From that point forward, I tried to keep her out of my father's field of vision.

"Oh, my God, he's super short! What was that he called you?" She was like a dog with a bone when I tried to shake her off again, her eyes widening in expectation of an answer.

"Boog! He calls me Boog. I have no idea why. He just does."

She laughed. So much so that I caved and began to laugh myself. Now we were laughing together at my expense which is something I would have typically been embarrassed by but wasn't. Jessica always made me feel comfortable. Thankfully, she never called me Boog. Over the next weeks, we hung out at the pool and at her parents' apartment; occasionally at mine but I tried to keep her away from *Boog's house*.

It was late August, and summer's heat was becoming less intense. It was in the afternoon one day when the doorbell rang. Alex was standing in the doorway, crying.

"Hi, Alex, are you okay? What's wrong?"

She had a hard time composing herself. "I fucking hate him. I swear to God I do. And my mom is a total bitch. Jessica isn't home, and I really needed someone to talk to. Can we talk?"

"Sure. Not here though. My dad's home and —"

"We can go to my place. My mom and *Señor Dickhead* went out."

We walked the stairs to the twelfth floor. She cried to me about how she felt lost. Being a person driven by emotion, I felt for her and consoled her as best I could. She collapsed into me, and I held her for a few moments. She pulled away slightly and started kissing me. I didn't resist. We kissed, and one thing led to another. I left her apartment only thinking of Jessica and my betrayal. I could not believe I let this happen and could only hope this event would pass without conflict. No luck, I got played. The next day, Alex told Jessica what had happened, and Jessica wanted nothing more to do with me. She wouldn't take my calls or talk to me when I saw her. It was now September, and Jessica still refused to talk to me. I ran into Alex in the lobby. We hadn't spoken since that day, and I stopped her and asked how things got so fucked up.

She smirked. "You got what you deserved."

"What did I ever do to you?"

"I was supposed to be the one to hook up with you. Not Jessica! You were supposed to like me. *What's wrong with me?*"

"Nothing. I just really liked Jessica."

"But you fucked me anyway, didn't you? I knew you would. All guys are the same. You took my best friend away."

"What are you even talking about?"

"You and Jess were together all the time, and she didn't have time for me anymore. You brought this on yourself. Fuck you."

There I stood, devastated. I no longer had Jessica, and it was all my fault.

Jessica continued giving me the silent treatment, and even though we lived in the same building, I never spoke to either her or Alex again.

Freshman Year

September was upon me, and starting school was creeping up too quickly for comfort. I was not prepared to enter a new school where I was an absolute stranger. I hated the sick feeling these thoughts gave me, but there they were, like a monster creeping out of my closet when the lights went off at night. I would lie in bed wide awake envisioning scenarios of the torture I might endure. —*Aw, look at the poor kid with the drunk dad and the mother that didn't want him.* My mother put me in this situation, and I was praying it was only temporary. —*Only until I get back on my feet, I promise.*

To my father's credit, he had given me five hundred dollars to go clothes shopping. This had been a few weeks before school was about to start. I went to Merry-Go-Round in the Cherry Hill mall and talked to a salesgirl not much older than myself. I told her to pick out outfits and that I had a five-hundred-dollar limit. I spent hours there as she kept throwing clothes over the door of the dressing room. I finally walked out with my new wardrobe and left the store confident. I was ready. Spending that amount of money for clothes was a ridiculous concept for me, but I needed to fit in. I was about to enter a school where kids came from wealthy upbringings. I had no money. I wasn't a trust fund kid. This thought hadn't fully sunk in; if it had, I think I would have shut down completely. My lack of privilege hit me like an avalanche on the first day of school.

It was the morning of my first day at Cherry Hill East High School, and I stood in front of the mirror wearing one of those new outfits. I felt my bladder would fail me at any moment. Since we used the address of my father's friend, I needed to walk about fifteen minutes to reach the bus stop. When I arrived, there were already a handful of kids talking and laughing. I stood silently and waited among them, petrified. The school bus squealed up, and we all piled in like zombie sheep. I sat in the front in a seat by myself and wondered how I was going to make it through this. The bus pulled into the high school parking lot, and when I got off, I felt certain I was not meant to be here. I looked around and saw a sea of luxury cars: BMW's, Volvos and Mercedes Benzes. *How do these people afford this?* I recalled the time I went to Wawa and bought lunch with food stamps and felt worse. Again, I had no business being at this place and pondered if my father did this to torment me. I went through that day in a haze, and I'm not sure if I said a word to anyone. I got off the bus and walked home, mad at my mother for putting me in this situation. I know she didn't want this for me. Still, she put me here. I went home and cried myself to sleep that night.

The next day I woke up and went through the same routine. I reached school, and the feeling I was trespassing continued. However, this day changed everything. At gym class, I began talking to the boy who would become my closest friend in ninth grade. His name was Ali Rahimi. He was Iranian-American and very welcoming. We talked during gym class, and I later found we shared the same lunch period. I sat with him and his friends, and I began to feel the nervousness wane. That nausea in the pit of my stomach departed. We spent the next few weeks talking and getting to know one another. I would say he was my best friend, but I was living a lie. He had no idea I wasn't well off and that I actually lived in an apartment on the wrong side of town with my father who was a glorified maintenance man. I shied away from those topics at all costs. He probably wouldn't have even cared, but I wasn't about to take that chance. I was, again, hiding behind a façade. I couldn't shake the feeling of inadequacy. I decided to embrace my disguise through deception and avoidance. I found myself spending all my free time with Ali, and many days I went to his house after school. He lived about a mile away from school in a house like those I'd only seen on *Lifestyles of the Rich and Famous*. It was enormous and Mediterranean in its décor. His father was a heart surgeon, and his mother was a lawyer. I felt out of place and happy at the same time. This rich kid was now becoming a very close friend. Ali had an older brother, Arman, finishing his senior year. Arman was one of the most popular kids in school, and I soon found out why. He was a dealer in the drug ring that infected the town. It didn't seem to bother me because I was just happy to "belong". The wooden rollercoaster I was on had stopped the click-click of the climb and was about to plummet over the top and begin a sequence of drops, loops and hairpin turns. All I could do was hold on and hope not to lose my shit.

Since I was a buddy of the drugs dealer's little brother, I became accepted by the "cool" kids. Overnight, I accumulated a stable of friends. All were popular and more than willing to talk to me, even seek me out. These people primarily consisted of juniors and seniors. I played the part, felt more comfortable, and wore the situation that had haunted me mere weeks ago like a tailored suit. Ali invited me to a party on the third Friday night in the school year. I told my father I was sleeping over a friend's and went to his house after school. I'm not certain dad cared either way. We hung out and ate dinner with his parents and Arman before heading to the party. It was within walking distance, and when we arrived, the party was in full swing. There were so many people packed into this house that we could barely move. The air was thick with mixed perfume, bad breath, and sweat. The music was low but through the chatter you could hear *Comfortably Numb* by Pink Floyd playing in the background. Ali led me through the crowd and seemed to know everyone. He introduced me to random people along the way. I wondered how the hell some high school student could hold a party like this. There were no parents to be found, and there was alcohol everywhere. I had never experienced anything like it, and the situations would only get more absurd. The house was a split-level, with the living room upstairs. In there, an otherwise empty, round glass coffee table contained a small white mound of powder piled in the middle. A few lines of cocaine were neatly cut away from the rest. Two boys sat on the couch on cleanup duty. They disposed of the evidence with a rolled bill. Panic set in, and I was unsure if I was going to be able to handle this scene. Ali nodded me over, and once we reached the kitchen, he tossed me a beer. This night was not like the one in that vacant apartment where I drank slowly and calculatingly. I drank quickly and often. I don't remember much of the end of that night except throwing up in a bush outside the house. We made it back to Ali's, and the next morning would be the first of many brain-melting hangovers.

The next few months would be much of the same scene, and my comfort level settled. I began smoking pot on a regular basis with Ali and Arman. Unlike the first time, I now knew what it felt like to be stoned. We went to a small party one night with a crowd of ninth graders. I really didn't know many of them, but Ali was the shining star in this crew, so I garnered much attention just being part of his inner circle. The house wasn't as glamorous as I'd seen recently, but it was still better than anything I had. Everyone crowded in the basement where there was a wet bar, a pool table and a pinball machine. They had a real pinball machine! I wondered how anyone could have a pinball machine in their house. The night went on, and it was fairly mellow. There were a few cute girls there, but my sights were set on a blond that reminded me of a shorter and younger version of Jessica. I found myself gravitating toward her and finally got her attention. The crowd began to filter out, leaving only a few of us remaining; it was after midnight. For the first time in my life I had become the predator, stalking my prey. She went upstairs to the bathroom, and I soon followed. I stood outside like I was next in line. When she came out, I momentarily grabbed her hand as she passed. She stopped and just looked back. I reached out and pulled her closer but didn't say a word. I leaned forward hoping not to make a complete ass of myself. She leaned in and kissed me. We made out in the hallway for a few minutes. I then really had to pee so I told her I would see her downstairs. I did. It was like our little secret as we sat there interacting with the remaining stragglers. She told me she was going to leave soon, and I nearly begged her to stay. She did. At the end of the night it was me, Ali, this girl *(I'm so sorry I don't remember your name)* and the girl who hosted the party. Ali seemed to be a lock scoring with the house owners' daughter. They ventured upstairs, leaving not-Jessica and me alone. We hung out for a while and started shooting pool. She stayed close as I walked the perimeter of the table. I stood there assessing ball placement for my next shot when she stepped in between me and the table. She wrapped her arms around me, and the games were over.

I put my hands on her waist, and I guided her, as she bunny-hopped back onto the pool table. She was barely four feet tall, and I towered over her. I looked down on her, waiting. I leaned slightly forward, and she lunged toward me, grabbing both sides of my face. Her attempt to kiss me failed as we clanged teeth. There was a momentary giggle and retraction, followed by a successful retry. As we kissed, I slid her further back towards the center of the table. Leaning into her, I could feel the table's scratchy felt between my fingers. She clumsily pulled her shirt over her head and threw it to the side. I didn't bother trying to take off her bra. Instead, I pulled it down, exposing her. —*She wasn't Jessica*. She didn't have the experience or attitude to tell me what I wanted to hear, but I heard it just the same. —*please fuck me*. Her shorts were too tight, and I couldn't slide them off. I pulled myself away so she could undress. She was now lying there with a black lace thong and a smile. I slid it aside and fucked using both sides of the pool table for leverage. I could feel the felt beneath my knees ripping at my skin with every thrust. After we finished, I excused myself to the bathroom to assess the damage. I would have war wounds for weeks to come. My knees reminded me of the time I flew over the handlebars of my BMX bike when I was eleven. The skin grated away, leaving miniscule blood droplets seeping through. I couldn't find peroxide in the medicine cabinet, so I doused a handful of toilet paper with rubbing alcohol and dabbed at the wounds. When I went back downstairs the girl was lying on the couch with an afghan over her. She was wearing my IOU sweatshirt and not much else. I flipped off the recessed lighting, leaving us in darkness except for the fixture over the billiards table. I slipped onto the couch beside her. I was the big spoon. I heard the light hum from the furnace in the closet across the room. Sleep quickly found me.

I woke up the next morning and she was gone. I had no more than a passing conversation with her after that night. It was surreal how she tied no emotion to our encounter. I guess I was beginning to succumb to the norms of my environment. It was my first casual sex experience, and I held no particular emotion for the sex or the girl. She didn't even have a name to me. At least, not one I remembered. I moved on.

The typical high school social cliques existed but since my friends dealt drugs across those classes, the lines blurred. I was a friend with the athletes, the outcasts, and the theatre people. The parties Arman brought us to were carefully chosen. Ali and I accompanied his brother to most of these, and I sensed he was trying to diversify his customer portfolio. Those cliques held parties, and they seemed to stick with their own, but we fit in no matter the circumstance. It was a confidence builder to be in this situation where I could weave in and out of these different social classes. As long as they had the money to buy the drugs, we were there to happily provide them. I don't say this to make myself look any kind of way but, for the record, I never sold drugs. Well, I didn't but I was riding a drug dealer's coattails so what's the difference, really?

I was at a party one night that seemed particularly hardcore. We got there late and found Arman already snaking through the horde. There was a huge bong in the basement. I had not seen anything like it before. It looked like a decorative vase; bulbous on the bottom, tapered through the middle and, finally, flaring out at the top. There were six octopus-like tentacles protruding from the neck, each one connected to the lips of people sitting in a sort of prayer circle. I realized they were smoking pot through it. Amazed, I squirrelled my way in and took a few hits before moving on. The night went along, and people were staggering around. I hadn't been to a party with so many fucked up people, including myself. Heading upstairs from the basement, I saw something I still have dreams about. This kid was freaking out and jumping around like an idiot. Kind of screaming but more talking gibberish to himself loudly. The next thing I knew he was diving through the front bay window. The crash of glass sent people into a hysterical frenzy, and everyone scattered like roaches. I made my way outside where I saw the kid lying there, convulsing, covered in blood. I was terrified and just started running. I had no idea where I was going, I just ran. I got a few blocks away from the party house and ducked down behind a car parked on the street. I heard sirens in the distance, which prompted me to continue my Forrest-Gump-like trek home. Finally getting my bearings, I realized I was now on Kresson Road. This was the street the bus followed to take me back to my "house". I was extremely high and drunk, so I was also dizzy and paranoid. I dove behind bushes whenever I saw headlights, thinking every passing car must be a cop. I reached the apartment in a couple hours and only later realized I'd run about five miles that night. School was buzzing all week. This kid was alive, thankfully, but had suffered serious cuts on his hands and face and was in the hospital. There was a rumor he had smoked a joint laced with LSD, and that's what flipped him out. Either way, I was paranoid every time I smoked from that point on. The partying calmed down for the next few weeks. I went to Ali's house many nights, and we'd get high with his brother and hang out. School was going okay, but I cannot say I was the greatest student. My grades were nothing to write home about, and I was more interested in the social access it gave me.

The weekly parties started up again. It seems like that's all I did that year, but I was having fun, maybe too much. I thought of how unhappy my mother would be to see me this way, but that didn't stop my actions. I found myself comparing my reckless behavior with that of my father. That didn't move the needle either. I continued working a few days a week doing odds and ends for the apartment building, and most of my money went toward chipping in for beer and weed. I even started buying my own stash.

We went to a party one night and it was bananas, borderline obscene. It was a party held by the football team, and the girls there were beyond beautiful. Football players are famous for attracting the prettiest girls, so it was no surprise, but I was still blown away. I was intimidated because these guys were all in great shape, and I was really thin. It didn't matter, I was gaining confidence! I talked to tons of girls that night. The party spilled outside, and even though it was freezing no one seemed to care. I drank, smoked, and bullshitted the night away. I made out with a couple random girls. It seemed like no big deal to anyone. Maybe not even me at this point. After having sex on a pool table with a girl I just met, I realized these girls didn't really ponder repercussions. I started hooking up with a girl in some random room. She had jet black hair that felt like silk. If I hadn't been underage myself, I might have questioned her age. Things progressed, and she countered my advances of sex with fellatio, something she stumbled through with, seemingly, no experience, and it ended up being the worst blowjob ever. It was clumsy and toothy and downright dreadful. I didn't finish and we both walked away a little put off. I'm not sure what went wrong. It's not one of my fondest memories. I brushed it off when I started talking to Michelle Laurent. She was about five-six with dark brown poker-straight hair, pinned up with barrettes on the sides. She turned out to be of French and Italian descent. Her speaking voice was almost too proper, leaving no doubt she came from money. I didn't have more than eight dollars in my pocket, but I had her hook, line and sinker. She laughed at everything I said. Her smile tore threw me like a cannon blast. Michelle was a sophomore and, unfortunately for me, dating one of the senior football players. He paid zero attention to her, so I was free to keep banging my head against the wall. I continued to pursue her even though I had no shot. After that night, Jessica lost pole position to Michelle. She was all I thought about, and I guess that's the point of teenage crushes. I found myself constantly daydreaming about her. I couldn't help it. We shared no classes and rarely saw each other except passing in the hallway. When we did bump into one another, we'd stop and chat for a few minutes about nonsense. I tried to be witty, but it was always rushed. I found myself walking away replaying those snippets of conversations and editing them for things I should have said in the place of the things I actually said. Nonetheless, she always seemed pleased to stop and talk whenever we could.

It was reaching spring, and the partying continued. I was now smoking weed alone outside the apartment building. I would go to the Wawa a few hundred yards from the complex and buy cigarettes. I had become a pretty regular smoker. I pushed down the recurring thoughts of how disappointed my mother would be. My grades were hovering just above the Mendoza line. I began experiencing moments of feeling worthless. I felt like I was just going through the same motions and not really evolving as a person. I think I was beginning to resent myself a bit for succumbing to the darker side I have, and I attributed that to my father's DNA. His liquid lunches made him oblivious to my current lifestyle and mental state. I'm not sure it would have bothered him anyway. He enjoyed the stories of some of my conquests. Dad now knew I was going to parties and hooking up with girls but had no idea I was smoking pot. I even confessed to him about my crush on Michelle.

In one of our hallway fender-benders, I found out Michelle was joining the swim club. Turns out, it was much like any normal high school club like the chess club or science club. When I talked with Ali, he thought I was joining the swim team. I wasn't that ambitious. I just wanted to be closer to

Michelle. This was the first of many manufactured ploys throughout my life I attempted to *get the girl*.

Today was the day. The bell rang, I rushed to my locker, dropped off my books, and got my backpack. I headed down to the basement excited to see Michelle. She was still dating the football player, but I didn't care. I just wanted to be around her. I scanned the pool and there she was, surrounded by four other girls, talking and laughing. She was in a one-piece bathing suit, and she looked beautiful. I went into the locker room and changed into my new suit. It had cost me a small fortune that I had to work extra to pay for. I stuffed my school clothes into the bag and headed out. She saw me as I walked along the opposite side of the pool. A whistle blew from a distance. The teacher overseeing the club was gesturing for Michelle to stop running.

"You just got me in trouble, Mister." Michelle was squinting at me in a playful, accusing way.

"What, me? Noooo. You were the one running."

"I never expected to see you here."

"I love to swim and thought it would be fun. Meet new people."

"And see me!"

"A fortunate coincidence," I said.

I befriended a few of the guys in the club. I tried not to reveal she was the only reason I joined. I was gaining traction and started sensing I was becoming more than a friend. One Wednesday when we were getting out of the pool, she told me not to leave. I got changed and headed back to wait. I stood a few minutes before she appeared from the girl's locker room. She handed me an envelope that had my name written in big bubbly letters. She kissed me on the cheek and said to not open it until I got home. I couldn't wait. As soon as I was safely on the late bus, I was like a bomb technician carefully deconstructing the envelope. The letter was six pages long and told a story about a girl who met a boy. It continued citing examples of events we had shared from her perspective and expressing what she thought to be an unrequited love. The final paragraph depicted a picnic that took place in a clearing in the woods where the couple made love. I was elated and at a loss for words having Michelle pour her feelings into that envelope. I spent the rest of the night wondering what it all meant and stared holes through the paper; I read it a dozen times that night. I was going back to school not quite knowing how to react. Fortunately, I guess, I didn't see her right away and thought maybe she was embarrassed and avoiding me. I may have even been relieved. Michelle was one of those girls that deserves to be put on a pedestal. She belonged there, but I could not give her what she deserved. Not even honesty, which is free.

That week before swim club she asked, "Do you have time to talk before you leave today? I really want to get a few thoughts off my mind. I told my mother to pick me up thirty minutes later today just in case."

"Of course," I said.

After swim club, we changed back into our school clothes, walked out the front doors and sat on a bench beneath the flagpole. She sat so close she was brushing against me as she spoke, her hands flailing in concert with her words.

"I'm really getting tired of Daniel. All he wants to do is drink and party every weekend. That's not my scene, but I have gone along with it. He never spends time with me. I have been weighing my options. And, if I am being completely honest, Brian, I can't stop thinking about you. Crazy, right?"

"Not to me." I just stared into her eyes. Moments passed with no words exchanged.

"I also don't want you to think I am some loose girl bouncing from one guy to the next. I'm not. I was thinking about breaking up with him before we met. You *have* given me more reason to do it. Again, being honest."

"I don't think that about you. I like you too."

Michelle smiled, and I reached and grabbed for her hand. Honking from the black Mercedes pulling into the lot broke our stare and ruined any chance I had to steal a kiss. It was probably my safest move since she was still dating someone that could break me in two.

I told Ali what happened, and I'm not certain he truly believed me, so I showed him the letter. He was stunned and said I should be careful messing around with a senior's girlfriend. I agreed it wasn't in my best interest. The paranoia was all for nothing. The next weekend Michelle broke up with Dan. From what I heard around school; it didn't bother him. In fact, there were rumors he was saying he ended it.

The next week we walked to a McDonald's not too far from school and grabbed something to eat. We talked effortlessly, and I was so comfortable with Michelle. She had her mother picking her up and offered to give me a ride home. I declined, and my heart sank. I realized I was, once again, living a lie. I avoided all talk of my personal life and turned all the focus toward her. I had told her I lived in Barclay Farms, the development near my building, with my father. I should have told the truth, but I was young and thought since she had money, I needed to play the part of having it too. I kept the charade going the entire time we dated. Much like my friendship with Ali, everything revolved around her world. She would never know I was a poor kid with a drunken, verbally abusive father living in an apartment building on the wrong side of the tracks. I did everything I could to hide my shame, and I played the role.

Michelle wasn't the partying type and didn't really get into the whole drug scene, so I struggled to balance my friendship with Ali and that crowd while finding time to hang out with Michelle. As the pendulum swayed farther in her favor, my friendship with Ali was slipping. I was still smoking weed and drinking, but never around Michelle. I was piling up lie after lie, although I never lied to her or myself about how I felt. I remember sitting in her living room watching television. I wanted in the worst way to tell her that I loved her, and even though it was the only truth I had, I couldn't seem to get the words out. We sat there on the couch holding hands watching MTV and singing along with the videos. We were singing "She Bop" by Cindy Lauper and laughing. I stole a few kisses that day, but our relationship was pretty tame considering what I had experienced over the last few months. I didn't care; I was content having a beautiful, sweet girl to call mine.

We talked on the phone every night, but this one conversation was different. Michelle told me her parents were going away for the weekend, so she invited me to stay over while they were gone. Michelle was an only child, so we would have the house to ourselves. We planned on my coming over early Saturday morning. I sleep-walked through school the next week and was too young to appreciate the concept of anticipation. The weekend was finally upon me, and I was coursing with excitement. She didn't live too far off Route 70, so I took a bus and walked the remainder of the way. I told my father that I was going to Ali's house and staying until Sunday. He didn't care and told me to have fun and be careful. I arrived at Michelle's house like a cat burglar looking out for neighbors. I dashed through the side gate leading to the backyard. I knocked on the sliding glass door and a minute later saw her coming toward the door. She was wearing cut off jean shorts and a Duran Duran t-shirt. So pretty. Michelle slid open the door; once in, I dropped my bag and immediately kissed her. I couldn't help myself.

"Sorry, I needed that."

"Me too," she replied.

It was about noon, so we ate lunch and lay together on the couch and watched MTV. I kissed and caressed her the entire time. We fell asleep lying there and woke up midafternoon. I remember waking up to find her staring at me, smiling. It was a feeling I will never forget and gives me goose bumps thinking about it. I woke to her looking, lovingly, at me and I felt total happiness. I hugged her tightly. She got up, grabbed my hand; and led me upstairs. We went into her room. The room's walls were pink, decorated with pictures of Ralph Macchio and Matt Dillon torn from *Teen* or *Tiger Beat* magazines. Otherwise, the room was tidy, barring scattered clothes on the floor. Michelle jumped on the bed and knelt down as I was standing in the doorway. I walked over and sat beside her. We began to kiss, and I eventually decided to steal second base. My heart was pounding through my chest. Moments later we were naked and fumbling under the covers. We were kissing for a long time before anything serious happened. She took control and as she moaned, I lost mine and it was over. She melted on top of me, and we lay there staring into each other's eyes. She whispered. "I love you," in my ear; I reciprocated. I really felt I did.

Now dressed and back downstairs, we were both famished. I was craving egg rolls, so we ordered Chinese. I spent every dime, including my bus fare home, to buy dinner. We sat in the living room feeding each other directly out of the

Chinese take-out containers with chop sticks, hysterically laughing and watching MTV. The night grew old, and we ended up back in her room, this time to sleep. The next morning, I left shortly after waking because I was paranoid her parents were going to show up early. I had spent all my money on food, so I had to walk the entire way. I replayed the day in my head to pass the time. It is still one of my favorite memories, and it saddens me to think I cannot even recall the sweet girl's real name.

It was the beginning of February 1985, and my freshman year, at least at this school, was about to come to an abrupt end. My mom called to tell me she was moving back to Franklinville the next week and wanted me to come home. I didn't hesitate. I packed everything I had and counted down the days. This had been a surreal time for me, but I always felt out of place. I had lost my virginity, partied entirely too hard, fallen in love a couple of times, and lied to everyone I cared about. I would be moving home on the twenty-second, and the Saturday before, I found myself in my room, alone. Michelle was with girlfriends, and Ali was away with his family. I was watching MTV and wanted to get high. I headed toward the kitchen and saw my father passed out on the chair. I grabbed a sheet of aluminum foil and went back and locked my door. I made a makeshift bowl with the foil and I took a baggy containing about two joints worth of pot and locked myself in the bathroom. I turned on the exhaust fan. As I exhaled, I caught myself in the mirror, and it struck me. What the fuck was I doing? What had I become? What had happened to the kid who came to this place less than a year ago? I didn't know, but I didn't like it. A memory of my brother flashed through my mind. —*Mom knows*. I buried the bowl in the trash and flushed the weed down the toilet and vowed to never smoke marijuana again. I didn't hold to that promise, but I did not smoke through the remainder of my high school years.

Moving day was here, and I brought my bags to the lobby and sat there waiting. Ironically, Jessica walked past me without a word. She glanced down at my luggage, looked at me with a wry half-hearted smile, and she disappeared into the elevator. A few minutes later my mother came through the front doors. Unable to hold back the tears, she was a sobbing mess as she hugged the life out of me in the middle of the lobby. I left that day and, again, ghosted everyone close to me, just as I had done a little over nine months prior. The only difference was I never saw any of them again. Not Ali. Not Michelle. I have often thought about them over the years but never spoke of them to anyone. I didn't tell anyone about most of what happened that year.

First Crush (reprise)

When I moved back to Franklinville in late February of '85, it was into a brand-new low-income housing development. My full-sized bed took up half of the ten-feet by twelve-feet room. It was about a quarter the size of the room I had in the apartment in Cherry Hill, but I wouldn't have exchanged it. My first order of business was to go back to Washington Avenue where my friends lived and see if anyone was home. The very first Saturday morning, I hopped on my bike, and took a ride over. There was only one person I was looking for, and she was there. Melanie was at her aunt's, Thomas's mother's house. She looked much different from the last time I had seen her, only nine months prior, a little haggard, stressed out maybe. We talked and headed up to the fort to hang out. The "fort" was located in the rafters of Thomas's rickety garage. The year before, we had hammered two-by-fours to the wall as a makeshift ladder and covered the cross boards of the a-frame roof with sheets of plywood. Thomas and I put this together shortly before I moved, and it now seemed very "lived in." I climbed up and noticed blankets, candles, magazines, and the familiar smell of weed, stale booze, and cigarettes. It seems we all grew up a little that year. Melanie entered before me and lit a candle. She crawled to the back and returned with a fifth of Jack Daniels. She gestured for me to take it and when I waved it off, she took a swig and replaced the cap. We talked for a while, and eventually the moment I had waited for more than two years to happen, happened. Melanie kissed me. I had loved this girl for as much as I had the capacity to do so back then. But here, in this moment, after so much had happened, everything had changed. I wanted desperately to go back to that time where we were both innocent and pure and just fueled by our adolescent emotions. That was not to be. I had loved her just a year ago; an innocent, unsullied love. It was now gone.

Brother

I spent my entire childhood idolizing my older brother. For whatever reason, we were never very close. It's funny, my mother and I were cut from the same cloth, emotionally. Brady was just different, and my mother would often say he was a "typical O'Sullivan." The O'Sullivan's were my mother's side of the family and mostly an unemotional clan, so my brother blended in perfectly. Mom and I were outliers, and towards the end of her life she would say she and I must have been adopted. Brady just seemed to find it difficult to express emotion.

My brother and I co-existed as the years wore on but never truly bonded. When we moved to Franklinville in 1981, he was going to be turning sixteen in September and beginning his junior year. *I was eleven.* Brady tried out for the baseball team, but with his rapidly deteriorating knees he did not make varsity. There was a point in time where he had been a shoo-in to get a college scholarship catching for at least a Division 2 school. Now he couldn't even make the varsity squad on a mediocre high school team. He gave up his dream and focused on being a grease monkey. He took shop classes in high school and realized he had a talent under the hood. My brother had been used to the attention from being a great baseball player, and now he could be found mostly wearing flannel, grease stained jeans, and obscurity. I didn't think too much about it until I was much older, but I can imagine how it must have affected him having his dream of playing meaningful baseball dissolve before him.

Right after high school, Brady enlisted in the Air Force. When he was going through boot camp, mom told me how homesick he was, so I wrote him countless letters. The following are shortened versions of his responses to my letters and my only windows into his world. These exchanges would be the most my brother has ever talked to me and, certainly, the most vulnerable.

8, Nov, 83

Dear Brian,

It was good to get your letter yesterday, (7, Nov, 83) it really made my day. I got mom's letter today. It was 9 pages long, that made me feel good too. Mom told me you got a 98 on your universe project because you followed my advice (which when you take my advice you can't go wrong). I'm glad to hear you did good. Just make sure you keep up the good work.

Thanks for letting me know about Steve crying on the way home. It just proves to me, in a way, that he is going to miss me, and he is a true friend. Whatever you do, don't lose or take advantage of your friends. If they take advantage of you, you don't need them.

Just do me a favor and write me as often as you can because I really miss you and your letters make me pretend you're here. It's always good to hear from you. Let me know if you need anything or advice for anything. You know I'm always here for you.

I love you very, very much and I miss you just as much. Write me back soon.

I love you,

Brady

I was surprised by Brady's openness and hoped we might become closer than ever through these letters. They made me so happy. He never told me he loved me when he was home. He certainly couldn't be bothered to give me a forum to ask for the advice he offered. My thirteen-year-old brain couldn't comprehend his current environment and state of mind. He was seeking the familiarity of home and trying to escape his current reality. I cherished this time and resented him later for not being the person he was in these letters.

20, Nov, 83

Dear Brian,

Thanks for the (Billy) Squier picture. It reminded me of rock and roll. We don't get to listen to any radio or watch MTV. I'm glad to hear you're pulling A's and B's in all your classes. Keep it up.

Your letter made my day. I don't have much to tell you at this point expect that I love you and I miss you. Beginning tomorrow, I have fifteen more training day left. I'll be home for Christmas. Talk to you later.

Love Brady

2, Dec, 83

Dear Brian,

How you doing? I can't wait to hear that Eddie Murphy tape, is it <u>really</u> funny? I hope so because he's a blast.

I don't care if you use my radio, just be careful with it, okay? I hope you have the money to pay for them tapes you bought. Get me a couple if you can. 350 comic books is a lot. Keep it up, Okay! I'm surprised you haven't gotten bored of it yet. How much money do you have tied up in them? I have to go, lights out in a couple minutes. I love you. See you when I get home.

Love Brady

We already established that I collected comic books. Tons of them. If fact, I ended up selling my collection in order to buy my first car which was a mint condition '72 Chevelle SS. It was orange with white racing stripes and a complete chick magnet for the two months I owned it before wrapping it around a telephone pole. This letter came before I was arrested for stealing comic books from the convenience store.

Lastly, the Eddie Murphy tape Brady referred to was called *Delirious*. It came out as an HBO stand-up special in 1983. It was also available on cassette tape, so I bought it. If you haven't seen it, shame on you.

24, Jan, 84

Dear Brian,

How's it going guy? I'm hanging in there, you know me. I hope you get the job you want because you can use the money, right. I'm studying diesels now, it's pretty interesting but complicated at the same time.

Why are you taking intro to small engines? Do you want to build a Kick-ass car like my Trans Am? Wait till you see it when I get through with it.

You should see me now; I'm really starting to fill out pretty good. I go to the gym every weekend and physical training three days a week which is a mandatory formation (which means I have to go).

I'm going to go. I have to do some studying and them I'm crashing out. Write soon. I miss you. I love you.

Love Brady

Dec,16, 86

Dear Brian,

How are you doing? I'm OK, I guess. Merry Christmas! Happy New Year! Hope you have a good xmas. Sorry I couldn't send you anything from here, but Margie will take care of you from the both of us.

Is It snowing there? It's 55 degrees on an average right now and rainy all the time. All they play on the base radio station is xmas songs. It's depressing but I'll get through. You know me, I can handle just about anything in one way or another.

I took the test for my European driver's license last weekend and passed, of course. I will pick it up this Friday. When do you get your driver's license? Good luck!

Well, I have to go for now. Take care of yourself.

Merry Christmas and Happy New Year.

Love Brady

This last letter was a couple years later but they were all I had managed to hold onto over the years. Brady was stationed in Italy at this time and I'd later found out he was dealing with an alcohol problem that stemmed from his inability to cope with the stress of being there. It just goes to show the façade people can present to hide an alternate reality.

The words Brady wrote in those letters were the most emotion I would ever get from him. I can't say he didn't feel them, but he was never very good at translating them in person. I'd like to say he tried to be the big brother I desired but not really sure his attempt resembled anything I had ever imagined to be ideal.

It's not like he was horrible to me. He really wasn't. He just didn't seem to have any desire to play the role, and when he tried it always felt forced. For instance, after Brady came back from Italy, he was stationed at Andrews Air Force Base in Maryland. He arranged for me to come down one weekend. I was still sixteen, so it was very exciting for me to go hang out with my big brother and his fellow airmen. He had one of his buddies drive me down, and he met us at the gate. We went to his apartment, and he immediately offered me a beer. Later that night we all hung out in one of his friend's apartment and played "Scarface." Never playing it before, I had questions. I came to find out it was the simplest of games. Every time Al Pacino's character, Tony Montana, said, "Fuck you," you drank. Simple. If you've seen the movie, you'll understand why I spent the majority of the night throwing up into a trash can. It was a confusing night on many levels and, maybe I should have been content with the bonding experience we just shared, but it was lacking. I've thought about this for years, and it is probably any sixteen-year old's dream to hang out drinking beer with his older brother. It wasn't the time we spent together as much as the hollowness that accompanied it. We simply never connected. I tend to be more outwardly emotional than most males, especially Brady. He certainly had the capacity for being emotional given the letters he sent to me, but not expressing his feelings was his downfall. And, ultimately, the demise of any meaningful sibling relationship.

In high school, I started participating in all the stage productions. I had lead roles in the dramas but smaller parts in the musicals due to my lack of singing skills. Nonetheless, I became fairly well known throughout the town. I am only speculating, but I feel this small-town success was not appreciated by my brother. I remember the day Brady told me "I wish people would shut the fuck up about you already!" I was devastated and really didn't understand the source of his hostility. I knew mom was proud and gushed about me to whoever would listen but apparently, he was hearing about me wherever he went. He wasn't home when I played Buzz Pennywinner in our production of *They Run in Our Family*. He came home one day and, out of the blue, asked about the time I got hit in the balls on stage. According to whoever told him the story, I was a *riot*, but it was obvious Brady didn't think so. The play is about a family obsessed with sports. I played Buzz, an energetic high schooler about to play his first football game. At one point I entered stage right, running, and misjudging where the couch ended and my testicles began, I crashed crotch first. Although blinded by pain, I was always taught the show must go on. Even if you flubbed a line, make it work. Make the audience embrace the moment. I had lines to recite and I recited them. I admit to hamming it up and realized I stole their hearts with the ovation I received that night. It was talked about for as long as I can remember, but even though I should have been happy to steal the show I was quietly embarrassed. And here was my brother giving me shit for being memorable. His resentment towards any accolades I drew became ever more noticeable. At the time, I didn't piece together that his resentment had less to do with anything I did but more of what he did not. He should have been behind the plate those short years ago with all the town talking about how tremendous a baseball player he was. That never happened. It was stolen from him, and I feel some pity knowing he never got to fulfill his dreams. I just grew more distant. I had a growing collection of very good friends that filled the void.

Over the years, the gap between us only seemed to widen. I'd always been my mother's favorite. Whether it was because I was the youngest, I'm not sure, but it was apparent. Mom and I were just much more alike.

Brady and Margie lived on the Air Force Base in Maryland for many years. He always gravitated toward his wife's family over ours. They were a large Irish Catholic clan that was still intact. It was the kind of stability he was missing, so he clung to it. It became apparent where his allegiance lay when he came home for the holidays. He would go visit mom for a few hours and then spend several days with his in-laws. The inequitable division of time was never lost on my mother, and she was quietly crushed by his actions.

High School Sweetheart

I just finished tenth grade and wanted to find steady work for the summer. I was hired as a dishwasher at the local diner. To that point, I had various odd jobs delivery bread and scrubbing pots at a bakery as well as two paper routes. All were before school and negatively impacted my grades as well as my ability to stay awake. I wanted to work to help my mother pay bills and have a little walking around money. Every fall, mom took me to Jamesway or some other low rent department store to buy school clothes. I never wanted to embarrass her, so I kept comments to myself, but I also I wasn't parading around like a runway model in the only clothes she could afford. Working made me feel like I was contributing to our household and my self-esteem.

The Lombardi brothers owned the diner. They were a comical Italian duo whose huge forearms and square jawlines reminded me of a cross between Rocky Balboa and Popeye. Frank ran the front of the house and the business side, and his brother Joe was, for lack of a better term, the chef. I worked in the dish room. You could practically taste the uneaten leftovers as I scraped them off the plates and into the garbage can. The smell from the decomposing, organic, trash pile was a combination of raw sewage, industrial strength sanitizer and a hint of vomit. It gets caught in your nose and you swear it will never dissipate. I got used to it. I had spent months cleaning dishes and pots when Joe asked me to peel potatoes. This was the first mundane opportunity at what would become my first professional passion, culinary arts. Joe provided no direction, so I took it upon myself to go to the stock room and get a fifty-pound bag of spuds. I grabbed a potato peeler and started tearing through this starchy mountain and was about two-thirds of the way through when I heard Joe cursing my name. I poked my head up, and he asked me why I couldn't follow "simple, fucking directions." I apologized, but I wasn't sure why. I found out he had a pot on the stove full of potatoes that were being blanched. He had left them and assumed I understood his intentions. Meanwhile, the potatoes were boiling away to nothing. After that incident, Joe never liked me, but I had potential, so I was no longer washing dishes. I was doing prep work fulltime. I was soon trained to work the fry station for dinner shift. I did not receive a raise but was able to eat whatever I wanted. Over time, I swapped places with the grill cook just to break up the monotony and eventually worked both stations on slower nights.

By the time my junior year began, I was working a set schedule at the diner. By then, the Lombardi brothers had sold the restaurant to a dentist. He purchased it as a gift for his wife. It was her favorite place to dine with her parents when she was a child. It's a stupid reason to get into the restaurant business, but stupidity was a low hurdle to jump for these folks. They had a daughter, and she was stunning, about a year older than I was. She was a beacon of light walking through the restaurant, and the only thing preventing her from being a celestial creature was her being a terrible human. She grew up on the right side of privilege but lacked humility. She could do no wrong in her parents' eyes. I'm a horrible person to admit how elated I was when I heard she had been knocked up by some random guy. The gossip tore through the diner like a brush fire. They sold the restaurant not even a year into their ownership. I never saw or heard from that family again.

When the new owners took over, we soon realized we were all auditioning for our jobs. The new owners were Greek-Americans and very demanding. They also knew what it took to successfully run a diner. After two weeks, only two cooks were left standing, me and Dijon. They fired everyone else. Dijon was the breakfast cook who worked the grill on the weekends. He was a god in my eyes. He was the inspiration and tutor I needed to handle Sunday mornings at the eggs station at Denny's years later. I worked the grill at night; on the busiest nights.

When someone was hired at the diner, their first thirty minutes consisted of being paraded around like a prize cow and introduced to the staff. This is how I met Valerie Smith. I raised my spatula as if to say hello as she was standing with the owner's wife. Her sheepish smile was accessorized with dimples and a cute crinkle in her nose. She would only ever be considered cute, and I really hadn't given her a second glance. Valerie was shorter than my usual type and would fall into the *solidly built* category. I could not have picked her out of a line-up after our first introduction. One of the waitresses told me Valerie took the job just to be close to me. I found the idea of having a stalker somewhat flattering. It *did* start the conversation, and over time I began to like this girl. She was timid at first but had a personality that drew me in. She called me on my sarcasm and challenged me on my opinions. I liked it, and I liked her. We began to date, and I soon became a fixture in her home. Her family became mine. Well, sort of. Her mother adored me. Her father was a hollow, emotionless shell of a person, and her brother, Mike, was a loner and unsure of his place in the world. No shame there, he was a kid. Nonetheless, I felt at home. I found myself eating dinners with them and generally feeling part of their all-American family. Since I didn't come from a traditional one, it was refreshing.

We were young and in love for what that's worth in those teenage years. Over the next few months, the relationship was heating up. In the living room late one Friday night, we were on the couch watching TV. Adhering to the *keep-one-light-on* house rule, the room was dimly lit. The rest of the family was fast asleep down the hall as the heavy petting began. We tumbled off the couch and hit the floor with a thump which was muted by the volume of the television. I pushed the coffee table away from the couch creating the much-needed space to work. Her father's XXXL scarlet Rutgers University t-shirt, black Umbro soccer shorts and cotton panties were her only defenses. I found myself hovering over her with my pants down around my knees. It was like a praying mantis trying to mate with a ladybug. I covered her small frame in dancing shadows. Being her first time, some discomfort was expected. The pain came but not for the right reasons. Initially, I saw the strain in her gaze. She went with it.

"Are you okay? Should I stop?" I said, feeling something was wrong.

"No, I'm okay." Val was wincing.

I could no longer feel the friction needed to keep going. Pulling away from her, I backed onto my knees using my hands for leverage. The carpet squished and I looked down to see the floor was soaked in a sea of blood. I told her there was a problem and when I withdrew my hand it was now wearing a liquid glove. The horror in her eyes matched how I felt.

"Brian, you have to *go!*" Val said in a trembled voice.

"I'm not leaving you like this."

"My father will *kill* you." Her voice was cracking and increasing in volume. Tears collected in her eyes. She was pushing me towards the door. I nearly fell backwards with my pants still sagging at half-mast.

"Go!" she said.

"Are you sure? I —"

"*Gooo!*"

I was terrified and confused. I sat in my car across the street silently freaking out and talking myself into going back in. I heard a low scream and saw her bedroom light come on several minutes later. Someone was in the room with her, but I heard no voices. I drove away. The next day her mother called.

"Hi Brian, it's Mrs. Smith." I could hear the exhaustion and worry in her voice.

"Hi, Mrs. Smith. How is Val?" I paused. "I'm so sorry."

"The doctors are keeping a close eye on her right now. She'll probably be here for a few days."

"Can I come see her?"

"That's probably not the best idea right now, Brian. Her father needs some time to process what happened."

"What happened to Val? I mean, I know what happened but not really sure, you know. I shouldn't have left."

"Leaving was the best thing you could have done. Valerie told me she went into the bathroom. She sat on the toilet thinking the bleeding would stop. She then went to lay down and that's when I heard the screams. When I went in her sheets were covered in blood. I yelled for her father to call 911. By the time we got to the hospital, Val was in shock. She went into emergency surgery to repair a laceration in one of her vaginal walls. The surgery went fine and she's resting in the ICU."

"I'm so truly sorry, Mrs. Smith. I don't know what else to say."

"You don't need to say anything. She's going to be okay. I just wanted you to know."

"Thank you for calling," I said. Mrs. Smith broke the connection.

After four days in Kennedy Memorial Hospital, Valerie was released. I was waiting outside the house when Mr. Smith's dark blue Chevy Suburban pulled into the driveway. I could only imagine how this man must have been feeling. His only daughter had sex for the *first* time and nearly died. My taking her virginity on his living room floor was plenty to take in. Still, I needed to face the situation. Mrs. Smith got out and opened the back-passenger side door to help Val. Her father gave a grim glance in my direction as he headed into the house. I jumped out of my car and rushed over to help. Val gave me a pained, thin-lipped smile and kissed me on the cheek when I hugged her. During our momentary embrace I caught the gaze of her mother and wondered if I made a mistake coming. I grabbed a duffle bag from the back seat and asked, "Is it okay if I come in?"

"It's fine, her father wants to talk to you anyway."

"Oh, mom, come on." Val was noticeably prescribed medication for the pain.

Mrs. Smith ushered Val into her room as I dropped the duffle on the chair in the family room. I saw Mr. Smith sitting at the dining room table staring at a rocks glass that looked to contain a couple fingers of whiskey. I never took him for much of a drinker, so I braced for impact.

"Hi, Mr. Smith. I wanted to—"

"Sit down," he interrupted in a monotone voice. I sat at the table directly across from him. I wondered if I was out of his swinging radius. He looked pensive, saying nothing for some time. He took the whiskey down in one gulp and said,

"You love my daughter, right?" His eyes were fixed on his empty glass.

"Yes, sir."

"I know you didn't mean to hurt her, but she's my little girl and we almost lost her." He then locked eyes with me and said again, "We almost lost her." His eyes were glistening and red.

"I'm so sorry. I never meant for... I mean, I didn't... I'm just really sorry."

"You're going to marry her, right?" he asked.

"Of course. I love Valerie very much. Can I go see her now?"

He nudged his head in the direction of Val's room. That was my permission for dismissal. I went in, and Val had succumbed to the situation and the medication. She slept until the next day.

You would think this was the end of the story, right? It wasn't. Surprisingly, the whole family was able to move past the traumatic event, and our relationship continued; it even grew stronger. Val and I spent most of our time together, and although sex was no longer an option, we were still boyfriend and girlfriend. I became closer than ever to the family. I ate dinner there practically every night, slept over from time to time, and everything was back to normal.

When I graduated high school, Valerie still had a year left. Our vastly different schedules put a mounting strain on the relationship. I was going full-time to college studying culinary arts, so, to compensate for our time apart, I spent most nights at her house. While I was *permitted* to sleep over, I was sequestered in her room; she bunked on the couch. I spent considerable quality time with her family, mostly by cooking dinner. I embraced the opportunity to practice what I was learning in school. Her mother shopped for groceries we would never have afforded at my house. Val was in school every weekday, but for me, classes were scattered at various times throughout the week, therefore it was not unusual for me to sleep in on days I could. She and her brother would be at school and her parents at work. I usually had the run of the house.

Until, on one particular morning, I woke up from a wonderful dream. Someone was going down on me while I slept. It took me a couple moments to realize it wasn't a dream, and I thought Val ditched school to spend the day with me. *Wait, Valerie never did this*. We hadn't had any sexual contact since *that* night. It was her mother. Over the next several minutes I experienced a wide range of emotion. The first was feeling uncontrollable pleasure. I wanted to grab her and take her right there. A final battle was being plotted between my carnal instincts and my morals. She was sitting on the bed leaning over me. Her ample breasts pinning my torso to the mattress. Her fingernails ran gently up and down my thighs as she worked. The conflict between emotions had now erupted into full-scale war. *What am I doing? Please don't stop*. There is a scene in the movie *Animal House* where Lawrence is about to have sex with a random coed. She passes out and the devil appears on his right shoulder telling him to fuck her. *FUCK HER!* An angel appears on his left encouraging the opposite advice. Unlike the movie, the devil sort of won. I didn't fuck her, but I continued to *sleep*. I couldn't help my hands from wandering and I'm certain she was aware of my consciousness. She was relentless and continued well after I finished, nearly to the point of discomfort. Then, when it was finally over, she did the unthinkable. She curled up next to me. While lying there, her head in the crook of my shoulder and an arm draped across my chest, I took a peek. She was wearing a black lace teddy. Was this all premeditated? Holy God, this is the mother of my girlfriend —*whom I nearly killed by having sex with for the first and only time*. My thoughts raced. The decent part of me thought, *What now! Oh my God, what have I done?* The sick, demented part of me regretted not embracing the moment in what was a once in a lifetime opportunity. My internal debate came to a screeching halt when she said, "I love you."

"What?" I prayed that came from my inside voice. My eyes still glued closed. —*I'm a teenager, dating YOUR daughter*. Now certain my thoughts were solely my own, I was spiraling. I then felt disgust towards her, briefly, but it was there. What was so broken in her that allowed her to do this to me? Although I had these conflicting thoughts racing through my mind, I remained "asleep" never uttering a word. Mrs. Smith's apparent frustration got the best of her, and, finally, she left. She whispered something on her way out. I didn't catch what she said, but it seemed to be in the tone of sheer disgust, assumingly, with her behavior, but maybe with mine. Either way, I felt relief; she was gone. I was paralyzed anticipating meeting her face-to-face. Twenty minutes later I heard her car fleeing the scene.

I have to go back for a minute and retrace the steps that may have inadvertently led me into that mess. The previous summer a group of us were swimming in the Smith's family pool. It was me, Valerie, her two best friends, Amy and Stacy, and her brother Mike. We were rough housing in the pool as teenagers do. I was throwing people in the air and watching them crash into the water. I even did this to Val's mom once she joined us. She went under, and when she rose from the water her bikini top had slid to the side, exposing her. When I looked up, I realized she had caught me staring. Mrs. Smith dropped into the water to "fix" herself. However, in hindsight, the drop *seemed* to come with a slight hesitation, and she was giving me *that* look. You know, the playful stare that lasts a second too long and is accompanied by a seductive grin. *I was recently at a wedding dancing with this married woman and she was giving me that look. Trying to yell over the music, she said, "If my husband wasn't here..."* Same look.

Now, remember, I told you the devil on my right shoulder sort of won the battle. So, it should be of little surprise that I soon found myself in another compromising situation with "mom." I know it sounds pretty screwed up, but remember, I was a teenager, barely out of high school, so the maturity of my judgment was suspect, at best. I had limited sexual experience; more than most my age, I suspect, but still limited. I was also fueled by an insatiable libido so how could I let this opportunity pass me by? Why should I have displayed better moral behavior then this grown woman? I know, it seems like a horrible thing to do, especially to my girlfriend, and again, in hindsight, it was, but *—and here comes the rationalization—* my girlfriend and I had begun to hit a rough patch. We barely saw each other, and our bond now seemed more of a habit than a relationship. Simply put, we were growing apart. We made every attempt to just be together and get along. It always ended in disagreements. I admit, my societally taboo sexual experience with her mother certainly did not help.

The second incident started out very innocently. Val and I went to a Friday night movie. We saw *Twins* starring Arnold Schwarzenegger and Danny Devito. We had fun. It would end up being the last time. We got back to her house, pecked out a kiss and said goodnight. She had to work in the morning, but since I assumed her father and brother were home, I felt *safe*. As it turned out, they went to a car show in Harrisburg bright and early the next morning. I was, again, left alone with Mrs. Smith just down the hall. This time I was awake and tried to relax my closed eyes as the door opened. She was back for round two. Walking towards her daughter's bed, she asked if I was awake, which I ignored. The thunderous pulsing of my heart surely gave me away. With no answer, she moved closer. I could feel the blanket and sheet slowly sliding away. I felt the cool air rushing over my body on this winter morning. With my eyes closed, I could not see her expression as she exposed me, fully engorged. She whispered, almost to herself, "Oh, Brian." Her tone was of anticipated regret. She knelt beside the bed and gripped me tightly in one hand. Warm breath blew across me, causing my stomach muscles to clinch tightly, as if ready to absorb a punch. My reaction must have snatched her back to reality as she let out a drawn-out sigh. She let go, flung the covers back over me. My erection now serving as the center mast pole for some make-shift tent. I heard her walking and she seem to pause somewhere between me and the door. After a few silent moments of reflection, she left the room. I laid there see-sawing my emotions, volleying between fear and self-loathing. *Would someone find out? Would she come clean and tell Val? Or her husband? Was I just being paranoid? Most importantly, I needed to get out of there.* The door opened again. She was coming back. Mumbling her way over to me. This time she tore the covers back with no regard for my make-believe slumber. I heard something swoosh to the floor. I later realized it was the nightgown she was wearing. Now fully naked, she climbed on the bed, her knees anchored on both sides of my head. She was taking her time, teasing me. Again, whispering to herself like a mental patient. With her positioned on top of me, I was free to open my eyes and take this all in. Her breasts reminded me of Jessica. She finally began, but slowly. Her knees sliding, inch by inch, ever so slightly away from my ears, causing her body to draw closer to the bed. She was now so close she was rubbing herself back and forth against my nose. Grinding faster, she sat bolt upright and thrust down harder, now in a full gallop. She was moaning wildly. The ride finally came to a full stop. I tasted her satisfaction on my lips, and she leaned forward again. When she was done with me there was no cuddling. She dismounted and walked out of the room with purpose. The door closed with a hearty slam. I was lying there, her scent all over me, and left wondering why she slammed the door. *Disgust? An unspoken challenge to wake up and face the situation?* I didn't know but was not planning on finding out. I waited about a half-hour for her car to back out of the driveway. She wasn't letting me off the hook this time. I realized I needed to drum up the courage to get out of bed. When I did, I quickly threw on my clothes. As I ran out the door, I said, "Thanks, I gotta go. Running late!" —*Thanks? I'm so stupid.* That walk of shame was indeed the most difficult one of my life.

After the second run-in with "mom", I figured the best thing to do would be to pull back. I went to the house once or twice to talk to Val. We stayed on the porch. We were all but over. We finally agreed the patient had died on the table some time ago. —*Time of death, two seconds past climax.*

Mailbox Baseball

When I was eighteen, Anthony "Ant" Girardi had become one of my very best friends. He was an unlikely candidate for the job given our varied tastes, but there were ties that bind. He was a headbanger and fan of 80's hair bands. "Go hard or go home," Ant would say. He spent every dollar he earned on rock concerts. Anthony's hair dipped a few inches below the shoulders, and his vast collection of Iron Maiden and Metallica t-shirts would convince you he was a stoner spending his time peeking under the hood of a '73 Plymouth. Truth be told, he was a fairly strait-laced guy, and I don't think he smoked weed until college. During high school, Anthony worked for a record store called Sam Goody in the Deptford Mall. It was there he developed the ability to rapidly gain friends. He was the kind of guy who prided himself on being the expert. In this case, the subject was his favorite, music, so he was wholly invested. Ant knew everything about any album you picked up and had a wise ass comment to retort to dumb questions and sarcastic remarks. The true draw to Anthony was his thoughtful and invested approach to every conversation. You always felt he was utterly present. His personality turned him from a solid seven to a nine. Many girls he dated proved he was able to punch way above his weight class. To be blunt, his personality is what got him laid.

Anthony and I started hanging out because I was in theater, and he was in the high school band. He played saxophone in the pit orchestra for all our performances. However, the shared passion that brought us close was playing billiards.

We ultimately ended up joining a Tuesday night doubles league in Atco, New Jersey. We tried to get together and play as much as we could. There was an old pool table in his basement, so, when all else failed, we would find ourselves down there knocking around balls and talking about life. His mother had passed away of cancer several years earlier, and his father, never really a nice man, only got worse after she was gone. To that end, Anthony and his father never saw eye to eye. He would vent about how he despised him and couldn't wait to move out. I often tried to lighten the conversation by talking about girls.

Anthony dated a girl, Lily Tocci. He immodestly told me stories of their sexual escapades. With Lily, nothing was taboo or off-limits. I never reciprocated by sharing the madness I experienced in Cherry Hill, and the exploits with my high school sweetheart's mother were still a year away. Lily was a true beauty, and every inch of her body showed she had spent most of her youth in a dance studio. Her meek personality was apparently a deception masking a caged tiger. She took part in the musicals but mainly faded into the background as part of the chorus. Theater was the only reason I ever met her. She was beautiful, but for whatever reason, maybe her seemingly reserved nature, I never really paid much attention until I heard Anthony's tales. I was then super envious and couldn't help but fantasize about Lily. I never told him, of course.

One night, there was a cast party at Macy O'Quinn's house after our Saturday night closing performance of *Oklahoma*, in which I had played Andrew Carnes. Macy was two grades behind me but always seemed to host the best parties. They reminded me of parties from my freshman year (without the blatant drug use).

I was standing in the kitchen with Macy and Dale Patrick talking about the show.

"Man, I can't believe it's over. I really *loved* that show," Dale said. Dale had played one of the leads, Ali Hakim. The character was Persian and therefore required an accent. He made it somewhat believable. Dale was half awkward, half rock star. He was typically the former, but given his powerful baritone voice, he usually landed lead parts in the musicals. Girls found him cute, so his awkwardness was overlooked.

"I know, I can't believe it myself. My favorite scene will always be the one where Carnes threatened Dale, I mean, Ali, with the shotgun. I think you got the most applause *every* night, Brian," Macy was gushing.

"*Hey*, I was part of that scene *too*," Dale said, seeking the spotlight. Along with being starved for attention, he had a nervous tic involving his inability to look at anyone when he spoke. He would look up, above you, as if there was some astral projection hovering on high and stealing his gaze.

"Relax, Dale. You did great. And we're down here, by the way." I was waving my hand in front of his face. "Why are you always staring at the ceiling when I'm talking to you? I gotta take a leak." I left before he could answer.

The house was packed, and I was fairly intoxicated as I weaved through the crowd towards the bathroom. Lily was in the front of the line, waiting. When she saw me, she started waving like a frantic air traffic controller. I went to her.

"Hey," I said.

Lily smiled and said, "Hey, you." When the bathroom door opened, she took my hand and led me in. She spun me around, pinning me against the wall and kicked the door closed behind us. In retrospect, it was a total drunken Fonzie move on her part. We made out and didn't say much. She was the aggressor, but I didn't pull away, so I was just as responsible. A few minutes passed and then people started knocking on the door. It was the only bathroom in the house, so it was sacred territory. We dashed across the hall to Macy's sister's room. She clicked the door lock and we were soon moving around the bases. At one point, I said, "What about Anthony?" but she cut me off by telling me to shut up. She was on a mission. I felt like I had no control. I didn't want it because it would have given me accountability. I was drunk, and I let it happen and would accept the consequences. Meanwhile, according to what I heard later, there was a conversation going on just outside.

Anthony was asking, "Hey, Dale, where's Lily?"

"I don't know. I think I saw her go that way a bit ago," Dale said and motioned toward the bathroom.

Anthony walked to the bathroom to a line of people eagerly waiting.

"Has anyone seen Lily?" Ant asked.

There was a collective *no*, but just as he turned to walk away, a girl came out of the bathroom and pointed to Macy's sister's bedroom door.

"She just went in there with Brian," the girl said.

Anthony listened through the door for a few minutes and then went outside to get some air.

My act of betrayal ultimately found Anthony arrested. The next day I learned Anthony had taken his emotions out on the neighbor's mailbox. The neighbor, as it turned out, was a county police lieutenant. Understandably, Ant was pissed off and did not speak to me for months. I made an unspoken vow to never betray a friend like that again. I wondered if I would have the self-control to keep it.

Denny's Family Restaurant

I enrolled in culinary school during my senior year of high school. When the time arrived to start classes, I realized just how ridiculous the schedule would be. The classes were broken into fifteen-day blocks and scheduled morning, afternoon or night. Needless to say, it was difficult to get a job with that kind of schedule. I ended up taking a job working the 11p.m.-7a.m. shift at Denny's restaurant. I spent my days learning classical cooking techniques and my nights preparing pre-packaged foods for drunken assholes. There were typically four employees on the overnight shift: a cook, two servers, and a manager. Over time I became a shift manager. The employee count suddenly went to three: a cook (me), two servers, and a manager (me, again). Diane Burke was one of those servers and ended up becoming a very influential person in my life, sort of another mother figure as well as a dear friend. We had great times, as those late-night after-hours crowds crawled through the door at two-thirty a.m. I lobbied for months to train as a server because I thought there was much more money to be made. I got my wish, and once I got the hang of it, Diane and I did nothing but fuck with the customers. It was glorious. On Thursday, Friday and Saturday nights, we had a packed restaurant and only two servers, so we were always in the weeds. When it was this busy taking shit from drunken customers wasn't tolerated. Fortunately, we both had the types of personalities which enabled us to tell them all to go fuck themselves without a riot breaking out. We used to have a deal. I would take the tables with just girls, and she would take the guys; we would split the rest. It didn't matter because we made an agreement to split the tips down the middle at the end of this chaos. One night we were divvying up the tips and I poured about twenty dollars in coins on the table. She said, "What the hell is that?" So, I told her the story. I waited on a table of four girls. I was buried and didn't have much time to waste, so I vaulted over the side of the booth and landed in an opening between two of them, straight *Dukes of Hazard* style. I landed perfectly in the seat. Now this may have been really impressive for a table full of drunk girls, but I was sober and on my game. Cocky, yes ... but it was true. Anyway, I flirted my ass off, my typical MO, and threw food in front of them. I didn't think much more about it except for the fact that they were hot and drunk. After all, I had fifteen other tables to worry about, and there were still people waiting at the door. I went back later to clear the table and found a mess of dishes and my tip. The tip was all coins which normally means you want to follow the people to the parking lot and beat them with a bag rusty nails. This time was different. They emptied their pocketbooks, finding all the change they could muster, and arranged it to read:

We love you Brian 555-555-5555

I don't remember the actual number, but it was one of the girl's numbers and I slept with her the following week. Sometimes shit works out.

As time went on, management realized the midnight shift line cook position was difficult to keep staffed. They offered to pay me much more than I was making to go back to the kitchen. I did it out of some sense of duty. They replaced me on the floor with another waitress.

Kathy Swanson was twenty-seven, blond, brick-house body, beautiful face and a southern accent. How was she even real? We worked together for weeks and I flirted but not too over the top. Mostly eye contact, a few comments here and there. I couldn't help it. She was a gorgeous woman. After a time, she began flirting back.

One night, I was in the stock room doing inventory when she came searching for condiments. "Gotta marry those ketchups," she said, smiling. I was thinking how she had one of those smiles that immediately put you at ease. You knew her all your life within the first few seconds of meeting her. We talked for a few minutes and sexual gravity pulled me closer. We closed the distance and stood face to face. Her lips were several inches away. She closed the gap. We spent the next couple weeks manufacturing our impromptu make-out sessions. Kathy was the sexiest woman I'd been with and the chemistry was explosive. She was the aggressor and made the first move. Kathy told me she was off that next Thursday night and had no plans. I told her I was free as well, so we made arrangements to spend time together. It was odd that she wanted to meet at ten-thirty p.m., but I didn't question it at the time. I met her in the restaurant's back parking lot. When she got into the car, we started basically dry humping in the front seat. Other than destination, the agenda was pretty clear. We ended up going to a motel not too far away. I knew the place because there was an underage night club sharing a parking lot where I spent many Thursday nights with a friend from college.

I went to the front desk while Kathy waited in the car. I was a nervous wreck, and it must have been obvious as the clerk assisting me asked if everything was okay. I must have looked like I just finished a marathon, but I said, "Yes, I'm fine, thank you." I ended up getting the most expensive room for no good reason other than I wanted to seem like I knew what I was doing. "Give me the most expensive room you have!" We walked into the room, and I was practically shaking. What did I know, and how was I going to satisfy this woman? After all, I was still only nineteen. Was it the fact she was an older woman? Did she in some way remind me of Mrs. Smith? I don't know.

Did I mention we had stopped at the liquor store, and she bought a bottle of wine? Thank God because I needed it. I was petrified thinking of what was to come.

I opened the wine. We sat, talked, and drank. Kathy got up and started to fill the Jacuzzi. I tried not to think about how many people must have had sex in this thing on a weekly basis. We would be lucky to walk away without contracting Necrotizing fasciitis soaking in that DNA soup. I stared as the water rushed out of the faucet filling the tub and I hadn't noticed she was already getting undressed. I turned and she was standing in front of me, naked and flawless. She walked to the Jacuzzi and slowly slipped in. It felt as if it played out in slow motion. I watched as every inch of her disappeared. My eyes traced the curves outlining her body during the decent, and as she settled into position her nipples were momentarily bouncing as if to decide whether or not they wanted to be submerged. They didn't. Brimming with excitement, I thought of jumping in fully clothed, but at the same time, I felt apprehensive about stripping down and joining her. My nervousness slowly eroded. She reached out a hand inviting me to join her.

"Come in." She took a sip of wine and set the glass behind her on a table next to the hot tub.

Without a word I sat on the edge. She moved closer, causing a miniature tsunami that splashed water on my jeans. I gave her an accusingly playful look. She said, "You're getting your clothes all wet, silly." She flicked her hand open, as a magician might, sending a dozen drops of water now racing down my face. We laughed in unison and I leaned in. We kissed as I undressed. The water was much warmer than I had expected. I knelt in front of her. Kathy scooched close and wrapped her legs around mine. She put her arms around my neck and pulled herself up, now resting on the top of my thighs. We were kissing deeply. Not out of control but with purpose, pure passion. I was as hard as steel when she leaned back to accept me. I was unsure if it was the warm water or the wine, but I felt like I could last forever. I flipped her around and she clutched the outside wall of the tub. She screamed that she was coming and commanded me not to stop. I obeyed her.

We ended up having sex two more times that night. The odd part came when she woke me up at seven a.m. and said I had to take her to her car. *What was the rush?* I drove her back, and she left in a hurry. I drove home replaying the night. I went to take a shower and felt pain as I pulled off my t-shirt, almost as if I were tearing it off. Looking at the slashes on my back in the mirror made me wonder how much skin remained under her fingernails. Did she even notice? Was she home cleaning her nails and feeling a bit guilty? I wouldn't fully heal for months.

We worked together again a few nights later. It was exciting to think about our hidden affair. Time passed and she befriended another coworker, Rhonda. Rhonda worked mostly nights but occasionally filled in for Diane on the graveyard shift. This was one of those nights. It was around two-thirty a.m. and the after-hours bar rush was dying out.

"Order up, Kath," I yelled through the pickup window. She took the two breakfast plates from the window and winked, "Thanks, hot stuff."

I saluted her with my spatula. Also returning her wink and smile. "Welcome."

After she dropped off the food and refilled their coffee, Kathy came back to the window. "Can I get another side of bacon for table 24? I'll ring it in after. Oh, and I told Rhonda."

"Told her what?" I was plating the bacon as I said it. When I looked up, she resembled the Cheshire cat. "What did you tell her?"

"About us." She blew me a kiss, took her bacon and walked away. She looked over her shoulder still smiling.

We agreed to keep the list of witnesses to a minimum. Only Diane and Rhonda ever knew of our secret romance.

Some nights when Rhonda was working graveyard, I would meet Kathy at Rhonda's place for mini sex marathons. The first night we walked into Rhonda's apartment, we just started going at it. We went into the bedroom and didn't make it to the bed. After it was over, we realized we'd just has sex on a pile of dirty clothes. I know, it's nasty and it reminded me of that scene in Porky's. I warn you; this is about to get a little weird.

Kathy invited me to meet her at a park in Pitman. When I arrived, she was sitting on the end of a park bench, so I went to sit next to her. She jumped up and walked a few feet away.

"I'm sorry, we can't sit *that* close."

"What are you talking about?"

It was then I realized there were two kids running around close by. She was paying a little too much attention to them, and then it hit me. They were her children. There was a boy about nine and a girl that looked to be no more than four or five. She confirmed my suspicion and told me she was dropping them off, and I should stay here until she came back. I waited twenty minutes, and she returned. We went to her house and headed straight to the bedroom. We were lying there naked in her bed when I told her I was surprised to find out she had kids. Then she floored me.

"I have to tell you something else, too." She now had tears collecting on her long lashes, threatening to jump. "I'm so sorry I didn't tell you this before. I have a husband."

I sat there staring questioningly at her, but I said nothing.

"You have every right to hate me."

"I don't hate you. I really don't know what to feel."

"He's not a nice man. He was, well, at least I think he was before, you know, before we were married. Now he is just mean. Not physically, well, not much. Mostly the way he talks. He's really nasty."

"So why are you still together?"

She glanced at a framed picture of her children on the dresser. "Them. And he would kill me. No, *really*, he would."

I have to admit I was in the middle of my own moral dilemma. Was I considering keeping this going? What the fuck *was* I thinking? I couldn't help but think, here we go again, another sordid tale to tell at parties while the flames tickled my feet in hell. She then reached down and grabbed me. I decided to give her what she wanted.

I saw her on and off for a few months. It was always on her terms now, and I assumed it was when she felt safe enough to sneak away. Kathy then told me I should go with her to visit her sister in Reading, Pennsylvania. *There is no way any good can come from this.* So, of course, I went. I met her in the parking lot at Denny's about nine-thirty p.m. I noticed her kids were in the back seat. Are you fucking kidding me? My brain was certainly not in charge here. I followed her. I drove behind her for about an hour and a half and she pulled into a McDonald's in the middle of nowhere. I got behind her in line. It was Kathy, her two kids, and another smoking hot girl that I later found out was her sister, Melodie. Apparently, her sister had recently moved to that area, and it was easier to find the McDonalds than her house. She whispered to me that I should park down the street once we reached the house, and she would come get me when the kids were in bed. I ordered a large Big Mac combo and went back to tailing her. We reached the house and I parked. Once I finished eating, I waited about thirty more minutes for her to come out and get me. It crossed my mind a dozen times to get the hell out of there. She came out and I followed her to a barn. It was a legitimate barn. The exterior stone shell looked to be a couple hundred years old. The massive a-frame roof was equipped with a traditional cupola in the center with what looked to be a brass weathervane protruding from its peak. It was pretty cool, although a little rustic for my taste. We went into the house, and an uncomfortable introduction was in order. I met Melodie and husband, Scott. They were welcoming and didn't treat me like the home wrecker part I was actively playing. We had a few drinks, and they went up to bed. We were going to sleep in the living room. I was fascinated with the pocket doors in this room. They were made of reclaimed wood and the antique door locks were equipped with skeleton keys.

As I locked the second door, I said, "I like your sister and Scott. They seem nice. Are you sure it's cool for me to be here?"

"Absolutely. Stop worrying. Everything is fine."

"What about tomorrow. Should I leave before the kids get up?"

"No. Mel is taking the kids out to breakfast in the morning."

This put me more at ease and I went to her. She had made a bed in the center of the floor with blankets and pillows. We fell asleep at some point and were woken by the sounds of children.

I shook Kathy awake. "What time is it?" I asked.

"Seven-twenty." She was pointing towards the clock on the far wall.

"When is Melodie taking them to breakfast?"

"Dunno, should be soon though."

Her sister ended up being a total fucking ditz. Apparently, she decided it would be a great idea to make breakfast for the family instead of going out to eat. So, while the kids were running around, we were butt naked on the floor. Kathy's son, Taylor, started looking for his mother. Taylor started hopping up and down outside the front window like a human pogo stick. He was tapping on the window with every bounce. I got a blanket, wrapped it around me and army crawled across the floor away from the window. Not quitting in his search, Taylor decided to pick the lock. And the little motherfucker did it. I couldn't pick that lock if you spotted me twenty minutes and handed me a fist full of fifties, but there we were. Kathy ran to the door as he slid it open. He turned and saw me sitting there wearing only a blanket and a smidge of shame. He then turned to see his mother standing fully naked. She was crazy hot to any man, but even I was embarrassed for him. She yelled and closed the door.

She got dressed in a panic and motioned for me to do the same. She spoke in whispers telling me to wait there until she came back. I was both nervous and cracking the fuck up inside, all at once. I guess I didn't realize the impact this event might have on our health and her marriage. She soon came back and said, *"Go! Now!"* I ran out the back door and didn't look back.

Since it was some time before GPS's were invented, I had no idea where I was. I tried my best to retrace my tracks from memory to get home. Four hours later I pulled up to my house. I went to bed and slept until six p.m. It was the best sleep ever.

I wasn't scheduled to work for a few days and had no other contact with Kathy. After thinking about the whole situation, I was a little freaked out by the experience and was ready to move on. I went back to work and everything seemed normal. She showed up as scheduled but had a man with her: her husband. —*I might be dying tonight.* He sat at the counter directly in front of me for the next few hours drinking coffee and smoking cigarettes. I messed up so many orders that Denny's food cost is still not leveled out. Fortunately, I was not a suspect. His attention was turned to all the male patrons my married girlfriend *serviced*. He was clearly agitated and on the edge of his stool the entire night. He finally left when the restaurant emptied. It was around three-thirty a.m. For the first time all night, she finally spoke to me. Earlier in the night, our conversations had been limited to strictly work-related subjects and even those were brief. Now that the crowd had died down, she explained the events that occurred following our trip to the barn.

Kathy explained they had driven home, and a day had passed with no conversation surrounding the events of that morning. The next night while they ate dinner, her husband asked how the overnight stay went. She told him it was good to see her sister and the house was coming along nicely. Taylor contributed to the conversation, saying the television repairman and mommy were naked in the living room. After the kids were excused, forcefully, from the dinner table, a heated conversation took place. She denied the allegations, but he evidently took the side of his son and took it out on her. I hadn't noticed until she mentioned it, but the makeup concealed bruising just below her left eye. He spent the next couple days showing her that she was his property. This scared the shit out of me. Here I was screwing his wife, and she was paying for it. He assumed, correctly, that since she only left the house to work that she was with someone from there. He spent the next week at that same counter-seat staring at everyone with contempt.

I had effectively broken it off the minute I left the barn that day in Reading, but I made it official after a couple uncomfortable conversations. She claimed she loved me, and I was the most caring lover she had ever known. It didn't matter; I was done. Don't get me wrong, the sex was great, but there was more where that came from when you worked at a Denny's family restaurant.

A few weeks passed, and I only saw her during work, but at this point we had fallen back into the role of coworkers. I was also beginning to work breakfast on the weekends as the main egg cook, so I saw her much less. Once in a while, I would find little treasures on my car. *No, not a busted taillight.* I would find single roses, cards, and love letters. My favorite memento was a Denny's coffee mug. It had a decal of the moon on it and when you put hot coffee in it, the decal transformed into a sun. I still have that mug and drink from it with mixed emotions.

When I started working day shifts, I realized Denny's was a colorful place to work and had a great cast of characters. There was Walt, the flamboyant middle-aged waiter that reminded me of the love-child Jack Tripper and Mr. Roper might have had working on the set of *Three's Company*. There was a blond named Beth with really big hair (it was 80's hair in the post 80's era). She reminded me of a younger version of Flo from the comedy, *Alice,* also of the late seventies. She was taller, probably in her late thirties, and strutted around like a peacock, tailfeathers in full bloom, thinking everyone was eye-fucking her. They weren't. She was like a back road that could stand to be repaved. Then there were the *Golden Girls*. There were three of them I remember the most, but I couldn't tell you their names. They were all adorable grandmother types, and a little naughty. They may have worn me out if they had the opportunity. Overall, it was a fun, roller-coaster of a job.

One particularly busy Sunday morning, Theresa Costa threw a plate back in the window. The plate slid off the edge and smashed onto the flat-top grill next to where I was standing. Only as the blood dripped down my forearm did I even realize there was a ceramic shard protruding from it. It wasn't very serious, but Theresa saw what she did and came back behind the line to check on me. Seeing her up close made me realize how pretty this girl was. She was very short, under five feet, which, again, typically doesn't get my attention, but I was intrigued. Theresa was a couple years older than me and in medical school at the University of Pennsylvania. She was out of my league intellectually. It only took a few conversations for that fact to reveal itself; however, she seemed drawn to me. Over the next couple of weeks, she made a point of checking how my wound was healing. I was actually becoming a little annoyed but wanted to see how far I could take the situation. If I could manage to see her outside of work the outcome might be worth the price of admission. I began to feign interest in her conversations with coworkers. We talked more as time passed. It was approaching mid-summer and Theresa asked me to come to her house to swim. I assumed there would be others. I arrived a little after noon on a Saturday. When she answered the door, she was wearing a sheer cover-up over her string bikini. Up to that point, I thought Theresa seemed to be a bit of a prude. I had seen her come into the restaurant in street clothes that were more fitting of a nun. Under interrogation, I would have described her style as super conservative. This bathing suit was at odds with that notion. We went out back to the pool, and I found we were alone. She told me her parents were out with her sister, Rebecca, and wouldn't be back for a few hours. We hung out, swam, talked and listened to music. I had fun just soaking her in, although I got lost a few times in her intellect. I went inside to use the bathroom and came out to find her waiting. She was just coming at me like she was on some mission. We started making out, but it was really awkward because I was about a foot and a half taller. I steered her in the direction of the staircase and sat down, so we were on a more even playing field. When I took off her bikini top, the longest nipples I have ever seen in my life were revealed. At the time, I didn't realize they were longer than what one might consider normal. I just thought they were spectacular. I paid them great attention and she flew off the handle. She started ripping at my swim trunks and I found myself with my shorts off and her fumbling around with my cock. She gave me a blowjob, and her efforts, although a little toothy, paid off. I left before her family got home.

Over the next couple weeks, I tried to meet up with Theresa, but it never worked out. She always had something going on. On the chance I might catch her, I stopped by her house one Saturday around dinnertime. I knocked on the door and a younger but prettier version of Theresa answered. After introductions, Rebecca explained that Theresa had just run out to pick up food and would be right back. She invited me in, and we sat and talked for a while. I always felt intimidated by Theresa's intelligence, but not Rebecca's. We seemed to be on the same wavelength intellectually, and there was an obvious attraction. It did not shock me when she came over and straddled me. She was just as aggressive and, seemingly, more experienced than her sister. When I warned that Theresa would soon be home Rebecca only said two words before leading me up to her bedroom: "I lied."

A couple weeks later, I was invited to dinner at the Costas' house and met the family. Theresa and I were far from dating, and I really thought of us as very casual. I was confused when she asked me to dinner. When I arrived, Rebecca was sitting at the table. I was introduced to her and her parents, and, without issue, we ate and had a great dinner conversation. I drove home that night thankful Rebecca didn't create some grand scene. I didn't see a relationship developing between Theresa and me. I avoided her whenever possible and let whatever spark we had, extinguish gradually. That dinner was the last time I saw Theresa socially.

Watch the Tram Car Please

In the fall of '90, Diane, my friend and mentor from Denny's, had scored me an interview at a new upscale catering place in Voorhees Township, New Jersey. I got the job and spent the next nine months working my ass off as an assistant executive steward. It was an impressive title for a crappy job. I'm going to simplify this a bit, but I was the person who polished the silver, ensured the staff got the equipment for the events and was in charge of the dishwashers. I poured my heart into the job and was fired. It was unexpected and not well deserved. I was fired for the first and only time in my life. I was twenty years old and hovering somewhere between pissed off and devastated. I decided to take the entire summer off and spend it at the Wildwood shore. A few friends agreed to go with me. Besides me, the people who chipped in included James Hale, Nelson Galvez, Anthony Girardi, Timmy Murphy, Robin Woolf, and Giuseppe Columbo. We rented an apartment on East Magnolia Avenue, two blocks from the center of the Boardwalk. I spent the next few months drinking too much and fucking everyone that said yes. Only James and I stayed the fulltime. Everyone else came down on the weekends and other arbitrary days, leaving a trail of dishes and filth in their wake. This place became a special kind of disgusting and could only have been disinfected with napalm. On the weekend, it wasn't uncommon to wake up to a house full of strangers. Sometimes I would find out the random houseguests' names over coffee in the morning.

The VHS tapes we made with James's camcorder memorializing the debauchery of that summer still exist. Those tapes prevent me from ever complaining about *the darn kids today*. There are a few incidents I would take back but, for the most part, I had the time of my life. I was able to hone my game and had more success with girls than I ever would have imagined. My buddy Timmy used to tell me I was good at *shooting the gift*. In fact, my success during the summer of '91 became something of a yardstick with my friends.

The building we lived in had three stories with six rentable units. We were the only summer-long renters and occupied the third floor in the rear. There was access to a common balcony overlooking Magnolia Avenue where we would often cat call and rate girls with makeshift scorecards as they walked by. —*Yes, when I read it back it sounds idiotic to me too.* It was no better than horny construction workers whistling to the dressed-up bypassing businesswomen in the city.

I often had coffee on that balcony in the morning. Like clockwork, every Saturday's departing tenants evacuated just hours before their replacements arrived. A team of older women systematically scoured the units some time in between; given the conditions, it was a heroic job. Most of the summer, the apartments were occupied with dudes and modestly attractive girls but one weekend in late July, three people graced our homely dumpster community. Regardless of their looks or gender, I always greeted the new neighbors. This week I was taken aback when I saw them. It was three friends, two girls and a guy, from Jersey City. They were all beautiful. They were Italian and followed the Jersey Shore motto; GTL (Gym, Tan, Laundry). I was the self-appointed live-in bellhop, so I hailed them from the balcony and went down to help bring up their luggage. At times, I felt like Mr. Roarke welcoming people to *Fantasy Island*. As far as our latest guests, if they had kept their mouths closed, you would have thought them the most attractive people on the planet. The New York/New Jersey blended accents were almost too over-the-top to take seriously. Marco was chiseled out of iron, a bronze god with a year-round membership to Gold's Gym and Hollywood Tans. You could never stand next to this man without feeling inadequate. I was a scrawny rail struggling to keep weight on at all. On the beach, I reluctantly took my shirt off around this guy. The two girls, Adriana and Maria, looked practically alike with the only difference being a couple inches. Their dark complexions only made their blue eyes stand out. *I would not have been surprised to find out they were wearing colored contacts.* They often claimed to be sisters when we were out. I knew the truth. Over the course of the week, I gravitated towards Adriana, the taller of the two. She spontaneously kissed me on the dance floor one night. We spend the next couple days together. On Thursday of that week, I had to go home and didn't return until Friday afternoon. When I came back, Adriana had ghosted me. She was either out somewhere or busy when I came around. I never talked to her again before they pulled out early Saturday morning. I was confused. That Saturday night we had a party, and after we were all fairly drunk, the guys had a funny story to tell me. Two nights prior, while I was out of town, they had a party, and our Jersey City friends were there. Timmy and Anthony told a story of how I was sexually confused and wavered between liking men and women. This fake news "grossed out" Adriana and, thus, the shun I was confronted with upon my return. My friends found this to be hysterical, but the joke was lost on me. I later found out Anthony was the mastermind behind it all and knew it was retaliation for an incident that had occurred earlier in June.

It happened in the second week of June. There was a girl from Runnemede, New Jersey, and her name was Julia Bach. Anthony had been crushing on her for months. She came to Wildwood for vacation with two girlfriends, Becky and Andrea. They rented a condo on Magnolia Avenue a few blocks west of our apartment. I spent quite a bit of time with Julia during that week. Anthony wouldn't be down until Friday night. I went to the beach a couple of the days with Julia and her roommates. We ate pizza and walked the boards. It was me, James, Julia, Becky and Andrea. James was into Becky. I'm not sure if they hooked up, but they disappeared a few times throughout the week. Julia and I did not. I assumed she and Anthony would get together once he arrived. I was just keeping her company. That Friday night, our house was brimming over with people, and the landlord who lived on the first floor came up once to ask us to turn the volume down. That was our warning. We obliged, and even though it was barely eleven o'clock, that seemed to be the first nail in the coffin of the party. The crowd dwindled.

"Can you walk me?" Julia asked.

"Sure, where are your friends?"

"Dunno."

"Where's Anthony?"

"Dunno. Passed out?"

We walked out of the house and Julia took a left towards the Boardwalk.

"Your condo is the other way."

"I'm not ready to go back yet."

"OK, where are we going?"

"I don't care. I just want to walk around. I'm not tired."

We were both pretty silent walking down the Boardwalk. From behind, we heard, "Watch the tramcar, please. Watch the tramcar, please." We had been walking on the concrete path of this trackless train. In Wildwood, the tramcar has been a staple of the Boardwalk since 1949. The tram is mostly yellow with blue trim with a dozen or so passenger cars connected to the engineer's car.

We stepped out of its path and Julia said, "Can we?"

"Of course," I raised my hand to signal to the tramcar driver, and the tram came to a full stop. I paid the attendant riding in the caboose, and we climbed on. We sat there for a few moments in silence again.

I finally said, "Julia, are you ok—"

Before I could finish, she cut me off and bluntly said, "Brian, I know Anthony likes me. He told Becky, and she told me. He asked her what he should do and if I liked him. She told him she didn't know. I like him... a lot! Just not in that way, you know. He's my friend, kinda like a brother or whatever."

—This became a recurring theme that summer.

"Wow. That sucks. I was sure you guys were going to be getting together. He is really into you."

"And I'm into you." Julia and I were now looking at each other, and, when she leaned in to kiss me, I couldn't resist. I never seem to be able to resist. We kissed for a few moments before I pulled away.

"This can't happen. I'm so sorry." The memory of what I had done with Lily in high school was too much to think about. "Listen, Julia, I do like you and if it wasn't for Anthony, I would totally be into you. I just can't do this to him. Not again."

"What do you mean?"

I paused and thought about what I was going to say to her. "Look, it's a long story. Let's just say I fucked him over in high school. I didn't mean to. I was pretty drunk."

Julia didn't say anything. We sat there in awkward silence for a minute or two, and she said, "Okay, then that's that." She clapped her hands like she was in a marching band playing cymbals. I could see the glassiness in her eyes as she wiped the tears away.

"I'm really sorry."

"No, you're being a friend. I get it. I just wish it were different. I liked you when we met that one time back home and really like you now that we spent most of the week together. I REALLY like you now. This fucking suuuucks. But I get it, I get it. I should go back. My friends are probably wondering where I am."

We got off the tram and started walking back to her condo. She reached out and grabbed my hand, lacing our fingers together, and we walked the rest of the way like we were sweethearts. When we arrived, we stood face-to-face holding both hands.

"Goodnight, Julia." I was smiling and wishing we had met under different circumstances.

"Goodnight, Brian." She let go of my hands and pulled a key from the back pocket of her jeans. Julia turned towards the doors for a moment, looking down at the ground. She turned back, gave me a lingering kiss and said, "But I really don't want to get it." She began to well up again, so she turned away, unlocked the door and, without looking back, closed it behind her.

I went back to the house, and a handful of guys were sitting at the kitchen table. I said hello and grabbed a Miller Lite from the fridge.

"Where have you been?" I heard from behind me. It was Anthony.

"I walked Julia home. She couldn't find you."

"She didn't look for me, dude. I was right here. This place ain't big."

"What is with the accusing tone, bro? Did I do something?"

"I hope not, did you?"

"If walking someone home is doing something, then, yeah, I did."

"She's only a few blocks away, dude. You were gone for almost two hours."

He was right. I hadn't even realized that much time slipped past. "We were talking. About you, actually. And maybe you should talk to her."

"Oh, oh, I will. I just want to hear it from you, friend."

"Dude, what am I getting accused of here? Nothing happened."

"Erm. Okay."

And really, in my eyes, nothing did happen. Yes, I kissed her back, I held her hand but did the right thing in the end. I'm not sure if he ever talked to her because she left the next morning, and I never spoke to her again. There was noticeable tension between us for the remainder of the summer.

Giuseppe or "Guy" lived at the gym. He was only down on the weekends but never took a day off from working out. He bought a weekend membership to a shithole gym around the corner. One day he brought home a stray. I don't know his real name, but Guy called him Tank. He became a staple at most of our weekend parties. One night there were four of us playing pinochle, and Tank was about twelve beers deep. He threw up in a trash can, and we were relentless. I couldn't grab the camcorder fast enough. Once he saw I was taping, he came back to life.

"This is Tank. I know, I'm fucked up. Zo what." He was grinning like an idiot, babbling incoherently, and his eyes were on fire. There was also a fair amount of puke on the collar of his shirt.

He continued, "I've been up for over thirty-six hours, and we just finished playing pinochle and drinkin' my ass off. Fuck you, dude."

"We didn't *finish*, dumbass. You threw up all over yourself, and we had to stop," I said.

"Whatever, I'm gone to bed right now. I'm just chillin' ya know. You know whad I mean? Hasta luego, fugger."

The camera didn't have a light on it and neither did the outside staircase leading down, so there was only an audio recording of the subsequent wreckage.

"Come on Tank, stay. You can't hang, pussy," I said.

"Fugyouguyz. I'm gonna get on my bike and go home."

"You can't even find your ass let alone your bi—"

There was a thunderous thud, and the stairs below us were bouncing as Tank tumbled down them. I set the camcorder down on the landing and ran to see if he was okay. He needed a few stitches and an IV but, otherwise, he was fine.

A few days later, Tank brought around a girl that he claimed to be dating. She was cute, and, if he was dating her, he had completely outkicked his coverage. Her name was Sarah Cohen, and she was a nice Jewish girl whose father owned a couple delis. *—I appreciate the irony here.* One was located in Wildwood Crest a few blocks away from their bayfront condo. She had a striking resemblance to Baby Houseman from *Dirty Dancing*. Sarah began hanging around the house even when Tank wasn't around. I didn't have a car, so Sarah let me use her car whenever I needed it. It was a cherry-red 1990 Ford Mustang GT convertible. I looked great driving it. It was the year "Summertime" by *DJ Jazzy Jeff and the Fresh Prince* was released, and, whenever it came on, I would blast the radio to hear the drum machine intro. Over the course of the next couple weeks, Sarah and I began hanging out more, since we were both at the shore fulltime. Whenever she wasn't working at the deli, she would come by the apartment. We would go to the beach, or she would bring over sandwiches from her father's shop. It wasn't the Carnegie Deli, but a free corned beef special was hard to beat.

Once a week, I went back to my hometown to cut a few lawns for a friend of the family. Sarah was working eight to four that day, so she told me to take her car. I did and dropped her off at work on my way. By the time I got back to the shore, it was well after six p.m. I drove straight to her condo. She answered the door in a robe and her hair was twisted up in a towel.

"Hey, how'd it go?"

"Fine, I just feel like my skin is crawling from the dirt and grass clippings. I may need to vacuum your car out tomorrow." I gave her a wide-eyed, apologetic smile.

"Don't worry about it. You hungry?"

"*Starving*. Did you eat yet? Where's your dad?"

"He's with his dumb girlfriend somewhere. He's probably banging her at her place or behind some dumpster."

I snorted out the laugh I was trying to hold back. "Kinda harsh."

"I love my dad, but he's kind of a douche. She won't be around long. They never are."

"So… what about food? Did you eat?" Now I was giving her a wide-eyed, clenched-teeth smiley face.

"No. Pizza?"

"YAAAAAAAAS, me like pizza. *And* I got cash today, so my treat." She always seemed to treat, so I was glad when she didn't fight me on it.

We ate and had a couple beers on the balcony that faced the bay.

"So, what's up with you and Tank?"

"Friends," she said matter-of-factly.

"You know, he *thinks* you're his girlfriend, right?"

Sarah let out a hostile growl. "We went on *one* fricken' date and he can't get over it. I only want to be friends. That's it. I *barely* even kissed him." She cringed a little.

"So, you've talked to him about it?"

"Oh, my God, like so many times."

"*Innnn-trest-innng*. I think that's why Robin hasn't made a move on you. I haven't seen him this into someone since tenth grade in high school. But he thinks you're taken. *Are you seeing anyone?*"

"Bri, I'm with you *all* the time when I'm not working. Who am I going to see?"

"That's true. Well, I guess Robin can now take a few swings."

"Uh, he would strike out. Robin's super nice, and I like talking to him. I consider him a friend, but he is *so* not my type. And I think he might be gay."

"Robin! *Nooo?*"

"Maybe he doesn't know it yet but, yeah, he's gay. So's his brother Phil."

"You're out of your mind."

"Am I?" She shot a mischievous look as she got up and walked by. "I'm grabbing beers. You need one."

"Sure, then I should be going."

I heard Sarah come up behind me and saw the bottom of a Miller Lite bottle floating just above my forehead. I leaned my head back and reached for it. As I did, Sarah kissed me. It was just a peck, but she hovered. She was measuring me up. Eyes staring intently, flickering side to side, into mine. I'd be lying if I said I never thought about hooking up with her. I guess, I too thought she was taken. Now knowing she wasn't, was I interested? I took my free hand and slid it under her hair and around the back of her neck and pulled her to me. She twisted around; our lips still locked as she maneuvered to make a safe landing on my lap. We sat kissing in the moonlight.

"Well, that was terrific. *And unexpected.*"

"I have wanted to kiss you for a while now, but I wasn't sure if it would be cool," she confessed.

"Sure of what? I wasn't sure. I thought you and Tank were a thing. And I usually get a vibe. You gave off no *vibe*!"

She laughed at me. "You're stupid."

I sat staring at her for a few minutes. Totally silent. My hand resting over my mouth like a baseball catcher meeting the pitcher at the mound and not wanting anyone to lip-read the conversation. I then told her the story about Sarah and Anthony and that even though Tank and I weren't that close, I needed to respect the friendship. Sarah took the fact that I put her in the friend zone in stride. I wish I hadn't, she was pretty great. We drifted apart after that night.

Labor Day weekend was only two weeks away, and most of the guys had had their fill of the Jersey shore. Attendance was at an all-time low the weekend before the holiday. That was the weekend I met my next girlfriend.

North Jersey Girl

Towards the end of the summer in 1991, I met a girl. I saw her almost half a block ahead of me on the Boardwalk. I yelled for her to *stop*. It was certainly a caveman tactic, but it got her attention. As I approached, I noticed her Italian heritage. She had perfect olive skin with dark hair and dark eyes. She was wearing a bikini top struggling to do its job, daisy dukes, and tan wedges. She looked even better than I had seen from a hundred yards away.

Once I approached, she asked, "Who were you *fucking* talkin' to?"

I liked that and laughed out loud. "Now, who the fuck are you *laughin'* at, asshole?" She seemed a little pissed.

I continued smiling, completely ignoring her curses, and said, "What's your name?"

She stared daggers through me for a solid thirty seconds and then cracked a thin smile.

"What is happenin' here? Who dis *mutherfucka* think he's tawkin' to? Fuck him, let's go, Sabrina." The thickly accented rant came from an alarmingly short blond girl who had a voice that could shatter glass. I would later find out she was Sabrina's cousin, Katie.

I ignored Katie and said, "Sabrina? Okay. Hi, Sabrina, it's nice to meet you. I'm Brian."

"*Are you being fuckin' serious wit' us right now?*" Katie was almost screaming at this point. I continued ignoring her.

"Cuz, give me a minute," Sabrina said to Katie without breaking our eye contact. Katie threw both hands up in disgust and walked away.

"So where are you staying, Sabrina?"

"My cousin and I are over on East Pine. What's it to you?"

"That's your cousin? She seems pretty annoyed," I said. Katie was sitting on a bench on the far side of the boardwalk staring at us, mumbling to herself. I couldn't help but laugh.

"She's fine. Just a little wound up. Your screaming for our attention didn't help. And *so* rude, by the way. You tawk to your mother like that?"

"Hey, it worked?" I said.

"*Did it?* You think so? Why should I not just tell you to go get bent and walk away?"

"Because you'll always wonder about me and think, 'What if I hadn't walked away that day?' It'll haunt you forever." My smile was now gone. I was being totally serious. I just stared into her brown eyes until she broke.

"*Fine*! What do you want from me?" Sabrina said. She was now smiling so widely her lips all but disappeared.

"I want to see you. How can I reach you? Can I see you later tonight?" We made plans to meet that night. Sabrina left and went over to her cousin. I waved and smiled. Katie gave me the finger.

After that day, Sabrina and I became inseparable. When I came home from the shore, I landed a job opening a hotel in Mount Laurel, New Jersey. It was conveniently a few hundred yards from Exit 4 of the Turnpike. I worked six days a week and even had my own hotel room when there was a vacancy. I was technically still living with Sophia, but, most of the time, I ended up spending nights in Sabrina's dorm room. She was a sophomore at Rutgers University, New Brunswick campus, studying political science. I would finish work around ten, go to the Burger King's drive-thru, and order, like clockwork, two Whoppers and a large Coke, before making the forty-mile trek north on the turnpike. We would stay up too late talking for hours. We shared everything about each other. I found out her mother had cheated on her father, and he decided to stay. I told her about my alcoholic father in disturbing detail. I found out her sister had two abortions with the same guy. I told her I saw the bodies of two men who died by my father's gun. Sabrina confided that her uncle had sexually molested her when she was eight. She told me he was released from jail and living the rest of his life as a registered sex offender. I probably would have told her about being molested by my cousin, but that memory was still buried somewhere inside me. No topic was off limits with us. Sabrina usually passed out mid-sentence from exhaustion.

Between working non-stop and going to see Sabrina, there wasn't much time left for my mother. She was living with a woman, Janette, in Philly, and I really despised my mother's latest partner, not an excuse but certainly a deterrent. In October of '91, a letter was sent to Sophia's house addressed to me. I picked it up about a week later. At the time, I had only read half of the first page. I just couldn't bring myself to read the rest. I only recently read it all the way through.

October 24, 1991

Dear Brian,

This letter is not easy for me to write and probably won't be easy for you to read, but it has to be done.

I know that you didn't ask to be born, but I wanted you, and even when I was carrying you, I loved you. I will love you and worry about you until the day I die.

I raised you and took care of you the best that I could. Always so proud of myself for raising two *great sons. But guess what, I don't know where my two sons are. Sons that have more time for friends, even strangers, than for me, their mother.*

You don't care enough to call to see how I am (are you alive, mom?). For months I have begged you to call me once in a while. But you are too busy, or you have to work. How about all the years I took care of you. I shudder to think where I would be if I didn't have Janette in my life.

You have your life and don't want me to be a part of it. I'll learn to live with that. You talk to me like I'm a piece of trash. Guess what, Brian, I don't deserve it, and I won't take it anymore.

I don't have two pennies to rub together, and yet you want to throw a bill on me that was made for you. I can't believe you are the same person that said to me, "Mom, I will never do to you what Brady did." Well guess what, you did. I wasn't even good enough to meet your girlfriend. Are you that ashamed of me? I am going to tell you the same thing that I told your brother. If you can't call me and come to see me and treat me like I am your mother all year long, then don't bother for the holidays because I won't be home. I will send birthday and Christmas cards because that my right as your Mother.

I am tired and ENOUGH IS ENOUGH.

Some day you will have kids, and I hope that they have more love and respect for you than you have for me. I can't be kind anymore. I will not let you push me over the edge. I won't allow it. I can't believe how you changed. I don't know who you are.

Love Mom
Get these people off my back. It's not my bill, and I won't pay it. Even if I could.

When I read it, I had to stop a couple times. I thought back to the day I first opened it in '91. I remembered only getting as far as mom saying, "sons that have more time for friends, even strangers, than for me, their mother." I remember throwing the letter aside. I thought she was being melodramatic and maybe even a little selfish. She was right though; I did not have time for her. The hotel I worked at was just opening, and the hours were demanding. I sometimes worked eighty or more hours a week that first year. I worked all the holidays, and when I wasn't working, I wanted to see Sabrina. It wasn't just my mother, I lost touch with all my high school friends as well. This was the first job I had since being fired. I swore I would never get fired from a job again, so I became consumed with it.

I stopped a second time and broke down in tears. When she wrote, "You don't care enough to call to see how I am (are you alive, mom?)"—*No, I'm dead. I died of cancer, remember. Don't you wish you had time for me now?* You always think about the how you *could've-would've-should've* after someone *that* close to you dies.

I gathered myself and continued until I got to the part where she compared me to Brady. Comparing me to my brother plunged the knife deep. It wouldn't have back then but watching the way Brady treated my mother over the years made the twenty-eight-year old comparison all the more soul crushing. The next time I paused was when she said, "*I wasn't even good enough to meet your girlfriend. Are you that ashamed of me?*" That part was more about self-reflection than sadness. I sat wondering if I really was embarrassed by her. We had always been poor growing up, and sometimes I blamed her. She was a lesbian, and during the seventies and eighties it wasn't as accepted, so my family was different. I had harbored some feeling, but it wasn't embarrassment. It was resentment. —*Did I resent my mother for my life?* The truthful answer is yes and no. I did when I was younger. I resented her for killing Santa Claus on that cold day in '79. I resented not having a normal childhood like most of the people I knew growing up. But then *I* grew up and realized it wasn't her fault. She wasn't to blame, and I didn't resent her at all. I'm thankful for her and would not have wanted to grow up under different circumstances. I learned to love unconditionally and be thankful for every little thing I received in life. The value of life is not in the possessions I accumulated. This life is about nurturing and cherishing the relationships I made, however broken. Without the people I have in my life, the ones I don't care to breathe without, what's the point? There isn't one.

The last time I paused had nothing to do with her and everything to do with me. She said, "*Someday you will have kids, and I hope that they have more love and respect for you than you have for me.*" The reason this part haunted me so much was that I never ended up having any biological children of my own. It's a sore subject that I often reflect on in the dark lonely hours of the night. It's my one true regret.

The rest of the letter was regarding some bill my mother received. The only thing that sprung to mind was a bill for my college loans. She cosigned for them, and since I took a break from school, the grace period had lapsed, and monthly payments were due. My mother spent most of her life poor, so I understood her worry, but more concerning was the tone of the letter. I am not sure where this came from or what place my mother was in mentally when she wrote it. I later found out Janette continued the mental abuse mom was accustomed to. I didn't feel like I spoke to her in any derogatory fashion. Since I hadn't read the letter, when I eventually introduced Sabrina to my mother, there was no awkward moment to prepare for. They immediately liked each other which made me happy.

Sabrina and I spent the next year in what felt like premarital bliss. I became a fixture in her family. She would come down and visit with my mom on her own. Sabrina was extremely bright, respectful, considerate and kind. I had thought many times of how I would propose. We needed to be more established in our careers, of course. It was only a matter of time.

As I said, I spent very little time at Sophia's, but when I was there it was getting uncomfortable. On several occasions, Sophia had friends over and listening to their escapades through the paper-thin walls was quite disturbing. I talked to my brother about coming to live with him and his wife until I was able to get my own place. He said okay, but I never really got a feeling one way or the other how he felt about it. I figured we would be able to finally develop a relationship since I was no longer the annoying kid he was always trying to avoid. Unfortunately, during the time I lived there, we barely spoke. Even though I paid him room and board, I felt like a freeloader the entire time. I stayed with Sabrina as much as possible during those months.

Eight months into our relationship, Sabrina and I searched for my father. I had told her what I could remember about him, and she felt closure would be good for me. We debated the topic many times. I saw no point to it but, in her mind, there were unresolved feelings, and, now, as an adult, I could handle him. She was wrong. We found my father. He was living in the same trailer park we lived in when I was a toddler. Full circle, I thought. He had inherited a trailer from Josephine, an old friend of his who died and left him this mostly condemned shack on wheels. I pulled up and knocked on the door. I stood there for a couple moments before I heard him behind me. "Boog?" My voice abandoned me as I turned around. I had no words. He walked towards the two-step platform that served as his porch and offered a smile. The skin on his face looked like well-worn leather. His early years of painting bridges had finally caught up with him. I hadn't seen him since I was fifteen, so now, at twenty-two, I found him to be a diminutive man. He was skin and bones. The fear I had harbored for years now seemed unfounded. How could this man hurt me?

"Hey, Dad, how are you?"

His eyes were now fixed on Sabrina. "Who's *this*?"

"This is my girlfriend, Sabrina," I said. He was already approaching her.

He took her hand and politely kissed it. "It's very, *very* nice to meet you." His obvious false teeth glistened as he gawked at her.

"Great tits," he said as he turned towards me.

"*Dad*, have some respect!"

"I'm not lying. Jesus, Boog, you struck gold didn't ya? You know how to pick 'em. Apple didn't fall too far from the tree, I see." He was staring at Sabrina's ass at that point. Her grace was my only solace as she gave me calm in this impossible situation.

"What are you doing here, Boog? You need money or somethin'? I don't have any if that's what you're looking for."

"No dad, I just wanted to see you. It took a bit to find you."

"I'm not hiding. I've been here since Josey died."

"What happened to her?"

"She got old. I don't know. She went into the hospital about a year ago and never made it out. What are you doing for work these days?"

"I work for a hotel as an executive steward."

"My Boog, the executive. Maybe you should give *me* a couple bucks."

"It's not that kind of executive."

"What's your story, beautiful?" Dad was still staring at Sabrina like she was an exhibit at the Philadelphia Zoo.

She pointed to herself and said, "*Sabrina.*" As if to remind him her name was not *Beautiful*. "I go to college."

"So, we have an *executive* and a *college* girl. What are you gonna be when you grow up?" The condescension in his voice was ever so slight but present.

"A lawyer." Sabrina said coldly. She was now the one staring at him. "What do you do?"

"I'm retired."

"*Okay*, well, we have a thing we have to get to so we're gonna get going. It was great to see you, dad," I said.

"Come give your father a hug and a kiss." I did and could feel just how frail he was under his long-sleeved button-up. He kissed me on the cheek. The scruff of his beard scraping my face and the stale smell of cheap beer ended up being the last memory I had of my father. He tried to kiss Sabrina on the lips, but she managed to turn in time.

"Bye, Dad," I said.

"Come back and see me soon, Boog. And bring *Beautiful*, here, with you."

A few years later, my mom received a call from the police. Since my mother and father were still legally married, she was his next of kin. They were calling to ask her to come identify the body. It was revealed that my father had been found by a neighbor several days after he died. He was curled on the floor beside the couch in his dilapidated trailer. He finally drank himself to death. The day prior to his death he was caught in an A&P Supermarket trying to walk out without paying. His haul included bologna, cheese and white bread. —*How ironic.* I wondered if he felt as embarrassed as I had been that day in Wawa. I also wondered if he would have survived had they pressed charges.

Sabrina spent the summer of '92 taking extra classes. Her goal was to finish college in three years and enroll in law school. She was determined, and her goals were set. Meanwhile, her father was on her for her spending habits. He gave Sabrina an allowance while she was in school, so she could concentrate on her studies. He was a retired New Jersey State Trooper, and her mother did not work. They were not wealthy and stretched every dollar. She was frustrated by the hold he had on her and wanted her freedom. It's funny because she didn't really need the money. Whenever we went out, I paid. She became obsessed about getting a job. She was a junior at Rutgers and tired of bumming cash from her parents. I recommended she get a job at a restaurant. With her looks and personality, she would make a fortune. She caved to the idea and ended up getting a job waitressing at the local TGI Fridays just off campus.

One day in late fall, I began work at six in the morning, and it was nearly eleven-thirty by the time I walked into her dorm room. She was doing homework, but when she saw me, she was bursting at the seams with excitement.

"Com'ere. Close your eyes. Close your eyes."

"Aw, Sabrina. Please. I'm exhausted."

"Come on. I've been waiting *all* day!"

I closed my eyes, so tired I'm surprised I didn't fall asleep. A couple minutes passed.

"Okay, open your eyes."

Sabrina was standing there with her TGIF uniform on, although not standard issue. From top to bottom, she had on a red headband, a black long-sleeved shirt, unbuttoned, no bra, a black lace thong and one black garter on her left thigh. Sabrina wasn't a very sexual person given her history with abuse, but she tried, and on this night, she seemed down for anything. It was a good night.

Some time passed, and between school and her job, Sabrina was never around. She picked up shifts constantly, and, with my work schedule, I saw her about once a week.

In February of '93, I had been suffering from the flu and called out of work for a few days. I phoned her one night.

"Hey, you," I said.

"Hi, how are you feeling?'

"Shitty. I just want to stay in bed and sleep for a month."

"Take care of yourself. Stay in bed."

"How's school going?" I asked.

"Fine. Just trying to make sure I get everything done with work and all."

"How's that going? You liking it?"

"It's okay. I'm making decent money. The people are cool. You should go to bed though. Get some rest and I'll talk to you tomorrow. I love you."

"OK, I love you. Goodnight."

"Night." She broke the connection.

After we hung up, I got a sick feeling in my stomach. It was a gut punch that came from nowhere. There was nothing in her voice telling me something was wrong. I can't tell you why, but I knew different. I jumped out of bed and drove ninety minutes to her dorm feeling sick to my stomach. When she answered the door, I could see it in her face. I said, in a very a matter of fact way, "You cheated on me."

When she broke down, I felt a cold sweat rush over me, and I nearly lost my balance. I clutched the door jamb to steady myself. I was disoriented by the sickness, the mucus sloshing around in my head. As she dropped to her knees, head down, her tears puddled on the concrete floor. My mind was cloudy, but my anger was growing to rage, fueled by adrenaline.

"How could you do this to me, you *bitch*. I fucking love you so much."

"I'm sorry, I'm s—"

"F*uck you! Dammit*, dammit. Damn *you*." I was trying to hold my voice to a low roar. I was standing in the threshold of her dorm room and didn't want to draw attention. I certainly couldn't let anyone see me lose control.

Sabrina was talking through her sobs. "It just happened."

"You have to be fucking kidding me. It just happened. That's the excuse? You dirty cunt. How? How did this happen?" I was now channeling the voice of my father.

"I was at a trunk party last week with people from work. There was a bunch of us. It just happened. I drank too much. I shouldn't have gone back to his apartment. It was a stupid mistake and didn't mean anything. I'm sorry. Please forgive me." She was lying there, at my feet, broken on the floor. I was about to unravel, so I walked away before anyone came out to witness the impending carnage. I feared what I might say or worse, do.

Years later, I would rationalize this as normal behavior for a twenty-year-old college student, but in that moment the wounds were too deep and fatal. I drove the entire way home screaming my darkest thoughts at the windshield. I spent months going through the rollercoaster of emotions that came with such a betrayal. I first blamed myself. I worked constantly, and we were spending less and less time together. This made me miss her more. —*did it make her miss me less?* My inward thoughts turned to outward venomous fury. Without realizing it, I would snap at people for no reason. I hated everyone. I felt like my life had come off the tracks, and I was plummeting into a ravine. Sabrina hindered my healing process by calling me every week to apologize. I took her calls with the sole intent of torturing her. I wanted her to hurt as much as I was hurting. She took every verbal blow like an adequate journeyman boxer. The calls went from frequent to nonexistent. At that point, I was sifting through the wreckage and began to realize the most important factor had little to do with love. It had everything to do with trust. In my heart, I knew she loved me. That no longer mattered. I stilled loved her, but I could no longer trust her. I reorganized my priorities for any future relationship. Trust was now on the top of the heap. Without trust there is nothing, and I find it is impossible to recapture once lost.

I was beginning to think less and less about Sabrina, and I threw myself back into work. I almost felt normal. Even if not happy, I felt I was on a more stable emotional footing. My brother threw me another curveball when he broke the news that he and my sister-in-law, Margie, were moving to Jacksonville, Florida. Brady had accepted a job offer which required them to move immediately. They told me I could continue living at the house until it was sold. They liked the idea of someone being there since they would be so far away. I took them up on the offer and, with work, hadn't realized six weeks had passed since they moved. I began seriously looking for a new place when I came home one night, and the electricity had been shut off. Apparently,

Brady had paid through the month, but that was it. He never mentioned it. I was literally in the dark. This lack of communication was typical of our relationship, and I guess I should have expected it. He never called to let me know, and then I realized my living there was more about having someone, anyone, there to make them feel better and less about me having a place to live.

Since I worked so much, I was able to keep a room at the hotel and stayed there until I got an apartment of my own. I even started getting my clothes and dry cleaning done at the hotel. I'm not sure when Brady sold the house.

I've often thought about Sabrina over the years. Songs play on the radio that still remind me how sure I had been. I was planning to marry her, have children, and live happily ever after. Guess not.

All the Wrong Reasons

I was twenty-three when I met my next jail sentence. I was waiting tables at a restaurant in Blackwood, New Jersey. There was a lounge connected to it, and the staff earned a drink ticket for each shift worked. I finished my side-work and cashed out. I heard an off-key voice as I reached the door, it was karaoke night. I've never been a fan of karaoke. Maybe it's because I am more of an introvert than I realize. More likely, the psychological need for people to see the best version of me trumps any desire to potentially make a fool of myself.

After someone performed a horrific version of "My Way," we got rick-rolled right into the voice I would hear for the next twenty-four months. She sang "I Will Remember You" by Sarah McLachlan. I have to admit, her rendition was haunting. I had my back to her like a judge on *The Voice,* so my critique was solely on the vocal. It was good.

I should have predicted she would be sitting two stools away, my own personal ancient Greek Moirai dictating the past, present and future, not of my life but of my relationships. I always find myself blissfully steering into the crash. I sent her another club soda and lime.

"Thank you, that was sweet," she said, offering me a head-tilt and a coy smile.

"You're welcome. I liked your song."

She blushed and was now leaning into the bar to see past the guy between us. He was facing the stage. I gestured behind his back in an attempt to ask if they were together. Her head shook and nose crinkled indicating she was not.

I asked, "Excuse me, would you mind swapping places?"

"Huh." He was looking at me over his shoulder in an attempt to put the pieces together. "Sure." We played a predestined game of musical chairs.

"Hi, I'm Brian, and it's a pleasure to meet you."

"Lauren Meyer," she blushed again. "Like, I'm sorry, I like don't even know why I said my whole name like I'm in grade school. I'm, like, so..." Her cheeks were fully flushed.

Chuckling, I cut in to save her. "Schreiber."

She looked at me as if I was now speaking in tongues. I told her, "My last name. It's Schreiber. It's only fair you know *mine* now that I know yours."

As we talked, I found myself wondering if she was even of legal age. It turned out she was only a few thousand exhales past her twenty-first birthday. This was her first time in a bar, and she had the nerve to come by herself. I liked the confidence that required. It's like going solo to the movies for the first time. For most people, there is a threshold of angst you must cross, and she had. We talked for another twenty minutes about nothing of substance.

"I'm sorry, but I have to get home. My parents will start to worry."

"Oh, okay. I'll walk you out?" I paid the tab –*both tabs*– and escorted her.

In the light of the parking lot, I could see Lauren's small frame much more clearly. Other than a constellation of freckles spanning both cheeks, her pale skin was flawless; mostly makeup-free, barring eyeliner and a touch of lip gloss. In the bar, I had thought she was a blond; she was more of a ginger, bordering albino. *I imagined throwing a sheet over her in the sunlight to avoid her bursting into flames.* She was a pretty girl, a seemingly talented singer, and I would come to find out she sprinkled in a bit of modeling. Lauren had performed at Disney the previous summer and had had aspirations to make a go of it professionally. She had the passable American Idol look, so I bought into the possibilities. What wasn't obvious that night was she was withholding a secret.

I had moved into an apartment in Turnersville, New Jersey. Lauren lived with her parents barely two miles away. I found myself drawn to her smile and how sarcastically funny she was. She appeared squarely between the date and danger zones on the crazy/hot scale. —*Google it, I'll wait.*

The first time I went to Lauren's parents' house for Sunday dinner, I stepped into a very traditional, seemingly normal, family who checked all the boxes. There were a mother and father, happily married, two older sisters, Mary and

Amanda, and one younger brother, Danny. Amanda's three toddlers were also there, but her husband always seemed to be working. They were all so very nice, and I think I needed that at the time. My own modeling and non-starter acting career had fizzled out like a Fourth of July sparkler. I needed to think about what I wanted to do next and if Lauren might fit into the picture.

> *I kind of fell into modeling after doing a side job with a soft drink promoter. The next thing I knew I was getting head shots and scoring small runway gigs here and there. My agent sent me to what turned out to be a casting call for extras of a movie ready to begin shooting in Princeton. I hadn't realized until I arrived that the movie was a period piece, and everyone was dressed in clothing of the 1950's. I was in jeans, a t-shirt and cowboy boots and looked like I was auditioning for a Wrangler jean commercial. There were at least a thousand people packed into the auditorium and lining the surrounding block. The process was my first, and as I finally made it into the auditorium, I saw it play out. The entire front row would step onto the stage in single file. A person, who I would later learn was the assistant to the casting director, and two other cronies walked the line pointing left or right. The people in line scattered into opposite directions off the wings of the stage. As the first row vacated it was replaced with the line behind it, and the process continued. When it was my turn, I walked self-consciously across the stage and settled in place. I was picked to go left with several others in the line but once off stage one of the cronies asked if I could hang around for a bit. Two and a half hours later the auditorium was empty. The assistant to the casting*

director came over and said they would like me to read. I read through a couple pages of lines with another person and was sent on my way. I was given no feedback other than, "Thank you, we'll let you know." Over the course of the next three weeks, I would journey to Princeton four separate times where I read for several different people in a trailer set up as a makeshift office. On my penultimate visit, I was told it was between me and another actor and was asked to audition one final time. Upon my arrival, the assistant director coldly told me they were going with a union actor. I cried the entire way home, and the whole experience turned out to be emotional quicksand. I would never let myself get trapped in it again. People have told me over the years the experience should have been considered a success. It wasn't, at least not for me. I tend to be very thin skinned when it comes to rejection as it is a reflection of my meticulously manicured image. I convinced myself I wasn't cut out for the entertainment business. I wish I hadn't given up.

In the spring of '94, I ended up taking a job waiting tables at Fowl Play in Philly. Lauren and I had been seeing each other for about a month. The restaurant was outdoors and fell victim to frequent May showers. Sometimes I would go home with barely thirty dollars to show for my efforts. To compensate, and pay rent, I picked up as many shifts as I could. Lauren had a key to my apartment so, sometimes, I would come home and find her waiting. She was twenty-one but sleeping over was a no-no in her parents' eyes. "Not while you live under my roof," her mother had told her. One night, I came home late, near the witching hour. Lauren was fast asleep on the couch while Jay Leno interviewed Henry

Rollins on *The Tonight Show*. I knelt by the couch next to Lauren and kissed her softly on the forehead.

"Hey, baby, how was work?" She was groggy and apparently had been sleeping for a while.

"Sucked. It rained *again* and I only made forty-seven dollars."

"Aww, I'm sorry you had a bad night." Lauren was still wiping the sleep out of her eyes. She hadn't been feeling well for last two weeks.

"You're here late, Laur, your mom's gonna *freak* you know."

"I don't care, she'll get over it. I needed to see you." She wasn't her bubbly self, and I realized there was something else going on here.

"Laur, is everything okay?

Lauren sat quietly, staring at the wall. Tears began to well in her eyes.

"Why are you crying? What happened? What'd your mom do this time?"

"Nothing, it's not her. It's *me*. I need to tell you something. I just don't know how."

"Just tell me, already." I was a little annoyed because sometimes Lauren was known to pour on the drama. This wasn't one of those times. She was now sobbing. I put my drama defense shield back in its holster and wrapped my arms around her. She was now gripping me tightly and heaving, virtually hyperventilating at this point. A few minutes later the whimpers subsided, and she raised her head.

"I have to tell you something."

"Okay." I was measured and cautious, unsure what news could possibly cause this emotion.

"I love you," she said. It was the first time she said it. I wasn't sure how I felt, but she needed me to return the sentiment. So I did.

"That's what got you so upset?" I was now laughing.

"I'm pregnant," she said, and spigot in her eyes opened fully.

My mind raced. We had had unprotected sex many times, but I tried to be careful. I realized we never talked about her being on the pill or protected in anyway. Actually, we never talked about protection at all.

She continued, "I should have told you."

"What do you mean you should have told me? You're telling me now."

"When we first started dating, I should have told you."

"*Wait*, it's not mine?" My response was equal parts, confusion, relief and disappointment.

"I was raped, Brian. Around two months ago. When I was doing the show in Hershey. There was a party after and one of the other dancers… he didn't take no."

"Oh, my God, I'm so sorry." I was now tearing up. I would go through a collection of emotions, but, at the time, I was heartbroken for her. I just held her.

"I understand if you don't want to see me anymore. I needed to tell you. This isn't going away." She was falling apart in my arms and all I could do was console her. No decisions were made that night.

"Do you want to stay here?"

"No, I better get home. My parents will have a flippin' heart attack if I don't. They are already freaked out about this whole situation."

I understood her point. Their daughter was raped two months ago, she was pregnant and now had a new boyfriend whom she loved. They didn't know the last part.

"I'll take you home. I don't want you driving like this."

"I'll be okay." She was trying to collect herself.

"No. I'll pick you up in the morning, so you can get your car. You're not driving tonight, end of story."

"I'm really sorry, Bri. I really am. I should have told you. Please forgive me."

"It's okay." I said it but I didn't know if I meant it. I was caught off guard. I hadn't expected any news that night. I hadn't even expected to see Lauren. When she finally told me, I thought I was finding out I was going to be a father. I wasn't, and now the word raped got tossed in like an emotional grenade. And then what she said hit me. *—This isn't going away.* She was planning to keep the baby. It took me a few days to process what was happening. I did like her, a lot. I said I loved her, but I can't say that was true. I felt I needed to help her. I decided to stick around.

Lauren's father, Barry, was an engineer working for a company that manufactured specialty chemicals. Rose Meyer was a stay-at-home wife who had dinner on the table every night and kept an immaculate house. She kind of reminded me of a shorter version of my mother. Like Lauren, she was barely five feet tall and needed rocks in her pockets to break a hundred pounds. Mrs. Meyer invited me to church one week; she insisted. That Sunday, against my silent protest, I met the family in the parking lot of the church just before nine. The two older sisters were not present. They had drawn their line in the sand long ago. It would be the first time I attended an Evangelical Christian church. I am going to judge here, and if I offend anyone, I'm sorry. The congregation was entirely white, and they all seemed to be drinking the Kool-Aid. They were a boisterous bunch and praised Jesus at every turn. The sermon's theme revolved around taking specific events out of the news and connecting dots to particular verses in the Bible. There seemed to be an emphasis on these being the "end times" and preparing for salvation. I didn't buy it, but I was respectful and endured the weekly service when I couldn't find a passable excuse. It was important to them, even though Lauren didn't seem totally sold either. Weekly service was what they did as a family, and she respected her parents.

Lauren's brother, Danny, was thirteen, and, with his grueling sports schedule, I didn't see him much. Her sister Mary was my age and a reservist in the Navy. She had neck length curly brown hair with hazel eyes and a body built by the US Naval Academy. Whenever her parents were around, she was quiet, maybe even demure. In their absence, she cursed like a truck driver and sexual innuendoes were a constant. My kind of girl. The oldest sister, Amanda, lived in a grungy apartment a few miles away with her husband and three kids. She didn't look anything like the rest of the family. She had a gaunt Olive Oyl look, and she and her kids looked like they could all use a bath. What she didn't share in familial appearance she more than made up for in personality. In that way, Lauren's two sisters were identical. Hysterically crude. I fit in well with them, and they respected me for sticking around through the pregnancy. They were extremely close knit. Maybe a little too much at times.

Lauren wasn't home when I got there one Saturday night. I no longer knocked, and the front door was usually unlocked so I let myself in.

"Lauren?" I called out.

From upstairs, Mary yelled, "She's not back yet. Come on up."

Amanda was in Mary's room, and they were both leaning into the mirror attached to a dresser. I could faintly hear Amanda's rug-rats downstairs terrorizing their grandmother.

"You guys going out?"

"If this slut ever finishes getting ready," Amanda said.

"Shut the fuck up, I'm getting laid tonight."

Amanda looked back at me with an eye-roll. "Whatever, whore."

Mary put lip gloss on and commented how it tasted like cherries. Amanda said, "Let me taste," grabbing Mary by the nape of the neck, craning her into a backbend and lapped her tongue across Mary's lips. "You're right!" Mary then sprung around and planted her lips on mine. Before she drew away, she stuck her tongue out, penetrating my closed mouth. She snorted out a laugh like she was amused by my response. My bulging eyes were not my only physical reaction to this gesture, and she was right, it tasted just like cherries. I heard the front door slam. I shook off the tingling in my jeans and ran down to greet Lauren. As time passed, I realized this behavior seemed normal to them. I wasn't interested in finding out where their line in the sand was drawn.

Lauren was now in her third trimester and constantly in discomfort. Her petite frame was struggling to contain the growing life inside of her. You never saw her without a smile, but she was beginning to struggle. Cocoa butter tummy rubs were now part of my daily routine.

Late in Lauren's seventh month of pregnancy, I went to her parents' house in the afternoon on my day off to surprise her. The door was unlocked, as usual, so I let myself in. It always felt weird, but in the beginning, I was constantly told to stop knocking *like a stranger*. Once inside, there were three options. To the left was the fake living room with plastic covered furniture. The stairs were straight ahead leading to the second floor, and the family room was to the right which got the most foot traffic. Before I called out my presence, something caught my eye in the fake living room. There was a folding table set up and a children's tea party was well underway. I stood there puzzled not really sure what I was seeing. Rose Meyer was sitting with her back to me, and the other chairs were occupied by stuffed animals. She was pouring tea and having a lively conversation, which I assumed had to be with the grandchildren lurking around the corner. No, that was it. Mrs. Meyer, apart from the stuffed animals occupying the three other chairs, was entirely alone. Lauren had been in her room when I arrived and must have heard me come in because she was now turning the corner and struggling down the stairs. Horror glazed over her face as she watched me standing at the threshold of the door listening to her mother ask Penelope the giraffe if she wanted more tea. As she walked past me, she grabbed my wrist and whispered, "Follow me." We got outside, and Lauren melted down in front of me. When she cried her cheeks turned bright red, and, as tears streamed, her eyeliner drew black lines down her face.

"I'm sorry you saw that!"

"Laur, I'm not sure what I just saw." I tried not to appear freaked out.

I walked Lauren to my car and drove around like she was an infant soothed by the hum of the engine. We didn't talk much, and by the time we returned her father was home. We went in, and Lauren made a beeline to tell her dad what happened.

"Hey, Brian, can you join me, please?" Mr. Meyer was already heading through the sliding doors. I followed him to the backyard.

"Are you okay?" he asked as if I had just been in a car accident.

"Yeah. *Yes*. Yes, sir."

"This was bound to happen sooner or later. I'm sorry it happened like this. You have become like a member of this family. It's insane to say that in the short time you have been around. Lauren really cares about you, and it's obvious you share her feelings." He took a pause as to measure his words. His eyes were kind, and this man truly loved his wife. "You should know my wife is dealing with some mental health issues which cause her to not be herself sometimes. Well, it *is* part of her. It's difficult to sugar coat the situation. I am just going to come right out with it. Rose suffers from multiple personality disorder."

He was very open about her diagnosis and said it was the result of *incidents* occurring in her childhood. My voice box paralyzed, I said nothing. I attentively listened to his words and felt his thinly veiled embarrassment.

"Now you know. If you see my wife acting strange… please just try to go with it."

"Okay, sir."

And I did. And it was *fucking* fascinating! Over time I witnessed several different people wearing her skin. There was the little girl that offered Penelope the giraffe more tea. She came out many times and talked as if she were four or five years old. A couple of personalities seemed to blend together, but I expect I couldn't differentiate them with my limited exposure. One night, Lauren's sisters were taking Rose out dancing. I went up to Mary's room as I usually would while they were getting ready. At that point, seeing Lauren's sisters in their bra and panties was common. Mary had once told me it was just like seeing them at the pool; I guess I couldn't argue with her. Rose was dressed more like Mary and less like Rose. I found out this was Megan, and she was twenty-four. She also possessed the sass of her daughters and mumbled, "Who's the hotty?"

"Megan, that's Brian, *Lauren's* boyfriend."

"Oh," she said with a semi-apologetic face. She then turned back to Mary and said in a whisper, "He's still hot."

I was flummoxed and went downstairs and talked to Barry. I was ordered to now call him by his first name.

"How long do these episodes last?"

"Depends." He was fully engrossed in the daily-double of *Jeopardy*.

"What happens when she goes out dressed as she is and switches back to herself?"

In the background Alex Trebek was saying, "In the New Testament it was said that 'His meat was locusts and honey'."

Under his breath Bill answered, "Who is John the Baptist?" As if almost a continuation of his correct answer, he replied to my question. "She's aware of it. Maybe not in the moment, but she knows what happens. She may get uncomfortable and need to come home."

"I'm sorry, Barry, this is just a lot to take in."

He broke the trance Alex had placed on him and looked at me and said, "No need to be sorry; this is our life, and if you are going to be part of it, you need to understand. We have an appointment with her psychiatrist later next week. It's a *family* appointment, and I would like you to consider being there."

Really? "Okay, thank you. I'll be there." I was too young to truly understand what I was getting myself into or why I decided to stick it out. Here I was, twenty-four, with a pregnant girlfriend —A girl I did not really love— having a baby that was not mine. I was now being considered a family member and invited to become intimately familiar with the details of my girlfriend's mother's disorder.

Lauren and I drove together to the psychiatrist's office.

"I'm, like, so happy you're coming. This is humiliating, but she's my mom you know. It means a lot. You *really* do love me." —*no, I don't.*

She was nervous. I just took her hand in mine. Our eyes met, and she realized it was going to be okay.

"I can't believe my father likes you so much. He like, never liked any of my boyfriends. The whole family loves you. You're so good for me." Lauren was now leaning across the car with her head on my shoulder.

When we arrived, everyone was there except Amanda's three kids. It was actually the first time I met Amanda's husband, Rick. He was covered in tattoos and looked dirty too. —*Did they even have running water in their apartment?* We went in, and mine was the only new face, so introductions were made, and for my benefit there was a preamble describing what was going on and why we were all there.

Dr. Flannery scanned us all and started, "You are all well aware of Rose's condition but for Brian's benefit, as requested by Barry, let us go through the diagnosis once again. Rose is suffering from a fairly severe multiple personality disorder. Through intense therapy, we have determined the condition was exacerbated by the long-term sexual abuse she experienced in her childhood and well into her teens. Are we all okay?"

Everyone muttered a collective, listless, "yes."

Even though Barry had prepared me, —*incidents occurring in her childhood*— the mention of sexual abuse was difficult to hear. I kept my eyes trained on Dr. Flannery to avoid looking into any embarrassed faces in the room. The doctor continued to explain they were in the middle of treating Rose, with the goal of integrating her alters. I won't pretend to be qualified in all the ins and outs of this treatment. I will tell you we were told this would take years of work, and our part would be to help her through it. To do so, we needed to try our best to accept all the alters and avoid any conflict between them. I walked away with a much better understanding of the situation and ready to help, but I wouldn't be honest if I didn't say I struggled with whether or not I could hang in there. The entire situation was a dense clusterfuck.

Over the next month, Lauren and her mother were at each other's throats for one reason or another, and the baby was very close now. I suggested to Barry that Lauren should stay with me. He hated the idea at first and then warmed to it, and within the next few days Lauren moved in. It was meant to be temporary.

Lauren was barely able to walk as her due date approached. The thin pretty girl I met was now replaced by a very bloated, semi-familiar replica. Only her smile was truly recognizable. On the day she gave birth we raced to the hospital. The *go-bag* had been sitting next to the door for the past week and a half and would now be called to duty. Since I wasn't the father, I wasn't in the delivery room, but I paced the waiting room as if there was no difference. She wasn't even born, and I already loved her.

The doctor came out to tell us we had a new baby girl in the family, and the entire waiting room applauded. I quietly gushed and failed to hold back tears. Once the baby was cleaned up and now in Lauren's arms, I was permitted in the room. As I expected, when I first saw this little human wrapped so tightly and wiggling in her mother's arms, I broke down. Lauren looked at me with tears in her eyes and said "Brian, meet Brianna."

The tears now streamed from my face as I realized that even though I didn't help conceive this child, we would forever be linked in some significant way. It was two letters off, but it was Lauren's way to give me a small piece of this angel. In isolation, this would be one of the most fulfilling moments of my life.

I was a proud faux papa.

Over the coming months we played house, and Brianna consumed our attention. Given Lauren's post-partem mood swings and physical state, our sexual relationship had diminished to non-existent. To be fair, she was willing and able; I was uninterested. I think back now and realize how horribly I reacted to her advances. Both of our sex drives were strong. I am an admittedly vain and a hyper-selective person when it comes to what I find attractive. She was no longer fitting my strict requirements. One Saturday, we dropped Brianna off with her grandparents and Lauren and I drove to the Cowtown Flea Market in Pilesgrove, New Jersey. We were on a desolate back road when Lauren slid her hands into my crotch.

"What are you doing?"

"What do you think I'm doing? She tugged at my belt buckle." She was smiling.

"Are you nuts? I'm driving here."

"No one's around. Pull over if you want."

"Stop it," I said and pushed her arm away. A few silent moments uncomfortably crept by.

"Why don't you have sex with me anymore? You look at me like I disgust you."

"What are you talking about? You just had a baby."

"The doctor cleared me two weeks ago. You were there, remember? And you don't *fuck* me anymore. Not like you used to. You haven't since I was five months pregnant." Lauren wasn't one to curse like her sisters but in this angry moment she couldn't help herself. "I know you are cheating on me. You make me feel like a fucking fat slob. You look at me like I'm trash."

"I don't know where this is coming from, but I'm not talking about this right now."

"Then when?"

The conversation stalled there and the trip rummaging through other peoples discounted possessions turned into a silent funeral march. We barely spoke for the next couple days. One night I woke up, and she had been fellating me as I slept. She mounted me once I was hard. I *woke up* and finished the job. She never realized my excitement was fueled by fantasies involving my high school sweetheart's mother, but it served her purpose. This contrived scenario happened more often that I care to admit.

While my relationship with Lauren was deteriorating, my relationship with Brianna and the family couldn't have been stronger. I became the father Brianna needed and the man their family thought a good influence in their daughter and granddaughter's lives. I was so taken by Brianna, but my relationship with Lauren was rocky, at best. Brianna simply wasn't enough reason to keep me faithful to Lauren. As the air turned crisp, I had already spent several late nights in the city that were not easily explained. This was one of them.

It was Friday night at Fowl Play, and the waiting list just spilled over to a fourth page. I had a station of six tables, one located halfway across the restaurant, but if there was anything I was good at in life it was managing people. I learned early how to read a room and appease folks accordingly. When we were this busy, it was impossible not to piss a few people off. I always tried to triage the situation as best I could. The kitchen was at almost a complete standstill and only salads were coming out at a reasonable pace. I personally bought a couple rounds of drinks that night for the more well-known tippers. They rewarded me for my efforts. It was around nine-thirty at night, and the kitchen was beginning to gain traction, but the new patrons were a restless bunch given the wait time they endured. A couple of solid sevens sat at one of my four-tops. I usually bitched to the hostesses for seating two people at my four-tops because I couldn't maximize the station. After taking their drink order, I realized I couldn't be upset with these two ladies from the Midwest. Both very well put together, they were here for some conference at the Philadelphia Convention Center and found themselves sitting with me; they were both starving. I got their salads out quickly given the two-hour wait they endured before getting a table. To this point, they were less than impressed with our city. I overheard them talking about the traffic and rude people they would never see in Nebraska. Once I had a hold of my station, I ordered three Jolly Rancher shots from the service bartender and delivered them to the table. "My treat." I sat down and *presented the shots in front of them and one in front of me. I explained I had overheard their conversation about Philly and couldn't in good conscience let them leave without some authentic "Philly" hospitality. "Cheers!" I quickly got up, explaining my manager would kill me if she saw me sitting there drinking with the customers and politely excused myself. I was sure to get a good tip from these two. Their irritated mood from waiting had washed away. Every time I walked by their eyes followed me. I dropped off their check. "Thank you, ladies. Enjoy your stay and come back and see me sometime." I dropped them a wink and walked away. They left and, soon after, my entire station emptied and refilled within about ten minutes, so I was on to the next batch of irritated customers. The busboys collected the checkbooks while clearing the tables and handed them to the waitstaff. I used to stuff them all in the back of my shorts and close the checks out once I had time to breathe. During one of those periods of peace, I began closing my checks out and came across my friends from Nebraska. They gave me a fifty-dollar tip on a ninety-dollar check. I then noticed they wrote on the back of the customer copy of the receipt, "Hope to see you soon! Philadelphia Marriott Downtown, Room 237." There was a hotel key behind the receipts. At that point I was shaken. This felt like Denny's all over again, but the tip wasn't in all silver coins. I spent the rest of the night figuring out what I would do. I had a girlfriend and baby at home waiting for me. The problem was I only worried about Brianna, and she would be fine without me for a few hours. I took a cab to 12th and Market. I walked through the lobby with purpose to the elevators. My pace slowed once I reached the second floor. I second-guessed this entire* *plan. Once I slipped in the keycard and heard the magnetic lock click, I knew there was no turning back. The night played out, and my first threesome as well as their first lesbian experiences were behind us. I got home in time to see the sunrise.*

Lauren's jealousy raged. She would often become angry, and I would equal and even surpass her to the point of verbal assault. I considered my words the weapons I used to win arguments. The reality was, they didn't. Even well-earned victories were lost in these tirades. My mouth betrayed me at every turn as my father's venom coursed through my veins. Our relationship was tumultuous, but as the Fowl Play's season wore down, I temporarily settled into the role Lauren wanted, an attentive partner. She had slimmed down a bit, and the attraction I felt initially was vaguely resurfacing. For the first time in a year, I initiated sex.

Brianna was the daughter I longed for, and even though she wasn't mine by blood, she was mine. Everyone treated me like I was her father. I did anything for this little girl and assumed I always would. Around Christmas, Brianna was suffering from a severe case of colic. She cried constantly. One particularly long night, it was snowing as consistently as she was crying. I pulled my favorite recliner next to the sliding glass door and sat rocking her in my arms. The sleeping and crying spells took turns through the dead of the night. We both eventually were overcome with exhaustion, and I woke up the next morning, alone. Lauren had taken the next shift.

Given my history, the Christmas of '94 was a memorable one. I woke up with a new daughter who was too young to appreciate the gifts under the tree. And yes, there was a tree. Her eyes, as big and joyous as her mother's, were full of life and happiness. We spent Christmas morning as any family might and by nine-thirty we headed to the Meyer residence. Other than the twenty-four stockings hung across the fireplace and banister, everything was normal. Some names I recognized and others I didn't. I realized the names I didn't were of the alters I had not yet met. Some were puffed with gifts and would be emptied as the alters arrived. The tree as well as some stockings would hang well into February.

Over the winter, the owner of Fowl Play called to discuss the possibility of my managing the restaurant for the upcoming season. After a couple lunch meetings with the ownership group, I accepted. I would begin in early March but wouldn't begin working twelve-hour shifts until late April. The job took me away from Lauren and Brianna. I only missed one of them. My long days turned into long nights. Lauren began badgering me about the extended hours away and how hard it was to take care of Brianna on her own. I was exhausted and not sympathetic. Her complaints of *being ignored* and *unwanted* were piling up like store circulars in the mailbox of an abandoned house. At home, Lauren's jealousy and irrationality was again bubbling to the surface. Her and my breaking points were edging closer to a formal introduction.

"Where were you?" the volume in Lauren's voice was rising with each word.

"Um. Work."

"You're cheating on me. I know you are. Who is she?" Lauren was grasping at straws.

"What are you talking about? I'm working my ass off here. I don't need this accusation bullshit."

"You must be cheating. You don't even *touch* me anymore."

It was true, I hadn't touch her in a while, but the allegations came nightly. Relentlessly. At times, she became unglued.

"You are leaving me here with *our* baby and out there fucking some other girl. You should be home fucking *me*. I thought you loved me." This behavior became normal for her and only pushed me further away. Most of those nights ended with Brianna waking up to her mother's rants and I would go into the nursery and rock her back to sleep. During the day, when we were home together, she would tell me working at Fowl Play wasn't good for us, and I should find another job. In actuality, nothing was good for us. We were not meant to be. I got into this relationship for all the wrong reasons. I stayed in the relationship solely for Brianna. It just wasn't enough.

Fowl Play was in full swing by May, and so was my libido. I left with a different girl every few days and often went home reeking of sex. *I'm not proud of it.* Chloe Scutari was a girl I'd had my eye on since her interview in April. She would later say she thought I was *slimy* when we first met. I wore her down. One night we shared a shift drink at the back bar.

That turn into six or seven. We parted ways, but a handful of shifts later, we turned shift drinks into drinks at her place. She and I were quickly entangled on her couch. It was a religious experience as we were so in tune with each other's bodies. As three a.m. approached, I was now totally sober and physically exhausted. However, I was expected home. We shared an extended goodbye, and I climbed into my car. Thankfully, I was sober because I was pulled over on the east side of the Ben Franklin Bridge and had to perform a full sobriety check. It was the last possible way I expected that evening to end. And yet, it wasn't over. I walked in to find a fiery ginger sitting on a chair facing the door; blocking my passage. Wide-eyed, and like a cobra, she was ready to strike. Brianna woke up crying five minutes into Lauren's tirade which gave me a reprieve. I spent the next hour consoling the baby and avoiding Lauren's tantrum.

As much as I loved Brianna, I could not continue living this way, and although I regret to this day not being there for her, I needed to move on. I rented an apartment in the Queen's Village section of Philadelphia. Through a tearful screaming match, I told Lauren I would pay the rent for the next six months, and they could stay until they figured out next steps. I packed and walked out without being permitted to say goodbye to Brianna. Lauren told me, among other things, I didn't deserve it. She was probably right.

I spent the next couple months working, endlessly, and trying to settle into my new apartment. I eventually went to the post office to collect my mail and submit a change of address form. I had placed a hold on it so it would be waiting for me. Nothing was waiting. I was told my *wife* had released the hold, and my mail was again going to my former apartment in Turnersville. Being young, and not quite sure how many federal laws were broken, I was merely pissed off and corrected the error. As shady as her act was, I hurt and betrayed Lauren, and I felt some responsibility for her deeds.

She not only redirected my mail but also obtained my credit card information. The list of her purchases included fifteen hundred dollars' worth of Bible videos from some place in Texas, a twenty-eight-hundred-dollar diamond ring, and various minor shopping sprees. In all, Citibank claimed I owed them north of five thousand dollars, a number I couldn't fathom at that age. I managed to get another credit card provider, MBNA, to negotiate my debt down to thirty-two hundred. I paid it over time and considered it a lesson learned.

The next meteor launched through my atmosphere was in the form of a domestic violence complaint accompanied by a restraining order. After an upsetting day in court, Lauren came to her senses and dropped the baseless claim. She admitted to just trying to hurt me. It was almost the end.

On occasion, over the next several months, I came out of my apartment and found her standing on the opposite corner or in her car parked, seemingly waiting. She now lived comfortably in the danger zone of the crazy/hot scale. I wouldn't hear from her again for years.

Chloe

By mid-summer of '96 I was feeling at home in my Philly bachelor pad. Living in a big city took some getting used to. For one, street parking was horrendous. Most nights, I had to circle blocks like a Gran Prix racer until I found a place to park. Street parking required feeding the meter by ten a.m. With the late nights I kept, I never woke up in time to pay the coin-operated warden. Oversleeping cost me approximately 700 dollars in parking tickets that first year. It was still cheaper than paying hundreds a month to rent a spot in a parking garage. Having a car, in general, seemed like more of a nuisance than anything. It was only worth having if you needed to go out of the city. Otherwise, you were paying to park somewhere. I found myself walking much more than I ever had in Jersey. Many of the bars and eateries I frequented were very close. The bar I would play darts at for the next twenty years was a half block from my apartment. Chloe and her two roommates lived right down the street on Pine. We were seeing each other more frequently, though, to her surprise, not exclusively. She began dropping by unannounced. One morning when the doorbell rang, I ran down to answer and found it was Chloe.

"Hey. Morning," she said.

"Morning back." I was standing in the doorway like the Queen's guard. "What brings you here on this *fine* morning, pretty lady?"

"I was at Pennsport taking a yoga class. I figured I'd stop by and see if you wanted to go to breakfast or something."

"Oh, uh, sure. Let me —"

"Excuse me, Bri," came a meek voice from behind me. I turned and a disheveled, jet-black-haired girl squeezed past me, chest-to-chest. She mouthed a kiss — *mwah*— and was off without a word. Chloe watched her cross the street, hair tangled, clothes from the night before, heels in hand.

"Who's *that*?" Chloe asked in a jealous tone.

"Umm, she's a—"

"Never mind. Bye, Brian." Chloe turned and walked away.

An hour later, I walked to her house and knocked. She answered.

"Can we talk?" I asked.

She came out, closed the door behind her and sat on the step. "Sure. Talk," she said bluntly.

"So, okay. I, I'm sorry for this morning. I never meant to make you feel bad or to put you in an awkward position."

"I guess I just expected more," she said.

"More what?"

"I don't know, I thought you were a total jerkoff when we first met, and then I thought you were pretty great, and now I'm feeling somewhere in between."

"Wait, why? What did I do?"

"I assume you had sex with that chick that did the walk of shame from your apartment this morning. I guess I thought we were kind of a *thing*. And I guess you don't."

"Is that what you want out of this?"

"*Isn't* that what you want? I guess that's a stupid question given this morning." Chloe was now being as sarcastic as I'd ever heard her. I kind of liked it.

"I just got out of a two-year relationship. Can we talk about this later? I have to go get ready for work."

"Sure, I'll be there at three for my shift. You owe me a great station tonight."

"*That*, I can do." I leaned in to kiss her, and she pulled away.

"You're not serious right now? *Ewww*. Did you even shower from last night?" —*I had not*. She got up and walked into the house without waiting for the answer, leaving me there humbled. I gave Chloe the best station in the restaurant that night.

Even though I said we would talk later, we didn't. Chloe never brought the subject up, and I avoided it. I really wasn't interested in anything serious just yet. Between getting my heart broken by Sabrina and breaking the heart of Lauren, I needed a break from serious. Don't get me wrong, Chloe was a lot of fun to be around. I tried to go out with her at least once every couple of weeks but working twelve-hour shifts six days a week made it a challenge.

Mondays were my only off day at the restaurant. I typically slept in and tried to rest up for the workweek ahead. If I woke up before ten a.m. I felt robbed. I didn't sleep enough during my twenties, so I needed to get it in when I could. With only a few weeks left in summer, the restaurant started slowing down. I began leaving at seven on Sunday nights. One Sunday, Chloe and I went to an *in-the-business* party at one of the local clubs. She drank me under the table, and we somehow made it back to my apartment. I woke up the next morning at around eleven-thirty. I hadn't slept that late in years, and my head was on fire. Chloe was still passed out when I got out of the shower. The bedroom was on the second floor of my two-story loft, and the sole bathroom was connected. When I came out, Chloe was sprawled out across the bed, naked. I thought back to when we first met at the panel interview in April. She looked so innocent with her long curly red hair and ocean-blue eyes. Her conservative dress that day showed modesty, a modesty meant only for the outside world. In my bed that morning, she was free. As she lay on her back, her breasts defied gravity. She was Italian with a fondness for tanning booths; caramel colored and not a single tan line. Finding out Chloe was a three-year veteran on the Temple dance squad gave some explanation to her chiseled curves.

"Hey?" she groaned.

"Hey yourself, how are you feeling?" I asked as my eyes traced the vertical line crossing over her six-pack abs.

"Like a *bus* hit me. Did a bus hit me?"

"Yes, the one that read Jägermeister on the marquee. It actually circled the block and hit you quite a few times last night." Laughing felt like lightning strikes.

"*Ooh*, I'll never drink that shit again. Can we just lie in bed all day?"

"Only if you keep wearing what you're wearing."

"You mean nothing?" She giggled. "Deal. But can you *please* get me a glass of water?"

"It's right next to you. There's a Gatorade, too. Hope you like orange. The Gatorade helped me. Oh, and there's Advil in the top drawer."

We spent that day in bed talking, well, mostly talking. I liked Chloe more and more. Over the coming weeks, we spent hours in bed after work, just talking. Chloe was one of the most sensual, deep-thinking girls I had met to that point. She wrote poetry and was extremely introspective. Whether it was her written word or her actions, she went to great lengths to try and express her feelings. She was much more successful with her writing.

I went to her place one night and found I had walked into a treasure hunt. There was a note on the front door that read, "Come get me." She had given me a key to her house on Pine Street, so I let myself in. The lights were all off and only the generosity of a few candles guided my way. As I walked toward the staircase, I noticed index cards climbing the stairs before me, each one clinging to the same sentiment with only one difference; the font increased. Except the final card.

Closer
Closer
Closer
Closer

I'm so wet

She was. I opened the bedroom door hearing Sade somewhere in the middle of "Smooth Operator." I found her masturbating. Waiting, impatiently. We listened to the *Diamond Life* album on repeat for hours as we soaked her bed sheets in sweat.

The next few months were much of the same. We were connected on some spiritual level for about six months. It should have ended there. It had reached the pinnacle of anything either of us could have expected. Instead, I offered for her to move in with me. Her roommates were both graduating, and she was basically on the street, so it was the obvious, if not the dumbest choice there was to make. To be fair to myself, it seemed logical at the time.

We moved her stuff into my apartment, and the seriousness of our courtship immediately became real. I was enjoying our dating phase but, once again, instant relationship. It seemed I couldn't help myself. Now that we were living together, I realized Chloe was usually drinking something. She was drinking daily. In fact, she was drunk most of the time, but had such a command of it that she could fluidly navigate her life without people ever noticing; the truest definition of a functioning alcoholic. I had been flying too close to the sun. I did not notice. Eventually, I confronted her, and this was when the angry man met the alcoholic.

"We need to talk," I said.

"Okay."

"Do you ever go a day without drinking?" I asked authoritatively.

"No." Her response was fraught with shame, and the revelation pissed me off.

I was finding myself getting angry. My ears burned as the blood pumped through them. I couldn't explain why I felt this way. I was incensed.

"Wow," I said. "So, you're like, what, an alcoholic? You could have told me that before I plucked you off the street like a stray."

She began to cry but not from sadness. She was furious. "You have no idea what I've been through. You have no right to judge *me*."

"I wholeheartedly *disa-fuckin-gree*. You came to live with *me*! I never signed up to get some Prospect Park gutter drunk as a roommate." I was out of line, but I couldn't control myself.

"You know what, screw you. You have no right to speak to me that way. If you want me out just say so. I don't need this."

I left and, ironically, went to the bar. I had a few beers and went back and apologized.

"Chloe, I'm really sorry I spoke to you like that. I didn't mean it. Will you forgive me?" I looked like the poster boy for assholes who abuse their partners. Spew hate and then go apologize later. Chloe forgave my unforgivable outburst, and we continued the conversation. She admitted she was drinking too much and needed to rein it back. She did, and selfishly, I ended up hating myself for ever suggesting it. The seductive, spontaneous, fire starter was gone. She had morphed into some unexpected depressive state of being, not living. What I came to realize over the first few months of cohabitation was just how damaged Chloe was.

We spent the fall of '96 adjusting to the new dynamic of our relationship. Chloe walked on eggshells, feeling like a constant letdown, and I was a trigger-happy bully. We should have both walked away. I think the only reason she stayed was because I reminded her of her father. He and I shared our special way with words, so I think Chloe had come to accept it as normal.

By Christmas, she was sober and seeking therapy for her diagnosed depression. The medication helped her from fading into the darkness completely, but she was a shell of the girl I had met. The sad reality was the medication and lack of alcohol caused Chloe to shed the seductive, crimson goddess persona and embrace something much less attractive. It embarrasses me as a human to admit, but it was true. I persevered out of nothing but self-assigned obligation. One more trap I would fall into without understanding the *why*.

The years between '97 and '99 became a constant bout with my fidelity. I tried, but to be honest, there wasn't enough to keep me punching out of that fight. Over that span, Chloe and I barely ever had sex, and when we did it was usually a response to one of my outbursts. I would get frustrated by her lack of interest. I was torn between trying to be understanding and needing to get laid. I fell into one-night stands and worked angles with girls constantly. Looking back, I was a fucking scumbag.

I had been, not so silently, crushing on this waitress, Mia Grosso, for weeks at work. Her flirtation was slight but unmistakable. Mia would needlessly brush against me as she passed by and made playful comments full of sexual innuendo. On one occasion, we found ourselves alone in the restaurant's back office.

"*So*, you finally have me alone," I said.

"Oh, my God, are you *crazy*? Chloe is right outside."

"Lock the door."

"Absolutely not," Mia said firmly.

"Tease."

"*I am not*! Shut up." Mia was squinting at me and seemed to be mulling over the possibility that my accusation was true. "Anybody could walk in here," she said and walked out.

Mia was in a committed relationship with Claude, a French citizen working in the US. He was super dreamy, and his panty-dropping accent only completed the package. I seemed to draw her attention, nonetheless. One weekend, Janine, one of our line cooks at the restaurant, was having a party. She was mostly gay and one of the coolest people I knew. She wanted, in the worst way, to hook up with Chloe and had no problems going through me to do it. Janine and I had made out at a party the year before, and she told me one day we were bound to have sex. She said she enjoyed a good dicking every now and again, but she preferred women way more. —*I don't need to have the leading role in every film, just squeeze me in the credits somewhere.* That night, Chloe and I arrived at the party to find twenty-five or thirty people crammed into this apartment, mostly co-workers but some stragglers I didn't know. I was looking forward to seeing Mia since she lived with Claude two floors below Janine, but she wasn't around. Claude told me she should be up soon. I wasn't interested in waiting. There were enough people for me to get lost, so, lost I got. I found a reason to go down to Mia's apartment. I knocked on the door, and Mia was noticeably uncomfortable when answering. It was evident I was the last person she expected to see. There I stood asking for ice. Looking into her eyes told me my ulterior motives were evident. She asked where Claude was.

"Upstairs, talking to some hot blond."

"Brian, this is *not* happening." She wanted to believe her own words.

Our eyes remained locked. I stood stone-faced. "I don't know what you mean."

"I would never cheat on Claude," she said, even though she knew he was incapable of returning the favor. I said nothing, just smiled back at her. Staring but saying nothing, I slowly closed the distance between us. Finally, face-to-face, we stood for a time, waiting each other out. She surged forward and aggressively kissed me. It lasted a few minutes, and her sanity, or maybe her morality, took control. She pushed me away just as aggressively as she had pulled me in. "You have to *go*," she said. I went back to the party, and we never spoke of the exchange to anyone. Luckily, I had not been missed. The party smoldered for hours and eventually dwindled to embers; only Janine, Chloe and I remained. I sat on a recliner nursing what became my last beer, totally preoccupied by the exchange with Mia, but now what was happening trumped the losing hand I had held hours prior. I was certainly a little fucked up, but nothing my youth wouldn't overcome. I watched, like a spectator at the Roman Colosseum waiting for the lion to slay its meager prey. Janine kissed Chloe and they clawed at each other's clothes. Janine commanded the situation, and, for a few minutes, I sat back and took it in. I watched as Janine stripped down, and Chloe's sweater and bra hit the floor. Chloe's tight jeans slid slowly down her legs. Janine glanced back at me with an expression of victory and maybe a little gratitude. She chewed at her bottom lip and smiled as she turned back toward Chloe. She pushed Chloe's naked legs forward and disappeared between them. Chloe's groans slowly rose and a few minutes later fell to silence. When Janine moved away, I was overcome and buried every inch I had into Chloe. This was the hottest sex we'd had since she stopped drinking. For me, the alcohol helped stave off the eventual outcome long enough for Chloe to utter words I never thought I'd hear. "You have to feel him inside you." Chloe and Janine switched positions. I continued until I had nothing left. I pulled out in time. Exhausted, I collapsed on top of Janine. I laid there watching the girls continue to kiss and couldn't help but feel I could get used to this scenario.

One important by-product of our three-way tryst was figuring out how tightly wound the depression was wrapped around Chloe. She always described it as suffocating and explained she participated not out of some bisexual curiosity but because she wanted to *feel* something, *feel anything*. Outwardly, I was sympathetic but, on the inside, would think to myself how weak she was. Regretfully, I didn't understand as I never suffered from depression. I ping-ponged between feelings of sympathy and hatred throughout our entire relationship.

My fifth season at Fowl Play was coming to a close. Autumn leaves changed and the shorter days seemed to affect Chloe's well-being. Her depression was, again, tightening like a boa constrictor. Chloe took a job at a Latin American restaurant called Casa Paco. —*The empanadas were fabulous.* She was also starting her senior year at Temple University. Enrollment had been touch-and-go, and I had to twist her arm trying to convince her to not drop out. Her depression was winning, but I was finally able to convince her to not give in. When she wasn't in school or working, she was glued to the couch staring at the TV. It usually wasn't on.

I was working at the Philadelphia Convention Center as a waiter doing catering events. I would often work double shifts keeping me out of the house for sometimes sixteen hours. We needed the money, so I tried to pick up as much work as I could. One night I came home, and all the lights were out. It was now winter and black-out dark. The first floor of the apartment was an open concept layout with the kitchen flowing into the living room. When I turned on the kitchen light, Chloe, startled, jumped off the couch. It was about ten-thirty at night. I assumed she had fallen asleep when in reality she had been there since the morning. She hadn't eaten, she hadn't moved. I went and sat next to her; I drew her close. I was fairly wound up and talking about work when she cut me off.

"I almost took all of them today." She was gesturing to the pill bottle that stood ominously on the coffee table. I didn't know what to say.

She had written about suicide in the past. She often wrote poetry and most of it was dark. A release of sorts, I thought. She wrote one poem in particular called "Pretty Hate Machine." You may remember it as the title of Nine Inch Nails debut album in '89. It was an interesting choice of title as a pretty hate machine was known as a person that was seemingly well-adjusted but trying to dress up and fit in somewhere they don't belong. This defined Chloe's life as she was always struggling to decide if she wanted to belong anywhere, or even exist for that matter. She dressed up daily to play the part of a well-adjusted human with goals and aspirations. Not that she didn't have them, they were all just entirely overshadowed by gloom. Some days were better than others. I seemed to make her happy, but she sensed I didn't feel the same and made constant efforts to try and improve. It was hard for me to feel happy and *in love* when I always felt like I was on suicide watch.

Another factor of Chloe not drinking was how it affected her social skills. When she was drinking, she was outgoing and had very few inhibitions, and when she wasn't, she became a recluse and very socially awkward. Her sister Paulina and brother-in-law Howard often held parties where a handful of couples hung out. The guys would play Texas Hold 'Em and the girls would collect in the kitchen and gossip. Most times, Chloe would be found sleeping on the couch or playing with the pets.

I started playing English darts at my favorite bar in September of 2001. One of my teammates, Gabe, and his girlfriend, Abigail, hosted a party at their apartment in Narberth. There were over twenty people packed into this one-bedroom place. It was cold out, so winter coats were piled on their bed. Abigail came over to me at one point and asked if I could follow her. She led me to her bedroom where the door was slightly open, lights out. She opened the door, and when she turned on the lights there was Chloe, shoes off, under the covers and sleeping with the cat next to her. It was precious and mortifying all at the same time. I appreciated Abigail's tact in this bizarre situation. I apologized, collected Chloe, and went home. This odd behavior sent me off the deep end, and I threatened a breakup. We went back and forth for a solid week. I screamed and dug fingers into her flaws. She pleaded and repeatedly read her scripted apologies. I conceded. I couldn't bring myself to let go. I also refused to let anyone know just how bad things were. To our family and friends, we were the perfect couple. It was a façade; I was very good at those. The problem with façades is that you need to keep them intact. At least I did. I needed people to believe my life was this picture of perfection. My mother always worried about me, and I needed her to see I was okay; more than okay, I was making all the right moves. She constantly bragged to whoever would listen about my successes in life, and I refused to let her down. I would go to the most extreme lengths, whatever it took.

Chloe and I had been seeing each other for a few years when I received an envelope in the mail that read, "Do not bend! Photos Enclosed!" They were pictures of Brianna at five years old. She had gotten so big and had lost one of her bottom teeth. There were four photos and a note that read,

> *Brian, Here's a few pictures. I hope you enjoy them. Hope we can get together soon.*
> *Lauren*

Chloe knew *some* things about Lauren and *everything* about Brianna. In a weird way, she was nearly as excited to see the pictures as I was. We opened them together and I decided, with her blessing, to see Brianna.

I got in touch with Lauren and planned to meet her and Brianna for lunch one Monday afternoon at a Lone Star restaurant not far from her apartment in New Jersey. When I got there, they were in the parking lot sitting in Lauren's car. Once they got out of the car, I had mixed feelings about this meeting. Looking at Lauren only brought back negative feelings, and Brianna was this adorable girl four times the size of when I last saw her. She didn't even know who I was. We went in and ate lunch, and it felt like Lauren was trying to use Brianna to manipulate me. The conversation seemed to keep going back to how great things had been between us. Lauren even successfully dismissed the mail fraud and stolen credit card incidents as desperate acts of a scorned woman. The mention of the domestic violence claim had no defense. We parted ways with the understanding we would keep in touch because she wanted Brianna to get to know me. I was happy with the outcome but weirded out by the experience. Over the next few months we became Facebook friends, and I was able to see updates. We even talked on the phone. However, the last time we talked, Lauren was talking, and Brianna was in the background. Lauren told me I was still hot, and I heard Brianna giggling. I'm not sure why this adversely affected me the way it did, but I blocked her number and unfriended her from Facebook. I never spoke to them again. I have to give Chloe credit where credit is due. I truly loved Brianna and seeing her after a few years and knowing I would have to let her go again was painful. Chloe helped me work through the loss.

About five years into dating, I decided the right thing to do would be to marry Chloe. I loved her, and I convinced myself it was the only thing I *could* do. I asked her father for his blessing and went ring shopping. I took her to the first restaurant we had gone to as a couple. I had no plan. I thought about proposing at the table. I didn't. When we left, I scrambled trying to make this romantic for her. We ended up stopping at a park just off the 300 block of Walnut Street. I expressed my undying love, and she said yes. We spent the next half hour walking home and calling anyone that might have cared.

On the way to the Bahamas in 2002, my best man, David, had to sedate me on the flight. I'm was terrified of flying. I'm not sure *what* he gave me, but I was knocked out before we even took off. We were staying at an all-inclusive resort, and about twenty or so people came down for the wedding. Everyone else was there for three days. We were there for twelve. The day came, and I watched the resort staff setting up the chairs and gazebo on the beach. We hung out at the pool all day knocking back Goombay Smashes. I was coming back from the bar with two drinks in each hand when David said. "Dude, the wedding is in an *hour*!" I sat there and finished my drinks then went up to get dressed. I was pretty well lubricated by that point, and I guess that should have been a sign. As I stood there on the sand, waiting for Chloe to come down the aisle, I wept. It was not out of character for me, but the reason for the tears is what I question as I think back. I believed they were tears of joy but understanding the relationship and what she added to it, for me, didn't warrant the waterworks. In fact, I probably should have jumped into the ocean and swum home before it was too late. I would have had better odds surviving the swim than that marriage. There was certainly a honeymoon phase where she seemed happy, but that wore off.

Living with Chloe was like being married to Dr. Jekyll; Mr. Hyde's appearance was unpredictable but coming. It was exhausting. I hadn't strayed from her since I hooked up with a coworker on a business trip to Atlanta about seven months before we were married. I was trying to do the right thing but for whom? I was miserable. It was all so sad, as everyone thought we had the perfect life. Publicly, we appeared to have so much going for us, but, behind the scenes, I was always looking for reasons to be happy, and my wife was looking for reasons to keep breathing. We were floating through life with no real collective plans for the future. I purchased a house for us in the East Falls section of Philadelphia with the sole intention of staying there for a few years, buying another home, and renting the first one. It needed work, and I spent much of my free time playing the part of underqualified contractor. As a couple, we would spend the next couple years circling the drain.

Premeditated

Since high school, I have habitually manufactured ways to meet women. This isn't the typical story of a pickup artist systematically knocking door-to-door like a traveling salesman playing a numbers game. While I possess the skill to talk to women, there are some encounters you don't want to leave to chance. I crafted scenarios and situations intended to stack the odds in my favor. This isn't about a simple one-night stand. Sometimes I'm using women as a vehicle to get where I need to go. Sometimes I just feel I need to know them. Sometimes I marry them. And, yes, sometimes it is just for sex.

In the fall of '94, after I graduated from culinary arts school, I enrolled at Rowan College to continue my studies. I had already gone through the class registration process when I received a letter in the mail. The notice was from my assigned counselor requesting I stop by his office to discuss my course load. I did and, after introductions, he asked very frankly, "What the fuck are you doing?" I was kind of blown back by his abrupt nature, but the question was no less valid.

After going through my transcripts and the classes I had registered for that term, he asked, "What degree are you pursuing?" —*Again, with these appropriate questions; I had no answer.* I explained my method for selecting courses was strictly based on interest. I was just enjoying college life. We talked through my current course load, and, after he questioned aloud my obsession with psychology, he told me there was an add/drop session the next week and gave me suggestions on classes I should pick as replacements.

A week later, I was standing in the grand hall where folding tables lined the perimeter, each marked with the course title and number. With two selections down, I scanned the room, still needing one more replacement. I did have a requirement left in English Lit, so that was an option. Or, OR! I could go stand in line behind those two very attractive girls over there. I excused myself and asked what line we were in. "Stats I." —*Excellent, I'm terrible at math, but these girls were very cute.* By the time we reached the front of the line, Lisa, Janelle and I were already fast friends. Lady Luck smiled in my direction as I had the slot open, and we all registered for the same day and time. I walked away fairly confident I would get to know at least one of those girls biblically.

After the second class, I realized I was in way over my head. There would be a quiz in a week, and I would certainly fail. Walking out, Lisa and Janelle were talking about going to eat. I invited myself, and we went to the campus cafeteria. I found out they both lived on campus, and Lisa even offered to tutor me.

"Oh, my God, would you really?"

"Sure, we can't have you failing out, can we?"

"Thank you so much. You have no idea. I feel completely stupid in that class."

Two nights later, I was knocking on the door of her second-floor dorm room. When Lisa answered, she was in baggy gray Rowan sweats, a gold and red Rowan t-shirt, and her thin blond hair was in a ponytail with, you guessed it, a Rowan scrunchy. She took school spirit to a whole new level. Lisa wrapped her arms around me as if we were long lost friends.

"Okay, let's get this." She seemed super excited. When I found out she had been a cheerleader since middle school it made total sense.

"Okay." I had forgotten my pom-poms.

She jumped on her bed, and I pulled the chair from her desk next to her. We both pulled out our textbooks.

"Okay, page forty-seven. Contingency tables. That will be on the quiz so let's start there." As she spoke, I was already uninterested in the discussion. I smiled and opened to page forty-seven.

"Okay, so contingency tables, also known as two-way tables, they let us know the relationship between two variables."

"Okay, relationship between two variables." I was echoing as I scribbled notes.

"It's important to remember the data collected isn't quantitative," she said in a matter of fact way.

I now felt like I was completely underwater. "Wait, what?"

"It's more about frequency." When she saw I was totally lost she said, "Come here," patting the place next to her. I jumped on the bed, leaning over her shoulder as she created a chart in her notebook. Lisa talked about marginal distribution but had lost me the minute she invited onto her bed. I occasionally said, "Mm" and "Mm-hmm" into her ear. As she talked, I fantasized. —*She could be a teacher one day. She's really good at math. Her hair smells like eucalyptus and watermelon. I wonder if her lips taste like cherries.*

"Brian?"

"Hi, Yes. Marginal distribution. Not sure I get it."

She laughed, "That was like five minutes ago. Did you fall asleep on me?"

I didn't think I had. Had I? "No, I don't think so. Honestly, I kind of got lost in smelling your hair. I'm sorry. You're being so nice trying to help me. I am terrible at math. I just can't seem to get it. And you are kind of a distraction being all cute. You have this whole teacher vibe going, and it's making it hard to concentrate."

She smiled and pecked me on the cheek. The peck turned into more and after Lisa deadbolted the door, it turned into much more. We hung out a couple more times with very little focus on Statistics 101. It was fun while it lasted. I ended up dropping the class before the deadline to avoid the failing grade. Turned out Lisa wasn't the best tutor, and I still had to foot part of the bill for the course, so I basically paid for sex.

I left the restaurant business before my thirtieth birthday for a real nine-to-five job. In November of '99, I took a job working for a software development company as a support technician. After spending four months taking courses and going through rigorous training, I was ready to begin performing customer installs. Up to that point, I was providing phone support from the office. Now, fully trained, I would be traveling to customer sites to install and integrate software. The only drawback was my fear of flying. I had only flown a half dozen times in my life. I always needed to get drunk or take pills to cope with the anxiety. My new job would keep me on the road almost fifty percent of the time which basically equated to two trips per month; sometimes more, never less. This would mean four to six plane rides per month. I needed to figure out how I was going to get through it. My first business trip was the worst. I had drunk about five twenty-two-ounce beers before the flight and needed to pee the entire way to Houston, Texas. What's worse, this was the first flight I had ever taken alone. During the takeoff, the stress sobered me up instantly, and I began to have a panic attack. I thought I might black out. We landed in Houston, and I swore I was handing in my resignation the minute I touched back down in Philadelphia. I picked up the rental, got to my hotel room and passed out. The install and training took four days, and the dread mounted as I continually thought about the flight home. *—I realize my fear of flying is an irrational one. I've gotten better, but not much.*

I got to the airport four hours before the flight was scheduled for takeoff. I had planned to get royally shitfaced in celebration to this being my last solo flight. I sat at the bar chugging whiskey and thinking about what I was going to do for work after I quit. I thought about going back into the restaurant business. It was something I enjoyed even though I hated the hours. I had polished off enough hooch to have the bartender pause when I asked for another. It was delivered with the check, and I was told, "Last one, buddy." This told me I was probably as ready for this flight as I could possibly be. I finished up, paid the bill, and headed towards the gate. I sat waiting for the agents to start calling people to board. After about ten minutes, I realized boarding was still over an hour away. I thought about going to buy a book to read but knew I would be too preoccupied thinking about the flight. I just sat there. I stared at all the people walking by. Some passengers from my flight began to fill the seats surrounding me. I made funny faces at this little girl two rows over; she might have been three years old. She would laugh and tuck her head down into the woman sitting next to her. The mother, I assume, would turn around, and I would divert my eyes as if I wasn't her daughter's playmate.

"May I sit here?" I turned and saw a tall, attractive, brunette woman walking towards me. She wore a blue pinstripe pant suit. Her red patent leather stiletto heels told me being sexy was still important to her. She held the extended handle of a small Louis Vuitton overnight bag with her left hand. I hadn't yet noticed if she was wearing a ring. She approached with purpose and I said, "Yes, please do."

I was no longer playing peek-a-boo with my toddler friend. I was now focused on the notes this woman was writing in her journal. I couldn't understand the words and curiosity got the best of me, "What language is that?"

"English," she said without taking a pause.

"It is? No, it's not."

"It is. It's shorthand. My mother taught it to me when I was in grade school, and I've been using it ever since. It's also good for keeping nosey people from understanding what I'm writing."

"Oh, wow. I'm, I'm so sorry. I wasn't trying to pry. I just glanced over, and it looked strange, so I asked. I'm sorry," I said nervously and probably a little slurred.

She turned and looked at me stone-faced for about ten seconds. She didn't blink. She then broke into a smile that showed all of her teeth and said, "I'm completely playing with you. Relax." She let out a snicker.

I then laughed out the nervousness I had. I realized it was the first time I wasn't fully absorbed by my fear of flying.

"Where do you hail from? Philly or Houston?" she asked.

"Philly, I was here for business. I work for a software company in the city, and they sent me down here to do an install of our software for this organization here, in Houston. I got here Monday; I mean Sunday. I started work on

Monday. I spent the first day on the install, of the software, I mean. Setting up the server and configuring it. It was my first time, so it probably took longer than it should have. And then I spent the last three days training the operators. It was my first one. I think it went well…They said it went well… I think it's my last one."

She looked at me like I had just escaped from a mental institution. "Are you okay?"

"Uh, yeah. Sure. Why?"

"You just seem, I don't know. On edge?" She questioned.

"Oh, well, yeah, I'm absolutely terrified of flying. It was my first time flying alone on the way here, and I didn't realize how hard it was going to be. I think I hyperventilated on takeoff. If not, it was definitely a panic attack. I tried to get drunk before I left, but it wore off super quick. I guess from my nerves. I tried whiskey this time. Not sure how that will work, but I'm not confident at this moment. I'm jus—" Before I could continue, she picked up my hand and placed it into her other hand. I could feel the soft skin of her fingers as they intertwined with mine. She was rubbing the back of my hand with her other one. All she said was, "Shh. It's going to be okay." Her voice calmed me, but her touch was the key. I realized even though this woman was at least a decade older than me, I was becoming sexually aroused. A few minutes went by.

"Are you okay?" she asked.

"Yes, thank you, that was helpful. Maybe you could hold my hand during the flight too," I joked.

"If you think that will help you, I will."

"Seriously, would you do that?"

"Yes, I'd be happy to. I'm Claudia, by the way."

"Brian."

She did, and we did. There was the small matter of our seats being in separate rows. Claudia asked the man next to her to swap seats with me. She held my hand through the entire takeoff. I felt anxiety but nothing like the previous flight. At one point, she was even stroking the back of my head. We talked throughout the remainder of the trip, and it kept me from obsessing about plane crashes. She told me the story about how she asked the man to switch seats with me. She said I was her nephew and was terrified of flying. It was at least a half truth. Claudia held my hand again through the landing, and that was when I saw her wedding ring. I had Chloe waiting for me at home, so I wasn't looking for anything other than a single serving girlfriend replacement on these trips, but the thought that these encounters could potentially lead to more was necessary to validate the believability of the distraction. There was no need to tell Chloe about my looking for a hand to hold during these flights. After all, they were only minor flirtations. At least, most of them were. The plane taxied and finally stopped.

Claudia patted my leg twice and said, "See, piece of cake." She winked and smiled. I wanted to kiss her.

"Thank you."

"Hey, one more thing. Before we got on the plane you said something about this being your last one. What did you mean?" she asked.

"Oh, right. Well, I was so scared of flying I figured I better get a job that doesn't involve traveling. I'm supposed to be away a couple times a month. Unless you'll be my travel buddy," I said with a smile.

She laughed. "Do not give up your job because you're afraid to fly. It will get easier. Just ask the person next to you to hold your hand. You seemed to be fine with me."

"Thank you, again."

"Anytime." She hugged me and kissed me as a mother might.

We deplaned and parted ways with a smile and a wave. As I watched the distance between us grow, I realized she was wrong. It wasn't mere holding her hand that calmed me. It was the sexual attraction I felt for her. I knew what I had to do. From that point forward, if I were going to stick with this job, all my neighbors for future flights needed to be premeditated.

My next business trip was scheduled a couple weeks later. I was headed to El Paso, Texas to do an install for the *Times*. The real kick in the teeth came when I found out this flight wasn't non-stop. I would have to pick up a connecting flight in Dallas. I tried to appear calm when the woman who booked our travel handed me the itinerary. I was starting to feel one of those panic attacks coming on. I went to the men's room and splashed water on my face trying to keep it together. I was heading out the next Sunday night at five p.m.

I had my luggage packed in the trunk and was on my way to the Philadelphia International Airport for the second time in three weeks. It was late February and still very cold, about thirty-six degrees. Luckily, it had been a mild winter to that point. There hadn't been snow in the previous weeks, so the roads were in good shape. Even though it was still very cold out, I was sweating through my hoodie. My anxiety was swelling once again. People that know me would never believe I would possess such a phobia. I tried very hard to present a persona of confidence and strength and this behavior did not fit the façade. As I drove down 95 South, I talked myself into a positive outlook. I tried to focus on how smoothly the last flight had gone. I parked in the economy lot and took a shuttle to the terminal. As I waited to go through airport security, my nervousness rushed back. I needed a stiff drink. I had, again, built time into my schedule to pregame at one of the airport pubs. I bellied up to the bar closest to my gate and ordered a beer and a shot of Jack. I went through that ritual a few times thinking about Claudia. I decided to try my best to recreate the trip home from Houston. I took my fourth shot, finished my beer and headed over to the terminal. I walked slowly as I approached the gate area and scanned for any woman who might grab my attention. To my dismay, there were none; there were a couple grandmother types chit-chatting; a decent looking woman I might have approached if she hadn't been clutching an infant. I needed a woman traveling alone. It was now ten minutes before the agents would begin inviting passengers aboard. I was psychologically losing altitude quickly. I continued scanning the room. I came up empty by the time the plane was boarding. I was on my own. I had an aisle seat on the back of the plane. With my height, I needed an aisle seat. The plane took off and I went through another panic attack. I tried not to show anyone, but I felt like I was slowly dying inside, little by little. The flight touched down in Dallas, and I was finally able to exhale. I wondered how I was going to will myself onto the connecting flight. It was taking off in a little under an hour. I rushed over to the terminal and grabbed another quick round at the bar. They were calling people to board as I finished the last few swallows of beer. I was one of the last people to board. I stowed my bag and found my seat. Whether it was fate or dumb luck, I don't know, but there was a very pretty woman sitting in the seat right next to me. I said hello, and she smiled. She was already settled in and reading a book, a pink foam donut secured around her neck. The pillow was in stark contrast with her short jet-black hair. As she continued to read, I was trying to focus on stealing glances at her, and not think about falling towards the earth like a fiery meteor. I fidgeted around the seat trying to get comfortable. She shot me a compassionate glance or maybe I took it as compassion. Whatever it was, I took it as an opening. We were now barreling down the runway and I caught her looking at me. I said, "I know this sounds crazy, but can I hold your hand? I'm really freaking out." I was holding the armrests of the seat with a pit bull's grip. I felt her hand slide across the top of mine, and her fingers slide under my palm. It soothed me. I looked at her again, and she just smiled. Once the plane leveled out, I was able to breathe normally again.

"Thank you," I said.

She laughed. "You're welcome. And thank you for having the best pickup line I've heard in a while."

"Oh, wow. No. No, that wasn't meant to be a pickup line. I'm not a good flier. Like, at all. Not that, you know, you are very pretty but I certainly didn't mean it that way. I was just struggling. I'm running my mouth again. Sorry, I tend to do that up here."

"Up here? Oh, you mean in the air." She laughed from her belly this time.

"I'm happy to amuse you." I smiled but was slightly embarrassed.

"Oh, I'm sorry. I don't mean to laugh at you. I really didn't mean it that way."

Yes, she did, but it was okay. I got what I needed. Jackie and I talked for much of the three-hour flight. She lived in Collingswood, New Jersey with her husband and two sons. I walked with her to the baggage claim and got a hug as we parted ways. "You're a life saver," were my last words to her. She just smiled.

I would love to tell you I had a one-hundred percent success rate sitting next to attractive women for every trip, I didn't. The flights home, El Paso to Dallas and Dallas to Philly, were all on me. I did a terrible job holding it together on those. I had mentally submitted my letter of resignation several times while soaring at 30,000 feet somewhere between El Paso and Philadelphia.

As I drove home, I did the math. I had been on six planes in the last month and of those six I was able to hold hands with a woman on two of them. That's a .330 batting average, an average that would make me a Hall of Famer in baseball. I figured finding a girl to sit with and hold my hand couldn't possibly be as hard as hitting a major leaguer's ninety plus mile an hour fastball. By the time I got home, I looked forward to my next road trip.

I had a couple rocky rides over the next month. There was one girl who helped me through but nothing noteworthy. My next trip would be a short flight to Boston. There was an annual newspaper expo at the Boston Convention and Exhibit Center, and I was going for the first time. I was booked on the same flight with three co-workers, including my boss, Peter.

It was seven in the morning the day before the expo was to open. We were leaving at three p.m., and I had a full day to stockpile my fears. The weather called for torrential downpours and lightning along the entire Northeast. I drove to the airport and needed to pull over at one point as bucketfuls of rain bombarded the car. The windshield wipers simply couldn't keep up. I had worked myself into a full lather by the time I reached the economy parking lot. I sat in my car, eyes closed, taking deep breaths. As I was walking through the terminal, it struck me. I would be traveling with co-workers. *How would they react to my consuming four or five rounds of liquid courage?* I was sweating again. I was the first to arrive at the restaurant where we agreed to meet. I ordered a beer and a shot of Jack. I downed the Jack and paid cash for the round. I had another beer when they arrived but not nearly what I needed. While we were sitting at the bar, I was talking to Chuck, one of our salespeople, and opened up to him about my phobia. He laughed at first and then, realizing it wasn't funny to me, got serious. He explained how safe air travel is and tried his best to allay my fear. I admitted what I had done on previous flights, and I'm not sure he believed me. In fact, he wanted to make a wager that I couldn't. There I was, not only desperately seeking a human crutch, I was being goaded into it with a monetary incentive. I took the challenge. I dropped money for the check on the bar and excused myself. After stopping at the men's room to freshen up, I made my way to the terminal gate. I stopped and scanned the room looking for the right situation; a girl, one I found attractive, by herself with an empty seat next to her. It would be ideal if there were no other seats surrounding her, so I appeared to have limited options. I did find a girl. She was sitting alone with nearly every seat around her vacant. In fact, she was in a row against the wall all by herself. Not sure what I was going to do, I walked over. As I approached, I noticed she was reading *Dreamcatcher* by Stephen King. It was his latest release and although it wasn't my favorite, it gave me an angle.

"How do you like it?" I said. She looked up not sure if I was talking to her.

I pointed at the hardcover book in her hands, "*Dreamcatcher*, how are you liking it?"

"Oh," she grinned. "It's okay, so far."

"Yeah, it's not my favorite either, but I'm a huge King fan and I like when he references characters from the 'King Universe'."

"You mean Pennywise?" She was twirling her sandy blond hair with her fingers, the book now resting, face down, on her thigh.

"Yes! You a King fan too?" I had taken the seat two away from her just to not appear too forward.

"I am. I haven't read everything, just the classics; *IT, The Shining, Carrie, Salem's Lot*," Ms. Avid Reader said.

"Oh, *Salem's Lot*! Loved that one. *IT* is my favorite but there are so many good ones."

"Yeah, I think *The Stand* is my favorite," she confessed.

"I didn't read that one."

"No way! You need to read that one. It's really good. Long, but good."

"Long like *IT* was?"

"No, I think it was a little over 800. Wasn't *IT* like 1200?"

"I think so. I'll have to check it out. I'm Brian, by the way."

"Colleen." As she answered me, I noticed Chuck, Peter and the other salesperson, Patricia, sitting a few rows over. Chuck was looking at me, and when we caught eyes he smiled and rubbed his thumb and index finger together. I realized we may have miscommunicated at the bar. I thought he was willing to put up twenty-bucks if I was successful but now, I was thinking he expected payment if I failed.

"You go to Temple?" I asked because she was wearing a cherry-red Temple Owls hooded sweatshirt.

"I *did*, I graduated last year."

We were going through the ritualistic Q&A session as strangers tend to do, when the agents announced they were going to begin boarding the plane. I had a seat closer to the front, so I boarded before Colleen. I sat, impatiently waiting for her to pass me. Finally, she came by and dropped me a wink.

"Have a good flight," she said and playfully pinched my shoulder as she passed.

The passengers were settling with only a few struggling with the overhead compartments. It was now or never. I got out of my seat and excused myself past a flight attendant who instructed me to sit down. I ignored her and passed two other passengers and finally got to the row where Colleen was sitting. She had the aisle seat, and there were two men next to her in the middle and window seats. I addressed the older businessman in the middle.

"Excuse me sir, would you possibly consider swapping seats with me? I would like to sit next to my girlfriend." I was gesturing towards Colleen and she sat there, wide-eyed but silent.

He looked at me for a moment, then to her. She smiled as if asking for the same favor. I added, "It's an aisle seat close to the front of the plane." I'm not sure if that was the deal breaker, or he was just a romantic at heart, but he agreed. When he left, Colleen moved to the middle seat and gave me the aisle.

"I can't believe you just did that!" she whispered.

"Me neither. I just enjoyed talking to you, and I despise flying. I figured I'd go for it."

"I'm glad you did. Well, we might as well play the role." She then grabbed my hand. I didn't even need to ask.

The flight was a short but turbulent one. During one of the stomach-flipping drops, I let out an audible groan and apologized for my sweaty hands. Colleen smiled and leaned her head against my shoulder. "It's fine," she said. Her free hand now resting on my chest. My heart was thumping frantically as we touched down. Once I heard the screech of the air brakes and felt the tug from the seat belt, I was able to exhale.

"You *suck* at flying," Colleen laughed, and I nodded in agreement.

While we were taxiing back to the terminal, she was scribbling her phone number on a torn-off corner from the inflight magazine she found in the pocket behind the seat in front of her. Colleen crushed the paper into my hand and told me it was really nice meeting me. We deplaned and I met up with my coworkers outside of the restrooms.

Chuck was holding a folded twenty-dollar bill in his hand. "Dude, I thought you were bullshitting me."

"Nope," I said with a smirk. I felt a combination of heroic and idiotic at the same time. My boss was sitting next to Chuck during the flight and they both witnessed what happened. Peter just shook his head in either amazement or disapproval. —*What was he really going to say to me?* I snapped the twenty out of Chuck's hand with a hearty, "Thanks, chump."

When we got to the baggage claim, I was watching the luggage carousel going round-and-round when Colleen jumped in front of me. She growled and had her hands up like she was a werewolf. I was fresh out of scares for the day.

"I forgot to give you something," she told me.

"What?" I pulled out the crumbled paper with her phone number on it.

"This," Colleen leaned forward with her lips pursed. She was only about five-four, so I needed to meet her at a lower altitude. She wrapped her arms around me and kissed me deeply.

She turned to walk away and said with a huge smile, "Bye, Brian. Call me. Best flight *ever!*"

"Who was that?" Patricia asked.

"Just a new friend." I said.

Russell Riley

I met Russell Riley when I was working at the Philadelphia Convention Center in the winter of '94. This was yet another job Diane Burke landed me. The three of us were banquet waitstaff and ended up working many double shifts together. There was plenty of downtime to talk as we set tables before events. Russ and I discussed all the Philly sports teams and were blood brothers with regard to musical taste. We soon began hanging out together after work, mostly frequenting sports bars even though he didn't drink. His vices were limited to Coca-Cola and Marlboro Reds. I'm fairly confident he received a Christmas card from Phillip Morris International every year. We would spend hours debating sports topics.

"Randall Cunningham is the best quarterback in the NFL," Russ said.

"You're delusional. What a 'homer' thing to say. Hello? Marino, Aikman, Elway, Young, Kelly. He's not even in the top three!"

"How could you even name *Aikman*? He's a stinking, filthy Cowboy!"

We would go on like that for hours across all four Philly sports teams. Sometimes we supported each other's arguments but not often. I loved to take the other side of an argument just to see him slowly simmer to a full-on boil. He was a very particular guy. His opinions were hand-carved into tablets of stone and he would stake his eyeteeth to validate his claims.

I was counting money one night, and I found his reaction a bit odd.

"Dude, what the heck are you doing? Give me that!" He snatched the money from my hand.

"What the fuck, bro?"

Russell proceeded to count the money turning the bills to face the same direction. Thankfully, I already had them in order by denomination. *Who knows what gate of hell would have opened if honest Abe were upside down?* He handed me the money like he had just performed some mind-blowing magic trick to an audience of eight-year-olds. I didn't say anything but realized something more was going on. It's nothing I could put my finger on, but I tucked it away somewhere in my subconscious.

The calendar flipped to a new year, and I would soon be back at Fowl Play for the summer of 1995. I had waited tables the previous year. However, over the winter, I had accepted an offer to manage the restaurant. It was a huge opportunity. It also gave me the influence I needed to hire Russell. He worked for me as a waiter that season and proved invaluable. His attention to detail was impeccable. We continued to get closer and began attending concerts together. We even became Philadelphia Eagles season ticket holders. The anarchy we witnessed in the 700 level of Veterans' Stadium was often better than the game.

In the fall of '95, we were back to working events at the Philly Convention Center. Russ started pitching these outlandish ideas of how to get rich. He would go through, in extreme detail, how we could make a video game for football where everyone played different positions. He talked about opening a daycare for dogs for all the single professionals in the city. He even talked about creating a website that would feature naked girls from the area. It became more than just conversations. He was equipped with arts and craft projects he had completed detailing his schemes. At times, his well of ideas seemed bottomless and mostly before their time.

February of '96 came, and I was again ready to open up shop on the Philadelphia waterfront. This year, Russ put his hat in the ring to be my day manager. The job was kind of a no brainer. I worked six days a week and was usually there by twelve-thirty p.m. This meant the day manager needed to open the doors at ten a.m. and run things until I got there. On my day off, Mondays, the bar manager would be there at twelve-thirty and look after things. I gave Russell the job. On Russ's two days off, Tuesday and Wednesday, I came in at ten a.m. to cover. Easy-peasy. Not to mention Russ also got a full station of tables to earn tips.

Three weeks into opening I had a handful of the staff approaching me about Russ. Apparently, he was too overbearing when it came to side work. Some of these people had worked for me the previous year. I trusted them, but I didn't see what they saw, so I appeased them by saying he was new and just wanted to make sure everything was perfect. A few weeks later, I came in early to a screaming fit directed at one of the waiters. When Russ saw me, he stopped his tirade. The waiter greeted me with an almost cartoonish eye roll before walking away. I whispered for Russ to follow me to the office. The trek took us through much of the dining room where the rest of the staff was setting up. The silence during our walk was deafening and uncomfortable. I was embarrassed for him. A typically jovial, talkative, group was reduced to a collection of the city's most beautiful mutes. I was slightly pissed at myself. People I trusted had come to me about this, and I didn't believe them. I failed them. Now I was angry. Once the office door closed behind us, Russ found out just how much.

"What the fuck was *that*?"

"Dude, it wasn't what it looked like."

I tried desperately to contain myself, but therapy for my anger was years away.

"I trusted you! What the fuck? It's the easiest fucking job in the world. They all know what they're doing. They don't need you to tell them. I needed a fucking babysitter. That's *you*, motherfucker. It's *not* hard!"

"Hey, that dude was being a total toolbag."

"Huh?"

"His station was in shambles. All the condiments were a mess. Ketchup half full. Empty salt. Dirty tables."

I sat there, thumbing my temples, assessing the oncoming migraine and trying to remember this man was my friend and I was just doing a job. This should not be difficult.

"I understand, Russ. I do. I have lost it on people myself, but we can't. We can't! Not everyone is going to be as critical as you. Constructive criticism is fine. Shit, demanding standards is *fine*. Screaming, however, is *so* not fine."

Like a dog beaten, Russ said, "I know."

"Seriously, bro, I *never* want to hear you raising your voice to the staff again."

I fired him a week later. He couldn't help himself and ended up thanking me a couple weeks after I let him go. He explained the job was too stressful and realized he needed a job where he didn't supervise anyone. "They can't live up to my expectations, dude." It turned out he wasn't owning any of the failure. He was actually thanking me for removing him from a situation he later would define as "beneath him."

Our friendship continued outside of Fowl Play, and since he seemed to forgive my firing him, we were good, truly good. I often met him after work at a sports bar a mile away. I loved this bar. The general manager was a friend of mine whom I hooked up with gold cards. This allowed him and his friends free entry and no wait to get into the club. In return, I never saw a check. *Ever*. No matter how many people I was with, it was *compliments of Dean*. The beneficiary was always the waitresses or bartenders. They, in turn, loved me. It was a continual cycle and the only losers were the restaurant owners. Russ would be sitting there at a table, alone, with three or four empty glasses: Coca-Cola. I would come in and order a Corona and a shot of Tuaca. He was usually mid-way through his second sentence by the time it registered he was even talking to me.

Fowl Play closed for the season, and instead of going back to the Convention Center, I landed a job as a front waiter at the CoreStates Center, the new home of the Philadelphia Flyers and 76ers. That fall and winter, I worked all the games and most of the concerts. I spent almost no time with Russ, who was still working events at the Convention Center. I worked there on occasion when the teams were playing away games. I always worked the flower and car shows. They were guaranteed paydays. Valentine's Day passed and I realized I hadn't seen Russell for a while.

I was walking into the employee entrance of the Convention Center when I spotted Russ, "Hey stranger!"

"Yo! How are you Bri, long time no see. What are you doing here? Slumming?"

I laughed and said, "No, I picked up a shift since both teams are on the road. What's it been, two months?"

"Wow, dude, I guess it has. How are things? How's Chloe?"

"Let's not ruin a good reunion," I said half-jokingly.

"Pitchers and catchers, *dude*. Next week! I'm so stoked." Russ was talking about the time of year when the Phillies pitching staff and catchers report to Clearwater Florida. The previous season ended in a letdown when the Phillies got swept three games to zero in the divisional series against the Colorado Rockies.

"I know, I have a good feeling about this year. Hey, we are starting to take applications for Fowl Play in the next few weeks. You should stop over and grab one. I have a stack at the apartment from last year."

Russell paused before finally saying, "I think I'm out this year, dude."

"What? *Shut up*."

"No really, I have other stuff going on and want to be more fluid this summer."

"Uh, ok," I was not sure how to react since the waitstaff almost printed money during the summer at Fowl Play, and I thought it was crazy to walk away from that kind of cash. "You sure? Everything okay?"

"All good, dude. All good things." Russ dropped me a wink and walked away.

I didn't see Russ again until late in the spring of 2008. My girlfriend (and soon to be wife) Chloe and I had moved to a different part of Queens Village. I was hoping the change of scenery would be good for Chloe's mental health as well as our relationship. During the first two years dating, she had the prescription that treated her depression changed at least three times. We were arguing one Monday about her non-existent sex drive when the doorbell rang. It was around six p.m., and we weren't expecting anyone. Absent a working intercom, I walked down the three flights of steps to find Russ waiting at the door. He brushed past me, talking a mile a minute. All I caught in the exchange was, "Hey neighbor, I need to talk to you about ..." By the time I caught up with him, he was standing in our apartment talking to Chloe.

"Yeah, I moved a block up on Bainbridge. Nice place, needs a little TLC."

He became the roommate we didn't need over the next few months. He was at our apartment at least two nights a week, sometimes bringing takeout when we were in the middle of cooking dinner or showing up for dinner without an invite. "That's great, come on in, Russ" were words I repeated dozens of time. Once Fowl Play opened for the season, I was working six days a week, but that didn't stop the visits. I would find out afterward:

"Russ stopped by with dinner tonight. We had Thai food."

"Good, I hate Thai food."

After two years, Chloe easily recognized the dripping sarcasm in my response. I still felt guilty —*I'm sorry, Russ, I have to let you go*— but I couldn't keep going on like this. Russ and I met late one night at our favorite sports bar.

"Do you believe that Flyers loss, dang it, they were terrible. We need a new goalie," Russ said.

"Hey dude, I really have talk to you."

"'Sup?"

"You know I love you right? You're my brother, you know, that right?" I was stammering.

"Of course."

"Okay, listen, you need to stop just showing up at our apartment."

The expression on Russ's face was stoic and slightly puzzled. He measured his words and said, "Oh, my God, of course. I didn't realize I was overstepping."

We left that night and I didn't hear from Russ. It was unusual.

I let a week pass before I stopped by his apartment early one Saturday morning. It took maybe ten minutes to get an answer at the door. It was a woman in her late forties in a t-shirt that had been washed one too many times. As she was talking it was hard not to concentrate on her see-through shirt. She told me Russ was sleeping, and while she droned on, I found myself scanning the apartment over her shoulder. *What the hell is going on?* I missed a few of her words, but she must have said goodbye before the door closed in my face. I walked away bewildered and spent the next few minutes trying to decipher what I saw. I went back to my apartment and told Chloe I thought Russell was in trouble. I didn't know how, but what I saw was odd.

I didn't hear back from Russ until the next week. We had planned to meet up at our spot after my shift. I got there, and he hadn't showed. He had told me ten-thirty and you could usually set your watch by him. I grabbed a seat at the bar. Russ showed up just in time to see the bartender writing her number on a Miller Lite coaster. I slipped it into my back pocket.

"What's up, stranger? Where the fuck have you been and what was that setup in your crib?"

"What setup?"

"All the camera equipment and shit."

Looking down, he said, "I started a business."

Basically, he had spent thousands of dollars —*that he could not afford*— to purchase a photo studio. He had maxed out his credit cards.

"Dude, you have no idea how much scratch I'm going to make doing this. I'm going to be *printing* freaking cash!"

I felt one of those migraines coming back and tried to figure out what the hell I was going to say next. This was fucking crazy. A manifestation of one of his get-rich-quick schemes.

"Russ, are you serious? What makes you think this is going to net you any money?"

"I've made three hundred so far. Just scratching the surface, dude."

I came to find he was using the newspaper and Craigslist to solicit girls to come to his apartment and take pictures. I was amazed; it was working. He had dozens of girls —*mostly fives and sixes*—willing to take a chance. He was building a porn site way before porn became a billion-dollar industry. It was genius, but he ended up drowning in unfulfilled promises. He had yet another great idea the world was not ready for.

After the business crashed and burned, I received word that Russ had totaled his brand new Mitsubishi Eclipse. Wait, when did he buy a Mitsubishi Eclipse? Two weeks prior, apparently. I ran down to his apartment the next day to see if he was okay. He answered the door in a ragged pair of Eagles pajama pants and a wrinkled white crew neck t-shirt. It looked like he'd been wearing this get-up for days. I'd never seen Russ like this. He opened the screen door as if to say come in. I went in and found all the equipment that had littered the apartment was now gone. That was fast.

"You okay, bro?"

"No." Russ was very short in his response.

"I'm here man. Fucking talk to me. What's up? I heard about the car."

"Screw the car!"

The room was heavy with thickening silence as I waited for his next words.

"What the heck do you want me to tell you, dude?"

"Nothing, bro. I'm just here for you. I just want to make sure you're okay. It's been a little crazy over the last couple months and I'm trying to make sure you're good. You good?"

"Brian, get the *fuck* out of my apartment!" It may have been the only time I ever heard Russell curse.

I left and walked home completely confused.

Another summer at Fowl Play had slipped by and still no word from Russ. Life moved on. Chloe was a grad student studying occupational therapy at Jefferson and had begun an internship at a local facility. She had been going there for several weeks when she came home and finally told me, "Sit down, I need to talk to you." I sat.

"What's up, Sunshine?" Sunshine was the nickname my mother had given Chloe.

She was professional, almost clinical when she spoke. "I have been working the last several weeks at a mental health facility. You know that, right?"

"Yes."

After an uncomfortable pause, "Russ is there. I wasn't allowed to tell you, but he's been there for weeks."

"What? Why?"

"I couldn't tell you, I'm sorry. He finally asked me to let you know, and he wants to see you."

I had no words. I thought back to the lunacy of the past months; maybe I could have connected the dots. They were far apart, and it was a stretch from anything I could have thought of, but I *could* connect them. Right? My friend is fucking crazy, right?

I took a cab to the facility on 8th and Locust. It was a nondescript building in as much as it didn't say "Nut House" on the marquee. I checked in at the receptionist's desk and waited roughly twenty minutes before I was told, "Mr. Schreiber, you can go up." I took the elevator (it felt the size of a dumbwaiter) up to the fifth floor, my mouth was dry as sand, and I was slightly claustrophobic. When I got off the elevator, a woman met me with a guarded smile.

"Can I help you, sir?"

"Hi, ma'am, I'm here to see Russell Riley. I think he's expecting me. My name is Br—"

"Good enough, please go through those doors there, and he's in room 503."

I did and he was.

"Hey, brother. How are you?" I said.

He was sitting in a chair next to the bed staring through the TV. We exchanged a *bro-hug* and he suggested going to the balcony to smoke. He pulled out his pack of cigarettes and gestured for me to take one. I had my own. We both lit up and took deep inhales, giving us the calm required to have this conversation.

"They think I'm bipolar." Russ said in a matter-of-fact way.

"What? Oh man, I'm so sorry. What does that even mean?"

"I'm not sure yet. Basically, they said I go through these manic and depressive states."

I could certainly attest to that and his behavior began to make more sense to me.

"They have me on Lithium and said it will take a couple weeks to kick in. It's supposed to level me out, even my mood swings."

"Bro, I've known you for a few years now and only saw this a couple months ago. Did this just come out now?"

"No, I'd been dealing with this since I was a kid, but I was basically high all the time."

"*What?* You don't even *fucking* drink! What are you talking about?"

"I was literally high all the fricking time. I would wake and bake every day since I was in high school. I stopped smoking weed a few months ago and I guess that sent me spiraling."

This was a lot to process. Russell had been one of my closest friends. I went home and told Chloe what was going on. She already knew but talking through it helped me. The relationship between Russell and me was never the same. Not because I wanted it to be; Russ was just different. Over the next year he stayed on the straight and narrow. Laid low. Then I lost touch with him until Facebook came around.

Kaleidoscope Eyes

My father was the ultimate behind-closed-doors racist. He might not have ever let you see it, but he was. My mother's father used the n-word more than I care to admit and never hid his feelings. Niggers, spics, dykes, faggots, queers. All atrocious slurs I heard by the time I was old enough to speak. I like to believe that living with my mother with her alternative, however closeted, lifestyle encouraged me to be accepting of everyone. I have always believed live and let live. I spent my youth surrounded by people of all different races and sexual orientations.

In 1982, growing up, I knew my place. When adults were entertaining, hanging around grown-ups just wasn't permitted. I was always told, "The adults are talking," which was my cue to go away. —*Scram, kid*. I was never told this more than when Denise visited. She was the coolest. Denise was the first woman I ever saw with lots of tattoos. Back then it wasn't typical for woman to sport a sleeve of ink. I found myself drawn to her. One night she offered to take me around in the city, and a couple weeks later I found myself riding the Frankfort line to her neighborhood in Kensington. To me, it was a new world. I had never been to Philly, so this was akin to traveling the globe. She bought me lunch and comic books. The memory is imprinted on my soul forever and I wish we had kept in touch, if just to say thank you.

When I worked at Fowl Play about thirty percent of my waitstaff were gay and mostly male. I always found gay men enticing for their overtly forward nature. Don't get me wrong, I truly love women and there were plenty at Fowl Play, but the atmosphere is just different around young gay men. I was a chronic flirt during my twenties. I didn't care what gender you were. Even though I wasn't interested sexually, I craved the attention. I found I needed it. When I lost that movie part in '92, I felt so rejected, not good enough. But just two years later, I felt like a sexual lightning rod. I became close friends with several of the waiters and we hung out after work. Woody's was a popular club in the "gay"berhood and I went there often. I was young, in very good shape and some people assumed I was gay. I didn't mind. My vanity was well served by doubling up the audience, male and female. When I was there, I didn't have to work for attention. Girls are just different. They are usually not as aggressive. Woman tend to like to be pursued, and, while I love the aspect of the hunt, I also like to be pursued. —*then again, my high school sweetheart pursued me and look how that turned out*. Gay men are not shy and will bluntly tell you what they want. I was propositioned for sex several times a night, and the *flirty eyes* were a constant. You know the ones where the stare lasts a little too long. They are usually accompanied with a slow-motion smile or a biting of the lower lip. This club was a room full of hunters. As much as I like to think it was just me, and I am something special, it wasn't and I'm not. It was just the atmosphere and hooking up was as easy as asking someone to dance. As it turned out, I was just the dick tease of the group.

Running one of the most popular restaurants in the 90's afforded me some perks. I would often bypass club waiting lines and get the next open table at a restaurant with a two-hour wait. In one case, I was pursued relentlessly by the bar manager of Woody's to guest bartend. Although I appear very confident and did love the attention, I didn't take the opportunity because I was scared. It was an irrational fear but just further validates the idea that you aren't necessarily the image you portray. I look back with regret because I would have had a fantastic time doing it and would have made a fortune.

One of my friends, Kurt, was an up-and-coming drag queen. He was off-putting to look at as a male. His hair was an orange-red, very long and straggly, mostly kept in a ponytail when waiting tables at Fowl Play. Kurt's eyebrows were pencil-point thin and he possessed no distinguishable features that confirmed he was male. But he had an infectious personality, and when she was onstage, she was outstanding! One night, there was a highly anticipated drag event at Woody's, and I wasn't about to miss it.

The emcee came out in a hot pink flamingo costume that must have taken weeks to sew. It was fabulous, and she was working the crowd. She was a beautiful black girl with pouty, fire engine red lips, lavender eye shadow and fake two-inch eyelashes. Fierce.

"Okay, are you ready?" She paused through the half-hearted applause. "I can't hear you. *Are you muthafuckin' bitches ready?*" The crowd roared. "Okay, let's get the ground rules set up in this bitch. Uh, huh. I'm talking to you, mister." She was talking very slowly for effect and pointing at some random person in the audience. "I want you to tip these bitches like you're their daddies. You hear me, sugar? Uh-huh. We clear?" She raised two fingers in a peace sign, "Okay! Second, the waitstaff and the bartenders work for a living and they got *rent*. So, don't make me come out there. Tip these bitches, too."

The crowd was working into a lather. "Okay, let's have some fun. Coming to the stage is my friend and soon to be yours, Avery Goodlay! Give it up for her."

Avery came on stage and did not disappoint. She was wearing a black leather cat-suit with six-inch stiletto lace-up, thigh high boots. —*Batman was hiding somewhere in the rafters coming in his pants*. The blueish-white blunt fringe wig she wore came to points at her jawline and was contrasted with black eyebrows, lashes and lips. There was a thin straight rainbow painted below her eyes that added a splash of color to an otherwise flawless black and white photo. Avery sang "Dark Lady" by Cher. She owned that stage, and the crowd showered her with money.

Diva after diva performed, and I became literally and figuratively intoxicated. The freedom of expression in the room was inspiring. But it was time. My red-headed friend was about to perform. He was a very funny guy with a great sense of humor. However, he tended to stay in his shell most of the time. I was slightly concerned. All these women before him were playing the crowd like a fiddle. I had no idea.

The Flamingo emcee was now back working the crowd and continuing to promote the financial well-being of the performers and bar staff. "Okay, bitches. This is my girl's first time performing, so I want you to put your hands together. *Get up and put ya fuckin' hands together,* and help me welcome my red-headed raven, the beautiful Phoebe!"

Phoebe came out and was not a person I recognized. She was in six-inch red patent leather heels and a sequined hourglass red dress. It took me a minute to realize she was the spitting image of Jessica Rabbit. The hair extensions added to her already long red locks gave the desired cartoonish look to a character born from animation. A ballad began with a piano, and Phoebe slowly sang about the rain and her love life boring her to tears. The song, No More Tears (Enough is Enough), was originally released by Barbara Streisand and Donna Summer back in '79. About sixteen bars into the song, a kick drum and cymbals sped up the rhythm to a familiar 1970's sound. The crowd lost their minds. I never looked at Kurt again without seeing Phoebe. He was transformed on the stage that night. She didn't get the "Best Queen" sash but she won just the same.

During my thirties, I worked for a software company with a guy, Sam Harrington, and he wore the pride flag like no one I had ever known. He wasn't the most flamboyant, just secure in his sexuality. At least he was now. The faint scars on his wrists told a different story. His valiant attempt at concealing them included a chunky black woven bracelet on one wrist and a watch on the other. We were sitting in the living room of his apartment on Walnut Street when he caught me looking.

"It's okay, you can ask."

"What happened? Did it hurt?"

"Honey, you don't know the half of it. I was full of pills, and it still hurt like a bitch. After I did it, seeing the insides of my wrists and the blood made me throw up all over myself."

"I don't know what to say, Sam."

"Sweetie, you don't have to feel sorry for me. It was a long time ago. I'm a different person now and stopped abusing myself a decade ago."

Sam knew my mother was a lesbian, and we talked about how hard it was growing up gay.

"My father and I never spoke about my being gay. *He knew.* I was a figure skater until my late teens, for Christ's sake! Whenever I did well and expected a positive, maybe even loving response from him, I only got, 'Well done, son.' His expression was more repulsed than proud. When I was in my twenties, I was always open for business. 'Buy me a drink, honey, and I'll blow you in the bathroom.' I've always been a bottom. My ass is so blown out I barely feel it anymore. I've been told looks more like a pussy now."

"I'll take your word for it," I said with a laugh. I tried not to look too grossed out from his overshare.

"After a while I just didn't care anymore. I had no real meaningful relationships. My parents were older to begin with when they had me. Their having a progressive attitude toward my sexuality was not going to happen. It wasn't premeditated. Cutting myself, I mean. Sure, the thought crossed my mind a couple times. One night I was in my apartment alone. This was when I was still in St. Paul. It was sometime in January, and you could freeze your titties off in the winter. Anyway, I was hooked on Percs and took however many were left in the bottle. Next thing I know I'm sitting on the floor in the kitchen with a steak knife in my hand and bleeding all over myself. And then I threw up and passed out. My roommate found me, and I woke up in a hospital with my arms tied to the bed."

"Too much information? You asked." His cathartic laugh seemed to tell me he was happy to be in a better place and relieved he could tell his story. I wondered just how black-out drunk I would need to be to do such a thing.

Sam was in his late forties when we first met. I was in my mid-thirties and hadn't been to Woody's in over a decade. It was about time for a reunion. On our walk there from his apartment, Sam convinced me to act like we were together. He said it would get him attention. We grabbed a pub table on the second floor and sat hip-to-hip. I went with it and guys kept coming up talking to me, then us. I can't say if I really made any difference, but I will say I played his wingman several times, and I was always the one that ended up going home alone.

Sam moved to Palm Springs not too long after and we remained Facebook friends but not nearly as close.

Vegas, Baby

Early in January 2004, Anthony, my mailbox-smashing friend, told me his bachelor party would be in Las Vegas that September. Of course, I was going, but, as it turned out, it wouldn't be the best timing for me. Well, maybe it would be the best timing; it's all about perspective, I suppose. I made the stage-gate payments as required and squirreled money away to ensure I was properly prepared for the trip. Twenty-one people planned to attend. If you saw Anthony today, you would see the clean-cut and slightly older-looking version of the headbanger he was in high school. Only now, instead of debating the merits of Metallica versus Mötley Crüe, he was describing, in delicious detail, the cocktail he was making you as a bartender. He can still own a crowd and does so in a more distinguished way as a bar owner.

August crept up on me, and I made settlement on the purchase of my first home. It was exciting and paralyzingly stressful all at once. By this time, I had been married to Chloe for a little over two years. She was still trying to get her life together, professionally. Her depression did not help, but it was mostly under control. In the end, I made the down payment myself and left her name off the mortgage application in order to qualify. Getting up from the table after signing my name dozens of times and knowing I was now a homeowner was a marvelous feeling. My mother was very proud. I could now focus on preparing myself for a celebration with one of the people I love most in this world.

We boarded a flight to Vegas that put us in Sin City about ten p.m. local time. We descended on the town with purpose, and I was with a group of fellows possessing little patience for taking a pause. I was a confident guy, but some of these guys were much more forceful in their tactics and loose with their morals. Not that I wasn't. A collection of cabs took us to the MGM, and, once registered, I was lugging bags to the twenty-first floor. I was one of the few to book my own room as I've never been one to enjoy sharing a hotel room with anyone but a significant other. I hung my clothes and went down to the casino. I sat at what I guess they would consider the main bar of the casino and ordered a scotch. I was playing video poker so I could "earn" my free drinks when the girl sitting next to me interrupted. She asked me how to play the game. I asked, "You mean poker?" "Yes," she replied. Now I'm pretty sure residency in the state of Nevada requires a general understanding of poker. Looking at her immediately gave away her disguise. She was immaculately dressed in what appeared to be a gown one might see on the red carpet of the Oscars. It took only a few seconds for it to register that she was a prostitute, however stunning. I fed into her game but would have never given her a dime. I spent my life embracing the same mantra. —*Never spend money on pussy*. Vulgar, yes. Sorry, no. Guys are always paying for it in one way or another. I would just rather have sex with a woman because she wants to, not because I've paid for the ride.

By this point, the hooker had moved on to the next guy and my friends began filling in around me. Once the group was whole, the energy level elevated rapidly. We spent the next few hours gambling and drinking. The night waned, but the next few days would be packed with drunken shenanigans. I slept in the next morning, trying to get acclimated with the time zone difference, and spent the afternoon at the lazy river of the MGM. You would think most of the guys had never gotten laid, as they were throwing every pickup line they knew at any girl within shouting distance. None of that nonsense worked. We were headed to the Pink Taco at the Hard Rock that night for dinner. Anthony was in trouble as Mitch Nowak, his former boss and now a well-connected Vegas resident, had a fairly ridiculous surprise waiting for him. Here we sat at the Pink Taco, twenty-one dudes present and accounted for, waiting for the top to fly off of this thing. We knew Mitch had something planned but what happened was a surprise to all of us. We were not disappointed. We had a room pretty much to ourselves except for a family in the back and a couple that appeared to be on a first date in the far corner. Drinks were flowing, appetizers started hitting the table, and then one of the waitresses came out and blindfolded Anthony. Game on! Everyone stood at full attention. Not sure what tomfoolery was about to transpire, we were all chanting Anthony's name. Our expectations could not compete with reality when a miniature Elvis walked through the door in all of his four-foot glory. He wore a full white, rhinestone studded one-piece jumpsuit, gold trimmed aviator glasses, and a pompadour Elvis himself would have envied. Elvis used the chair adjacent to Anthony as a stepping stool to climb onto the table. There he stood, mere feet away, striking the King's familiar windmill pose; both arms extended, one over his head both pointed at Anthony, fingers splayed flickering wildly. The crowd cheered. I hadn't noticed, but the entire Hard Rock staff and some other patrons had made their way in to witness this spectacle. Mitch pulled the blindfold away revealing Anthony's human gift. The look on his face was a mix of amusement and confusion, and that moment flicked over the first domino in this four-day bonding experience. That night we went to the Spearmint Rhino. Every place we visited, Mitch had an inside connection, making us VIPs wherever we went. In the club, we had a private section all to ourselves. The drinks flowed, the strippers were endless, and Elvis was the icing on top. At one point he was so fucked up he was dancing on yet another table with one of the dancers. It was only then I realized the most spectacular part of Elvis. He was missing his two front teeth. How did I miss that detail? It was now so glaring and fan-fucking-tastic! He would become the hit of the entire trip. As I write this chapter, for inspiration, I have a picture on my adjacent screen of Anthony posing with Elvis and two girls. Nothing more to say here other than Elvis blacked out and he needed to be fireman carried out of the strip club and thrown into a cab.

The next night, we were all meeting at the center bar. This time, our destination would be in the MGM itself. I almost spit the scotch out of my mouth when I spotted our buddy Nelson Galvez walking across the casino floor with Elvis perched on his back like Master Blaster from the movie *Mad Max Beyond Thunderdome*. I half expected to hear the crowd start chanting, "Two men enter, one-man leaves!" As they approached, I noticed Elvis had a backpack strapped to him filled with what we learned to be cans of beer, his personal contribution to the night's festivities. Once everyone was accounted for, we ventured up to the suite Mitch had booked for the night. I walked in and immediately imagined how the Rat Pack lived during their heyday. The front door opened up to a foyer and built in bar. Mitch had hired a girl to sling drinks. I looked left and saw a galley style kitchen equipped with all stainless-steel Viking appliances. To the right was a spacious living room with a gas fireplace, fifty-five-inch flat screen and a full rack of Pioneer stereo equipment. There were speakers hiding everywhere, and the music could be heard from anywhere in the suite, as well as outside. In the middle of the living room was a winding staircase leading to a loft-style second floor. There were three bedrooms and a full bath above us. I grabbed a scotch from the bartender and walked out to the sprawling terracotta-tiled balcony. There were several round granite-topped tables with chairs and a jacuzzi tucked under where the building jutted out, which strategically provided a sense of privacy. The suite faced the back end of Vegas strip with stellar views of the Mandalay Bay, Luxor, and Excalibur casinos. About an hour later, after taking a few group pictures, the first show was about to start. Mitch arranged for two sets of girls, staggered by an hour and a half. The first set of girls I don't even recall. They gathered us in the living room and slow-played a contrived lesbian show incorporating several sex toys. During the show, the guys were only permitted to throw money. I felt like our presence was only incidental. Both were attractive girls, and once their performance was over, they walked the grounds, drinks in hand, looking for buyers. It was surreal watching them standing bare ass naked on the deck in conversation as if they were clothed. My personal favorite moment was when I noticed one of the girls had inserted a long black horse tail anal plug. She was deep in negotiations, but I can't say whether it helped her sales pitch. I remember sitting on the deck for a while and smoking a cigarette when the next crew came in. My eyes had never been very good, so I approached to grab a closer look. I noticed there were two girls, one was a taller brunette with masses of dark curls and golden-brown skin. The other, a short blonde, was the most beautiful girl I'd ever seen in person. She had short, platinum blonde hair and was wearing a white leather bikers' jacket, black leggings and white cowboy boots. Certainly not Sunday church attire but she fit the part for the occasion.

We again gathered in the living room. These girls were more interactive and even introduced themselves. Lexi was the brunette, and the blond was Bobbie. At least, they recognized there was an audience and played to it. They put on a show that made you think they might be more than friends outside of work. There was some element of tenderness present between them. The bachelor had a strict pact of celibacy that weekend, so the girls took a volunteer to lay down in his place. He was instructed to lay flat on his back with his hands at his sides and his knees bent. Bobbie took her last stitch of clothing off, sat on this guy's chest and laid back against his knees. Her knees were also bent but had fallen out to the sides leaving her fully exposed. Lexi knelt next to the volunteer and shared his unique vantage point. She whispered in his ear, "This could be you later," and went in for the kill. She climbed over him, pinning his shoulders to the floor with her knees, and took Bobbie with her mouth. Lexi worked her over for a while with delicate precision. There was a special appearance by a fairly intimidating hot pink dildo before Bobbie decided she had enough. Once it was over, they made their rounds as well. I was outside talking to one of the guys when the blonde stopped and stood in front of me, staring. I stopped, smiled, and said, "Hi." She asked if I wanted to talk inside. I politely declined. She went on her way only to come back a few minutes later. This time she wrapped her pinky around mine and led me inside. As we walked, I told her, "I don't pay for sex." She looked back at me, not breaking stride, and said, "I wasn't planning on charging you." She now had my full attention. Bobbie guided me inside and up the staircase. She led me into the bathroom where she checked her makeup. I sat on the edge of the clawfoot tub. We made small talk for a few minutes, and then she turned and kissed me. It was tender and loving and something I would expect from a person I was connected with emotionally. She slid onto my lap and we made out until Elvis's voice broke our embrace. "Wanna get high?" he said. She and I stared at each other and without breaking eye contact, I said, "Why not?" So here I was, making out with this prostitute and suddenly smoking weed with her and miniature Elvis in the master bathroom of a two-story suite in the MGM, Las Vegas. *Gather the kids around, folks, it's story time.* So, Bobbie was still sitting on my lap, and Elvis was standing well into our personal space as we passed around this joint. She and I were caught in a staring contest when Lexi came in screaming, "He owes me fucking money!" I broke our stare and looked to see Lexi standing in the doorway, naked and ranting. Mike came through the door as she began to explain, "I fucked him in the hot tub, and I want my five hundred dollars." She would not relent, and I had no idea what the truth was, or who she was even talking about, but I knew I needed this problem to go away. I caught Mike's gaze, he nodded, and we had already non-verbally decided to pay this woman just to shut her the fuck up. We did, and Elvis and Mike left the bathroom, leaving me and the two hookers. With Bobbie still on my lap, Lexi said they needed to leave. After some back and forth, they were leaving but before she got off my lap, she asked how long I was in town. I told her a couple days. She got up grabbed one of the boxes of soap from the counter and wrote her name and number on the box. I laughed, "You don't really think I believe this is your number, do you?" She gave me a sarcastic stare and held it there until I cracked. "Okay," I gestured with my hands for her to back down, and to her friend I said, "You write her number on the other side!" I laid the soap box on the counter. She approached asking, "Bobbie, are you sure?"

"I am," Bobbie replied.

She handed me the box and on one side was the name Bobbie, and her phone number. On the flip side was the same number. Bobbie told me she had to go, but she would be home the following day if I wanted to hang out. They both left, and I needed to get really drunk. After all, I had just paid two hundred and fifty dollars to a hooker I never even touched and nothing to the one I had.

The next night we were going to the Palms Casino. Mitch was dating the general manager, and there was some fashion show. A limo bus came to pick us up around seven. We piled in and were on our way when Billy Paul came over the speakers. He belted out, "Me and Mrs. Jones, we got a thing goin' on!" Years prior, this was the song the guys used to sing when the subject of my high school sweetheart's mother came up. This time, the moment was particularly awkward. One of the other guys on the bus dated my high school girlfriend after we broke up. He was apparently much more into the relationship than she was but more importantly, he had found out from Anthony what happened between her mother and me. It was obvious he didn't like me very much but there was really no cause for his disapproval.

We reached the Palm and poured out of the bus. As we walked in, I spotted Pierce Brosnan using the courtesy phone outside the entrance. The internet claims he is 6'1" but I will tell you in person he appeared no taller than five-ten. Tops. We walked in like rock stars and had a private section to ourselves. The night was cool but mostly uneventful. There were a few topless models cat-walking throughout the event but nothing spectacular. I decided to call Bobbie. She picked up, and we talked for about fifteen minutes. She gave me her address and told me she was about a twenty-minute cab ride away. She was planning to hang out and watch a movie with her roommate. The roommate happened to be Lexi, the same girl that extorted 500 dollars from us the day prior. I was still going. After I hung up the phone, I told Anthony I was bailing. He announced to the group my intentions of leaving to meet Bobbie. The idea was met with a collective group opinion. I began listening to how they thought I might be led into a trap, killed and buried in the desert never to be found again. It was plausible and other than having another conquest, there was very little upside. What was the point? I cut my losses. But I will tell you I sometimes rummage through my box of memories and come across that soapbox. I think about Bobbie and wonder. She was, after all, the most beautiful girl I have ever seen.

Splintered Family Tree

I was thirty-four the year my mother celebrated the ten-year anniversary of being cancer free. Jeannie Schreiber had been diagnosed with breast cancer in her early forties. She made the decision to get a double mastectomy. The doctors claimed the procedure would drastically increase her chances for survival. Mom was a proud woman, and the choice not an easy one. She suffered from both the treatment of the disease as well as the mental anguish of removing what made her feel like a whole woman. When the surgery and rounds of chemotherapy were complete, she was eventually given a clean bill of health. Mom took amoxicillin for five years. Given her history, she went for checkups every six months; fingers crossed. She had struggled to quit smoking but never truly got the monkey off her back. Margot later told me she found out my mother would sneak to the neighbor's house and bum cigarettes. Mom tried.

Early November in 1994, Margot took mom to her oncologist for a routine checkup. The results were not good. The cancer was back, and it was now stage three lung cancer. My brother visited from Florida, but, as was Brady's way, he wasn't really present, not emotionally. I'm sure it upset him, but he was who he was, and that never changed. Mom felt his distance, and it broke my heart.

Six months passed. Mother's Day was approaching, and the situation was becoming surreal for me. I understood the road we were traveling, but I wasn't prepared. Concerning my mother's mortality, we were really *far* down that road. If I'm honest, I am ashamed to say I didn't see my mother enough over those last few months. I don't think it was on purpose or done out of avoidance, but I wish I had handled it differently. One honest, open conversation was exchanged about a month before she died. It was a precious moment in my life and one that helped provide the strength I would need in the future. This was my pre-therapy era, so I had yet to understand the *why* behind some of my life choices. I found myself questioning them.

It was around nine-thirty on a Saturday morning late in May. It had been raining overnight and made this day unseasonably cool. You could feel the dampness in the air like you were walking through invisible mist. My mom was sitting in the back yard drinking coffee, staring into the wooded area beyond the back fence.

"Hey, Mom."

She was slow to turn and look but said, "Hey, monkey." Unlike the nickname my father gave me, I liked it when mom called me monkey.

"How are you feeling? Much pain?"

"Not much, I'm good. *I am.*" She wouldn't have told me anyway. But, as always, her eyes never lied. She nervously lit a cigarette. It was too late for *that* to matter.

"You okay, Brian? You're not yourself. What's going on?"

I now stared out into the woods beyond the fence. I wasn't sure how to approach the subject. How do I tell my mother I made the biggest mistake of my life? In the matter of seconds, hours of thoughts went through my mind, as I whittled down what I needed to say.

"I fucked up, mom. I did. I never should have gotten married. I don't love Chloe. I'm pretty sure I never have. I don't think I truly loved anyone since Sabrina. She broke my heart. I've been living a lie for so long I'm not even sure what the truth is, but I know, for sure, I don't love her. I can't keep this charade going much longer. Everyone thinks we are the perfect couple, but they don't understand. They can't see it, and I can't tell them. How do you tell *anyone* your wife thinks about taking her own life? I just can't do this anymore. I don't know what the fuck is wrong with me. How do I put myself in these situations? *God damn it*, I'm sorry. I'm just really struggling right now." I sat there numb, no tears, just utterly deflated. I was waiting, desperately, for her to say something. She looked at me. Her eyes always told vivid stories, and there was a rainstorm brewing. She sat there for at least a minute before she spoke. She leaned forward grabbing my hand —*three quick pulses.*

"Oh, Brian. Monkey, it's okay. It's *gonna* to be okay. There is nothing wrong with you. You have a sweet soul. I think you just keep finding birds with broken wings. You can't fix them." She paused for a couple minutes and leaned back, measuring her thoughts.

"You need to do whatever it is that makes *you* happy. It took me forever to find Margot. You know this. I'm not telling you stories. She is the first person I could truly count on. Someone I know loves me. Unconditionally. You'll find it. I promise you, monkey. You'll find it." In that moment, my mother had forgotten she was suffering from terminal cancer and just focused on me. It was the purest love you can ever hope for. A mother's love. I knelt before her and hugged her tightly. Her tears fell warmly on my shoulder like they had done many times before. She told me everything would be all right. And she was right, everything was okay for a little over a month.

On June 22, 1995, Mom was having problems breathing, so Margot drove her to the hospital. Margot later called to tell me they were admitting her. I left work and headed to Kennedy Hospital in Stratford, New Jersey. When I got there, I entered the room; it was cut in half by a curtain separating mom and someone's great-grandmother. The old woman didn't see my sympathetic smile as I passed the paper-thin wall. She was on a respirator and wasn't in good shape. I saw my mother sitting up in bed, and her smile lit the room when she saw me. "Hi, monkey." Her smile attempted to hide the fear, but her eyes told a different story. We were both scared. My attempts to lighten the mood were half-hearted and just as successful. I sat next to her on the bed, and her hand found mine. When I was younger and upset by something, she would hold my hand in the same way as she was now. Her four fingers over mine, thumb tucked into my palm, gently rubbing, and she then squeezed tight —*three quick pulses*. One pulse for each word: I love you. My eyes were down. She was ducking her head, signaling for me to look at her. Our eyes met. At that moment, I didn't see a woman dying, I saw a mother and her unconditional love. I stared into her eyes and knew neither of us would break. We needed to be strong for each other. She knew it, and I knew it. Mom was the person I loved most in this world, and I struggled to accept reality. Margot, Mom, and I talked for an hour before the nurse came and said my mother needed some rest. Margot would be staying, so I left them, planning to return the next day after work — *I thought we had more time.*

The next morning, Margot called to tell me mom was deteriorating fast. I was there in a blink only to find her sedated. Apparently, the cancer had progressed rapidly and caused her agonizing pain. They had pumped her full of morphine early that morning. She was brought to a private room in the intensive care unit. By the time I got there, she had already been intubated. When I first saw her, I practically collapsed. I sat on the bed beside her. I was now holding her hand in the same fashion she held mine all of those years — *three quick pulses.* Please do it back. That would not happen, ever again.

The doctor came in to tell us my mother's cancer had metastasized, and her condition was worsening rapidly. She would no longer survive without continuous life support. Margot was a rock. I don't know how, but this woman was watching the love of her life slowly dying in front of her, and she was able to maintain some order in this nonsense. She began calling my mother's family and loved ones. I called Chloe and my brother and sister-in-law in Florida. Considering the sudden turn of events, the news came as a shock. I explained to Brady that mom was on life support, and we would need to make a decision soon. He told me they would pack up the car straight away and get on the road. *Wait, what?* So, yes, my brother and sister-in-law decided to drive the thirteen hours to New Jersey instead of hopping on the next flight. I wouldn't really become angry about this until later. At that point, I was just bewildered. Margot and I paced the room listening to the rhythmic hiss of the respirator and the sharp piercing beeps of mom's heart monitor. I kept wondering if she was still in there somewhere. I would periodically sit next to her and stroke her hair, not realizing she wasn't feeling it. Half her face was covered with tape holding the breathing tube in place.

My blood relatives began showing up. My mother had six siblings; four sisters and two brothers. Several of my cousins were there, and the waiting room in the intensive care wing was now overrun with family. Margot and I went out to let the family go visit two-by-two. As people shuffled from room to room, the chatter increased. My mom's youngest sister, Louise, started talking under her breath about bringing mom out of the morphine induced coma.

"Louise, what did you say?" her brother Bobby asked. Bobby had become the stand-in patriarch of the O'Sullivan's when my grandfather died of cancer in '82. He never liked me much. I reminded him too much of my father. My mother used to tell me to ignore his "smartass" comments and told him to stop picking on me. The snide looks bothered me more.

Louise said, "I was talking to the nurse, and they can wake Jeannie up so we can talk to her."

"Whoa," I barked. "They gave her the morphine for a reason. Mom was in too much pain."

Louise, as self-serving as ever, said, "I want to talk to my sister. What if it's the last time I get the chance?"

Bobby concurred. This conversation escalated until Margot calmly stepped in and said, "No, that's *not* happening. I refuse to allow Jeannie any more pain than she's already had. This isn't up for debate." Margot walked out and went back to my mother. I was so proud of her for standing up to these people. They continued to mull over the possibility, and I followed Margot back to my mom's room.

"I cannot believe these people. They only think of themselves."

"Brian, there's no need to get mad at them. They'll never change."

"I hate them. I hate every last one of them. I've spent most of my life being shunned by these assholes because I remind them too much of my father. *Fuck them.* Look at all the times they were mad at mom for one reason or another. Over nothing. Family, my ass. They are a joke."

Margot was now rubbing my arm almost like she was sanding a wall. She wanted to comfort me, but I realized she was focused on the love of her life. I was now stealing the attention. This wasn't about me or my dysfunctional blood relatives. This was about my mother and her last hour on earth. "I'm sorry, Margot. We need to worry about mom right now." I hugged her, and we wept for a few minutes together, preparing for what came next.

"Now's the time, Brian. We have to let her go."

"I know," I said.

"I'm going to go talk to the doctor and tell them to take her off the machine."

"Okay." I was now alone in the room with her, and really starting to fall apart. I sat next to her.

"I'm gonna miss you so much. I don't know how to live without you." I kissed her on the forehead and held her hand until Margot came back.

"It's time, Bri," Margot said.

"Bye for now, mom. I love you." —*three quick pulses*. I walked out of the ICU room completely broken.

My mother's last wish was to die in this woman's arms. She waited most of her life to find Margot and now, in her final moments, they would share her last one together.

I was in shock walking the hallway towards the waiting room. As I approached the door, I refocused and heard familiar voices. It was my relatives in the waiting room talking. I walked in as my Uncle Bobby exclaimed, "I'm her brother, I'm going in there!"

"You can't, mom just wants Margot to be there."

"Bullshit, I'm going in." Bobby was storming down the hallway.

About a minute later he was walking back toward the waiting room. I stared at him as he passed me. "Fuck you," he said. *Where was my brother when I, again, needed him the most?* This thought wasn't a fair one since Brady wouldn't have made it here in time no matter what form of transportation he took.

"She threw me out, do you believe it?" Bobby was saying.

"Who did?" my mom's sister Betsy asked.

"Margot. She was yelling at me." Bobby snapped. None of them got the point. This wasn't about them. This was about my mom.

I exploded. "Who the fuck do you people think you are? You act like you were all so close to my mother when you've spent years passing judgment on everyone, including her. *Fuck every single one of you.* She wanted Margot there for her final moments and for you (*looking at my Uncle Bobby*) to ruin that by thinking you have some entitled right! Goddamn you! You all fucking disgust me." I walked out and waited to be able to go back to be by Margot's side.

Not that I expected it to, but the situation didn't get easier. My brother finally showed up and was angry we had pulled our mother off of life support before he got there. I was close to punching him but heard my mother in my head, "he's an O'Sullivan." Of course, Brady and Margie went to stay with

Margie's family, so I didn't see them until the next day at the florist. We were there to pick out an arrangement for the viewing. He and I disagreed, once again, because I picked out an expensive arrangement. Avoiding his protest, I handed the florist my credit card and paid for the arrangement I wanted for her. I left in disgust. On the day of the viewing, I was there with my wife. I hadn't expected it but at least twenty friends showed up to celebrate my mother. My entire dart team attended. Russell Riley showed up. Most of them had never laid eyes on my mother before that day. My heart was full. I went to the casket and knelt before her. It was the moment I had dreaded most. At viewings people always say "they look so good" or "how peaceful" they look. It's all bullshit. My mom wasn't lying there in front of me. This was the painted husk she left behind that day in the hospital. I wanted to look into her eyes one more time and hear her say everything was going to be okay. I wanted to hear her call me monkey. I took her cold, lifeless hand. —*three quick pulses.*

Standing in the receiving line with my relatives was cruel torture. They all hugged me like we hadn't been screaming at each other the day mom died. This wasn't about holding grudges for a single event. Most of my relatives had been assholes to me my entire life.

Back at Mom and Margot's house were all my friends and Margot's family. My blood relatives mostly didn't bother coming, and the ones that showed up did not stay. Ironically, I had more friends there that had never met my mother than blood relatives. It just goes to prove my philosophy of how irrelevant blood relation can be. Not always, but in this case, it spoke volumes. That day I made the very conscious decision to disown my mother's entire bloodline. Everyone I knew to be family would now become strangers. They all deserved nothing less, and my friends and Margot's family became my *true* family. Bloodlines mean *nothing*, and despite their attempts to reach out over the years, I haven't spoken to any of them since. As expected, Brady never reached out, and that totally validates everything I ever thought about him.

Toxic

June 23, 2006 marked the one-year anniversary of my mother's death. I had been reeling through the previous six weeks as the day approached and told Chloe as much. To that point, we had been married for 218 weeks. A handful of them were good, but it felt like sleepwalking. When I finally woke up, I had a vague memory of our last four years together, mostly highlighted by arguments and apathy. This day, however, would burn bright as my mother's voice echoed from the grave. It was a Friday, and Chloe decided to go to happy hour with coworkers. She forgot the significance of the day, and how I had dreaded it. After finding out she wasn't coming home, I met a buddy in the city who didn't want me to be alone. By the time I returned, it was after midnight, and Chloe was fast asleep. I didn't sleep a wink that night. I was incensed. My mother's voice kept speaking to me —*You can't fix them*— and I knew what I needed to do.

It was around six-thirty in the morning when I heard Chloe's footfalls descending from the second floor.

"Brian?" her muffled voice called out.

"Down here." I didn't realize it was morning. I had been sitting, in a trance, on a folding chair in my unfinished basement since I got home from the bar.

Chloe came half-way down the stairs. "You okay? You didn't come to bed last night. Why are you down here?"

"No, I didn't." I looked up at her in disgust. I had been chain smoking all night, and with no ventilation in the basement, the smoke collected like smog over the Los Angeles skyline. The scent of stale cigarettes and whiskey stained the air.

"Why not? What's wrong? You're scaring me." My lack of anger is what scared her. She knew me to quickly fly off the handle and scream vile profanities when I was mad. Little did she know, I was a cauldron on the verge of bubbling over with hate.

"You really don't know? Nothing? You've got *nothing*?" I wanted another swig but the bottle of scotch I brought down had been emptied hours ago. "Yesterday? Ring any *fucking* bells to you? Stupid bitch."

It finally dawned on her and hit her like a shot causing tears to well in her eyes. "I forgot, I'm sorry."

"I don't want to hear you're sorry. You're always sorry about something. I've been talking about it for weeks. *You are such a fucking selfish bitch.*" In reality, she wasn't. She just didn't have the capacity to be there for me. Chloe spent so much mental energy navigating around the potholes of her depression that she never looked over to see if I was bleeding out in the passenger seat.

"I don't know what to say. I'm sorry, I feel terrible."

"You should. When have you ever really been there for me? The entire time we've been together? *Give me a time. Any fucking time? You're useless!"* I could feel the migraine growing behind my eyes as I unleashed an expletive-laced tantrum. Her heaving sobs did not slow my wrath. *"I'm sick of this. I refuse to do it anymore. I deserve better than you."*

The room stood silent for a few minutes except for my deep and consistent exhales of smoke from my Marlboro light. Chloe finally broke the silence.

"What are you saying, Brian?"

I was now beginning to break. My head was pounding, and tears of anger and sadness were leaking from the corners of my eyes. I had thought of this moment so many times. What I might say if I ever had the strength. All I could do was repeat myself.

"I can't do this. I can't do this anymore, Chloe." I sat there staring at her. She stared back. My tirade was over, but I would not relent this time. I wanted a divorce.

Chloe left the house that day and didn't return until late the next night. Over the coming months, her shock and disbelief eventually morphed into anger and vindictiveness. I spent that time sleeping on the couch and living like a homeless person in a tent city with my clothes in piles around me.

Over the years, Chloe had seen several psychologists. I went with her on occasion. They had all told me I needed to be patient and understand her perspective. I tried. The last woman we saw even spoke with me privately. She counseled me to seek help for my anger. She was right, and I started seeing Michael later that year. Of course, it was too late to save our marriage, it was too broken. It turned out we were both pretty broken.

In the midst of all this, Elena Blackstone was about the worst thing that could have walked into my life. Right after the Fourth of July holiday, she began working for my company as a graphic designer. Elena was a terrific artist and not terrible on the eyes. I later found out she had been a model in New York for a couple years. Her career highlights included appearing in a couple of music videos and a cameo in an episode of *Law and Order*. She was always something like pretty-girl-number-three in the credits. Elena was about twenty pounds heavier since her days in front of a camera, but you still saw remnants of the runway strut in her walk. Pleasantly, she was more down to earth than most of the models I'd come across. Bright, very witty, and as sarcastic as I was. The office had a very casual dress code, but Elena didn't adhere to it. She was usually dressed for a night on the town. Even on dress-down Fridays, her blue-jean and t-shirt ensembles were accompanied by four-inch heels. The men in the office were beginning to do daily drive-bys just to see what she was wearing.

Elena often came into my office to kill time with my coworker Doug and me. I found her hilarious and so much fun to be around. I had been notorious for getting involved with coworkers, and, given my mangled home life, I was primed to make more bad decisions. Elena was a good distraction. In this case, the flirting began a couple weeks in, and we ended up going to happy hour after work. There was an Outback Steakhouse on the first floor of the building. We hung out for nearly two hours, and I realized then she could put away serious amounts of alcohol. She ordered a shot kicker with every round and never broke character. In that way, she reminded me of my first six months with Chloe. I was over my shot drinking days, so I stuck with my go to, a Corona with lime. When we left, I asked if I could drive her home and offered to pick her up for work the next day. This way, she would get home safely. She declined, jumped in her car, and sped away. No hug, no kiss, no thanks.

The next morning, I had caught up on email and was working on my second cup of coffee by the time Elena arrived. She came straight into my office. "Morning," she said with a smile, her face perfectly painted and accentuated with red lipstick. —*I wondered if it tasted like cherries*. I was in meetings and calls for most of the day. A few minutes before five, she came into my office and asked if I wanted to do happy hour again. I had to decline since I was going into the city to play league darts. She made some noise with her mouth in disapproval and walked out. Over the next week we really didn't talk but constantly caught each other's stare. She asked if I wanted to hang out one night. I said yes and invited her to dinner that Friday after work. Chloe was still living at the house, but she had gone to Rehoboth Beach for the week with her sister and wouldn't be back until Sunday night.

I had a meticulously manicured back yard furnished with a gazebo, bottom-lit koi pond, and a couple hundred well placed twinkle lights. My friends teased me relentlessly when I described using a shop-vac to vacuum the bricked patio. It was true, I was obsessive, but it was an impressive hundred square feet tucked away in the middle of a Philadelphia suburb. I left work at four that Friday and went to the market. I bought six-ounce salmon fillets, ingredients to make homemade Caesar salad, asparagus and fingerling potatoes. I was marinating the potatoes in shallots, extra virgin olive oil, and fresh thyme when Elena knocked. When I answered the door, she was holding a bottle of Grey Goose and a half-gallon container of cranberry juice. It was mid-August and still light until about eight o'clock. She poured herself a healthy cocktail as I went out to start the grill. I came back in to find her pouring a second drink. It was certainly a sign, but, true to form, I ignored it. I turned music on outside and told Elena to go relax under the gazebo while I was preparing dinner. She went out, grabbed a seat, and lit up a cigarette. I watched her through the kitchen window and imagined all I would like to do with her. Probably tonight. I paced the cooking, so everything was finished at the same time and filled the time in between by setting a proper table.

"Dinner is served." I set a perfectly plated entrée in front of her and a bowl of Caesar salad just to the side. "Fresh cracked pepper?" I pulled a pepper mill from under my arm.

"Please and thank you. This looks awesome!"

"Thanks."

As she was eating, "Oh, my God, this is seriously fucking delicious. Where did you learn to cook like this?"

"Blame my mother." For whatever reason, I didn't tell her I

studied culinary arts after high school.

"So, tell me about yourself," I said.

"Uh, okay. Well, you already know I lived in New York for three years. I actually came home because I got *married*." This was news to me.

"Oh. Still?"

"Separated," she said. "He's living in Cinnaminson with his parents and I'm back with my mom for the time being."

"Irreconcilable differences?"

"Yeah, he was really abusive," she admitted.

"Physical or verbal?" I asked.

"Yes," she said with a wince.

"Oh, I'm sorry," I said. I thought to myself I was at least fifty percent better than he was.

"What about you? I know you're going through a divorce now, right?" Elena asked.

"Yup. I can't wait. I need this sentence in purgatory finished. At least I got a break this week."

"This week?" She looked confused.

"Yeah, Chloe still lives here. She is still looking for a place."

Elena's eyes grew as big as saucers. "Wait, she still *lives* here? That's fucked up. I shouldn't be here. I thought you were way further along."

"Listen, it's been over for a long time in my eyes. I just finally pulled the trigger." I held back most of the details of my dissolving marriage.

We spent the next couple hours talking, and she had knocked the waist off the Grey Goose bottle. It was impossible not to notice the cranberry was making less and less of an appearance in her glass. She then excused herself. I thought she was going to the bathroom but after about ten minutes, I went in only to find her passed out on my couch. Well, not getting laid today, I thought. It was fairly early, so I went back outside, smoked a couple cigarettes, and finished the bottle of wine I had opened for dinner. When I came in, she had not moved a muscle, so I covered her with a blanket and headed up to bed. I woke up the next morning and Elena was gone. She did not leave a note. I assumed she had somewhere to be, and at that point realized I didn't have her phone number. I had no way of knowing if she was okay and only knew the town where she lived, not the street address.

I went in to work on Monday expecting to find out why she left so early without saying goodbye. She never showed up and had called out sick that day.

We were seeing each other at least once a week over the next couple months. Always at a bar. Chloe wasn't moving out until the first week of November, which nicely coincided with my cousin Tabitha's wedding. It was in Mexico and would double as the vacation I sorely needed.

Carved pumpkins were randomly hatching on porches throughout the neighborhood. I picked up Elena for dinner one night, and we were heading to Chickie's & Pete's for lobster pizza and a few drinks. Elena got in the car and leaned over to kiss me. I had barely rounded first base with her to that point. It was merely lack of opportunity.

"Hey, beautiful, how are you?"

She blushed. "Aww. I need a fucking *drink*. Get me out of here."

"Well hi to you too," I said sarcastically.

"Don't be a tool," she fired back. Smiling. She reached out to hold my hand and it rested, interlaced with mine, in my lap. Her fingers wandered and, abruptly, almost as if she was telling me to watch out for an oncoming train, she said, "*Oh, my God*, did you see the news?" Without my reply, she continued, "This guy's son was kidnapped."

"That sucks. And came completely out of left field. What made you think of that?"

"I don't know. He was the son of a senator or something like that. Myers? Maybe."

"John Myers? He's a state legislator. Wow, crazy."

"*Right?*" Elena said.

"Hey, I have to ask you something. And I know it's kind of soon, *maybe*. I don't know." I kind of trailed off.

"What, stupid?" she asked. Elena and I got into the habit of calling each other stupid. It was always playful and would become a term of endearment between us.

I laughed. "*You're* stupid, but I like you. *Seriously* though, listen. So, I have a wedding to go to in November. It's my cousin's wedding. Well, she's not really my *cousin*, not by blood. I disowned all those assholes. This is my mom's partner, Margot's, niece. I consider them family so that makes Tabitha my cousin. Sorry, that was convoluted. Anyway, I was wondering if you'd go with me."

"Oh, my God, I would totally love to go."

"There's only one thing, it's in Mexico. And we'd have to make sure we can still get decent airfare, but I already have the room."

"Oh. Shit. I probably can't go."

"Aww, that sucks. How come?"

"I don't have enough vacation time to take off." She made that funny noise with her mouth again. "And that would have been the perfect place for us to have sex for the first time."

"No way! You're gonna make me wait until November. You are torturing me." I was only kind of kidding.

Elena let go of my hand and gripped the crotch of my jeans as she said, "I'm worth the wait." She ended up being right.

That next Monday, Elena came sprinting into my office.

"Guess what?"

"You're pregnant?" I fired back with my best poker-face.

She laughed, "I hate chu, stupid. *No!* I talked to my boss this morning, and she's going to let me borrow vacation days from next year. I can go with you! Isn't that awesome?"

"Aw, shit."

"What? There are no flights. Right? Dammit, fuck my life."

"No."

"Then what is it? This is great news." She was looking at me like I was an idiot. I was about to tell her I had already asked another girl but thought the joke would go over flat. I abandoned it in my mouth.

"Nothing, just playing with you. That *is* awesome news. Let's check for the flight." We found a flight on the same day as mine, but a few hours later. Against her protests, I paid for her ticket.

We went to a Halloween party the Saturday before leaving for Mexico. I was still suffering from a terrible case of blue-balls and Elena's sexy nurse costume wasn't helping. I spent the entire night pawing at her and all she kept saying was, "Five more days." I was elated, not just with the thought of that, but Chloe would be moving out the weekend I was in Mexico.

I arrived at the hotel in Playa del Carmen, Mexico with two dozen or so of Tabitha's family and friends. Elena wouldn't end up getting to the hotel for another four hours. The group checked into their rooms and gathered at the pool bar.

Sometime later I heard, "Hey, *stupid*," from behind me.

I swung around in time to catch Elena. She had jumped into my arms and wrapped her legs around my waist. This leap of faith could have gone badly. Instead, I stood there getting passionately attacked. When we finally came up for air, I saw Margot with my other cousin, Carla, standing by the bar smiling at us.

"You have to meet my family," I said as I set her back on her feet.

"And then you are fucking me! At least once." There was no uncertainty in her raw declaration.

"*Deal.*"

Elena and I spent the next six days celebrating and making up for our *lack-of-opportunity*. Everyone loved her because she was the life of the party. Vacation Elena took drinking to a whole new level. She wasn't sloppy, but she was blackout drunk every night in Mexico. I should have thought more deeply about whether or not this rebound relationship was healthy —*I always find myself blissfully steering into the crash*— but I was having too much fun.

When I got home, the house looked like burglars had been interrupted midway through their heist. The master bedroom was empty except for the California King. Half the pillows were gone. The third-floor loft was mostly vacant. It was an unused room where we stored all the unopened gifts from our wedding, mainly kitchen appliances and cookware. Chloe taking them was odd since she never once cooked a proper meal throughout the entirety of our relationship. She used to say she could burn water, and, since I was a *trained chef*, I should do the cooking. I didn't mind. She even took the Kitchen-Aid mixer my mother bought me the Christmas before she died. It was surely out of spite. I surveyed the rest of the house, mentally noting what had been taken, and rationalized the losses as being worth it. The divorce wasn't final, but I was finally free.

With Chloe gone, Elena started spending nights at my house, sometimes entire weekends. We were having fun together, and she eventually became my girlfriend. We attended two more weddings during the spring and summer of '07. Again, everyone adored her, but there was a disease growing inside. A little over a year into dating, Elena stayed at my house more often than not. She even had a couple drawers in the dresser and a few feet of closet space. Unfortunately, when she was there, she was usually in one of two states: drunk or blacked out. When she was sober, we were like best friends. This wasn't one of those days.

One rainy day in August, we drove to work together. At lunch, she was disappointed to hear I wanted to go straight home instead of going for drinks. I drove home that day and, needing gas, stopped at the station to fill up. For whatever reason, I went into the car's center console, and found an empty fifth of Smirnoff Vodka. When I saw it, I looked up and caught her guilty glazed-over gaze. I hadn't seen it before, but it dawned on me that she had started drinking at work. She made other arrangements knowing we weren't partying that day. When we got to my house, I was trying to remain calm. It didn't last.

"Are you drinking at work now?" I asked matter-of-factly.

"No!" she said, but the indicators were there. Her eyes were bloodshot, and she swayed slightly as if she was listening to invisible music. Elena headed into the kitchen to pour herself a drink. "I asked you to go to happy hour, and you said no."

By the time I followed her into the kitchen she had already taken a couple gulps. I later wondered if she did it to mask her earlier drinking.

"You're fucking *unbelievable*," I said in disgust.

"Fuck you, dickhead." She downed the rest of the glass,

poured another and walked out the sliding glass back door. She was smoking, and I didn't want to broadcast my business to the neighbors, so I waited for her, stewing in my own boiling blood.

She came in about fifteen minutes later with an empty glass and an attitude.

"I don't know who the fuck you think you are. You're not my mother. Stop acting like it. You don't fucking *own* me. It's my body, I'll do whatever the hell I want."

Whether she realized it or not, Elena was now basically admitting it to me. I lost it.

"You're a drunk whore! If you want to kill yourself do it somewhere else. If you don't like it, you can get the fuck out. You're Port Richmond trash that I should never have picked up."

"Fuck you. I don't need this bullshit." She took her keys, slammed the front door, and squealed out of the driveway.

For the next week, we avoided each other at work. I saw her sitting in her car one night on my way home. She was lighting a cigarette. I caught her looking, and our eyes locked. Never one to learn a lesson, I went over and got in the passenger seat.

After a few seconds she said, "You're *stoopid*." She made that sound with her mouth. "And I'm *stoopid*, too."

I couldn't help but laugh. "I'm sorry I said that awful shit to you. I didn't mean it. I was just angry you lied to me." The craziest part was I was angrier about the lie than I was the drinking. I thought about talking this over with Michael at my next session.

"I'm sorry too." She was less descriptive about the reason for her apology.

We alternated between being best friends and mortal enemies for the next couple months. During the good times, Elena *really* liked me. Actually, the word love became the replacement. And I grew to love her too. She was really a great and caring person when she was sober. I started to relate much more to what my mother went through with some of her life partners.

Elena was certainly a girl who lived on the edge. A week after Thanksgiving, she asked me to go to a strip club. She said she used to go a lot when she was modeling in New York and always had a fantasy of being with a girl. She promised the best sex of my life after getting home. Who was I to say no? Win/win, right? We went to Club Risqué around nine p.m., took seats at the bar, and ordered drinks. Electricity was pumping through her, and it was a sight to watch. The girls at this club were mostly pretty to very hot, and her eyes were locked on every dancer that came on stage. At one point, a very athletic girl was center stage and climbing the pole. Elena pointed this stripper out to me, and I tried to act like I hadn't already noticed her. If you have ever been to a strip club with a hot girl, then you know they are magnets for strippers. So, true to form, every stripper stopped to talk to Elena. I realized why she liked going, the attention. She truly loved attention, and she would take it anywhere she could find it. —*We were a lot alike in that way.* Elena and I sat on stools face-to-face, and every stripper pulled the same move. They would approach, step between her and me, fall ass first into my lap and begin a conversation with her. They would tell her I was cute, but ultimately the play was to ask for me to pay for a dance for Elena. It must have happened a dozen times. Thankfully for my wallet, she declined, every time. There was only one girl that had a chance that night. Her name was Alexis. She was the stripper Elena had noticed earlier working the pole on the center stage. She came by but didn't pull the same move. She actually asked me to buy her a drink. Bold, yes, but effective. I bought her a drink, and she spent the next forty-five minutes shooting the shit with us. She was very cool and very topless. I had been around countless strippers in my twenties but had not seen one walk around topless. It was actually against the rules, and at one point, one of the bouncers came by and told her to put her top on. I was relieved because I no longer had to make the effort to not look. They were magnificent and expensive. Alexis was very up front. She lived in Delaware and worked Thursday through Sunday. She was married but in an open relationship and had a daughter, four or five years old. She was also interested in spending time with us but couldn't that night. She told us to come in on a Thursday over the next couple weeks, and she could stay late. Elena and I spent the drive home talking about whether or not she really wanted this. She suggested we go in two weeks not to appear desperate. I was just happy she was interested in pursuing this; shit, she was driving this.

Two weeks later, I found myself going to the liquor store, stopping at Anthony's bar to pick up wine glasses, and at the hotel to get a room. I was being fairly presumptuous. Elena and I headed over to Club Risqué about ten-thirty that night. We sat on the complete opposite side from where we were the last time. We grabbed drinks, talked, and listened to the music. The girls circulated through, but there was no sign of Alexis. In my head, I was calculating how much I spent on the hotel room that night for what might turn out to be no reason. I think we were there for close to an hour when we heard the emcee say, "Alexis, coming to the main stage." Elena was super excited and a little drunk. I was purposely keeping myself sober for performance purposes. Alexis came over after she got off stage and told us she was glad we came back. I told her we were staying in a hotel down the street in case she wanted to hang out after work. She smiled and said she would like that, kissed Elena, and went back into the dressing room. We left and went back to the hotel. This was my first planned threesome, so I was overcome by my OCD and had to have the perfect setup. I would laugh the next day about the amount of alcohol I had brought for three people. About ninety minutes later there was a knock at the door. It was Alexis in gray sweatpants and a pink Victoria Secret sweatshirt. Her hair was pulled up in a ponytail. She was still hot but in a much more girl-next-door way. She was also a few years older than I thought but still way younger than me. Alexis turned out to be twenty-six; the same age as Elena. She hugged me on her way by and came in. I offered her a drink and poured her a glass of red wine. We talked for a few minutes, and Elena was noticeably fading. She has been drinking pretty heavily and while that wasn't unusual, she seemed to go the extra mile tonight from what I considered were nerves. This was an experience she had imagined for some time, but unfortunately, she wouldn't remember it the next day. I, however, would take full advantage of the situation. Alexis was certainly into guys but had an obvious sweet tooth for girls. At one point, as we were talking, I was sitting on a chair next to the bed where Elena was lying, and Alexis cozied up next to her. It was intensely hot to just watch these two girls cuddling. I was half aroused over the thought of what was to come. We talked for a while longer. I got up to get a drink and once it was poured, I looked over to see the two of them were kissing. I sat down in the chair and watched. Elena was in shorts and a t-shirt in the beginning but now the t-shirt was off, and Alexis's hand was working its way into her shorts. Much to my appreciation, Alexis kissed her way down Elena's stomach until she only had the shorts to contend with. They were no match. The next thing I saw was Alexis burying her face and tongue into Elena. I could barely contain myself, but I sat there and watched. Elena convulsed, orgasming. Alexis was kneeling against the bed, engulfed in her invasion, I decided to join in. I knelt behind her and pulled her sweatpants down. As she drove deep into Elena, I did the same with a single finger. She buckled her back in response. As she moistened, I added two more and drove deeper. She was no longer able to concentrate on Elena as she spasmed wildly. Alexis slid up on the bed and began making out with Elena as I continued penetrating her. She knelt on the bed, ass in the air. I found myself needing to taste her. Her legs trembled. I grabbed her like an inmate might the bars holding him captive as she convulsed and came. She collapsed on the bed and as I climbed upon her, I noticed the alcohol had finally taken everything from Elena. She was stirring but barely conscious and missing the memory she longed to experience. I was throbbing and could no longer contain myself. I drove deep into Alexis. I threw her legs over her head allowing me to go deeper and the angle now made her squeal. She screamed that she was going to come, and I continued for as long as I could. As she panted and squirmed, I pulled out and came on her stomach, but she wasn't quite done. I drove three fingers inside her, sliding them along the topside of her vagina and she lost all control. She squirted everywhere. I had never yet seen anything like it and would not have believed it possible if I hadn't experienced it for myself. It poured out with such force and only made me go harder. She finally pushed my hand away and collapsed beside Elena. It was only then that I noticed Elena was now totally passed out. She missed out on her fantasy, so drunk that she would hate herself the next day. I persisted trying to extract every ounce Alexis had to offer me. She was a puddle when I was done with her. I curled up next to her and had my arm around both of them. At some point, she gathered herself and said she needed to go. I walked her down to her car. We kissed for a few minutes and she left. I went back to the room and realized what a disaster I was stepping into. Elena was passed out on the right side of the bed. I flopped on the left side and immediately realized it was drenched. I was lying on a mattress soaked with Alexis's come. On one hand, I was pleased with myself for inducing such pleasure, and on the other hand I was just trying to get some fucking sleep. The mattress was so saturated I needed to pull Elena off the bed, flip the mattress and put her back. As I fell asleep, I noticed the flip side of the mattress was a bit damp. We really did some damage that night, and I felt bad for the unlucky guests who would be staying after us. I quickly drifted off to sleep. The next day Elena felt guilty, jealous, and unfulfilled. She thought she knew what had happened but was too drunk to enjoy it. She said she felt and heard me having sex with Alexis next to her, and that was all she focused on. She didn't know the half of it.

Over the next few weeks after the threesome, our relationship was like a powder keg, and Elena eagerly provided the spark. My rational mind knew I needed to distance myself from her. Call me stupid, I was torn. — *you're stoopid*. I still wanted to be with her.

Untangling myself from the gummy web Elena spun around my life over those couple years was trying and messy. I spent that last year lying on Michael's couch pouring my heart out and describing, in disturbing detail, just how fractured our relationship was, and yet I continued to clutch the handrails through the descent. To be fair to Michael, he repeatedly advised me to end this relationship, describing it as toxic. I wasn't ready to listen to reason. Elena and I had hit our pinnacle, and even as the damage mounted, I refused to get off this ride.

Elena had called out from work one day and spent it at my house. When I got home, I found her on the recliner watching the six o'clock news.

"Hey, miss me?"

"No." She smiled and continued, "Of course, now get over

here and kiss me like you missed me, stoopid."

"Give me a minute." I ran upstairs and changed, and when I came back down, Elena had poured herself a drink and was on the back-patio smoking. I went out and sat across from her and took a sip to confirm my suspicions. She was no longer mixing the vodka with anything. Not even ice. I walked away without a word. I was watching the news when she came back in about twenty minutes later. I had been working through keeping a lid on my anger, and these times were my truest tests. She stood there staring at me and then began screaming at how I needed to jump down off my soapbox because I was just as bad as she was. In truth, it wasn't far from reality. She was just outpacing me, and I didn't see my growing problem. My lack of reaction flipped a switch in her head. Her screams did not provoke me, so she turned and grabbed the top outside corners of the 50" flat-screen and was pulling it towards her. I leapt over the coffee table in time to catch it. She was incensed that I reacted to the TV but not her. "You care so fucking much about that thing, and you could give a shit if I lived or died!" She grabbed a picture off the console table that stood guard against the banister and smashed in on the hardwood floor. Glass scattered and she threw herself on the ground. The cuts weren't too severe, but her hands were bleeding and there was a trickle of blood on the highest part of her right cheekbone. "I hate you," she muttered in a breathless voice. Minutes later she called 911. When the police arrived, all I thought about was Lauren and the bogus domestic violence report she filed back in '95.

Elena showed the officers her cuts and claimed I threw her

to the ground onto the broken glass. She told them she wanted me out of the house. *My* house! She didn't even really live there. One of the cops took her outside while the other stayed behind to question me. It became obvious she was too drunk to file an official complaint, and once they found she didn't actually live with me they took her back to her mother's house. They told me she would be instructed to file a complaint once she sobered up. She never did and came crawling back the next day to apologize in her usual fashion. This may have turned out to be the first argument I ever had with a significant other where I didn't lose my temper. Contrary to claims, I was never physically abusive, but my words back then could slice like a surgeon's blade. The ability to hold my tongue that day proved therapy was actually helping with my self-control, but certainly not my decision making.

In my relationships, I seemed to go through breaking points where I could not take anymore. Not that I couldn't handle the nonsense, I did that quite well, but there needed to be an *event*, some tangible reason for me to finally throw in the towel. It took entirely too long to get there. Believe me, I understand. My breaking point wasn't getting the cops called or the daily and belligerent drunkenness, the sloppy mess that reminded me of so many prominent figures in my life.

A few weeks later, I went to play darts in Philly, leaving Elena in the house alone. It was any normal Tuesday with the boys. We won the match despite my terrible performance that night. I beat myself up the entire drive home even in a victory, remembering a handful of missed throws I had hit a million times before. When we won, if I shot poorly, the self-loathing was short lived. True to form, by the time I pulled into the driveway I had forgiven myself. I remember seeing my breath in the cold of the night, and I ran from the car to the front door. It was open. Not completely but it would have given way if pushed. I walked in cautiously but with purpose, not sure what I was stepping into. Elena's car was still in the driveway. All the lights on the first floor were on. I ran into the kitchen, thinking of a couple recent break-ins in the neighborhood. All I found was an open flame on the stove. It took a minute to focus on it given my wildly running imagination of what might be occurring.

No one was there, just the glowing flame of the front right burner.

I imagined what happened. We both smoked when we drank, and I pictured her drunk and craving a cigarette. When I was home, we would light up with the flame from the gas stove and go out to the back patio and smoke. I am certain this is how the night played out for Elena. Only this time, she was a little too fucked up to remember to shut off the burner. I went over and turned the knob to extinguish the gas. As I did, I notice to the right of the flame was a stack of mail. Don't ask why I kept mail next to the stove, I just did. I never thought it would be a problem. It still wasn't but there it sat. Leaning ever so slightly left toward the calling flame. My imagination was uncontrollable. I pictured my house in flames, and in the darkest parts of me, I pictured her asleep through it all, engulfed and all that remained was sifting through the ash. Of course, my rational mind would never wish this on anyone, particularly someone I loved. Needless to say, this was the event I needed! I was then able to move forward. Although, as you would imagine, it was not without drama. Elena left to go back to living with her mother. In the fallout, I found dozens of empty plastic vodka bottles throughout the house. It was like a demented Easter egg hunt and actually pretty impressive how many plastic grocery bags I filled with the empties. This was only the beginning of my true descent.

Taxicab Carousel

With Elena out of the picture, I was left alone with my vices. I brought the best impression of my father to the forefront. I was thirty-eight and on the verge of becoming a full-fledged alcoholic. I would routinely get home from work, go into the basement and write, drink, and smoke cigarettes. At some point, it became more about the drinking than anything else. If I had drunk myself to death at that point I would have truly walked in the footsteps of my father. Looking back, I feel like I gave it a hell of an effort.

The divorce from Chloe was finalized a month after I kicked out Elena. It was twenty-one months in the making and ended in my buying out her equity rights to our house. Later in 2008, the housing market collapsed, and the value of my home plummeted. In the divorce, I had basically given Chloe half of the equity that was reduced to nothing.

I fell further down the hole, and the days began to run together. *—worked, wrote, drank, smoked, passed out; rinsed and repeated.* This went on for several months. I was still seeing Michael once a week for therapy. I managed to hide my alcoholism. I was able to keep it quietly contained within the walls of my house and, mostly, in the basement where all my truths were exposed, bleeding onto these pages. And it was in that dungeon where I began to unravel the damage that had rampaged through my life. I began writing about some of my deepest pain and darkest memories, as well as incidents that may have seemed to be enviable by some people but were mostly hollow and unfulfilling. My life was becoming a cesspool and I was drowning in it.

As it turned out, I didn't accomplish much. I had thoughts down on a page but no real depth. It seemed I was more interested in finishing a few drinks and getting on to the next day.

One Thursday night, I was a couple beers deep and starving. The cupboards were bare, and I had sense enough not to drive, so I walked to the pub down the street. I had never been to Harry's Bar & Grill. My friends spoke highly of it, but I just wanted a burger so who cared about their Yelp reviews? I walked in around six-thirty to a mostly empty restaurant. I sat at the bar and ordered a beer and food. I drank and ate. The crowd thickened. An hour and a half later, I was surrounded by college kids. I was certainly not blending in, but I am not one to fade into the background either. I began a conversation with the people surrounding me, and the next thing I knew I was in an intense political conversation with some girl around half my age. I guess I won the debate because I found myself walking Political-Science Girl back to my house.

It was around 12:30 in the morning when I turned on the music and twinkle lights in the back yard. I cracked a couple Coronas and led her outside.

"Wow, this yard is super chill," she said.

"Thank you, I like it. So, you said you go to Temple, right? What are you studying?"

"Political science. I hate it."

"Oh, so why'd you pick that major?"

"My father. He's a lawyer downtown. He wants his little girl to *follow in Daddy's footsteps*. It's super boring."

"What do you really want to do?" I asked.

"Not too sure, actually. I think I want to work with kids. That will really piss him off. There is like no money in education."

"Not sure you should pick a career based on pissing off your father. I'm sure there are better ways to do that."

"Yeah, like right now. He would lose his shit if he knew I was here." She made herself laugh.

"What do you mean?"

"No offense but you're like my father's age. Or at least close."

"Does that bother you?"

"Oh, no. If I wasn't into you, I wouldn't be here. And you're super cute —so."

"Nice. Thank you."

An hour later in my California King, her age meant less to me than the warmth of her soft skin and the tickle of her breath on my neck as I thrust into her. I felt content, maybe even happy. Later, I got up to pee and then headed downstairs to get a glass of water. I stayed down there for some time, cell phone in hand. I went back upstairs.

"Hey. Hey!" She looked adorable lying there in just my shirt, but she had to go. "Your cab's outside."

"Huh? Are you serious, right now? You want me to leave?"

"I do. Nothing personal. I'll pay for the cab." I watched as she got dressed. She had turned her back to me and mumbled something about my being a middle-aged jerk in crisis. To be fair, I wasn't yet middle-aged, but I understood her point.

I went back to Harry's the next night. The bar wasn't as busy but there was a table of three girls across the room.

"Hey, Jack. Can you send that table drinks for me?" I asked the bartender.

"For all three of them?" he replied.

"Yeah, I think that's the move. Although, I'd like *that* girl to know I'm interested." I was pointing.

"Which one, dude?" Jack asked with a chuckle.

"Oh, yeah. The girl on the right, with the red shirt."

"Got it." Jack talked to the waitress, and I waited.

I casually watched as the waitress was talking to the girls. Red Shirt Girl glanced over and painted a smile on her face. I dropped her a wink, smiled back and turned my attention to getting myself a refill. About ten minutes went by when I felt a light tap on my shoulder.

I turned and smiled, "Hey, how are you?"

"I'm well, thank you. I'm curious why you didn't come talk to me. My friends said to say thank you for the drink."

"Tell them it was my pleasure."

"You *could* tell them yourself. We don't bite."

"Is that an invitation?"

"You're really making this hard, you know," she said.

I laughed, "I'm sorry. I just get intimidated in groups. I'm Brian, by the way."

"I'm Emma, you coming or what?"

"Sure, let me just settle up here." I paid Jack for my drinks and walked over to Emma's table.

"Hello, ladies."

Emma said, "This is Brian. Brian, this is Lucy and Maggie." They greeted me with smiles and hellos.

"Pleasure to meet you both." I shook hands with them. "And I can't leave *you* out." I shook Emma's hand, holding it for a beat longer than the others.

We spent the next hour laughing and talking. I found out the three of them were nursing students at Thomas Jefferson and it was Lucy's birthday. I bought a round of shots and we had most of the bar singing "The Birthday Song."

Shortly thereafter, Maggie said, "I gotta get up early. You guys want to go soon?"

"Sure, we can jet. I have to go dress shopping with my sister in the morning anyway," Lucy said.

I put on a pouty face. "Aww, that sucks. Lucy, you can't leave *your* birthday party." I gave her a wide-eyed smiley face hoping to change her mind. It didn't work.

Emma said, "Guys, it's *super* early. I don't want to go home yet."

"So, don't. Stay here with me," I said.

The girls were now looking at each other, passing thoughts through the air. Their expressions were saying, "Are you sure?" and "This is a bad idea!"

"It's *fine*, guys, really. I want to stay," Emma said convincingly. The girls said their goodbyes with hugs, kisses and whispers, presumably about me. They waved goodbye and were off.

"They worried I'm some psycho? I really felt they were reluctant to leave you here."

"No. It's not that. *Okay*, full disclosure? I have a boyfriend. Well, have, had, I don't know. We might be on a *break*. Whatever you want to call it. He is just too needy. Uh, no, not needy, *I don't know*. He wants to get married soon, and I'm totally not ready for that yet. I'm too young. Jeez, uh, I really just need to stop talking. I'm sorry."

I grabbed both of her hands from across the table, "It's okay. No sorries required. Do you want to get out of here?"

"Yes." She was, once again, convincing.

Emma and I retraced the steps I had performed with Political Science Girl the previous night. The difference was, I actually liked Emma. She was a nice girl, and other than a fairly noticeable gap in our ages, I could see myself with her. I didn't trust myself.

We were lying in bed, and I just blurted out, "I should probably call you a cab."

"*Excuse me?*" She was entirely caught off guard. "You *must* be kidding."

"I'm sorry, I'm afraid not. I think it's for the best." My voice was monotone.

"For the best? For *who*? Fuck you." She was dressing at light speed, shaking her head in disbelief. As she sprinted down the stair I called out, "Wait, let me at least get you a ride."

"Fuck you, jerkoff, my car is around the corner." She slammed the door hard behind her.

I realize the picture this paints of me, and I resembled every brush stroke. I felt guilty, but it got easier. This scenario repeated itself over the next fourteen months in an exhaustive fashion, an embarrassing number of times. Some were beautiful girls and some, not as much, but they all succumbed to my bullshit and followed me home like I was the Pied Piper of Hamelin. But they all left with the same callous dismissal —*your cab's outside*. I imagined my mother looking down in disappointment. My shame didn't deter me; however, I became more and more uncomfortable going to Harry's. I kept running into previous play toys. I needed a change of scenery.

Facebook

I gave up my bar stool at Harry's and retreated to the basement where I continued writing about my life. In 2009, I discovered Facebook. Over the course of a month, I was in contact with people I had not spoken to since high school. The reconnections were overwhelming. I was even talking to people who had been both above and below my social pecking order back then. It was astonishing how time had leveled the playing field. I had hundreds of contacts both new and old. A crazy explosion occurred when I posted one of my modeling pictures from my early twenties. My friend requests skyrocketed to close to six hundred, mostly women. It didn't seem to matter that it was a dated picture. The fact I was once worthy of a camera seemed to be enough to garner attention from random girls everywhere. I accepted the requests from women I found attractive. And now, the nights spent in my basement, fueled by scotch, writing my memoirs was interrupted by these newly found Facebook friends. The conversations came out of nowhere. Some innocent, some not so much. Of course, they all start out innocent. I brought another laptop home from work and was now double fisting my efforts. I had this journal on one screen and Facebook on the other.

One conversation was in July of '09 with a girl I really did not remember from high school. As I read it back, it was indeed corny; however, effective. These are just excerpts copied from the website so take them at face value. I will provide color where my memory serves.

> *LeAnn – It's LeAnn Richter. We went to high school together. In the same graduating class. I forget too. It was so long ago. You look GREAT. Hope life is treating you well. PS: In your pic, you look prettier than me! LOL.*
>
> *Me – I guess senility is setting in for all of us. Thanks for the compliment but you seem to have kept yourself together over the last 20 years. Are you living in Philly or Jersey?*
>
> *LeAnn – I live in Chester County, PA. Lived here for 22 years.*
>
> *LeAnn – Why are you single?*
>
> *Me – Temporarily self-imposed due to years of bad choices.*

For a couple weeks the conversation stalled.

> *LeAnn – Hey, did you get a woman yet? And, if not, what's the hold up? You are gorgeous sweetie!! You must be saving yourself for me, huh? Awww, I love you too!*
>
> *Me – It's not finding one that's the problem. It's finding one worth keeping around. All the good ones are taken, including you.*
>
> *LeAnn – I'm sorry Brian. I am picky too! You need to broaden your horizons a bit and keep trying.*

Not sure what she saw on Facebook, but her next comment began to change the rules.

LeAnn – I guess you are a piece of meat! You are definitely hottie McHotterson! If I wasn't married... OMG... that's all I can say. And we don't live that far apart so it would be easy to see you!

Me – Hmm, that's true.

LeAnn – LOL, you're bad! We should NOT get together for I fear the worst.

Me – Me too

About a month later and out of the blue.

LeAnn – You are so hot.

Me – Aw, you're so sweet. What brought that on?

LeAnn – LOL! Got your attention. Just wondering how you're doing. Haven't heard from you in a while. What's new? (and you are a handsome devil)

Me – Not much. Same old shit. I'm probably go to bed soon. Not sure why, I haven't been able to sleep well lately.

LeAnn – I know a good sleep aid. Sex is the best medicine. I will have sex with you for medicinal purposes only. What do you think? Although I'm not sure my husband would approve but I'm sure he will understand under the circumstances.

Me – What he doesn't know helps me. Stop teasing.

LeAnn – I am not teasing. I really think a sexual experience will help you sleep better.

Me – OK, give me my medicine.

LeAnn – You lie like a rug. You would never do it.

Me – You're kidding yourself.

LeAnn – You would take advantage of a married woman? I think not. You are too good of a man. Besides, am I really your type anyway? You never noticed me in school. We both live in PA Where would we meet? Delaware County? Chester County?

Me – You're right. I am really not that type of guy. But something tells me it would be pretty hot if you got me past my morals.

LeAnn – Oh, my God. Do you dig me or what? You want me, don't you?

Me – Is this something you really want?

LeAnn – Do you?

Me – So what are we talking here? Specifically?

LeAnn – You couldn't handle me. In three weeks, I will be able to get away. If you are interested. Name the place. We should meet first before we do anything. Got it? Well, actually I am a good girl. I don't know if I could be with another man. But then there is you. I've been with my husband for 16 years. I haven't strayed. But you are so pretty. I can't help but wonder what it would be like. Wow, it's getting hot in here.

Me – You wouldn't regret it. I have to head out. Talk later.

LeAnn – Hey cutie, it's been weeks since we talked. Everything ok?

A couple more weeks passed, and I hadn't really been on Facebook.

LeAnn – Hello? What the hell did I do?

I finally checked Facebook and got her messages. It seemed a little desperate and I was juggling a couple girls, so I ghosted her. I wouldn't hear from her again for a while.

Scumbag

It was Thanksgiving morning, and my temples were throbbing. Thanksgiving Eve is notoriously the biggest party night of the year, and college kids lived for this shit. I had decided to go back to Harry's Bar, and ended up with some random chick in my bed when I woke up the next morning. I was too fucked up to call her a cab the night before. I don't even think we had sex. I didn't remember her name. Did it matter at this point? These countless encounters were stacking up like a cord of wood. I went downstairs and brewed a pot of coffee, still trying to wipe the cobwebs from my pounding head. Random Girl came down at some point and said she had to go. Bye. She wasn't even very attractive. I was starting to question my motives but more importantly, my judgment. I was no bottom feeder. This girl was definitely below my normal standards. What the fuck was I doing?

I can feel you judging me, and it's okay. I am too.

I knocked back the pot of coffee and tried to straighten up the house a bit. I didn't need to be at Margot's for dinner until four, and my cousins were habitually late to everything. Not sure why, but I guess it is just how some people are wired. I have the hardest time being late for anything. Besides, I wanted to talk to Margot.

I arrived at Margot's at two-forty-five p.m. She met me at the door with a hug and a kiss. We went into the house and sat in the kitchen.

"How are you?" she asked.

"I'm good. You? How are you feeling?" Margot had had a heart attack when mom was still alive, and the doctors had been keeping a close eye on her ever since.

"I'm good, too. A little tired but I feel okay."

"Can I help with anything?" I asked.

"No, everything is done but the turkey. Just waiting for the girls to get here, but you know they'll be late," she said, laughing.

"Yeah, I was hoping we could talk."

"Okay. Everything okay, Bri?

"Yeah, yeah, of course. I've just been writing recently. About mom, you know. Um. I don't know how to even bring this up." I paused for a good thirty seconds. "Okay, so I was at Michael's and I remembered some *stuff*. You know, about mom." I was pausing, constantly, trying to find the right words. Margot hadn't known I was going to therapy, so I explained how he helped me recover buried memories. I didn't mention the anger issues.

"I remembered the time when I lived in Oklahoma. Mom had told me we lived there, but I hadn't remembered the gun until recently."

When I finished and saw her perplexed look I asked, "Are you okay?"

Margot asked, "Did Mom ever tell you why he was chasing you?"

"No," I replied.

"Well, I think it best to forget it," Margot said.

I refused to let it rest. I had so many broken memories, and any way I could fill in the blanks, I would take, even if the words were better left unsaid. She took a deep breath before a long exhale and with love and pain fighting for control in her eyes, she began. "Mom told me about the time your father chased you guys with that shotgun. It was you, Brady and mom. Well, your father used to get mad when she didn't do what he wanted." Margot was welling up in tears and trying to compose herself. She finally continued, "He made her have sex with other men, and he would like to watch. Whenever she resisted there was hell to pay. She couldn't win because when she went along with it, he would be furious that she was enjoying it too much. One ugly day, they were fighting about her and a guy he forced on her, and when the gun came out, she grabbed you and Brady and hid behind some bushes."

Margot had no further detail. I'd like to say the story surprised me, but I had become fairly numb to the evils of my father.

"Let's not talk about this anymore. Mom would want this to be a happy day," I said, feeling sorry I ever brought it up.

"Good idea," Margot said. She grabbed my hand. —*three quick pulses*. My mom taught her well.

This would end up being the last Thanksgiving at my mom's house. Since my mother's death, and, with Margot aging, it was getting harder and harder for her to keep up with hosting holidays. If I'm being honest, it never felt the same after mom left us.

My cousins Tabitha and Carla arrived. The three of us were laughing and enjoying drinks while Margot was putting the final touches on dinner. We eventually sat down at the dinner table and dug in. The conversation went around and around as typically expected at family functions. Of course, always being one with the honesty, I unintentionally turned the conversation on its ear.

My cousin Tabitha asked, "Any love life news?"

"Not really. I met this girl at Harry's Bar a few weeks ago and ended up taking her to dinner," I said and continued, "Actually, Carla, I was in your neck of the woods. The White Dog Café in University City. You know it?"

Carla said, "Yeah, good spot. That's really close to where I live."

I replied, "The food was great. I ended up going to hang out at her place. It was somewhere called Myer Hall."

"Ew, what floor?" Carla asked as if already afraid of my answer.

"Second," I said.

"*Ew*, that's my building and *my floor*! You're a scumbag! Who was it? I bet it was Melissa, oh, my God, it was Melissa, wasn't it? *Ew*. Well, at least she's pretty." Carla was totally disgusted.

It was the girl Carla thought, and maybe I had become a scumbag? Some creepy older, coed predator. I have to say I was not embarrassed. Not that it was a particularly proud conquest, but even though I am an emotional person, I am also quite vain. I felt this made me still young and viable in some way, so I took it in, silently, as a victory. The rest of dinner went as planned, and I managed not to offend anyone else that night.

Long Distance Lust Affair

My friend, Dillon Black and his wife love to host holiday costume parties. I'd been going to them for years, and the '09 Fourth of July celebration had been a redneck theme. The Confederate flag was less than politically correct, but, otherwise, it was a riot to see everyone in costume, poking fun. Dillion is the tattoo artist that did all my ink, and his commitment to these parties is off the charts. His cutoff denims, sleeveless red-checked flannel and fake buck teeth were spot-on, but the real showstopper was his hair. He had had long flowing locks for over a decade and had decided to cut them into a proper mullet just for the occasion. It was glorious. Although he set the bar, the twenty or so guests did not disappoint. I knew about twenty percent of the people and wished the other eighty were hot strippers looking for discounted ink. No such luck. My friend Paul Spencer came in with his girlfriend, Maria, and another girl.

"Yo, Paul, over here!" I yelled.

"Hey, Brian, what's shakin', dude?" Paul said.

"Not much. Maria, nice to see you."

"Hi, Brian, this is my sister Jillian." Maria was always nice to me, but it never seemed genuine.

"Hi, Jillian, very nice to meet you," I said. She smiled and returned the sentiment.

"She's visiting from Michigan, so we figured she needed to experience one of Dillion's costume parties," Maria said.

"Cool. They are always a good time. Halloween is the best, so if you're ever around you should come to one of those," I said.

Jillian replied, "Ooh, that sounds fun. I *love* Halloween."

Jillian was not much to look at, but she was packing a punch from the neck down. She was also wearing cut-off jean shorts, and a skintight tank top that read, "Blink if you want me." Her cowboy boots sold me. Over the previous year, I had been fucking twenty-something coeds like a factory worker pounding out fidget spinners. I was always in *hunting* mode. During the course of the day, the eye contact between Jillian and me acknowledged a mutual attraction. She turned out to be the aggressor. Jillian followed me into the bathroom and pressed me to the wall. I found her forward nature attractive; there was something sexy about her. We made out until there was a knock on the door from someone doing the pee pee dance. We left and, before the end of the night, we exchanged numbers.

The next day, after several back and forth texts, Jillian called me. I tried to talk her into coming to my house before going back to Michigan, but my pleas fell on deaf ears. In fact, she had been talking to Maria and was convinced I was a *player* just planning to use her for sex. I didn't realize Maria felt that way but, it was probably the truest moniker I could have been branded with. I insisted she come over, and I could feel her close to caving to my invitation. I had her on the hook but not enough to get her driving in my direction.

Jillian was back in Michigan by the time she contacted me again. I had given her my email address and we soon became Facebook friends.

She wrote to me one day,

> *Hey Brian,*
> *I promised you a picture. I don't go around showing these, even though I don't find one thing wrong with it! I think only two people have ever seen them at all, so I'm like a picture sending virgin! So... Shhhh*
>
> *Jill*

The picture was of her but not revealing. Although she was naked, the picture was pretty tame. It made her look much prettier than I remembered.

I wrote her back and said, "By the way, you mentioned *them* when you referenced the picture. Are there more?"

"Who gets naked in front of a camera and takes just one picture? Laugh, but I may have misplaced them... Getting out of dodge for the weekend, talk soon."

Days went by without any contact.

"I'm so sleepy tonight and in the mood for a snuggle partner. You came to mind. Just a thought," Jillian wrote.

"You've disregarded me so long I almost forget what you look like. It's shameful the way you've ignored me," I responded.

I soon received an email with the subject, "This was kinda fun." The email included seven pictures of her from the neck down mostly dressed in a see-through bra.

I replied to her email. "You seriously need to jump on a plane. You're killing me with these pictures."

Jillian wrote, "I just took care of a little business thinking of you. What is it with you anyway? You're like the mystery man that I crave. We have to really consider getting together!"

"The next time you decide to 'take care of business' would you mind sending *that* to me? And I enjoy the fact that you *crave* me because the feeling has been very mutual lately. Let me know when you get that plane ticket."

"You are so damn adorable it's not even funny. Yes, I do *crave* you. So much actually it's driving me crazy! Don't doubt I'm coming. "

A couple weeks passed with similar conversations which only heightened the sexual tension when I got the following text.

"I actually got a plane ticket! Am I crazy? You didn't think I was going to do it, did you? I'm kinda surprised at myself actually. We're keeping this hush hush correct? Have a good weekend," Jillian wrote and seemed excited. I know I was.

"That's cool. What's your drink of choice? Only 10 days away. Tick, tick," I said.

"You don't need to get me drunk first, I'm sure you'll get lucky even if I'm sober."

The day came, and I pulled into the Philadelphia International Airport on Saturday, September 12, around ten-forty-five a.m. I drove down to the US Airlines arrival gate, and she was waiting right under the sign as promised. I jumped out, gave her a quick hug and put her luggage in the trunk. We were off.

"You didn't say anything to Paul about my coming, did you?" Jillian sounded concerned.

"No, I haven't even talked to him. When we're not in the middle of dart season, our communication is touch and go."

"Good, Maria would give me hell if she knew I flew in to see you."

"She really thinks that poorly of me, huh?" Her lack of answer told me all I needed to know.

We pulled into the driveway and I wasn't even in the house when she pushed me through the door. Her anticipation was overflowing, and I needed to calm her rising tide. I didn't want to play the end of the movie before the opening credits started, so I decided the only way to satisfy her was to give her an orgasm. I realized she was going to be insatiable. I kissed my way down to her waist and her hands guided where she wanted my lips next. Several minutes and convulsions later, she was satiated, temporarily. We spent a few hours talking and then got dressed to go out. I took her to Buddakan for dinner and then Helium Comedy Club for a show. I can't recall the show because my concentration was on her hands diving under the table. This girl was unquenchable. As we drove back to my house, she was completely naked by the time I turned into my cul-de-sac. Thankfully I lived on a quiet street, and it was a couple minutes past eleven. She was standing there beside me, naked and only holding her heels, as I fumbled to put the key in the front door. She ran straight upstairs and once I followed, she was lying spread-eagled on the bed. We spent the next hour and a half fulfilling all the promises we had made in weeks of text exchanges.

She drifted off, so I went downstairs, poured a drink, and walked out on the patio to smoke a well-earned cigarette. I had just finished a second when she came out in my black terrycloth robe. The sash was not cinched in the middle, so she was walking across the patio like Darth Vader with perfect tits. I went inside to refresh my drink and poured her a glass of wine. She had helped herself to my stash of smokes. We both raised our glasses and smiled. She would be on a plane back to Michigan by four p.m. the next day, so we were running out of time. We talked for hours and I realized she was much more than a horny woman. She seemed a little lost and lonely and maybe a touch vulnerable. Tears began streaming down her face as she told me she needed to find happiness. True happiness. All the sexual tension had dissipated, and I was left with a person I hadn't seen coming. A person I wasn't prepared for and, certainly, not a person I needed. She lived 800 miles away, and I was at least that far away from being ready to handle something serious. She continued to apologize for the waterworks.

"You have nothing to apologize for, Jill. I understand where you are coming from."

"I just need to find someone who will make me happy. My previous relationship crashed and burned in fantastic fashion. I moved to Michigan for him, leaving everyone I knew behind. His friends became my friends. My *only* friends at that point, and when he moved out, I was left with nothing but a job I hate, in a place I hate and my son, who I love dearly. I need more. I need tenderness and intimacy. Not just a good fuck. Don't take that the wrong way. It was great and I am so happy I came, several times actually." She laughed at her own pun. "You know what I meant. And then you had to go and turn out to be this great guy. I didn't expect you to be a total asshole, but I didn't see me feeling like this. God, I'm pathetic."

"Stop it. I'm glad you came too." Now I was laughing. "This has been so much fun, and I really needed it. You're a great person, and you will find someone great to share your life with. You certainly are a catch."

Jillian came around the table, plopped into my lap and planted a big kiss on my cheek. As she was draped over me, the robe hung open leaving much of her body exposed. I wanted to have her again, but I restrained myself and gave her what I thought she really needed at that point, a hug. I took her back up to bed and held her through the night.

When Jillian woke up the next day, I greeted her with the best Dunkin' Donuts had to offer that morning. We drank coffee and shared a bagel. We had been up fairly late, so by the time she woke up, it was eleven-forty-five in the morning. I needed to get her to the airport no later than two, so there was no time for extracurricular activities, not that they were appropriate at this point. The conversation that transpired that previous night took the wind out of our sexual encounter. I drove her back to the airport and after a warm hug and close-mouthed kiss goodbye, she was off.

When she got back to Michigan, I got a text that included a wide range of emotions. The *I'm sorry's* beat out the *thank you's* by a wide margin but for no good reason. She was human, after all, and it was obvious that even though she came to visit a player that only wanted her sexually, she got to know someone that had much more feeling than she anticipated. It was flattering. The idea of a long-distance booty call partner was now in the rearview mirror. Over the next month we exchanged emails, and, although they were flirtatious, there was a more serious tone. She was confessing to liking me more and more. I sent her an email telling her I didn't have the capacity for anything serious. I didn't hear from her for almost a week.

I then received a voicemail stating how she was concerned about the existence of all the graphic photos and the masturbation video she had sent. She asked if I could delete all traces of them. When I didn't return her call right away, she emailed.

> "Since you knew it was bothering me, I just want to say thank you 'friend' for confirmation of the received message… You're awesome! I kind of figured you didn't care either way if I dropped off the face of the earth but did hope you had some care for my feelings. Maybe I put too much on you, totally my fault."

I responded, "Jill, I'm really sorry I didn't get a chance to get back to you earlier. My life over the last two weeks has been nothing but a blur. I did receive your message and I will obey your wishes, but I honestly was a bit confused by your voicemail as it seemed a bit out of left field. I was in no way avoiding you. I'm not sure why this is bothering you all of a sudden but, again, I apologize for not being prompt with my reply."

Jill responded, "Thanks for getting back to me. Not sure why it bothered me all of a sudden. All I can figure is that life is caving in on me, and I'm falling into a very unhappy place and truly not used to being unhappy; usually pretty optimistic. You've been the only person I've had to lift me up, and that's not fair to you since you don't want to be that person anyway. Being in your arms was the safest I felt in a long time, and that can play with your head.

Removing myself is for the best while I have my life breakdown. Thank you for the last few months."

I replied, "I'm sorry to hear you are having a tough time. I really don't have the capacity to give you more of a presence. I'm not close to ready for any of this. I wish you well and thank you for the fun memories we shared."

Jill wrote, "I wasn't planning on writing you back, but it bothered me how I may have come across. I honestly expected and wanted nothing other than a little fun. You smell so good too. I could melt. You were my escape from reality and my excuse for not dealing with the tremendous loss I've experienced the last few months. After a few cries and a new future plan I will be fine. Sorry for throwing my stupid, shitty drama on your lap. It's not really my style and kind of embarrassing. No need to reply."

I didn't.

Two days later she wrote, "I'm drinking and watching sad movies and can't help but to write you and say, Why? Why are you always on my mind? I guess email is harmless enough. It could be worse. I could be leaving cookies on your doorstep."

I was getting irritated and decided to reply. "Jill, I'm sorry I haven't responded. I was a bit put off by some of the things you said and with all the craziness I've experienced over the last few years I really am trying to avoid the drama. I was in no way trying to be a dick to you about it, so avoiding the situation was the way I dealt with it. It probably wasn't the mature way, but I always find myself in fucked up situations, and after the great conversations and times we shared I wasn't expecting the reaction I received from you. I hope all is well in your world. Good luck."

Jill wrote back. "What did I say? I would really like to know. It's hard for me to say sorry for being passionate and having high emotions. I'm sorry if I said something that hurt your feelings or pissed you off. I ache even thinking that is true. I understand what you say and agree with the craziness my life has been lately. I really don't like it either. Honestly, a lot of it has to do with confusion. And YOU (like it or not) have been in the mix of all of it. I'm venturing into new territory and unfortunately, we haven't been friends long enough (if EVER) to know me as a person, which is unfortunate."

Aaaaand, here comes the crazy.

"YOU KNOW, the more I think about it, were you just using the situation with me as an ego boost? How did that totally and completely escape me? You hate the fact that I actually began to care for you. As soon as I had any actual emotions you got uncomfortable. Now *I'm* a little put off. So, we weren't really friends after all. Maybe you are just as shallow as I heard. I sensed something in you that was so special but maybe I was out to lunch. Well, add me to the list, I suppose. I'm just really sad right now because all I want to do is hug someone that doesn't want to hug me back. Sorry if I have too much emotion for you. If I feel sexy and want to send pictures of my pussy, they will go to you! JUST FUCKING DELETE ME ALREADY!"

I finally tried to end this nonsense. "OK, I think this is getting out of hand and as I said before I really can't deal with the drama. My life has enough of that already. Did you boost my ego with your attention? Sure, but please do not think that is foreign to me. I fed into it because it was fresh, fun and exciting. I appreciated everything you said and thought you caught a glimpse of who I am. I also thought you realized I was not the person previously described to you. If you feel that was a front, I don't know what to tell you, but I feel no need to defend myself. You can think of me what you feel you need to. I know who I am and who I am not.

As far as emotion is concerned, I was totally up front with you regarding my ability to give anyone any kind of emotion past what I have to this point (however minimal that may seem to you). I am nowhere near giving anyone true love at this point in my life. My wounds from previous failed relationships dictate my actions. As far as sending me anything further, please do not. It was fun and lighthearted in the beginning, but those terms no longer apply and have been replaced with angst, hurt feelings and dialogue that could not be further from where it began.

I think you're a nice person and have no real problem with you on the whole. I feel at this point maybe we should part ways and focus on the happiness we both deserve. I'm sorry if I, in any way, made you feel bad about this situation. It was definitely not my intention. Be well."

Jill wrote back, "I was extremely attracted to you, wanted to fuck you, desired & dreamed of you, finally got to fuck you, then missed you, needed a friend, turned to you, shouldn't have, my fault (I suppose), still in this time wanting to fuck you again. My fault. Sorry for the drama. Hope we can meet and fuck in better circumstances. Be well. I won't bother you anymore"

Jillian continued to write emotionally erratic emails over the next couple months. I cannot tell you why I didn't delete or block her. If I'm being honest with you and myself, I needed the attention. I needed someone out there to care. As unhealthy as it may have been, I needed it. Ultimately, she was harmless, but she was probably right in some ways. Maybe I did need the ego boost. I never responded, and she was months away from suffering the same fate as forty percent of my Facebook friends.

Finally, True Love

I had been going to therapy for about three and a half years to deal with the anger that plagued me. Going to see Michael became a balancing act, as I navigated through my past and did my best to hide the depravity my life had become. I found I juggled truth and deceit effortlessly. Although I went there to deal with anger, I learned so much more. I clawed through seven layers of battle-tested armor in those sessions, exposing the experiences of my childhood and adolescent life. Many recollections involved my parents and the subconscious reasons behind my life-mate choices. I had grown up watching my mother struggle to find happiness in her relationships.

My mom was a woman of stature, standing at five-foot-ten inches. Her blue-green eyes told the story of her life. You could see just how much she loved you. You could also see the pain. Her smile was infectious but not always present. I thought, through the eyes of a son, she was mentally one of the strongest people I knew. I would later realize just how broken and dependent she was.

My mother grew up always knowing she was a lesbian. It was a time in our country when living an alternate lifestyle wasn't just frowned upon, it was believed to be immoral and judged accordingly, even within her own family. She was the oldest of seven. It turned out she had a gay younger brother, Bobby, and according to accounts from my father, a sister that "dabbled in her fair share of pussy." My mom had explained that being with my father was a combination of social pressures and true attraction. Apparently, before the alcohol took hold, he was handsome, charming, and, she would say, "could sell an Eskimo ice chipped from their own igloo."

Mom married Ray Schreiber at some point based on pictures I saw, and she gave birth to my brother around the same time. My mother was eighteen when Brady was born. I would show up roughly five years later, and we lived for a couple of years as a typical nuclear family. My father's mental and physical beatings eventually took their toll on her. Infidelity was the least of mom's concerns. Ray's charm wasted away, and our escape had become about survival.

Over the next fourteen years, mom went through relationships with Sophia and Janette, but, mostly, she was repeating history. The only real difference was their gender. These women were certainly not as mentally or physically abusive as my father had been, but they caused her damage, nonetheless. These women drank and fought with her until there was nothing left but to say goodbye.

After she left Janette, Mom moved in with my brother, but, within a few months, she was moving again. My mother was jumping into another quick relationship. This time would prove different. I spent the next dozen years watching, with envy, the true joy. I'm sure they argued as lovers do, but Margot was not cast from the same mold as the women that had come before her. Margot didn't really drink, and for the first time my mom found someone who only saw her. That didn't change my mother's dependence. She still needed someone to take care of her, financially. She paid her way by keeping a clean house and making an award-winning meatloaf. Margot and Mom spent their time proving to me true love was possible. I had convinced myself I would never find it.

All the tales leading up to this point are meanderings of a man on a rudderless journey to nowhere. I'd amassed an exhaustive collection of stories to tell at a bar and have men envy, but I really had nothing. Nothing meaningful. At times, I felt as though I was reliving my father's life. I was taller, slightly better looking, and, in comparison, more successful professionally, but at my core, just as damaged. I was haunted by his memory and in some subconscious way, his equal. I maintained my self-awareness and recognized the collision course I was on, but I was not strong enough to keep the train on the tracks. I stumbled into a bottle like clockwork, daily, and used every girl I convinced to say yes as a temporary companion to combat the loneliness. Toward the end of this period, I was drinking and fucking so much that getting an erection was like pulling a single yes out of a hatful of *no's*. In the dead of night, with a belly full of whiskey, I cried uncontrollably, wondering when I would finally drink myself to death. My mother was gone, I had fathered no children, I had disowned my entire bloodline, and although I was blessed with a vast compilation of close friends, I felt utterly alone.

And then everything changed. My life went from being an airliner with two blown engines falling from the sky to one now jetting toward salvation. I no longer needed to write this book. Finishing it would not be my destiny or my legacy. I never intended to be an author. I wrote out of sadness, a loyal bottle of scotch at my side. As it turned out, this would be my true love story.

Broken Window

I had been at work on an otherwise uneventful day, when on my way to lunch I saw a beautiful woman crossing the parking lot. I wanted to know her. She got into her Ford Taurus X and was gone, but I never forget her long, poker-straight, dark brown hair, legs that went on for miles only concealed by an impeccably fitted black pencil skirt, high heels, and a smile I would never *unsee* again. I had no idea who this woman was and spent endless lunches leaving at the same time, hoping. I even found myself grabbing lunch and eating in the parking lot. Still hoping. On the day I first saw her, she could have been a transient passing through, never to return again. Those thoughts went through my mind. I pushed them away. I never forgot her smile. I was left hoping, but not quite obsessed. My resiliency wore down as the weeks passed, and I eventually stopped basing my lunch on the time and only scanned the parking lot as I drove off. But ever still, hoping.

Weeks later, she appeared and was walking though the office as though she had a purpose. *What was it?* Today she wore a navy pantsuit. Her hair was now in a ponytail and her smile brightened the entire room. She took my breath away, and then she was gone. I saw her speak with my co-worker, Rob, before she fled and immediately went to finally find out this mysterious stranger's identity. I needed to know her. I guess at this point, I was a little obsessed. Rob told me her name was Veronica. She was the building's property manager and here to promote a blood drive. *Great, needles.* I coerced Rob to get me on the donor's signup sheet directly below her. This was my premeditation.

I was nervous when I woke up the day of the blood drive. Talking to women was never my issue. Maybe I was anxious about having a steel rod jammed in my arm as the life blood was sucked out of me. Or maybe she was just *the one*. Nervous or not, I was about to meet her.

I took the stairwell and walked two floors down to the same parking lot where I had spent weeks on a daily stakeout. This time, there was no doubt she was there. I arrived a few minutes early to ensure we would cross paths. There was a huge Red Cross sign on the bus, mocking me. I climbed on, and there she was sitting on a gurney with a needle taped to her arm. The nurse told me to sit tight, so I grabbed a seat across from her. I sat there waiting, staring at her in an attempt to catch her gaze. Veronica was in another pair of navy slacks, this time pinstriped. She wore a tan long-sleeve blouse, a single button undone, the left side folded up neatly to accommodate the nurses work area. She had both legs stretched out across the gurney and was clicking the tops of her candy-red heels, Nine West stamped on the bottom. A cell phone was clenched between her ear and right shoulder the entire time. Her eyes were focused on the blacked-out window of the bus. I watched as her blood collected into the bag. It felt like an eternity. *Look at me!* Not even a fleeting glance. She was wholly immersed in her phone call. The nurse came back and freed the shackles that were draining her, and she left. No hello, no goodbye. Nothing. She was gone. I was devastated. I sat there momentarily stunned and wanted to run off the bus to force the encounter. Before I could make a run for it, the nurse was in front of me and as I refocused back to reality, I heard her say, "You're next." It took two glasses of orange juice and twenty minutes before I was allowed to leave. I haven't given blood since.

It was a beautiful spring day. My office housed three floor-to-ceiling, double-hung windows. I opened the first window. The second was behind my desk, so I hopped over it and propped open the window. I felt an unexpected weight as the top frame gave way and came crashing towards me. I was able to catch it in time without the glass breaking. I managed to safely set the window back in its tracks and secure the latch. I wasn't hurt. The office manager called maintenance. I imagined my father walking through the door and saying, "Hey, Boog, what's the problem?" He didn't, and neither did any maintenance person. I looked up to see Veronica walking through the office, and then she was coming toward me. My moment was finally here, and I had not planned for any of it. Serendipity in its truest form. I was speechless and then not. We talked about the disagreeable window, and ultimately, I had demands. I felt it only fair for her to at least take me to lunch as reparation for the actions of her offending window.

Veronica conceded and told me to meet her in the parking lot.

"I'll be out front in a gray Ford Taurus SUV," she said.

I went out the front doors and, as promised, she was waiting with *that* smile.

"Where are we going?" I asked.

"This is *your* extortion, not mine. You pick. And I'm not from around here anyway."

"Extortion? I could have been killed. Have a little compassion."

"*Please!*" It was the first time I heard her laugh. I later added it to the list of things I adored about her.

"KitchenBar, it's up here about a mile on the left. You'll have to pass it and make a U-bee," I instructed.

She made the U-turn and pulled into the restaurant's parking lot. She said, "Thank you, kind sir," when I opened the front door. The hostess ensured there were only two of us, and we sat at a table meant for four people. The menu was placed on the seats facing each other, but I chose to take the seat next to her. She was not in her typical attire. That day, she wore tight blue jeans and a thin, multicolored long-sleeve top. The arms were tight but the material around her body was loose and flowing. She had on brand new low-top white Converse sneakers.

"Is it dress-down Wednesday?"

She squinted her eyes at me and said, "No, smartass. I wasn't supposed to be here today. I left my calendar when I was here yesterday and had to pick it up. I can't live without it." I could see her measuring me up and trying to figure out if I was an asshole or not.

"Why are you staring at me?" She said.

"Because you are very pretty. I'm sure that happens all the time. Does it bother you?"

She said, "No, but it doesn't happen all the time. It never happens."

Her misplaced modesty made me laugh. The waitress came by and took our orders. Two iced teas, a turkey club and side salad for her, dressing on the side, and a cheesesteak with mushrooms for me.

"I have to say, it was kind of neat how you conned me into a date," she admitted.

"A *date*?"

"Well, I mean lunch. You know what I mean. Don't twist my words," she said defiantly. There was a hint of sass in her voice. I liked it.

"Hey, *you* said date, not me." I held my hands up as if to surrender.

The waitress brought out our food and I picked on it. I had no appetite for anything but Veronica.

"What's your deal?"

"My deal? What do you mean 'my deal'?" She seemed annoyed by the question.

"You know, are you single, married, kids?"

"I'm separated and I have two girls. Fifteen and five."

"You seeing anyone?" I continued to badger the witness.

"Not currently. It's a little complicated. What about you?"

"I was married for four years. Didn't stick. No kids. Regretfully."

"Regretfully?"

"Yeah, I always wanted them. Girls really. Just didn't work out. She wasn't the one."

"There's still time." She said it but I didn't believe her. "Okay, so you are divorced with no kids. Girlfriend? Or *girlfriends*?"

"No one special."

"What are you looking for?"

"Twenty-seven, not married, no kids." *Yes, I really said this and, yes, I'm an idiot, I know.*

"Huh? Seriously."

"Kinda, yeah. I guess." I was already regretting saying it. Veronica was looking at me wondering why I had even conned her into lunch. We sat there as if we were in a staring contest. She blinked but didn't turn away and smiled in defeat. The smile I will never *unsee*.

"I'm not sure I get you. I'm not sure I even *like* you."

"Oh, you like me. You would have declined my offer for you to buy me lunch. Politely, but you would have said no. Made up some place you had to be. Something." She knew I was right. She would have blown me off as I'm sure she had done to others many times, probably without realizing it.

The waitress cleared our plates and dropped the check. I picked it up and was taking out my wallet to pay.

"Oh no, that's *not* happening. You blackmailed me into this and I'm not going to have you holding it over my head that I didn't end up paying."

"I'm beginning to get offended. That's rude. I was just trying to be chivalrous."

"Save it for the twenty-seven-year-old with no kids."

"*Ouch*, you're mean."

"You said it, not me," she said. I couldn't tell if she was truly being sarcastic or serious. As I got to know her, I would think back and realize it was a mixture of both.

We pulled up to the same spot where she had picked me up.

"Door to door service, nice. Thank you for lunch."

"You're welcome, now get out. I have to be back in Jersey by two."

"Can I at least get your phone number before you throw me out?"

"I'm not twenty-seven."

"I'll make an exception."

She gave me her business card and told me her cell was on it. I reached for the card and grabbed her hand before pulling away. My heart jumped a little.

"It was very nice to meet you, Veronica."

"You too, Brian."

I hopped out and watched her drive away.

We exchanged texts over the next couple weeks and she showed up to the building more than usual. Veronica always made me need to catch my breath a little.

About a month later, I was pulling out of the parking lot and noticed her car two ahead of mine. I decided to follow her even though she was heading in the polar opposite direction from where I was going. In hot pursuit, we got to a point, on Cottman Avenue in Philadelphia, where she made a right-hand turn. Barnard Avenue to be precise, and I'll never forget. She stopped in front of some random house. I pulled in behind her. We got out of our cars and walked towards each other. We did not speak. We exchanged smiles right before the embrace. I could have held her forever. I wish she never let go that day.

"Can I take you out some night?"

"You sure I'm not too old for you?" she asked sharply.

I didn't say anything. I just stood there biting my lip.

She relented, "What were you thinking?"

"Dinner, maybe a movie. You like movies?"

"Sure," she said. We were now in the midst of another staring contest.

"How's Friday, seven?"

"No good, Saturday would work if that's good for you?"

"That works. Seven o'clock. Where do you live? I'll pick you up."

"No, too soon, I'll meet you," she said.

I hadn't even realized we were holding hands. She was swinging them into her hips to some beat or rhythm in her head. We were done here. I winked and she let go of my hands. As Veronica turned and walked away, I asked, "That's it?"

She turned back and said, "For now." We drove away in opposite directions.

Over the next few days we texted often and about everything. I was getting to know her, and I liked her more and more. She was now a real person and not just a celestial creature donating blood on a bus. We decided to meet in the parking lot at the Lowe's Theater in Cherry Hill. I felt like a teenager when her Taurus X pulled up next to me. I jumped out of my Acura TSX to greet her. She reminded me of Sandra Dee in the carnival scene at the end of *Grease*. It wasn't the outfit but her presence. In that moment, I embodied Danny Zuko in his letterman's sweater. She made me feel like I didn't need the cool guy façade, and we hadn't even started our first date. Veronica Hurenko stood slightly over five-seven. She was wearing a fitted, off-white button-down blouse, skintight jeans and black four-inch heels. My knees practically buckled when she approached me. With heels, she was only a couple inches shorter than I was, so the kiss she placed on my cheek was effortless. When she said, "Hi," as she pulled away, I could almost taste the peppermint on her warm breath. I broke from her hypnotic spell and opened the passenger side door of my car. We drove to dinner. The conversation was effortless, and I was both comfortable and excited. Her smile was intoxicating. She had me if she wanted; I was all in. After dinner, we sat at the exit of the parking lot, movie theater to the left, my house, in the distance, to the right. Our eyes met and, silently, we agreed we wouldn't be watching *Toy Story 3* that night. We arrived at my house a little after ten. I locked the front door and turned to see she was sitting on the carpet-lined staircase taking off her shoes. "They're killing me," she confessed. I fell to my knees before her and helped her slip them off. We were now at eye level. I went in for our first kiss. It was slow and tender. The flowery scent of jasmine from her Burberry perfume drew me to her neck. Veronica inhaled sharply as I gripped the crest of her hip bone protruding from the top of her jeans. We slowly made our way up the stairs, a couple at a time. When we reached the top, I motioned towards my room. She ran into the bedroom and flung herself backwards on the California King. We spent the next few hours never satisfying an unquenchable thirst. We drove back, admitting to each other how hard it was to abstain. I dropped her back at her car, reluctantly, that night about three-thirty in the morning. Wanting more. She always left me wanting more.

Over the next couple weeks, I pretty much stopped writing, but I kept drinking. It was a problem, and I was hiding it from everyone. Veronica and I were texting frequently, but I didn't see her. At the time, I had been casually dating a girl named Susan. I went to her house a couple times between my first and second dates with Veronica but avoided sex. I had had only had one date with Veronica, but it was enough to know I wasn't really interested in anyone else, so I broke it off with Sue.

Our second date might have had me running in the other direction. We went to dinner at my friend Gabe Franco's house. He and his wife, Abigail, were my bullshit detectors, and I needed to get Veronica under their watchful, protective eye. In Gabe's usual fashion, dinner was about an hour later than planned, and as fate would have it, Veronica got a call that pulled us away before dinner was ever served. The call was from her Uncle Roman. Baba —her grandmother— had gotten hurt and was in the hospital. Baba was in her late 80's and not in the best health. As we raced to Hahnemann University hospital, Veronica also raced to set the scene for what I was about to witness. Uncle Roman was a very intelligent, talkative drunk who would hate me on first sight. Baba would never hate me but probably not understand why I was there and, since she was blind, she would never see me at all. Roman spoke English, Baba did not. We reached the hospital and found Baba's room but not Roman. Veronica rushed to her grandmother's side, and as she spoke in Ukrainian, their hands effortlessly connected as if for the millionth time. Veronica turned to me, as I would see her do in our future, with pain and sorrow in her eyes. Although she was visibly upset, her Baba would never know it. She spoke as if she had full command of herself and the situation. Once Uncle Roman's voice called to Veronica, she jumped up, and the desperate look on her face vanished. She met Roman halfway in the room, and before she could introduce me, he said rudely, "Who's this?" Veronica had warned me in advance, so I paid him no mind but jumped up to greet him with a handshake.

Baba asked who was in the room, and from what I later learned, Veronica told her I was *just a friend*. Roman added comments as well, but Veronica claimed to not recall what he said in their native Ukrainian tongue. Roman kept taking turns between sitting by his mother's side and on a bar stool across the street from the hospital. He was much more open about his drinking problem than I was. During one of his absences, Veronica received a call that got me out of this situation. It at least provided a temporary reprieve.

It was Bella, her oldest daughter and she needed safe passage. She explained to Veronica how her father was supposed to take her home and now that he was drunk, she refused to get in the car with him. *I wish I had been so wise when I was presented with the same choices back in '84.* Veronica pulled the phone from her ear and with a pinched face, hesitantly asked, "Do you mind going to get her?"

"Of course not," I replied.

Bella, her father, and the rest of his clan were at her Uncle Will's house in Port Richmond. The house was two blocks from toxic Elena's mother's house, and when I pulled up, I thought Elena's mom could probably feel the pulse of the bass from her couch. At least a dozen people spilled out of the house onto the porch. Through the crowd, a short, brown-skinned girl separated from the pack. She was crossing the street, and although I didn't immediately see a resemblance to Veronica, I thought this was Bella. She presented me with a little wave, and I smiled. When she smiled back, I was sure it was her. She got in, and when she thanked me, I could sense the frustration in her voice.

I asked, "You want to talk about it?"

"No."

I had literally met Bella five seconds before, so I understood. After a few minutes of silence, I tried to crack the ice. "So, this is super weird. How's your night going? Mine's been… interesting." I said very matter-of-factly.

She laughed. "Stop it. This has to be, like, so awkward for you," she said.

"Lil' bit," I admitted.

As we drove down Route 95 South, the streetlights sparkled in her glazed-over eyes, and, in this moment, she looked like her mother.

Now serious, I said, "It's all good, no judgment here. Just happy to be able to help. And, hey, nice to meet you." Our eyes met and we exchanged a smile as she wiped a tear from her eye.

"Thanks. Nice to meet you too. Mom really likes you."

"Oh, so you've heard about me. Okay. Cool. Good, I hope."

"So far."

My cell phone rang, and I put it on the blue-tooth speaker in the car.

"How's Bella?" Veronica asked.

"I'm fine," Bella responded. "Daddy's an asshole."

"Well, you know how he gets. Baba is going to have to stay overnight. Roman is shitfaced. Brian, would you mind taking Roman back home and then dropping us off?"

"No, of course I don't mind. Do you want us to come up to the room?"

"No, we'll meet you outside the main entrance on Broad Street. Is that okay?"

"Absolutely. We should be pulling up in a few minutes. See you then." Veronica broke the connection.

I pulled in front of the hospital entrance on Broad Street, and Bella jumped out and got in the back. Veronica opened the back door for Roman and then got in the front. She clutched my hand as if it were the only thing stopping her from exploding. She held it tight the entire way back to her grandmother's house. Roman was slurring something in Ukrainian the entire way. I'm not sure I would have understood it in English. I think he thanked me when he got out of the car. Veronica got him safely into the house and when she returned to the car, she lost her composure.

"Oh, my fucking God. I'm so sorry, I didn't mean that, God. Bel, you would never believe it. Roman was so drunk. He had apparently been drinking all day and stepped on Baba's foot. He ripped the nail off her toe, and it wouldn't stop bleeding. It was still seeping a bit when we left. She'd not in any condition for this. That motherfucker. Brian, I'm sorry. I didn't mean for you to see this. At least not so soon."

"Welcome to the family," Bella said from the backseat. She continued, "What an absolute train wreck."

Veronica was still holding my hand. I looked over to her and squeezed in three quick pulses.

"It's not even funny, I'm so angry right now." Veronica was stewing the rest of the way home.

We pulled into Veronica's driveway. I was exhausted by this experience, so I can only imagine what they were going through.

"Fun time, thanks," I said and chuckled.

"I'm sorry," Veronica whispered.

I then realized Bella had fallen asleep in the back of the car. "It was a rough night, but a memorable second date. Hard to top this one but let's try, okay?"

"Okay." She leaned in and kissed me on the cheek. "I wouldn't blame you if this was too much, you know."

"And miss all this, not a chance." I lean in and stole a quick kiss on the lips.

Veronica woke up Bella, and they made their way into the house. Regardless of the lunacy of the night, I went home and poured a tall scotch thinking what it would be like to have these girls in my life.

I met Veronica's youngest, Samantha, on May 8, 2010. It was Saturday morning, and I was running a 5k in tribute to a friend lost to a drunk driver in high school. Veronica and I had been dating for nearly a month, so she was comfortable enough to let me meet Sam. They showed up, and I was surrounded by friends when they approached. Sam looked petrified. She was skinny as a rail with mid-length brown curls and enormous plastic-rimmed glasses. Like her mother's, her features were very small. They made her smile all that more pronounced and the gaps in her teeth made her all the more adorable. Other than a bashful wave and a mumble of a greeting she was silent and clinging to her mother's hip.

"She okay?" I whispered in Veronica's ear.

"Just shy, she's fine."

I gathered with the competitors and readied for the race. I looked over and saw Veronica with Sam in front of her. Both now smiling. Veronica smiled —*that smile I'll never unsee*— and I was off. I finished the race in a little over twenty-six minutes and found them at the finish line offering me an orange Gatorade. They didn't know it was my favorite, but they gained points just the same. I asked if they wanted to go to lunch after, but they had other plans. One of my closest friends from high school, Danielle, asked me to come by her house. She said her kids were home and would love to see me. I agreed and went over. Once I got there, I saw the abundance of cars, and some I recognized. I walked into a surprise fortieth birthday party. My closest friends all stood clapping and smiling. And then I saw Veronica and Samantha. Danielle got in touch with Veronica and invited them to come. While we were out back playing lawn games, telling jokes and drinking, Sam began gravitating toward me. She never ventured too far from Veronica, but the ice was breaking. I couldn't have asked for a better surprise party.

I spent more and more time with Veronica. As time passed, we grew closer, and Veronica would text me and say they were ordering take-out. It was my invitation to eat with the girls. That grew into a couple times a week ritual.

Veronica came to my house one Friday night and planned to stay the weekend. Sam was with her father and Bella was staying with a girlfriend. I had an oversized chair and a 50" flat screen TV in the third-floor loft. Since Chloe moved out, it had become my favorite room in the house. That night, Veronica and I sat side-by-side on that chair and fed each other lo mein right out of the container. She cheated and used a fork.

"Great lo mein, right?" I asked.

"Very good."

"Golden Palace. They're the best. Do you want that egg roll?" I effectively willed her to say no.

"You said you have a brother, didn't you?" Veronica asked.

"Yeah, Brady. He lives with his wife in Jacksonville. Well, I assume he still does."

"Assume? When was the last time you talked to him?"

"June 28th, 2005."

"That's *very* specific," Veronica said.

"It was the day of my mother's funeral. It's a long story that I can tell you about later, but basically, I disowned my entire family the day we buried mom. So, what about you? You have siblings?" I tried to change the subject. I hated talking about my blood relatives.

"I didn't *disown* anyone. Well, okay, you know my Baba. She is my heart. She basically raised me. Um, you know my Uncle Roman. Unfortunately." She laughed at herself. "I have a brother, Ray. We were never close until he got clean a few years ago. He lives with his wife and daughter in Pittsburgh."

"Ray. That was my father's name. There's another *doozy* of a story. Sorry, go ahead," I gestured for her to continue.

"Can't wait to hear about *that*. Okay. Well, my mother died on the operating table eight years ago during surgery."

"Oh, my God, I'm so sorry." I was holding her hand. —*three quick pulses.*

"I'm okay now. It feels like a long time ago. And my *father*, he died on the train tracks in Kensington after overdosing on heroin. I was a teenager when that happened. He was never really around, anyway. My mom was dating a Philly cop after he died. It was only after Joe died. The cop, Joe was the cop. Anyway, after he died, I found out he had a wife and kids living across town. My mom knew it, and that was weird. That's it. My family. Well immediate family. I have a couple uncles in Florida and my crazy Aunt Lucille and Uncle Gary. Also, I'm really still close to my mom's best friend Yana. Like Baba, I might have been closer to Yana than I was to my mom. You'll meet them all at some point."

We continued to talk for hours, we made love sporadically, and I told her I loved her. I actually think I fell in love with her the day she crossed that parking lot.

"I love you too, Brian," she told me and laid her head on my shoulder.

"You really make me happy. I can't remember ever being this happy." I was on the verge of tears.

"Me too. I don't care if we ever leave this chair again."

Veronica and I continued to date, and the seriousness of our relationship grew as quickly as our declaration of love. I got along well with both Bella and Sam, and it was only a few months into the relationship when the subject of me moving in came up. I was still living in the house in Philadelphia while it was being renovated in preparation to become a rental property. I was over for dinner, and the girls had excused themselves, leaving just Veronica and me at the table.

"The hardwood floors on the first floor are installed. The contractor finished yesterday," I said.

"That's great news! What's left?"

"Just the tile in the hallway bathroom on the second floor. Then it's ready."

"Have you thought about where you're going when you rent it?"

"You know, I've spent the last two years so focused on getting it ready, I haven't thought much about it. I guess I never thought I would be done. Maybe I'll buy a condo."

"Maybe in Jersey?" Veronica said with a smile.

"Maybe not! My days in New Jersey are over."

"You could move in here? Is that crazy? Too soon?" She smiled and looked closely to gauge my reaction.

"That never entered my mind to be honest. I never figured you would entertain such a thing, with the girls and all."

"The girls like you, *I love you*, and we're together so much it's kind of stupid to pay for another house." Her logic was sound, but we decided we would both think about it. She also needed to talk with the girls.

I moved in right after Halloween. I'm sure it was strange for Bella and Sam and everyone else in our lives, but it felt right to Veronica and me. I guess I took after my mother. — *You know what they say about lesbians and second dates.*

Veronica's daughters had different biological fathers. Sam's present, Bella's, not so much. I slowly tried to fill in the gaps as best I could now that I was the live-in boyfriend. I kind of knew my place. Bella was sixteen, so my influence on her was pretty minimal out of the gate. When she didn't have tennis or cheerleading practice she came home from school and slept until dinner. I constantly harassed her about getting a part-time job. That was the extent of my parenting for her in the beginning. Samantha was a different story. When I moved in, she looked at it like she had a new audience member. She danced and sang around the house; showed off for the new arrival. I was her buddy in the beginning. I eventually became the disciplinarian missing in their lives, something they sorely needed. Veronica and I rarely disagreed, and when we did it was only ever about the girls.

"Veronica, you can't just treat these girls like they're your friends. They need structure. Rules."

"Don't tell me what my kids need."

These were the type of disagreements Veronica and I had. Some more drawn out but at the end of all of them, I caved. They weren't mine, after all, as much as I wanted them to be. Punishments were never followed through with, and

Veronica admitted she felt guilty for the failed relationships with their fathers, however justified the breakups. I felt that impacted her actions somewhat. The kids needed discipline. She and I were raised differently, so we saw things from different perspectives. Over time, I began correcting and reprimanding the girls. There were chores to be done. I like to think they benefited from the structure and expectations.

> Years later, we took a trip to Florida when Bella was twenty. Samantha, eleven, made a smart-mouth comment to Veronica and I barked at her.
>
> "Sam, I never want to hear you talk that way to your mother again. Do we understand each other?" My tone was stern but not quite a yell. She groaned and said something incoherent.
>
> "I'm sorry, I didn't hear you. I asked if you understood me."
>
> "Yes," she said in a defeated but slightly defiant tone.
>
> Bella then said, "One day you're going to appreciate the fact that he cares enough to correct you." It was such a small statement that meant so much. I felt, in some way, validated.

Veronica had always been affectionate with me, and it took a while to see she wasn't the same way with the girls. In fact, I began to realize this family barely ever expressed emotion. They never hugged or kissed and infrequently said I love you. It was something I was not used to, having been brought up by a mother who was just the opposite and taught me the same. I quietly noted the behavior and was determined to change it. It's not that they didn't love each other; they did, desperately. They just never showed it; maybe they had never learned how.

The first time I made dinner for the family was totally to win over Bella. Her favorite was chicken Parmesan, and that was something of a specialty of mine. I looked forward to my first actual home-cooked meal with the girls. It didn't go as planned. I was dismayed but couldn't say anything; it was too soon. I served dinner and the girls collected around the table without a word. Bella had her phone in one hand below the table, in constant communication with everyone but us. Veronica and Sam were staring at the TV laughing at whatever antics *Hannah Montana* was up to. There were no other conversations, at all, at least not of substance. I sat there, staring at my plate. After dinner, I collected the dishes and began washing them. Veronica helped me clean up, and the girls evaporated into thin air. I couldn't tell if they liked or hated the meal. In my eyes, this family was a work in progress.

A monumental step in our relationship was when Veronica and I agreed we would be having Thanksgiving dinner at her grandmother's house. Baba was mostly bed-ridden by that point. I had gone a few times to visit and was beginning to develop a relationship with Baba. Veronica translated between us, but I felt a sense of connection none the less. She was a precious soul. Due to her blindness, her eyes were always closed, and her words were slow and measured. Baba's family was Ukrainian, and my father's ancestry was

German and Polish, so we shared an adoration for similar cuisine, pierogi and kielbasa being in the forefront of that affection. Veronica had always said her Baba's pierogi were the best. I needed to get the recipe and did on one of our visits.

I took the day before Thanksgiving off work, so I could prepare dinner. We would be making it at our house and transporting it to Baba's in Philadelphia. Veronica, Sam and I set out to make the pierogi based on the recipe Baba gave me. We settled into a makeshift assembly line where I was making the dough, and Veronica and Sam were cutting and filling them. By the end of the night, we had made dozens of pierogi. I also prepared coleslaw and macaroni salad and brined the turkey. Early the next morning, I put the turkey in the oven, and we prepared the rest of the dishes for the day.

We arrived at Baba's house a little after three in the afternoon. Baba was asleep on the hospital bed in the living room, and Uncle Roman was sitting at the dining room table. We had tried to finish most of the cooking at the house since Baba's kitchen was mostly in disrepair. The refrigerator and the gas stove-top worked but the oven only got lukewarm. There was a small microwave that helped us heat up the canned corn. By the time the table was set, Baba was up and mostly alert. Roman set up a TV tray next to her, and Veronica made her a plate. I was elated when Baba raved about the pierogi. She was gumming away at them enthusiastically.

Roman was fairly sauced when we got there. He had a tumbler he was filling from a 1.75-liter plastic bottle of vodka, the type large enough to warrant a handle. He was harassing Bella and Sam about the finer points of soccer, which is what was on the television across the room. Bella was buried in her phone, and Sam was trying to conjure up an invisibility spell. The six of us sat down to eat.

Roman complimented Veronica on every dish. She deflected all credit my way which led Roman to second guess his praise. I mostly kept my mouth shut for the sake of the girls and out of respect for Baba. We thankfully left shortly after cutting the pumpkin and apple pies. Veronica told me on the way home she told Baba we were now together. Baba gave her blessing.

Our first Christmas together was just around the corner. Between work and chauffeuring Sam and Bella around, Veronica and I didn't see each other much until bedtime. It was my favorite time of the day. I was at absolute peace when Veronica and I would go to sleep. She would turn in the other direction, and I got to be the big spoon. I enveloped her, and our bodies seemed to fit perfectly together. She told me I was her missing puzzle piece. One night, we were lying in bed and she said, "I love you, goodnight." I responded, "I love you more." From that point forward, I would always just say the word *more*. I would randomly write it somewhere for her to find or text her out of the blue. I just needed her to know how much I adored her.

It is important to remember roses have thorns. This fact is not to be forgotten. Somehow, I forgot. I was at work one day during the week between Christmas and New Year's when Veronica sent me a text around lunchtime.

The text read, "Brian, please call me. It's very important."

When I got the text, I closed my office door and called her at once.

"Hey, what's going on? Everything okay?"

"No, Not really. You want to tell me anything?"

"Uh, no. what's going on? Why do you sound pissed?"

"Um, Sam was using your laptop. Why do you have all these naked pictures on there? Who are these girls?"

I didn't know what to say. "I had forgotten there was anything like that on there. That was from a long time ago, and I guess I never got rid of them. It's only one girl."

"I don't care about how many *fucking* girls it is. I just don't want Sam to have to see porn at six years old." She was pissed off. She was right, but I also never thought she was going to go searching through my laptop. I had left that seedy life behind and was a family man now. *Thorns*. Veronica was livid, and there was no controlling the narrative. In the eyes of someone I respected and loved, I was once again a scumbag.

After a rocky couple of weeks, the event blew over and was forgotten but it did not come without consequences. Veronica's jealous streak had been exposed. At one point, she read a Facebook Messenger conversation between me and an old friend from high school. In the thread, my friend revealed she had had a crush on me back then. Veronica took this as an invitation, and the existence of this friend's husband and two children would not convince her otherwise. It got a little weirder when Veronica received a private Facebook message from another girl, LeAnn.

"Who's LeAnn?" Veronica asked.

"LeAnn?" I was confused by her question. I didn't remember a LeAnn.

"She's one of your Facebook *groupies*." Her comment might have sparked my pre-therapy self. I was bothered by her use of the work groupie, but anger wasn't the emotion. It was frustration. I then recalled LeAnn and our past conversations.

"LeAnn is a girl I went to high school with. I haven't seen her since I graduated over twenty years ago."

"Well, she certainly thinks you're *still a cutie*. She responded to one of my posts. And then this girl messaged me *privately!* Saying some shit about you being a *good catch and scooping you up before you deserted me?* What the fuck does that mean?" Veronica was playing the lawyer, and I was on the witness stand.

"Veronica, I don't know. I've had some crazy girls in my past."

I really had no words and was struggling to keep some of my previous bad decisions from tainting my present happiness. I was willing to do anything. I ultimately unfriended both of these women and over three hundred others to prove my loyalty and commitment.

Veronica always claimed to possess an uncanny ability to never hold a grudge. She just wiped the slate clean each day and moved on. I guess I believed that at the time. The incidents with the laptop and the Facebook groupies were never brought up again.

We were months removed from the naked picture fiasco. I was finally beginning to feel at home and less like a stranger. I was building closer relationships with Bella and Sam, and the conversations felt more natural. I felt like I belonged and was becoming part of the family. I was still harassing Bella about getting a job, and she finally gave in. She took a job at the Deb Shop in the Deptford Mall. Between school and work, she was almost non-existent in the house. Sam, on the other hand, was always in the house. She was shy and had a hard time making friends and tended to gravitate towards her mother. For better or worse, Veronica was kind of Sam's only friend. Sam tried to keep herself occupied by dancing and jumping around the house. At some point, Veronica sold Sam on the idea of going to try gymnastics. After complaining and several panic attacks later, Sam tried out and found she loved gymnastics. She spent hours a day, several days a week, at the gym. Veronica and I would alternate dropping her off and picking her up. Veronica went back to college to work on her degree, so there were nights it would just be Sam and me. I made the most of those times together. We would go to the diner for dinner after practice, and that was the beginning of the closeness we began to share. For our second Christmas, we bought Sam a trampoline for the backyard, so she could practice tumbling. It was hard to keep her off the damn thing.

One of the traits I loved most about Veronica was her strength. She had an iron will and the ability to persevere through anything. When Baba died, that will was tested. It was then that I realized Veronica also maintained a façade. Not like mine. Hers was built with masonry bricks, several layers deep. And just for a brief time, those walls came tumbling down. She was inconsolable. Even before Veronica's mother died, Baba had become the focal point of her life. Her mother favored her son, and she and Veronica were constantly battling over something. They never saw eye to eye, and Veronica went to live with Baba at the age of fourteen. Her grandmother was everything, and she hadn't gone a single week in the last ten years without seeing her at least once. And now, at the age of eighty-nine, Baba was gone. Veronica only saw her once more lying in a casket. I compared the close relationship she had with Baba to the one I had with my mother. I'm still not over my mother's death completely but, at the time, I mourned her for months. I found it odd how quickly Veronica was able to bounce back after the funeral. After that day, she never broke down in front of me. Never showed weakness for losing the person that meant so much. I thought her internal strength knew no bounds. Life returned to normal as we knew it.

In the summer of 2013, we rented a house in Ventnor, New Jersey. This is where Veronica was happiest. She loved the shore so going to the beach was what she most looked forward to doing. Bella was nineteen and would come down on occasion, but mostly it was Veronica, Sam and me. That summer Sam got an iPhone for her birthday, and it was the same summer I instituted "phone stack." I should have been hired as the national spokesperson for this concept. I advocated it to anyone that would listen. Basically, a phone stack is when all phones are off limits during meals. This immediately changed the dynamic of dinnertime. Maybe it was not very popular but as everyone that has kids knows, it's impossible to get time with active teenagers, and family time at the dinner table is a dying tradition. The hardest to convince to buy into phone stack was Bella. Her hands seemed to be surgically attached to her phone. She relented, and our meals were richer for it from that point forward.

About three years in, I tried to convince Veronica to marry me. She was not interested in the slightest and told me it would never happen.

"Why?" she asked.

"Because I love you and I want you to be my wife."

"I love you too. Getting married won't change how I feel. We've both done that before. It's pointless."

"Yes, I did do it before and for all the wrong reasons. I want to do it with you. I want to marry you. I cannot imagine my life without you in it."

"I'm not going anywhere." She said this with a finality that told me this topic of conversation was closed. We were at an impasse for almost two years.

One Sunday, Veronica came home from her usual trip to Philadelphia to take care of Yana. Yana was in her 70's. Since Baba died, Veronica had transferred her weekly ritual and now took care of Yana. Yana was quite the curmudgeon, but I would later be indebted to her. One Sunday in early 2013, the conversation of marriage came up, and for one reason or another Veronica came home convinced it was now a good idea. We went ring shopping soon after. Veronica did not want a traditional engagement ring. "Been there, done that," she said. We ended up finding what is typically an anniversary band encrusted with three rows of diamonds. On May 14, I went to a jeweler and placed the order. Now I began to plot how I would pop the question.

Two of our closest friends were planning to take a cruise in July of 2013 to the Caribbean. They were recruiting family and friends to go with them, and we decided it would be a perfect family getaway. We planned and prepared for this cruise for months. No one knew my secret plans. As our vacation neared, I was nervous and absent-minded; not traits I typically possess. We packed the car and drove to northern New Jersey where we were to board the ship. Five minutes after boarding, I was much more relaxed as I was with friends and drinking Coronas. My drinking had slowed down exponentially. We sat around all night on the main deck drinking and telling stories. In my mind, I had finally figured out my plan to propose and would have to wait two more days for the Captain's dinner. It turned out to be a perfect plan with terrible execution. Over those two days I became insufferable due to nerves. Veronica grew increasingly frustrated with my behavior. Finally, the day came, and we were getting dressed. At the Captain's dinner, there was a strict dress code, so I brought a suit. What I did not bring were socks or a tie. Veronica managed to buy black and green socks in the gift shop that said, "Jamaica" on them. Now I needed a tie. I scrambled down the hall to my friend, Mark's, cabin. He opened the door and could see I was in distress. "You okay, bro?" "No, I'm a fucking mess." I continued telling him, at a mile a minute, about my plans and how everything was collapsing around me. I was immersed in the middle of a full-blown panic attack. I thought he was going to slap me but instead he laughed and congratulated me. He then pulled, in his typical OCD fashion, a tie holder with about a dozen ties dangling from it. I chose one, thanked him, and left. Once dressed, I left the girls in the cabin and went to the bar for a much-needed glass of courage. We gathered in the dining room at the bow of the ship. Earlier that day, I had talked to Bella and Sam about my plans. They gave me their blessing and were truly excited. They were sitting at the next table but directly behind Veronica and me. My memory of the moment is fuzzy, so I cannot tell you whether it was before or after dessert, but I found myself kneeling beside her, the ridiculous Jamaica socks peeking out. She turned to see me, and then she realized what was happening. Veronica never saw it coming. She said yes, and, as word traveled throughout the cavernous two-level ballroom, thunderous applause erupted. I was now the happiest man alive.

In 2014, my birthday fell on Mother's Day, and I was really missing mom. It would be the first time I took to Facebook and wrote her. The first half was the story of how Veronica and I met, and the rest went like this.

> *So, I sit here over four years later. I have two daughters, Bella and Samantha. Bella is turning 20 this month and Samantha will be 11 in June. They are such great kids. Trying? Yes. But I love both of them very much. They are the girls I always wanted. Well… sometimes LOL. And then there's Veronica. She's become my rock. She is my favorite person in this world. You would have loved her. She's fantastic. I can't even describe how happy she makes me feel. I hit the gas when I'm a couple blocks away just to be with her for a few more minutes. Time goes by so fast and I don't want to miss it.*
>
> *We're getting married next year. She finally said yes. I asked her, well hinted for quite a while. I knew I needed to be with her, but she didn't see the point in getting married again. I think I wore her down ;) So now we're getting married and we're both so excited. She's made all my dreams come true. She finally gave me what I saw when I looked at you and Margot. She gives me what I still see in Margot's eyes whenever your name comes up. A love that conquers all. The love you see in movies and don't really believe it's possible. It is. I have it. And I'm never letting it go.*

I'm putting this on Facebook and people will call me crazy but if they knew you, they know you would have been hooked on this shit. So, there you have it. You're mostly caught up. I just felt like I needed to talk to you today. Somehow the days when my birthday falls on Mother's Day it's extra special. I just wish I could hug you one more time. I miss you so much. Happy Mother's Day Mom!

Bye for now,
Brian

By for now was what my mom used to always say to me after she was diagnosed with cancer. It was her way of telling me she would see me again.

Veronica was the type of person who loves lists and loves to cross off the items on those lists. Our wedding now warranted its own list. In her previous marriage, the wedding plans were not under her control. She was married in her first husband's church with a Catholic ceremony. My first marriage was on the beach in the Bahamas; very different paths. Veronica is mostly a religious, God-fearing person, and, although I consider myself spiritual, I am a huge skeptic. Nonetheless, Veronica wanted to get married in her church and have a traditional Ukrainian ceremony. There was a stumbling block. What resulted was a sixteen-month journey in search of an annulment for her first marriage. There were times we thought it would not be possible, but if I learned anything about my future bride, it was that she would not relent. If she wanted something, she would do everything in her power to get it. Finally, she did, and once the annulment was finalized, I needed to get right with God, so we met with Father Demkiv and scheduled our day at pre-Cana.

Time flew and everything was set; the bachelor/bachelorette parties were in the rearview mirror. We were having the ceremony at the Catholic Cathedral of the Immaculate Conception. I could not have been more elated to marry Veronica and officially call my three girls family.

On May 10, about six weeks before the wedding, I was sitting in the backyard.

> *Happy Mother's Day*
> *Well, here we are again. Another year has passed but I still miss you as I did yesterday and the year before that and the year before that. Dammit, this still hurts so much. But I get to talk to you here. I know you're here with me in some way. You have to be. My life is so blessed now. But I'll NEVER take it for granted. It's too precious. Veronica and I are getting married next month. I can't believe it's nearly here. I can't wait. It's going to be perfect. Almost. You won't be there, and that kills me. You are supposed to be there for this. It would have been the proof that I'm really OK. I remember that summer day when I came over, and I talked about how I made mistakes in the direction my life had taken. I remember you telling me that I had time and that I was going to find what I was looking for. I remember at that time not believing you, lol. Well as you always seemed to be... you were right again. I did.*

Anyway, the wedding is on June 27th if you can swing by to see what a beautiful family I have now and celebrate the day it all becomes official. When I think of Veronica, I have no words. She amazes me every day. She makes me a better man. She makes me whole. I'm so thankful for that because I wasn't sure that would ever happen for me. God knows I had some dark days before I met her. She saved my life, but I won't dwell. There's too much to be thankful for right now.

Bella just finished her sophomore year of college. I love her so much today and will so much more tomorrow. She's becoming such a beautiful woman. I see so much of her mother in her. She's turning 21 soon. It's hard, I know. You were not very fond of me during those years, but she'll come around just like I did. And one day… A day that I can't think about… she'll miss Veronica as much as I miss you. It's life, right? And that's the way this thing goes. A depressing reality. She's a smart kid. She's quiet and I'm trying to break that shell. I'll get there. I have to. I love her like she's my own.

And Samantha! Wow, that kid amazes me. Every day she surprises me. She's so smart. Hates to read but since they make her in school, she's chewing through books like there's a money taped to the back covers. She never complains about homework. Just does it. She'll come home from gymnastics practice, eats dinner and knocks out her homework. Assuming Dancing with the Stars isn't on ;) She's becoming such a free spirit and just feeling out who she is. She'll be 12 next month. We're having a candy bar, "Samantha's Candy Bar", at the wedding as a tribute to her birthday on the 20th. Bella's Bar is going to be the actual bar, lol. Anyway, Samantha changed gyms this year. It was tough because the gym she went to previously was a bit laid back and didn't push the kids enough. Not that I want them to be tyrants because at the end of the day we just want her to have fun and be happy. But Samantha wanted more. She wanted to go there so bad. She went to work out for them and started shortly after. Guess what? She HATED it. They were all MEAN! They all hated her. She just wasn't used to having someone yell at her, so she wasn't sure how to take it. She calloused and then was fine. In fact, she was more than fine. She collected lots of hardware at meets during the season and for all her hard work took the most important one at the end. She won the all-around medal for States. Broke the state record! I could hardly contain myself. I actually had to walk out at one point because I started tearing up and didn't want anyone to see me. She impresses me so much. Her dedication is incredible. Right now, gymnastics makes her happy. That's all we can ask for, right? Happiness. If she decides she wants to do something else tomorrow... we're behind her. She's my little gym rat for now and I love her so much.

I'm so lucky to have these three beautiful creatures in my life. I'm just fortunate to be able to be around them. They complete me. I just wish you were here. Until next year mom, Happy Mother's Day!

I love you, Brian

PS. If you're in the area on the 27th of June stop by. I have some wonderful people I'd love you to meet.

I woke up on the morning of my wedding day alone in the hotel room. Veronica wanted the house to herself to get ready with the bridesmaids. She had a gift bag waiting for me in the room that read *open on 6.27.2015*. The text of the card read, "I'm marrying my best friend." The inside read, "In you, I've found my best friend for life. A strong, brilliant man who challenges me, supports my dreams, and shows me happiness I never thought possible. Together we embark on our greatest adventure. There will be laughter, encouragement and love. SO MUCH LOVE. And it begins today."

The inscription she wrote was,

> "I hope you love the gift. I was scared at first but wanted you to know just how much you mean to me & how much I trust you with every part of me."

I opened the gift to find a photobook. There was stunning picture after picture of my soon-to-be-wife. She was dressed provocatively but tastefully. I sat in awe and wept. I'm not sure anyone will truly understand what this meant to me, and her going through with something this risqué was entirely out of character. She is a modest person. My heart was full. I must have flipped through the pages a dozen times before realizing I needed to get my ass moving. I had a pretty big day ahead of me, after all.

I met the groomsmen and best man at a diner in Stratford, NJ. We ate and headed back to the hotel to get ready. It was pouring rain and the national weather service predicted heavy downpours throughout the day and night. I thought it would bother me; it didn't. The limo bus arrived, and we headed over to the church. I was numb with excitement, and when I got to the church the photographer grabbed me for pictures. He was setting up for "the reveal." If you're not familiar, photographers love to get a picture of the groom when he first sees his soon-to-be bride in her wedding dress. I did not disappoint. I stood there in the church, and she came up behind me, grabbed my waist, and whispered my name. When I turned around, I shattered into a million pieces. She was breath-taking, and I swelled with emotion. Once I finally pulled myself together, we took pictures with us and my *daughters*. They are some of my favorites.

We went through a traditional Ukrainian ceremony complete with crowns for each of us to wear. They were really dollar store tiaras so I looked a bit ridiculous, but it goes to show there were no lengths I wouldn't go to for this woman. My groomsmen were particularly amused. After the ceremony, we all went back to the hotel and waited for the bus to take us to the reception. It was all in all an amazing night, and I will never forget the smile on her face from that day. *The smile I would never unsee.* She told me she had never been happier; neither had I.

We spend the next two weeks honeymooning in Paris and London. It was the first time abroad for both of us, and other than my fear of flying the trip was brilliant. We stayed in a quaint hotel called the Duminy Vendôme. The entire hotel had a pleasant powdery scent that was unmistakable. That first morning, I woke up as a married man in the most romantic city in the world.

"Good morning, wife." I said. I had been up for at least an hour; taking her in as she slept.

"Good morning, *husband*." she melted my heart.

"I read about a tea house around the corner from here. We can go for breakfast when you're ready."

"Emm, okay. I just want to stay here for a little bit longer." She nuzzled into me and fell back to sleep for another half hour.

We got ready and walked around the block to Angelina's Paris on the Rue de Rivoli. At eight-thirty, there was already a wait for a table. We admired the pastries in the display counter as we waited.

"Wow, looks at the profiteroles!" I'm not one for sweets but they looked delicious.

"No, no, no, look at the macarons!" Veronica was already ordering them from the clerk before I even acknowledged her.

The hostess sat us at a round marble table meant for two. The leather bound arm-chairs were inviting.

The waiter was attentive and present within seconds of our arrival. *"Bonjour, monsieur et madame. Est-ce que vous parlez français?"*

I remembered enough French from school to know he was asking if we spoke French. I responded, *"Très peu. En anglais s'il vous plaît."*

"Very well, monsieur, what can a bring you both? *Café?*"

"Yes, for me. Baby, what do you want? Tea?"

"Tea, please," Veronica said. The waiter smiled very professionally and was on his way. Moments later, another younger man came and filled our water glasses. The waiter returned with our hot beverages, and we ordered hot chocolate and croissants. The croissants were the best I'd ever tasted, and the hot chocolate was literally chunks of chocolate slowly melted in a double boiler and whisked with a few tablespoons of hot water. It was divine.

> *Two years later, on our anniversary, Veronica planned breakfast for me where she bought a wrought iron pub table and chairs in the style you would see in a Parisian café. We sat down and Samantha, who was thirteen, served us hot chocolate and croissants. Our own personal garçon. There was also a candle on the table that was the same smell wafting through hotel Duminy. Veronica had it shipped from the hotel. It took me right back to Paris and I felt so blessed to have this life.*

When we returned from our two-week honeymoon, it was back to the hamster wheel. Between work and Samantha's extracurricular activities life was busy, and Veronica and I didn't spend much alone time together. I looked forward to bedtime where she would crawl up close to me. So close, I was practically hanging off the side of our California King. The same one from the house in Philly. You could have fit three people on the other side of her, but you couldn't wedge a piece of paper between us. I used to tease her all the time about moving over. We would end up scooching to the middle of the bed while attached at the hip. This occurred every night, and I wouldn't have had it any other way. She would remind me I was her missing puzzle piece.

Late in 2017, my company wasn't doing very well; there were lay-offs and part of the savings included consolidating the office. We had a fifteen thousand square foot space that was initially leased with the aspirations for growth. When it didn't happen, the office was a financial burden. This resulted in many of my team working at home as we consolidated into a smaller corporate footprint. I had about an hour commute, so I embraced the ability to work at home most of the time. I initially scheduled visits once a week just to be present. As time passed, I decreased the frequency as my team was getting adept at holding Skype conferences and proved to be very attentive from afar. Another factor affecting my work stability was initially thought to be a good revelation. An investor, an old competitor from Australia, had invested in the company and now owned a majority share. There were expectations of great times to come. Meanwhile, Veronica was doing exceptionally well in her career but wanted to move out of her regional manager position and back into building management where she had been really happy in the past, a position she held when we first met. She was skeptical about applying because it would be a step back and down. I encouraged her to be happy and not worry about the cut in pay. After some time and lots of soul searching, she decided to go for the job she coveted. She got it easily. A previous boss of hers was the hiring manager, and looking back, the job was hers for the taking. She accepted the position and the unexpected result was a ten-thousand dollar raise.

Meanwhile, I was struggling professionally. I saw the instability within my company even with the influx of energy and money from the new investor. The tenor continued to trend south, and I started looking for another job. I had worked my way up the ladder over the last eighteen years to a director's position but found it difficult to find anyone interested in hiring me. I didn't want to appear vulnerable, so I kept the job search to myself.

Our oldest, Bella, had been talking about moving to Florida for as long as I could remember and yet she came up with every excuse not to go. In the summer of 2018, opportunity fell in her lap. Veronica's Uncle Rich owned a couple of rental properties in Daytona Beach. They were not the glamourous backdrops I remembered from 80's music videos, but they were only a block from the ocean. One of the houses became available, and Bella decided to finally take a leap of faith. Veronica and I told her we would support her in the move. In the beginning of July, Veronica took off a couple weeks and drove Bella and Sam down to help Bella get settled. I couldn't sneak away from work. I was silently drowning with the stress of my job, and I really could have used the break. We packed Bella's and Veronica's cars, and I said a tearful goodbye. I held her close and tight to let her know I loved her and promised to do anything to make sure she was okay until she could thrive on her own. The girls drove away, and I was left on the driveway feeling a little empty. The next two weeks were hell. Work was deteriorating around me. My family was in Florida, and I couldn't be there to help. All I could do was offer a credit card to help buy necessities. It wasn't even close to enough; I needed to be there with them. Every night, I sat in the back yard, lit a bonfire and watched Netflix. I thought I would never feel more alone. —*I was wrong*. Veronica was in constant motion getting Bella set up in two weeks' time. We didn't speak much. I was homesick. My home was these girls, and they were 1000 miles away. I needed them to return. Veronica sent me a card that stemmed my longing. The card read,

> *I did it again. I got caught up in the little daily stuff and lost sight of what matters most – you. I let too much time go by without doing what I really enjoy best – putting you first and sharing like we used to before life got so busy. I let you go too long without hearing "I love you" and "I appreciate you." I'm sorry for neglecting you and our relationship – and I promise to show you that I mean it.*
>
> *Even when my heart seems everywhere else, it's right there, next to yours, every single minute. And it will always be.*

She wrote this inside,

Brian,
Missing you made me realize just how much I need to focus back on "us" time. I love you and can't wait to see you.
XOXO
Veronica

I stood outside as Veronica's 2018 Black Ford Fusion pulled into the driveway. It was the longest two weeks I had experienced in a long time, and it was finally over. My baby was home. Samantha got out of the car, exhausted. She collapsed into my arms, and I held her until Veronica came and joined our group hug. I hadn't left the house in weeks but now I was home. I was whole again. It was the first time they had been away from me for that long, and it only made me miss them more. We talked for a while about the ins and outs of the trip and the experiences they had had.

Vows You Took

A few days after returning from Florida, Veronica thought she felt a lump in her breast. I couldn't feel what she was feeling, but given her family medical history, I suggested genetic testing. We went through the testing and found she had DNA markers which increased her chances for breast and ovarian cancer. It was not as dire as BRCA 1 & 2, but there was concern enough to begin scheduling tests every six months, alternating mammograms and MRIs. I silently broke a little inside given my mother's bout with breast cancer and eventual death. Veronica always showed the world a sturdy exterior but again, much like my mother, her eyes told the story. She was scared. I told her we would do whatever we needed to, and, although I may have gone overboard with all my suggestions, I refused to stand idly by.

On July 28, Veronica went to the gym and when she got home, she told me we needed to talk. I followed her in the bedroom and sat down next to her.

"What's going on, you okay?"

"No." Her eyes were outlined in red and bloodshot.

"Baby, what's wrong? Why were you crying?"

She handed me a printout with the results of the mammogram. It revealed several masses. I had no words. I held her and had a hard time holding it together. The vision of my mother lying in a casket swept over me.

"When did you find this out?"

"This morning. I looked it up on the SJRA Patient Portal," she said.

"Why didn't you tell me this morning?"

"I needed to get myself prepared for your emotional reaction." Her comment staggered me.

Without realizing it, I must have been following her around the house over the next couple hours, and she eventually screamed, "Can you *stop* crawling up my ass!" I retreated to the couch like a kicked dog. I had never felt uncomfortable around Veronica until that very moment. She scheduled an MRI for the following Monday. Before making it to the doctor everything would change.

It was August 17th and a *shitty—fucking—day*. Everything went wrong that day at work. I needed to walk away. I left the home office and collapsed onto the couch. I sat there thinking I needed the weekend to recharge the batteries. I promised myself I would not to obsess too much about Veronica's medical situation. I needed to be strong for her. Moments later, she walked through the door, already describing her terrible day. She went on for the better part of twenty minutes. After finally taking a breath, she asked how my day went. I just replied I would tell her later at dinner. Veronica had been suffering from stomach issues for the last couple weeks, so I thought it would be better to go out and give her choices. I then sat there on the opposite side of the couch, only a few feet away, staring at her. Staring directly in the face of something I never expected. There was something wrong. I couldn't put my finger on it, but now I was thinking maybe her distance the past week was more than the possibility of cancer.

"There is something wrong. What is it?"

She sat there across the room just staring back at me but not saying anything.

"What's going on? Are you okay?" My mind was racing.

The blood then ran from her face. Seconds seemed like hours before her response. "I'm not happy, and I don't love you anymore."

The floor dropped out from beneath me. "What? What are you talking about? Where did this come from?"

As tears fell from her eyes, all she said was, "I'm sorry."

I spent the next twenty minutes trying to remember how to breathe. I don't remember what else was said in those moments. On complete autopilot, I sprang up and headed into the bedroom. I needed to get the hell out of there. I needed a drink. I was rummaging through a drawer trying to find my house keys when she said, "You don't have to move out right now."

Wait, what? "Did you really just say that? I'm not moving out right now. I'm just trying to find my keys, so I can get out of here."

I rushed out the door not really sure where I was going. I had been talking to two of my best friends, Doug and Mark, over text earlier that day and sent them both the same thing, "Veronica just told me she doesn't want to be with me anymore." Within the next hour, Doug and Mark were sitting on bar stools on either side of me. They plied me with beers and shots, but no matter how much I drank I was sober. My adrenaline would not permit me to miss a single second of this nightmare. Doug dropped me off at around eleven-thirty that night, and when I walked in Veronica wasn't to be found. The lights were out, and the house was quiet. It was Samantha's father's weekend, so she was with him. On a chance, I went down to the basement and found Veronica there. She had taken the bed from Bella's old room and created a makeshift bedroom. What was happening? She said hello in a low, meek voice.

"What are you doing? Did you really make a bedroom down here in the couple hours I was gone?"

"What else was I supposed to do? I can't sleep in the same bed with you."

"How did this happen, Veronica? How do you just turn off your emotions like this?"

Before she could answer I turned and walked away. I fell into bed and spent the night aimlessly staring at the walls.

There would be no sleeping. The Saturday sun was rising and eventually Veronica came up and sat on the opposite corner of the bed. She looked sheepishly at me but was no longer saying she was sorry. She explained that she didn't know what happened. It just happened. We had gone to a brew pub and to Atlantic City for dinner and a show over the past couple weeks. All dates she planned, and her motivation was to try and feel something for me. *Feel anything*. The spark was just gone.

That night we had tickets to see a 90's freestyle concert at the Wells Fargo Center. We were going with a few other couples and Samantha. Later that morning, Veronica came into the bedroom and said, "You're still going tonight, right?"

"What? Of course, I'm not going. You just put my world in a wood-chipper. The last thing I want to do is go to a *fucking* concert!"

"But what do I tell Ann and Mark?" She didn't know Mark had been with me the night before. I was shocked to hear Veronica hadn't told Ann. She was one of her closest friends and had been for the past twenty years. How could she not know? She didn't.

"Tell them whatever you want."

"Can we not tell Samantha until tomorrow? She is really excited about this concert."

"Sure, Veronica. Tell her I'm not feeling well."

Samantha came home from her father's a few hours later, and I went in the kitchen to talk to her. I wanted to have one last conversation where our lives weren't completely different. Samantha and I had become much closer over the past year. In fact, it had been around two weeks earlier when Samantha had said, "I love you" to me without being prompted. I always had to say it first. I had finally broken through.

We talked for a while, and I started to get choked up, so I hugged and kissed her and told her to have a good time at the concert. Veronica was outside pulling weeds when I walked out. When I got in the car, she told me I didn't have to leave. I ignored her. I did have to leave. I drove over to Mark's house where he had a beer already open and waiting.

Ann came down the stairs and gave me a tight squeeze along with a heartfelt, "I'm sorry."

"Me too."

"What the hell is up with her? Is it the cancer scare? Did you hit her?"

"*What? Fuck! No.* I didn't do anything. I don't understand. This came out of nowhere."

"I can't believe she didn't tell me there was anything wrong. But I guess if she didn't tell you then, I don't know. This is all so fucked up."

I told Ann that apparently the only person that knew was her best friend.

"Figures. I don't even want to go tonight, but I feel like I have to," Ann said.

Mark chimed in stating he didn't care if he ever saw her again.

"*Mark*! That's not nice," Ann yelled. Mark smirked negatively.

The circular conversation continued until Ann had to leave to pick up Veronica and Samantha. Mark and I spent the rest of the night knocking the knees off a bottle of Johnny Walker Platinum. Sometime around ten-thirty, he started to fade, so I went home. It would be another sleepless night, and I was really itching to talk to Veronica. *She cannot really do this to me.* I texted her at seven-fifteen the next morning.

> "I can't accept this Veronica. I deserve MORE from you and you can't just throw in the towel without any explanation at all. That is not fair to me or our family. You need to figure out why you can just turn off your feelings so quickly. Why am I not worth fighting for? My heart is destroyed."

She came upstairs and walked into the bedroom a few minutes later.

"I don't know what to tell you. I tried to get my feelings back for you, but they just aren't there. I don't feel anything for you. *At all*. It's not what I wanted to happen."

"Why didn't you give me some sign? Or tell me before you got to this point? Can we go to marriage counseling? Can we work on this?"

"There's nothing to work on. You're a great husband, father and friend. I just don't love you anymore."

That broke me. We both talked to the girls, and I did my best to hide my devastation. When I called Bella in Florida, I cracked. She told me that I was the best father she ever had. I was her third given her biological and Veronica's first husband, Robbie, so that really meant so much. I did my best to avoid running into Veronica as much as I could. She went out much more frequently, many times taking Samantha and other times on her own.

On August 23, I had a business trip to New York City to meet the sales team at our new satellite office. At least work seemed to be climbing out of the nosedive that had been stressing me out for the past twelve months.

On August 29, Veronica was going to be taking Yana food shopping after work. It was unusual for Yana to be out late, so when Veronica came home at eleven-thirty that night, I was curious. When she opened the door, I was standing there, and she began to smile. It wasn't a nice smile, it wasn't the smile I'll never *unsee*. It was a taunting smile.

"What are you smiling about?"

"Why are you standing here waiting for me?"

"I thought you were going over Yana's? It's a little past her bedtime."

"It's no longer your business." Now, she was almost unable to contain a laugh.

"How can you be so cold to me? What did I ever do to you?"

"I just want this over and want you out. I'm living in the *fucking* basement!"

"That was your decision, and you even said you made this choice and should be the one to stay down there. I didn't ask for any of this!"

The conversation continued to devolve, and she became angry when I said her relationships seemed to have an expiration date. She was now infuriated because she knew I had spoken to her favorite uncle. He had told her the same thing. Uncle Rich had called me when I was in New York. He wanted to tell me how sorry he was to hear the news and that Veronica had done this very thing with her first husband at about the same point in the relationship. Veronica lost her composure and was now screaming at me. She then threatened to not let me see Samantha and stormed down to the basement. She stopped at the bottom step, looked up and me, and said, "And I want a divorce!"

In the first week of September, I went apartment shopping. I decided I wanted to be close to Samantha, so I found a community a town away. I put down a deposit for a place that would be available on November 2. It was about two months away, so I started packing my belongings. I spent the rest of the time either in the bedroom or the garage to avoid seeing Veronica.

Veronica retained the services of the divorce attorney she had used for her first divorce and had a property agreement drawn up. I signed it, and we were legally considered separated. Looking back, I certainly lost in the deal but wasn't thinking clearly at the time. It was all happening so fast.

November 2 came, and I took a few trips back and forth packing stuff into my car. I was trying to get a jump start since my real moving day was the third when my friends were coming to help out. After all was said and done, we drank beer and ate pizza for a while before everyone left. The silence was the first thing I noticed. This was going to get worse before it got better.

Thanksgiving was just around the corner. Veronica, Sam and I had originally planned to go to Florida to celebrate with family. Veronica and Sam went, and I spent the holiday with Margot's family. It would be the last holiday Veronica would text me to wish me well. Christmas was just as difficult. Years before, when Bella was still living at home, we had started a tradition where we got matching pajamas and took a family photo on Christmas morning. I knew the tradition was changing when Bella moved away, but I never pictured this outcome.

On the morning of New Year's Eve, at around seven-thirty, I received a phone call from one of my co-workers. Besides being a personal friend, he was in charge of our corporate IT. He was calling to tell me that our company was dissolving as of that day. I was not only out of a job, it also meant that the girls and I were no longer covered for health insurance. In a span of four months, I had lost my wife and my job.

Now collecting unemployment, I was back in touch with the former CEO and assisting him in trying to sell off the corporate assets. For helping, he was gifting money to me to avoid any tax implications. I took Samantha to dinner every couple weeks, and my friends were keeping me busy, so I didn't go insane. I just couldn't seem to get past how my marriage had failed. I spent endless nights going through everything I could think of trying to figure out what had gone wrong. I received the paperwork that Veronica was suing me for divorce on April 10. Ironically, it was the anniversary of when Veronica and I started dating back in 2010. I decided I needed closure, so I wrote the following letter to Veronica pleading for answers. I dropped the letter off at her house that afternoon.

April 10th, 2019

Hi Veronica,

I received the paperwork for the divorce, and I have to be honest with you, I can't sign it. Not yet. Your actions since our separation have proven how easy it was for you to move on, but I have found it impossible. I am still trying to make sense of all this and cannot find the answers on my own. I need your help. I need you to give me closure.

You have stated on many occasions that you don't owe me anything. You actually said much, much worse. I would like to believe you said most of it out of frustration and did not actually mean those hurtful words. I know I didn't. I just cannot wrap my head around the chain of events that led us here. Your timeline does not add up. You claim you began "losing" feelings for me in May.

Why would you not bring it up then?

Why would you get a tattoo of our wedding date during June if you were having these feelings?

What changed so quickly? I realize I was under a lot of stress with work and maybe not myself for a while. Was that the trigger? Did you really not care enough to be by my side?

I never saw weakness in our relationship. Maybe I was naive. Maybe I was just blinded by love. Honestly, I always looked at you differently than any other woman I ever had in my life. When I fell in love with you, I realized, for the first time, I needed no one else. My former ways of cheating and my wandering eyes were always looking for something better. With you, there was nothing better. I was unbelievably happy and wanted the world to know it. You were everything to me and the only reason I cared to breathe.

How did you get here?

I'm so angry at you for not loving me enough to say something before your love melted away. I deserved better from you.

How could you move on so fast?

The couple of flare-ups we had, I regret. But you had the perfect ammunition to fight me off. You used the girls. Telling me that I wouldn't see Samantha was enough to have me back down every time. I love the two of them so much. As you so callously pointed out, they are not mine. Not by birth. I understand, but I feel like they are. You always knew how I wanted children and how much I love Bella and Samantha but were so cold to throw that in my face. Why would you use them to hurt me? All I did was love the three of you.

You then moved at lightspeed to get me out of your life. It was the complete opposite of what you did when you decided to say yes to marrying me. You put all your energy into getting the annulment and planning our wedding. Then you put all your energy into erasing me from your life. I died a little inside the day you burned all the cards I ever gave you. You did it with no regard to how I would feel. I loved you more and more every passing day, and because you no longer felt the same you never thought enough of me to do it another time when I wasn't around. It was a very unsympathetic move. When I asked you about it you told me you wouldn't have the room to store them. Really, a shoebox of memories for a person that at one point you so loved.

Why didn't you think enough of my feelings to spare me that pain?

I finally left 77 days later. I know it was a relief for you that I was finally gone, and it probably felt like much, much longer. For me, it was the realization that I had lost the love of my life. Truly. All the ideas of possible reconciliation were erased as I was being erased from your world.

Only four months later, seeing pictures of you on Facebook with someone else where you seem very intimate and happy only fueled my confusion about how we got here without a single conversation towards saving our relationship. You know I am not a religious person, but you are, and I at least thought you would have given me a chance to help repair whatever you were losing. If only even for the vows you took.

If you ever loved me, have mercy. Help me make sense of this and give me closure.

Forever MORE,
Brian

She texted later that night and said, "Hi. Sorry it took so long to get back to you I have been sick the last two weeks and today finally feel better. I'm not sure if you want to talk in person or just have me respond via text. I wish I had an answer for many of your questions. I don't, but I want you to know I would never stop the girls from seeing you or talk badly about you to them. I apologized to Samantha a few times for that blow out we had which was totally unacceptable the way I reacted and even worse that it was in ear shot for her."

"Hi. I'm sorry you were not feeling well. I would prefer to see you in person. I am just seeking closure. Veronica, I loved you more than I ever loved myself and cannot seem to get past this sudden change in my life. I am hoping you can give me that."

"Hi. I understand and can meet to talk. I hope tomorrow afternoon."

"Ok. What time and where"

"I'm at the cancer doctor's now for a follow-up (all is fine). I should be done by ten-thirty. Wanna meet at eleven? Where do you want to meet?"

"That works. Wherever you feel comfortable to talk."

"How about the Meadows Diner on the Black Horse Pike?"

"OK, see you then."

I drove to the diner with sweat soaking through my clothes.

When I pulled into the parking lot I backed into a spot and caught Veronica's gaze through the window. Seeing her, I could tell from a distance this meeting wasn't going to fulfill my needs. I walked into the diner with my heart in my hands and as I closed the distance to the booth where my wife sat, I dropped it on the floor.

"Hi," she said.

"Hi."

We sized each other up for the first minute or so. She finally broke the ice and reiterated she was not sure what she could offer me as answers for the defection of her feelings but would try. She gave me nothing through her words. Over the next hour, with the waitress jockeying for position, we ordered our last meal together and spoke about the last few months of our relationship. She offered nothing of consequence, but I began gaining a perspective I had not had in the past. I had been too close to it and, until now, it was not easily seen. But there it was. Witnessing her lack of empathy, I realized she might not be equipped with the same type of emotional responses most humans possess. It was beginning to become clear to me, but nothing I had considered or could have comprehended before that moment. I began to realize she was not like me. I am a very emotional person who wears my feelings on my sleeve. My wife had always been the opposite, but I believe her strength was the tractor beam that drew me in initially. She was certainly affectionate enough, but I ignored all the signs that had been present all along.

For instance, Veronica went, religiously, to Philly to take care of her mom's best friend, Yana. She had previously gone to church but in recent years would confine the trip to taking Yana shopping and out to lunch. This occurred almost every Sunday barring some pre-planned event. I never went. This was one of those rituals that was Veronica's and Veronica's alone. Not that she wouldn't have allowed me, but it just felt like it was their time. One Sunday, I asked her to do something for me and she said, plainly, no. She had to meet Yana and would be gone for the remainder of the day. I was bothered because I rarely asked for anything and exclaimed how I felt I was never prioritized.

> *"It was the girls, then work. And sometimes those two are swapped. Then it's everyone else, and then me. Why am I always last on the list of your importance?"*
>
> *"You are being ridiculous!"*
>
> *"Am I? When have you ever put me first?"*
>
> *"But you don't need me."*

Ah, there it was. In my frustration, I missed it that day, but it was always there. She spent her life problem solving and taking care of people in need. When her Baba was alive, she tended to her constantly. Her age and blindness gave Veronica the perfect patient. She took care of her grandmother for the first few years we dated, and once she died, Yana was next in line to be "tended to." She tried to take care of her Uncle Roman, but, with his constant drinking and massive gun collection, you could never be sure it was safe to go into the house. But me? She never thought I needed her the way others did. They depended on her. What she didn't know was I *did* need her. In fact, I had been waiting my whole life for her, and now I needed her most of all. Only this time, she was not only not coming to the rescue, she was deserting me entirely.

We finished eating, and I ran out of things to say. I tried to resuscitate the conversation. We were done. I paid the check and we left. There was an awkward few moments on the stairs outside the diner where we didn't know what to do or say. —*Should we hug?* We said a simple goodbye, barely maintaining eye contact, and walked in separate directions. I guess we had been doing that for longer than I realized.

Emotionally drained, I went home and signed the divorce paperwork.

Postmortem

Over the next month, I received text messages from the few friends Veronica hadn't evicted from her social media world. They would text pictures of her, smiling, out with her new boyfriend. *I was slowly dying a death of one thousand cuts*. One was dated the day after our meeting at the diner. She was posing with him in a pair of high heels I had bought her, flashing the smile I would never *unsee*, only now she was no longer smiling for me.

Our interactions had become a work in progress. For me, not her. Over the years we were together, I watched her shut off emotionally. I knew what she was capable of, but I never thought it would happen to me. We still had financial ties and were technically still married even though the property agreement had been notarized and put to bed in her divorce attorney's filing cabinet. I held the loan for her new car since she was currently in the throes of chapter thirteen and could not secure one herself. She often texted me about her plans to trade it in and pay off the loan.

Her text messages were as they were when we were together without the word *more* at the end. It was clear she no longer loved me more than I loved her. *—at all!* Since our meeting at the diner, Veronica had been much more accommodating. Several times she had asked me to pick Samantha up from school. It was a step in the right direction. I tried to see Samantha at least every two weeks. One day, Veronica texted me about Samantha's sixteenth birthday party. She was extending an invitation to her house. "It would just be family," she said. I didn't respond to the text straight away. I wasn't sure what I was feeling at that point and pondering how crazy I must be for even entertaining going. Remember, this woman broke my heart with very little remorse. She began dating a person who became her boyfriend before I even moved out of the house only two months after the bomb dropped. However, I was considering it. I polled several trusted friend groups for their opinions; they were certainly mixed. I decided to go and finally texted back, "Thank you for the invite, I would really like to be there for Samantha."

"You are still her step-father."

I counted the days trying to decide whether or not my attendance would be worth the fare my heart would pay.

Opposite to my OCD tendencies, I arrived fifteen minutes late. I didn't want to be the first one there and felt lateness would provide a buffer. It did. I walked in and was greeted by Veronica's extended family, Samantha, and finally Veronica. She was very nice to me in the way you would be to someone you invited to an event but didn't really know. For me, it was extremely awkward. Everyone else seemed fine. Maybe a little too fine for my liking. Samantha clung to me whenever she passed. It was either her way to tell me she was happy I was there or her way of protecting me from the emotional mind-fuck I was going through. I left that night needing the tallest glass of scotch I could pour. I spent hours replaying the complete emotional disregard Veronica showed. I could never be so callous. Wait, that's not true. I could. I could to people that I no longer cared for and, maybe, even loathed, like my first ex-wife. I got to the point where I said whatever I was feeling without regard for her feelings. Was this my penance? Or more likely, the karma police coming to collect a fine I incurred so many years ago?

I've now gone through a birthday and Father's Day praying I would not be forgotten. It's a lonely feeling waking up alone on those days with bated breath. I heard from both Bella and Sam on both occasions, but I cannot say they were ideal holiday greetings. I would have preferred a card, maybe a call. I got text messages. Sign of the times, I suppose. At least I heard from them. I think if I were sitting on Michael's couch and talking about this, he would tell me I was trying to get validation of the impact I had on them while I helped raise them. And I would agree. I am starved for their attention and do seek validation. I would like to think I was a good influence. I would like to think when they reach an age of enlightenment, they'll truly see the impression I had in their lives. In the meantime, I would settle for an occasional unprompted text.

Felo de se

Some months ago, I wrote a post that was met with sadness and concern from some of my Facebook family. I'm sure others reserved comment and thought, "Here he goes again with this depressive nonsense." I don't think I'm a depressed person. I tend to write when I am alone in the emptiness of the night. On occasions of vulnerability, the door concealing the chamber where these dark thoughts live creaks open. When I combine knocking the shoulders off a bottle of JW Black with surfing Facebook, sometimes there is an unfortunate consequence. I have made promises not to do it again, until the next time, of course. I've thought about any possible reason for posting seemingly needy messages, and I truly do not think it's a cry for help or seeking pity. I never look back and think differently about the posts as they all seem to reflect my feelings. However, it makes me ponder my potential subconscious motivations.

Whenever someone calls me out for posting something too *needy* or *wanting* on Facebook, I can't help but think about my friend Dale. We were friends throughout high school, but he was always hanging on the fringe of our inner circle. It felt as if I couldn't truly connect with him. I always busted his balls for staring at the ceiling when he was talking to me. When I think back, I think that may have been part of the reason we never connected. Eye contact is important to me and it always felt like there was just something missing.

When we all left for college, I lost touch with Dale until Facebook came along. On Facebook, I found he was still playing the same role. Dale was always one needing attention. Facebook is perfect for attention seekers. He had a unique way of telling people he was not doing well while leaving them lacking details. His posts were cryptic and left room for people to inquire, "Are you okay?" He would never explain. His posts required no explanation to me. I recognized depression from a mile away. He was in pain, and his friends tried to answer his call and salve his wounds. He lost Facebook friends over the years with what was perceived as *nonsense just posted to garner attent*ion. Maybe it was. Maybe it was just cries for help. Maybe it was trying to find reasons to just hold on. He couldn't find those reasons, and eventually hanged himself on a doorknob just to ease his pain. His Facebook profile remains, and people still write to his memory wishing they could have done more. His daughter's posts are the most heart-breaking. I've often wondered if anything could have saved him.

Brianna Revisited

Brianna is now twenty-five, and I tried to see how she's doing through social media without anyone knowing. I still often think about rocking away her cries throughout that cold snowy night. She doesn't even know me and that makes me sad. I recently reached out to her through Facebook Messenger.

Hi Brianna,

I know this is coming out of left field, and you can totally blow me off. I don't even know if you remember me. I would understand. The last pictures I have are when you were 5. I'm looking at them as I write this note. All I can tell you is my life has had ups and downs and you were part of the ups. I was there when you came into this world, and I've since sat in the wings and wondered how you were. I can see your on Facebook page (you should secure your profile!!). The relationship your mother and I had crashed and burned. I take responsibility for that, but I never forgot about you. It was messy. I've held back contacting you over the years because I didn't want to cause any problems. I still don't, believe me. I would prefer that if you even entertain talking to me that we keep this between us. I am solely interested in talking to you. Let me know. I would love to see you. If not, I understand.

Brian

Hi Brian,

I didn't want to just ignore your message and leave you wondering if I ever saw it. I just wouldn't really feel comfortable seeing you. I know who you are, but obviously I was little and don't really 'remember' you. And seeing that you're my mom's ex.. it would be a little awkward honestly. I understand you reaching out though, being around when I was born, and I appreciate it. I'm sure you wonder how I've been, and I've been great. I'm living with my family (fiancé and two children), and we are expecting a third within a month or so.
I hope you're doing well. Thanks again for reaching out

Brianna

Brianna,

Thank you for getting back to me. I appreciate it and completely understand. I only ask you keep this between us. I would never want to stir up any drama. I am very happy you are doing great and congratulations on your pending wedding and children. I won't message you anymore. Continue to have an amazing life.

Brian

I'm so happy she responded, but I would have loved to have been able to meet her without stirring up the ghosts of the past. I guess I got what I deserve.

Closing Credits

I sit here today, my pen metaphorically running out of ink, looking back at the dumpster fire I called life. I realized no matter how much therapy I underwent or how I tried to rationalize human emotion and human nature; the answers eluded me. I thirsted for years to have a *normal* life. What did that even mean? I wasn't unique. Everyone experiences peaks and valleys. Everyone ponders what life would have been if they had made different choices. George Michael had a song called *Different Corner*. He sang about the possibility of never meeting someone had they turned a different corner and whether anyone would even care. You can only care about the choices you made and ponder the possibilities of the ones you did not. In the end, you choose whether or not to live with the results of those decisions. I have regrets as many of us do. I regret getting married the first time. I regret staying in that relationship for as long as I did. I regret not having biological children. That one hurts the most, but the hardest pill to swallow is that I would have never met Veronica and lived my happiest life for eight and a half years had I not made all of those previous decisions. I would have never had the two beautiful stepdaughters who made me smile every day. I'm desperately torn how everything played out.

So, what have we learned? Good question, maybe nothing. Maybe my life was way more fucked up than yours, and you can take comfort in that. Maybe you feel you slowed down just enough to see the gory details of a fatal car crash. The splintered fiberglass scattered across two lanes, flickering jackpot lights, and the blood splatter at the impact point of the driver's side windshield. However you decide to characterize my life is fine; it's your choice.

So how does this all end? The answer is, I don't know. I guess I have a few breaths to take and another chapter to write. Maybe I'll stumble upon a woman that will take my breath away before Father Time gets his turn. I'm sure now that you have finished reading this you have come to the same conclusion I did. I was the most broken toy of all.

Epilogue

When I found this file on the desktop of Brian's iMac, I wasn't sure if it was more like a diary or something he truly meant to publish. If I hadn't seen a name I recognized, *Broken Toys*, I might have missed it entirely. When I opened it and read the first chapter, I knew what I had found. When we were together, I heard about it. He told me he no longer had the desire to finish it. He also didn't want Bella and Samantha to see it. I had no interest in reading it. I do have the jealous streak he mentioned. And I always look forward, never back. I finished reading the whole book a few days ago. It took me almost a week to get through the chapter he wrote about me. It was hard to read and was a great love story, and I did adore him. After reading everything that came before, I realized he was an entirely different person when he was with me. He always told me I saved his life. He never told me the sordid details of the rest of it or about his anger, and now I understand why. A few years ago, before we were married, Bella was dating this kid. She was about nineteen. They were hanging out, and it was getting late so she asked if her boyfriend could stay at the house. Sleep on the couch. I didn't have a problem with it. Brian put his foot down, something he rarely did. I took the kid home, and when I got back, he told me the story about the high school girl's mother. I got pissed because I thought he was implying I would make a move on this kid. I think I understand now.

I would be lying if I didn't admit to feeling some sense of responsibility for what happened. I know how much he loved me. When I told him he was the best husband, father, and friend anyone could ever ask for I truly meant it. I just didn't love him anymore; I wanted to. I swear I didn't mean for it to happen. He was right, I completely cut him off emotionally. It was easier for me.

When we first started dating in 2010, I was over the moon for Brian. He was so attractive and had a way of talking to me like I was the only one around. When he guilted me into taking him to lunch that day, he did actually tell me he was looking for a twenty-seven-year-old girl with no kids. I thought, "Oh, my gosh, did he just say that?" I left thinking he would move on. I did go to the building a couple times a month after that lunch date. Before I met Brian, I usually went once every month to six weeks. He had his hooks in me. The whole story about giving blood; I did not see him. I was going through a separation with my first husband. I can't say it would have been different, but it is a great story. Whenever people asked about how we met, I always made Brian tell it because he told the story so much better. He always had a way with words.

When the police called me, I didn't believe it could be real. They asked me to come down and identify Brian's body. I almost dropped the phone twice. When I walked into the morgue, I saw him laying on a slab encased in a white zip-up body bag. I couldn't tell it was him from the contours of the body until they unzipped the bag. His face was unrecognizable, and I had to identify him by our matching tattoo. I broke a little as they zipped him back up. *He's really gone.* The officer said he had been found approximately eight days after he died. The neighbor below Brian's apartment reported a leak coming into her kitchen and when maintenance went in, they found him. No one missed him for eight days. Eight days he laid there, alone. He was found hunched over on the floor of the standup shower. There was a razor knife encrusted in blood lying next to him. Brian had cut himself on both arms from his wrist to his elbow. There was no coming back from it. There was an empty Johnnie Walker Blue bottle on the floor of the bathroom. It was the bottle Mark had given Brian and me at our engagement party. The officer then told me something I was unprepared for: "There was a note."

Hi Mom,

I know it's been a couple years and I'm sorry. My life has been pretty fucked up lately. Work went straight in the shitter and then this stuff with Veronica. I just can't seem to get through it. I've been leaning more and more towards not really wanting to. I'm not going to be melodramatic about it and ask for pity. I see that in my friends' faces and I've had about enough of it. I thought I had found the true love you and Margot had. I actually did but it didn't last. I look at Margot now and see her longing for you. Stuck in time. Stuck in your memory. That's where I am now only Veronica is alive and well. And dating someone. I guess I deserved it. I was never faithful to anyone until her. Fuck you, Karma. I could go back to fucking everything with a pulse like I did before. But why? It's not what I wanted in the first place. I wanted a love that would last forever. I had it, I thought. I still love her and always will. I tried to get over this. I really did. But I just can't do it. I'm sorry and I'll see you soon. Bye for now.

Love,
Brian

There was a second page.

Dear Veronica,

I'm sorry you need to deal with the fallout of all this. Since we are still legally married you will need to come see me. I'm sorry for that too. I am making you the executor of my will. Yes, I actually executed a will. The girls are the sole beneficiaries and the assets get split between them. You will need to sell the rental house in Philly and split the proceeds. My lawyer has all the details, but, basically, I want Bella to get her money now and Samantha's will be put into a trust she can begin drawing from when she turns 25. I wish this had all turned out differently.

More,
Brian

I had mixed feelings about including these notes in this book. They seemed too personal. I didn't think they were anyone's business. I ended up adding them only because he included various other letters and social media posts he'd written. He was never shy sharing his feelings, and it felt like something Brian would have wanted. I'm still not sure.

I am going to publish this book under his name and make sure any proceeds go to the girls. I see the influence he had on them and love him for it.

Brian, I am so sorry things worked out this way. I did absolutely love you once. ~Veronica

Author's Note

When I started this project over twelve years ago, it was written more as a journal. The idea of it becoming a book evolved over time. It was only this year, one of the most difficult times in my life, that I decided to dig in and pour my heart onto these pages. As I write this, it's three a.m. and I am still a revision or two away from finishing. Yet, I cannot help but think of you with gratitude. You are not simply my editor but a mentor and a cherished friend. This book would not exist without you and your honest, if not brutal, commentary. Sometimes you were not even kind, but I needed your truth to help me tell mine. The original collection of stories was disjointed and raw. You endured my defiant revolt against the rules of the English language. You purchased for me a lifetime subscription of commas knowing that I, at some point, had run out. The evolution of conveying my life's journey blossomed and crystallized through our conversations. This book is as much yours now as it is mine. So once again, I say thank you to you.

Brian Schreiber

One Last Thing

If you enjoyed this book or found it useful, I would be grateful of you would post a short review on Amazon. Your support really does make a difference and I read all the reviews personally, so I can get your feedback.

Thank you again for your support!

Made in the USA
Coppell, TX
24 April 2021